By Xenia Melzer

GODS OF WAR
Casto
Love and the Stubborn
Ummana

Published by DSP Publications
www.dsppublications.com

UMMANA

GODS OF WAR: BOOK III

XENIA MELZER

DSP PUBLICATIONS

Published by

DSP Publications

5032 Capital Circle SW, Suite 2, PMB# 279, Tallahassee, FL 32305-7886 USA
www.dsppublications.com

Ummana
© 2017 Xenia Melzer.

Cover Art
© 2017 Aaron Anderson.
aaronbydesign55@gmail.com
Cover content is for illustrative purposes only and any person depicted on the cover is a model.

ISBN: 978-1-63533-361-9
Digital ISBN: 978-1-63533-362-6
Library of Congress Control Number: 2016915375
Published July 2017
v. 1.0

Printed in the United States of America
∞
This paper meets the requirements of
ANSI/NISO Z39.48-1992 (Permanence of Paper).

To Eva, my sister. The best beta reader ever.

ACKNOWLEDGMENTS

AGAIN I have to thank a bunch of people for getting *Ummana* out. My husband and family, for their unwavering support. Dr. Richard Marranca for his valuable input and patience, and all the people at Dreamspinner who work so hard for the sake of producing the best possible book. Aaron Anderson for the great cover art, Paul Richmond for everything that has to do with graphics and all the things I have no clue about. Last, but definitely not least, the best editors in the world! Anne Regan for her limitless patience with all my mistakes and her ability to drop me a cheerful note whenever I need it most, Kelly who has a fierce eye for details and no fear to point my mistakes out to me, and Liv for her keen knowledge of grammar (I don't know how you do that…). Without you, the book wouldn't be as good as it is. Thank you all!

SUMMARY OF BOOKS ONE AND TWO

A LOT has happened in the lives of Casto and Renaldo so far. After being taken prisoner by Renaldo, Casto has fought his master at every turn. Their explosive relationship has seen many ups and downs that would have broken weaker men. The worst came when Renaldo fell for the schemes of Damon, a priest of the Good Mother, who convinced him that Casto had been unfaithful. In a fit of rage, Renaldo sent Casto to the mines in order to kill him. But thanks to Sic's courage, the scheme was revealed and the magic spell clouding the divine brothers' sight broken. Casto has returned to his master's side, no longer as a slave, but as his lover, heart, and future husband.

To bring Casto down, Damon had used Sic by blackmailing him into bringing Damon a cloak pin that would prove Casto's guilt. When Sic finally finds the courage to tell Renaldo what has happened, he is punished for his treason. Noran wishes to see his apprentice dead and it is only thanks to Casto's interference that Sic is allowed to live. Deeply hurt by Sic's deed, Noran starts losing control of himself and tortures Sic cruelly by using the young man's love to force him into absolute subservience.

Daran, on the other hand, is more than happy with his two masters. He has overcome his shock after Kalad was almost killed during the battle of Ki't and knows now without a doubt that he belongs to Aegid and Kalad for the rest of his life.

The divine brothers have found out that the followers of the Good Mother, who had infiltrated the Valley, had been trained in Medelina. Now the Wolf of War wishes to get his revenge on the city.

PEOPLE OF ANA-DARASA

THE VALLEY
Lord Canubis, the Wolf of War
Lady Noemi, the snake witch and wife to Canubis
Lord Renaldo, the Angel of Death
Prince Castolus of Ummana, husband to Renaldo
Lysistratos, "Lys," Emperor of the Storms

THE EMERIS
Lady Hulda, the Mother Superior of the Sisters of the Night
Lord Wolfstan, armorer of the Pack and husband to Lady Hulda
Lord Aegid and Lord Kalad, the desert brothers
Lord Noran, master smith
Lord Bantu and Lady Cornelia, siblings

OTHERS
Sic, slave of Noran
Daran, slave of Aegid and Kalad
Frankus, master of the sauna

UMMANA
Princess Anesha, Casto's sister
Lord Aran, Casto's father
Voltara, Lord Aran's right hand
Captain Aktan, leader of the Royal Guard
Lord Nambuno, member of the Council
Lady Amicia, member of the Council
Jago, master smith
Cassia, Jago's wife
Heljia, Jago and Cassia's daughter
King Erac of Medelina
Lady Vespia, ambassador of Medelina

MEASUREMENTS

MEASUREMENTS OF LENGTH

1 hand = 4 inches = 10.2 centimeters (1 hand is the unit still used to measure
    the height of horses.)
1 span = 9 inches = 22.9 centimeters
1 ell = 45 inches = 114 centimeters or 1.14 meters
1 pace = 5 feet or 60 inches = 1.5 meters
1 league = 3 miles = 4.8 kilometers

MEASUREMENTS OF MASS

1 ore = 0.85 ounce = 24 grams
1 clove = 6.4 pounds = 2.9 kilograms
1 quarter = 2 stones or 28 pounds = 12.7 kilograms
1 hundredweight = 8 stones or 112 pounds = 50.8 kg

AS TO readers who are familiar with the various measurement systems during medieval times, I would ask them to kindly turn a blind eye on any inconsistencies they may find.

UMMANA

GODS OF WAR: BOOK III

XENIA MELZER

PROLOGUE

"Isn't she the most charming creature?"

Ana-Aruna watched the small girl her sister had brought to the Green Lands, full of love.

"She is. I knew immediately that you would like her."

"Where did you find her? She's not part of our creation, and her light is well hidden if you don't know how to look."

Ana-Isara smiled while the girl chased after the butterflies that were dancing across the lush green fields like drunken gems, her laughter like silver bells in the warm, scented air. Here in the Green Lands, her light was clearly visible, unlike on Ana-Darasa where it had been hidden so well.

"Chance. I saw her playing by a lake with nobody else around. For a moment her light shone so brightly I had to avert my eyes. She feels like pure magic."

"You're right. She's more than special. I'm tempted to keep her here."

Ana-Isara touched her sister gently.

"You know this isn't a good idea?"

The Empress of Life sighed. "I do know. Watch well over her, out in the world."

"Of course. And when her time comes, you can welcome her here—if she chooses to come."

Ana-Aruna watched sadly as her sister took the shining creature's hand to take her back into her own world. The purity coming from her had touched the goddess deeply and she could only hope that the girl wasn't the only one of her kind.

THE KING OF UMMANA

1. WEDDING DAY

THE DAY the Pack celebrated the wedding of Lord Renaldo, the Angel of Death, to his heart, Prince Castolus of Ummana, dawned in splendid glory. The sun's rays cut through the chilly air like swords ripping an enemy's body apart, and they transformed the snow into a sparkling carpet of diamonds.

Excited anticipation ruled over the huts, the stables, and the main building. Even the slaves were affected by the nervous energy permeating the morning.

In Frankus's chambers, Casto stood in front of a huge, almost man-sized mirror and studied his body that, in only a few hours, would be scarred in the most barbaric way imaginable. Behind him, Frankus was busy arranging all kinds of oils and ointments on a table. While doing this, he kept rambling on in hushed tones.

"I explicitly told you to drink some wine so you could have a good night's rest. But why listen to somebody who's had as much experience with weddings as me? You had to brood the entire evening, as if today wasn't the happiest in your life. You probably wanted to put my skills to the test, didn't you?"

Completely unfazed by the scolding, Casto kept staring at himself in the mirror. Since he had fled from Ummana, his body had changed dramatically. During his year on the run, he'd still resembled a child, with the long, slender limbs of a newborn foal, though showing signs of his later build. After the Barbarian had taken him prisoner, the awkward adolescent body had transformed into a muscular, elegant weapon already forged in battle.

His skin was still as flawless and soft as back then, the studs in his flesh the only difference. Of course Frankus was right; he had seen better days, ones without those dark circles beneath his eyes that told of a night spent in useless musings. Then again, how often did one marry a god? If anything, those circles were well-earned.

Frankus pushed him away from the mirror, prying him from his useless pondering. "To the bath! You've got half an hour to clean yourself. Then we'll see what I can make of this disaster."

Without a word of protest, Casto obeyed Frankus, knowing that the man was probably even more nervous than Casto himself. The wedding was important in more than one respect, and Frankus was aware of all the implications that came with it.

The warm water managed to soothe Casto a little, and his thoughts went back to the day he fled from Ummana.

Most of his memories about that night were blurred because he had been so emotionally high-strung, not knowing what would become of him when he left the only home he'd ever known. The one thing he could remember clearly was the agitating mixture of wild triumph and utter fear swamping his senses as Lys galloped through the storm he had summoned.

At that time, Casto had been used to the feeling of being powerless. His father and Voltara, the torturer, had seen to that. While the gusts tugged at his cloak as if they wanted to tear him apart, Casto had experienced what it was like to control such powers through his connection with Lys. The ambiguity of those emotions left a deep impression on him, one that had influenced his actions more than he wanted to admit.

Now, too, he felt as if he were riding a storm, but this time he was alone, without Lysistratos to calm and protect him. And it wasn't an escape either, or at least, not a proverbial one. It was a step—no, a leap—into a whole new life that would permanently sever him from his past. Perhaps it would even banish the demons still haunting him—or so Casto hoped.

At the end of that day, he would be the mate of a barbarian god from the North. This fact would shape and change everything Casto had ever been, his entire personality. His whole identity was going to be created anew, not by him, but by the people around him. By the way they looked at him. It hadn't been easy becoming who he was, and Casto wondered whether he could make that change a second time. He was deeply afraid of losing himself to the Barbarian, of drowning in a different kind of helplessness.

Renaldo was just too much of everything, too intense—which was also the reason Casto loved him.

When he was honest with himself, all these thoughts were idle, an endless repetition of fears that he hoped to escape today. Becoming the mate of a man as overbearing and dominant as Renaldo would help him slay those demons from his past. Determined, Casto left the bath to let Frankus take care of him.

An hour later, Kalad and Aegid arrived to escort Casto to the main hall. The desert warriors were wearing identical clothes dyed in a vibrant dark green, their personal color. The seams of their shirts, as well as the jerkins, were embroidered with golden threads; their heavy coats and black boots were lined with otter fur.

Both men had superb ceremonial swords tied to their hips and golden vambraces decorated with emeralds strapped to their arms. They bowed to Casto, and he was almost sure they meant it. With those two, one could never tell.

"You're stunning, Casto." Kalad's voice was full of unrestrained admiration.

Casto wore dark blue silk trousers that caressed his body like a lover's touch. His black boots, dyed blue at the seams, were made from mountain deer leather lined with rabbit fur. The cream-colored shirt and dark blue jerkin with golden embroidery told Renaldo's story in the runes of the Ancients, and were also made of silk. Casto's eyes, highlighted by kohl, looked almost innocent in this getup. His wheat-blond hair was tamed by a broad leather strap, and the ends dipped in gold dust made the light explode every time he moved.

The contrast between Casto's stunning appearance and his contradictory character posed a deception Aegid deemed fitting on this important day. It emphasized how perfectly suited the young man was to become Renaldo's mate.

"Just now I'm regretting we weren't able to defeat Renaldo five years ago." There was a hint of longing in Aegid's voice.

"My words, brother." Kalad grinned.

"Perhaps you want to rethink your decision, Casto? We would take good care of you."

Only a few weeks ago, that saucy comment would have made Casto furious for two reasons: that he was regarded as a trophy, and the implication that back then he had chosen slavery freely. Luckily for Kalad, Casto had learned to see the words for what they were, a compliment wrapped in good-humored banter.

He bowed to them in mockery. "It would be my pleasure. But it would be your task to explain to a notoriously short-tempered and jealous god why the object of his desire has chosen to elope with two male hookers."

The desert brothers made indignant faces.

"Uh, that hurt. Hookers? I'd call us sexually open-minded." Kalad grinned when he said this, fully aware of his and Aegid's reputation.

Casto snorted. Kalad's and Aegid's promiscuity was legendary within the Pack. "Please, when we first met, you were changing your bed partners so fast you didn't even bother learning their names. You were worse than the Barbarian!"

"That's not true—not entirely." Kalad managed to let his voice sound hurt, although the twinkling in his eyes betrayed his amusement. "And since we've met Daran, we're fidelity incarnated."

"It's the truth!" Aegid came to his brother's aid. "The little thief is special in many ways. Ever since we got him, I haven't longed for diversion."

Casto rolled his eyes. He would never admit how much he enjoyed their relaxed bickering. Among all the warriors of the Pack, Kalad and Aegid came closest to what Casto would have wished for as brothers. "All right, I understand. You're the embodiment of sexual fidelity and devotion. Nevertheless, I have to decline your generous offer. I'm fully occupied with one self-righteous Barbarian and have no intention of trading that for double trouble. It's my pleasure to leave that honor to Daran."

Kalad and Aegid started laughing out loud. Their amusement was like a breath of fresh air to Casto's tense mood.

"Then we better get you to your barbarian while you're still determined. I've no intention to chase you through the snow should you get cold feet." Aegid sounded a little too serious for comfort.

"Those I already have. Why does it have to be so cold today?"

Casto hadn't planned to start lamenting, but he still resented the cruel irony that made the days with the most radiant sunshine those where the cold was especially biting. It almost seemed as if nature itself was having a good laugh at his expense.

Aegid and Kalad nodded in silent agreement. Aegid grabbed Casto's wrist. "Let's go. The sooner we start moving, the sooner you're in the main hall, and if nothing else, it's warm there."

Beaten by this valid argument, Casto followed them out into the cold.

THE MAIN hall was almost bursting at its seams. Every warrior in the Valley, as well as many of the slaves, were present to witness their god taking his mate.

When Aegid opened the gigantic doors, the excited murmuring from hundreds of voices was like a wall forcing Casto back a few steps. Then all noise died. The silence was so heavy, it made him wonder whether his heartbeat could be heard.

Aegid and Kalad left his side to take their seats next to the other Emeris at the far end of the hall.

Casto stood alone in the aisle. The stares from all the people almost hurt. All the expectations tied to his person threatened to weigh him down. He felt as trapped and chained as he had been in Ummana, confronted with a burden he was not ready to take on. If he started to run now, he could probably make it to the stables and Lys before anybody realized what he was doing. He could leave it all behind—

No. He had already tried that. There was no turning away from Renaldo, not anymore. Casto straightened up. He had come this far; backing out now would be even worse than staying. After all, this was no different from the official appearances he'd made in Ummana. He would neither shame himself nor the Barbarian.

At the end of the aisle, Renaldo and Canubis were waiting. They had gotten up from their wooden seats as a gesture of respect and were watching him expectantly.

Casto glimpsed the hunger in the features of his future husband, and everything besides Renaldo vanished from his sight. The Barbarian was breathtaking. His eerie perfection was enhanced by his dark blue ceremonial clothes.

Renaldo's shirt was made of the finest silk, highlighting the outline of his muscular arms, broad shoulders, and chiseled abdominal muscles without being vulgar. The leather trousers hugged his slim hips, and the black boots enhanced his long legs. Renaldo's only jewelry was a headband made from pure gold, formed like two wings holding a blue diamond between them. His eyes were smoldering, a mirror of the lethal fire blazing inside the demigod.

Casto was the only one who did not fear that fire. On the contrary, he loved it since it was so incredibly similar to his own.

Gravely he proceeded along the lines of warriors toward the two demigods, every inch a royal prince. When he reached them, he bowed. Only when Canubis and Renaldo had returned the formal gesture did Casto bend his knee to swear his fealty as a free warrior of the Pack.

"I plead my loyalty to you, Lord Canubis, and to you, Lord Renaldo, as my leaders and commanders. I swear to follow your orders and fight by your side until Ana-Isara claims me for the Green Lands."

In return, Canubis and Renaldo promised to protect and help him whenever he needed their aid.

"We accept your pledge, Casto. We offer you the protection of the Pack and swear to look after you until your time has come to return to the Mothers."

Once the words were spoken, the other warriors in the hall celebrated the pact they all had made with the Wolf of War and the Angel of Death with deafening applause. It was the pledge that bound them all as brothers and sisters under the sword.

After the cheering died away, Canubis approached Casto with a blade in his hands, the symbol for the alliance they had just made. The forbidding Wolf of War girded the sword around Casto's hips. His voice was loud and clear. "Welcome to the Pack, Prince Castolus of Ummana. You are most welcome."

The agitated hush following these words was proof that the brothers had kept Casto's identity a secret until today. It was one of the oldest, most effective tricks in politics. Always stay one step ahead of friend and foe alike, and surprise them when they are least expecting it to demonstrate your superiority. Casto nodded at Canubis in silent recognition that was met by a conspiratorial wink. Then Canubis stepped aside to make room for his brother, who took his place next to Casto.

As a greeting, Renaldo pressed a kiss on Casto's temple while he took his hands in his own. "You're doing really well, my own."

"I told you so. I'm used to presenting myself."

Smiling, Renaldo rolled his eyes before he turned his attention to his brother. Canubis regarded the two men standing in front of him with affection. It was an emotion that seemed alien to the usually unrelenting man and showed how much he loved his younger brother.

When the Wolf of War started to speak, the people in the hall fell silent again. "Some hundred years ago, it was me standing in front of Renaldo, harboring the same love and probably the same fears in my heart. Yet it was the happiest day in my life, and I can still recall it as if it happened yesterday."

He paused to give everyone a chance to recognize the importance of the moment. "I wish you, my brother, and you, Castolus, the same. That in a hundred or two hundred years' time, even for the rest of your life, you will think of this day and it will be as crystal clear in front of your inner eye as if it had happened only yesterday. You are about to take your vows of fidelity and love, with phrases given to us by the Mothers themselves. May these vows see the end of time, unsullied by treason or hatred."

Canubis took a silken cloth, dark blue and embroidered with golden runes, and wove it around Renaldo's and Casto's intertwined hands. Casto looked at Renaldo with a mixture of love and defiance when he started to recite the ancient vow.

"Ne, ana blod brester stratatos, renosor an treano net aremao te memoso net elendio, ana Renaldo muaro. Ne rono unemaso la na re anoso tare. No risuo, ne ledeto. Ne ratodio an no."

I, the kindred of the wind, swear my undying love and fealty to my mate and god, Lord Renaldo, the Angel of Death. I will be your heart from now on until time itself will end. Your will shall be my command. I belong to you.

Casto was not too happy about the wording of the vows, but seeing the love igniting in Renaldo's eyes made him bear them a little more easily.

"Ne, ana elendio muoro no Ana-Isara te Ana-Aruna, elendio da nort, paretao no adeso. Ne torinos memoso te aremao net uromeo da adoso an anas net permaso da unemaso. An anoso tere, no heloso da ne."

I, Angel of Death to the Mothers, God of the North, accept your vow. I welcome you as my mate, and I swear to love and protect you as asked by the Mothers and as is befitting for my heart. Till the end of all time, you are mine to cherish.

Renaldo's voice was clear and steady. He had waited all his life for this moment.

Canubis placed his hands on the ribbon between his brother and Casto.

"Ne, ana elendio remaro no Ana-Isara te Ana-Aruna, elendio da nort, tureano elene te irao asuendo. Ne torinos brester unemaso da riano."

I, Wolf of War to the Mothers, God of the North, bless this union and recognize it as eternal. I welcome my brother's heart to the family.

Heralded by the thunderous applause from their fellow warriors, Canubis took the ribbon away and hugged first Renaldo and then Casto before he turned back to the audience.

Renaldo raised a hand to get everybody's attention and start the next part of the ceremony, the presenting of the gifts.

Casto took a deep breath and touched his mate's arm. "May I have a word, my lord?"

Renaldo furrowed his brow in surprise, then nodded almost imperceptibly and retreated a few steps. The interruption wasn't planned, but he doubted that even his capricious prince would ruin a moment like that.

For a few heartbeats, Casto contemplated the sea of faces in front of him before he turned to Renaldo, because what he had to say was mainly for him to hear. "As you all know, we didn't have an easy start."

Laughter erupted in the hall, accompanied by whistles and howling. Renaldo smiled lovingly at Casto, who went on.

"Neither of us is what you might call easygoing—" More comments from the crowd interrupted Casto, only this time he ignored them and kept on talking. "—which is why I'm still surprised that I'm standing here today. Truth be told,

I've gotten used to our arguments, and no price in the world can tempt me into living even one day without your love. You gave me a home when I was without an anchor, you showed me consistency when all I knew was insecurity and doubt, and you loved me before I even knew I was able to feel so strongly myself. My life truly began when I met you, and I will always be grateful for that. To show my appreciation, I have prepared a gift for you."

That was Kalad's cue to hand Casto the box. Casto gave it to Renaldo, who regarded him with love and a hint of suspicion in his gray eyes. Even though the occasion did call for some pathos and a certain amount of subservience, Casto's unusually tame statement had alerted Renaldo. Casto's following words did nothing to ease his doubts.

"I do hope you are pleased with my gift, my lord."

"I'm sure your gift will please me plenty." Renaldo's voice was soft, with a barely audible strain in it. He opened the lid.

His eyes widened. Silently he stared at the content of the box, his jaw muscles clenched visibly. When he looked up, the perfect, impenetrable mask he normally wore was gone. "You shame me, my mate."

Casto smiled, satisfied. He enjoyed making the Barbarian uncomfortable in front of all his followers. It was a small revenge for all the things he'd made Casto endure since they met. "It is my gift for you, my lord."

Behind Casto, Aegid and Daran brought the brazier. Kalad approached Casto to help him get out of his jerkin and shirt. Renaldo took the iron from the box and buried it under the glowing coals with a rushed gesture. His face betrayed nothing of his feelings.

When the assembled warriors realized what kind of gift Casto had chosen, they started applauding again. After what seemed like a small eternity to Casto, Canubis made a gesture and absolute silence ensued. Only the sizzling of the iron and the soft crackling of the coals were still audible.

With his chest naked, Casto knelt in front of his mate with his back to him and swiped his hair over one shoulder. Aegid and Kalad grabbed his upper arms. Renaldo took the iron out and exchanged a glance with the desert warriors, who tightened their grip around Casto's arms so brutally he thought his bones would break any moment. In the audience, the mercenaries started hammering a dark, steadily increasing rhythm on their shields with the hilts of their swords.

Renaldo hesitated for one more moment, then pressed the glowing red iron between Casto's shoulder blades. Casto tensed in agony. His body jerked forward, and a muffled whimper escaped his lips but was swallowed completely by the noise in the hall. Casto had known he was facing serious pain when he decided to make this move, but he hadn't anticipated how bad it would be—worse than being whipped in public, *a lot worse*. Even the broken arm he'd had to endure at his father's court could not come close to the white-hot agony flashing through his body, assaulting his nerve endings, and swamping all his senses with the burning desire to scream and somehow escape the pain. If it hadn't been for the audience and his own unbreakable pride, Casto would have given in. But he would not scream, not in front of so many witnesses, not after he had forced Renaldo's hand to get his way. And so he gritted his teeth until he thought they would crack and imagined how good his triumph would feel once the pain subsided.

Mere agonizing moments that felt like a lifetime later, Renaldo tossed the iron aside and helped Casto to his feet and refastened his garments, surreptitiously wiping away the involuntary tears. The warriors started cheering again as Renaldo kissed him.

His voice was raw, only audible to the young man who was still shivering from the pain he had just endured. "We're going to talk this out later, O husband mine."

Casto's answer was equally challenging. "I'm counting on it, my lord."

Renaldo turned to the mercenaries. "Since my precious mate has gifted me so generously, I can only hope my presents for him are equally suitable."

He waved his hand imperiously, at which the great doors swung open and row after row of slaves started carrying heavy wooden trunks into the hall, the lids open so everybody could see the contents. First came twenty chests with clothes: silk and linen, velvet and exquisite leather, everything of the finest quality, all dyed in the dark blue color that was Renaldo's own. After the clothes had been carried outside again, twenty more chests were brought in, filled with gold and gems; expensive, intricately crafted wine cups; cloak pins, rings, sumptuous necklaces, and other jewelry. Another twenty trunks followed, and those were filled with books, each bound in leather with golden lettering on the cover. Then the slaves brought a complete set of war equipment: several swords, daggers in various lengths, bows and arbalests, an array of spears, chain mail, leather jerkins, and solid leather boots.

These unbelievable riches were followed by forty slaves and twenty of the best horses Renaldo owned, each with its own saddle, bridle, and several blankets.

Lysistratos was the last to enter the hall. His majestic appearance was highlighted by the gifts Renaldo had bestowed on him. The stallion wore a saddle made of dark blue chamois leather, one of the rarest and finest in the world. His bridle was of the same material; the headband was pure gold studded with three blue diamonds. The saddle fittings were gold too, and the stirrups were ornamented with lapis lazuli.

Speechless, Casto took in all the riches spread in front of him. The Barbarian had just made him one of the wealthiest men in the Pack, announcing his status with the highest impact possible. The assembled warriors felt it as well, for the looks they gave Casto were no longer just admiring. Now they carried a kind of awe that would soon turn into the respect Casto deserved as the mate of their god.

For once truly overwhelmed by Renaldo's generosity, Casto knelt in front of him, the gesture less graceful than usual due to the pain in his back. "You're the one shaming me, my lord. You're spoiling me."

Renaldo helped him up, genuinely pleased with this honest reaction. "I'm only giving you what is rightfully yours, my own." He smiled radiantly.

"I think it's time to declare the feast officially opened." With his arms stretched wide, he turned to his brothers-in-arms. "Let's celebrate!"

The invitation was met with frenetic joy. The doors opened once more, and this time slaves brought food and wine. Renaldo led his mate to the waiting Emeris, and Noemi was the first to hug Casto. He could feel a soft prickling from her, and the pain in his back subsided into a tolerable throbbing. Noemi couldn't heal him completely, because then the branding would be gone, but with her power she sped the process along so that it felt as if the wound had already healed for days. He flashed her a grateful smile.

"I'm so happy for you two, Casto. My best wishes to both of you!"

"I thank you, my lady. As always, you're as kind as you're beautiful."

Pleased with the answer, Noemi kissed him on the cheek. "You're so cute! What have we done all these years without you?"

Hulda pulled Casto into her arms. "We were appalled by our men's lack of manners. But truth be told, before we met you, we didn't even know what we were missing."

Casto took her hand in his own and kissed the back. He enjoyed this little game immensely. "How can anybody be unruly when confronted with so much grace?"

Wolfstan stepped up to his wife, smiling broadly. "Casto, stop it already! You make us look bad!"

"Don't fret it, darling." Hulda caressed her husband's arm lovingly. "You do realize this is all a game, don't you?"

"Of course, my precious, but it's fun to catch you off-balance now and then."

On and on it went. Casto drowned in congratulations and good-humored banter. Even Noran added his good wishes, though still rather grumpy, as always. Sic had been allowed to follow the ceremony from the farthest corner of the hall, and he expressed his joy with a nod and a broad smile before he left. Casto was sure the young smith had paid a high price for his participation, but that was a topic he would address once the time was ripe. Until then, Casto maintained a mental list of everything Noran made his slave suffer, so that he would not forget even one insult when he took his revenge.

The feast quickly turned into an orgy, which was the hallmark of any group activity in the Valley, as Casto had come to accept by now. It was not as bad as during the Spring Ceremony. Most of the warriors stuck to one partner and nobody was completely naked yet, a fact that would change as soon as the alcohol consumption reached a certain level.

Renaldo, like Casto, let his gaze wander through the hall, touched his hand lightly, and nodded at him reassuringly. There had been a major fight between them about the question of whether they should share intimacies during the feast, something that was considered mandatory for a wedding by many members of the Pack. Casto had finally won the argument by phrasing an ultimatum: should the Barbarian insist on that part of the ceremony, he could go and find himself another fiancé. Knowing there were some lines Casto would not cross, Renaldo had wisely acquiesced to his demand and promised not to lay a finger on him in public.

Around midnight Renaldo took his husband's hand, wished the other warriors a pleasant night, and then retreated to his chambers, where they would be undisturbed for the next three days. The time span was considered sufficiently long for the newlyweds to test their compatibility. Once it was over, the pair was expected to either confirm their union or annul it straightaway.

That was not an option for Casto, but he and Renaldo would still have their time of retreat.

The door hadn't completely closed when Renaldo slung his arms around Casto. His lips closed over Casto's, and Casto had some trouble evading the sudden assault.

"What do you think you're doing, Casto? I want you right now. Ever since you entered the hall this morning, I've been craving your body. Waiting this long was torture."

Casto couldn't suppress a smile. Renaldo's eagerness was a promising start to their wedding night. "I want you too, Barbarian. But before we get down and dirty, I want to give you something."

Renaldo glared at him. "I'd say you've given me plenty already. And don't you dare think I don't know what you've done."

Casto looked down, slightly flustered. He knew that forcing Renaldo's hand as he had done was in stark contrast to the vows he'd made. "I had to do it, Barbarian. For myself, for my self-esteem."

"Believe it or not, I do understand you. But I warn you, don't ever push me like that again. Do you have any idea how hard it was for me to hurt you in such a brutal way on our wedding day?"

Casto raised his hands in a conciliatory gesture. "I'm sorry, really. I'll make it up to you, I promise. Here, this is for you."

"Another present?"

Renaldo glared at the package in Casto's hands with open distrust. Finally he took it and opened it. He wasn't able to hide his surprise. "Are you serious?" Renaldo held up the leather cuffs Casto had sewn for him.

Casto held his gaze steadily. "I'm deadly serious. We both know why I allowed you to brand me today, and love or subservience have nothing to do with it. But as I said, I do love you, and I want this day to be as perfect for you as it is for me—well, most of it, anyway. We always have fun between the sheets, and I'm aware of how much you have to hold back. Tonight you don't have to do that. I'm going to do anything you ask of me. I'll be whoever you want. Tonight, you can let go."

Renaldo shook his head as if somebody had hit him. Deep in his eyes, a hunger awoke, so irresistible, so terrible it aroused Casto immediately and dragged him into depths he'd avoided till now.

"You're going to do everything I ask?"

"*Yes.* Everything you want. You can do with me as you please. I've sworn fealty to you today, and I don't want anything to stand between us, not even unexplored sexual fantasies."

"What about tomorrow night?"

Renaldo had put his finger on the crucial point. Casto treated him to a lazy, seductive smile. "We'll see, Barbarian. If I were you, I'd concentrate on the here and now."

Snarling, Renaldo pulled his mate closer. There was no doubt about Casto's sincerity. "I will, my gorgeous victim, you can bet on it."

His hands trembling with excitement, Casto helped Renaldo out of his ceremonial clothes and then undressed when Renaldo ordered him to.

As soon as he was naked, Renaldo fastened the cuffs around Casto's wrists, put his arms at his back, and locked the iron rings sewn to the leather. "You're completely helpless now, my own. How does that feel?"

Casto whimpered. He felt strange and a lot more vulnerable than he'd anticipated. His own strength was no match to Renaldo's, a fact Casto was always aware of, but it was a huge difference between just knowing and actually *experiencing* it. The lust Renaldo was practically oozing seemed more intimidating to Casto, more threatening—and also more arousing. Before he knew it, Casto was caught up in the insatiable passion that made his relationship with Renaldo so fulfilling.

"Please, my lord, don't torture me."

"Oh, but we're just getting started—slave."

Renaldo's lips caressed Casto's right cheek, then started wandering down, grazing his neck, pausing for a moment at his throat before Renaldo playfully bit the tight muscles at the junction between neck and shoulder. Casto squirmed in his embrace, trying to rub himself on Renaldo's thigh.

Renaldo kept him at a distance. "Don't rush it, my own. We have all the time in the world. Literally."

He started to push Casto toward the bedroom, never stopping with the kisses. Although Renaldo felt as if he were about to explode, he placed his mate gently on the bed and took his time to explore every inch of Casto's skin until he begged to be taken. With the aid of some cushions, Renaldo lifted Casto's rear to a height he found appealing. Then he entered him with first one, then two oiled fingers, massaging and teasing Casto until his hips started to buck in helpless pleasure. It was a heady feeling, seeing how the proud young man succumbed to the pleasure only Renaldo could give him—as only Renaldo was *allowed* to give to him. Moaning, Casto lifted his lower body, presenting it to Renaldo like a gift.

"Please, my lord, I'm begging you! Stop with the torture. Please!"

Satisfied, Renaldo withdrew his fingers, knowing from experience that his difficult lover would not refuse him anymore. He nudged Casto's entrance with his hard cock; his muscles bulged with the strain of holding back, of drawing out the teasing. "Is this what you want?"

"Yes, please!"

"What do you want me to do?"

"Take me. I'm begging you."

Renaldo shook his head. He enjoyed this game immensely. "If you want me, you have to go into more detail. *What* do you want me to do?"

Casto groaned in frustration. He already doubted the wisdom of his actions, but it was too late to back out now. He was too aroused, too eager. With only a hint of resentment in his gaze, he indulged the Barbarian. "I want you to enter me deeply. Take me hard and brutal. I want to feel that I belong to a god. I want to beg for mercy, knowing I won't get it. Hurt me, be cruel."

"As you wish, my delectable property."

Renaldo had been determined not to lose control completely, to keep that last strand of restraint, but when he heard Casto begging so deliciously, when his lover welcomed him so willingly, all reason evaporated in a red haze. This was not the ecstasy he'd felt the first time they had sex, and it wasn't the feeling of happiness, bordering on insanity, that swamped him every time he took Casto. This was a torrent that buried everything underneath, that only knew his hunger, his wish to own Casto, to mark him as his property for all time. Renaldo wasn't capable of clear thought. All he knew was that Casto was his and his alone. Laying Casto facedown, with brutal thrusts he took what nobody else was allowed to have. When Casto came for the first time, the fever running through Renaldo's body increased.

Renaldo dragged him up, glided his teeth over Casto's throat, then bit down hard enough to draw blood. Casto yelled and reared up, forcing Renaldo's cock even deeper into his body as he was overcome by his next orgasm and shook like a tree in a storm.

When Casto's muscles tensed again, Renaldo pushed harder, forcing his own rhythm onto the young man as his lips bathed in the delight of Casto's blood running hotly down his throat. It was the most feral part of him, the beast slumbering deep inside that reveled in this brutal consummation of their marriage.

It was what they had been made for: Renaldo to possess Casto entirely, Casto to absolutely belong to the demigod.

Renaldo continued to take Casto with regular movements, subduing him like a young horse that had to learn how to yield to its rider's will. It was no gentle teaching; for that, their need was too urgent. Renaldo reached his own climax and made Casto drown with him in the void of unrestrained, all-consuming lust.

Exhausted, they lay between the cushions, still connected, panting and sated.

When his breathing finally slowed, Casto gave a soft groan. As Renaldo came back to himself, he retreated from Casto's body, and his heart constricted with guilt when he assessed the damage he'd caused. Casto was covered in sweat. Even though Noemi had sped the healing along, the wound from the branding had turned a deep, angry red in reaction to their salty fluids and the chafing of the sheets. The bite wound was swollen and a thin trickle of blood ran down Casto's shoulders; the skin on the inside of his thighs was covered with Renaldo's semen. Renaldo hastened to open the cuffs and turn Casto around.

Tears stained Casto's eyelashes, and Renaldo was close to beating himself up for what he'd done.

"Casto, my own, my precious, I'm so sorry! I lost control. Is everything all right?"

Casto cocked an eyebrow. He was always hard to read, and right then he didn't seem to know what he should think himself. "I feel a little sore. I have to admit, I'm overwhelmed. You've never taken me like that before."

"And for good reason. I'm sorry for pushing you so far."

A puckish smile was the answer to that. "It's fine. I hardly felt any pain since I was busy having the greatest orgasms of my life."

Renaldo didn't seem to hear him. "That's the first time I ever subjected somebody to my full power. I simply don't know what to say. I've never lost control like that before."

Much to Renaldo's surprise, Casto seemed satisfied with that answer. "Good. I wouldn't like it if you had any means of comparison for what we just did."

"You're not angry? I thought you'd lose it completely."

"Why should I? It was my idea. I explicitly asked for it. Besides, I was curious what it would be like when you could do whatever you want. I'm surprised how much I liked it."

Overwhelmed, Renaldo pressed a gentle kiss on his lover's temple. "When will you stop surprising me?"

"Never, I hope. I don't want you to get too comfortable."

Renaldo furrowed his brows. There it was again, the slight discomfort he felt whenever Casto challenged him, even when it was hidden in a joke. Since Renaldo had no intention of ruining his wedding night by provoking a fight, he made his own words sound lighthearted.

"You've just been subjected to your god's full power and yet you dare be cheeky again? I can't fight the impression that you *want* to be punished."

Casto undulated alluringly, but his tone was dismissive. "I've been wondering when you'd realize it. Even though you're supposedly a god, you're not the sharpest dagger in the rack."

A growl escaped Renaldo's throat. Then he bent over his daring husband and kissed him.

Until the first rays of the sun tinted the sky a glorious shade of red, Casto got no more chance to defy his husband.

THE NEXT night, Casto woke because the bedroom was lit by a flickering light as if a candle were burning in the wind. Next to him the Barbarian slept soundly, sated by their lover's games.

Just when Casto had decided to wake Renaldo, he glimpsed movement in the corner of his eye. A tall, beautiful woman emerged from the dancing shadows. Her white hair moved softly, like cobwebs caught in a breeze. Her equally white dress hugged her body like a living thing, and it was impossible to tell where the cloth ended and the hair began. Black eyes dominated her pale face, and her bloodred lips parted in a friendly smile. Her voice, when she spoke, was a melodic whisper, like the autumn wind when it caressed the trees.

"It is not necessary to wake my son, Casto." She eyed the sleeping Renaldo, her gaze full of love. "He is very tired."

Casto got up from the bed. "You're Ana-Isara, the Empress of the Dead." He bowed respectfully.

The goddess smiled again. "I am, Prince Castolus of Ummana, and I'm glad we can finally meet. It has taken us some time."

Involuntarily, Casto lowered his gaze. He had never met a goddess before, but he learned quickly that her presence did not allow any pretense. "I know. I was quite stubborn."

An amused laugh was the answer to that. "You were as stubborn as a mule and as defiant as a three-year-old child. In other words, you are my son's heart."

"Is that really true?" All of Casto's fear and all the hope he had nurtured were bared in that one crucial question.

Ana-Isara looked at him, rather surprised. "Don't you feel it, Casto?"

"I'm wishing for it so desperately I can't tell whether it's true."

"What would you do if I told you your doubts were justified, that you are not my son's heart?"

The pain reflecting in Casto's eyes moved the goddess, but it was the graceful dignity of his answer that made her bow to him.

"I would die."

Ana-Isara caressed his cheeks with her cold fingers. "You *are* my son's heart. There can be no doubt about that. And you are a worthy member of the Pack. I did not want to hurt you, Casto, but you had to find out certain things on your own. You know now that you can trust Renaldo, that you love him, and that you are able to obey him. Of course, first and foremost he is your lover, but he is also your god, and you owe him obedience."

Casto nodded. As much as he resented it, he could not deny the truth in Ana-Isara's words. "I know."

"This does not mean you cannot criticize him. On the contrary, it is your duty, or he would become too conceited. But once he has made a decision, you have to bow to his will."

Again Casto nodded, slightly hesitantly. About that matter, the last word had not been spoken yet. "Yes."

The goddess flashed a radiant smile. "Come to me. I want to welcome you into my family."

She opened her white arms.

Casto approached her slowly. Cool like the grave was the embrace of the Empress of the Dead, but not uncomfortable. Casto felt safe and pampered, as if the world's challenges lay far behind him. Ana-Isara murmured close to his ear, "Death is nothing to fear. It is the door to another truth. Those walking in my footsteps do not have to fear getting lost. In the end, every pain we endure is only an illusion on our way to ourselves."

After having spoken that riddle, the goddess pressed a kiss on Casto's forehead. It was unexpectedly warm, almost searing.

"Don't worry, my son. My sister and I are with you. From today, you will never be alone again."

The light flickered and winked out; the goddess's hair flew up like a flock of birds in a storm and then settled like a coat around her.

When she stepped away, the pain set in.

RENALDO WOKE when he heard Casto scream as he had never screamed before. His gaze darted wildly through the room and stopped at the sight of his mother, who was just about to leave.

"Why are you doing this to him? Hasn't he endured enough yet?"

Ana-Isara's features hardened. "Indeed he has, and it has made him strong. Strong enough for you. This will make him even harder, more unbending. He is what you need, what your brother needs."

"But it's not fair."

"It's never fair, my son. You should know that better than anybody else. Take care of him. He needs you now."

Renaldo turned away from his mother and slung his arms around his screaming lover.

Long after the sun had risen, Casto's wails finally subsided. Panting, he lay in Renaldo's arms. Shudders ran through his body in a desperate reaction to a pain he'd never even imagined before.

Renaldo stroked his sweat-soaked back soothingly. "Shh, shh, my own. Everything's fine again. It's over."

Casto snuggled closer, still overwhelmed by what he had just gone through. "I'm sorry, Barbarian. I thought I was stronger."

"You stubborn idiot. You've been touched by a goddess. That's no triviality. You've done well."

"If you think so."

"I do. And now get up. I wish to see how you were branded."

Groaning in protest, Casto got up. He just wanted to sleep, but he could sense how important it was to Renaldo to find out what Ana-Isara had done to him.

With his fingertips, Renaldo traced the two black runes carved into Casto's flesh, right above his heart. "The sign of the Mothers and the rune for a rider. How fitting."

Gently he turned Casto around so that he could see himself in the mirror. Gingerly Casto touched the two dark symbols. Pride and resentment fought for dominance while he studied the signs that were proof of another person's will, not his own. "It doesn't hurt anymore."

"No. Being branded is brutal, but once it's done, the pain quickly becomes a fading memory. Look at your back."

Casto turned and stared at his back reflected in the mirror. The branding from the wedding was healed, the skin smooth and flawless again. Now the design glowed from within in the same color as the runes above his heart. Starting at the end of the *R*, a rune was engraved over every vertebra of his spine, telling the world that he was Renaldo's possession, his beloved heart.

Casto shuddered. This was too much to be pondered in his current state of mind.

Renaldo embraced and kissed him lovingly. "My precious heart. I am truly happy."

Sighing, Casto snuggled up to his mate and god. If half a year ago somebody had told him that one day he would be branded like an ox, visible for all the world to see that he was the Barbarian's property, he would have thought the person insane. Yet here he was, bearing the marks of a barbarian god from the North, and he was not unhappy about it.

Casto fought this disturbing, atypical thought and tried to concentrate on the lust Renaldo was stoking in him anew. Strictly speaking, he was too tired to be in the mood, but all he wanted was to be with Renaldo again without wasting time on things too complex to consider after a night like that.

2. REVENGE

A LONG time ago, the Emperor of the Storms stared down from a rise into the broad river valley where the Umman flowed lazily toward the sea. In the distance, he could see a glittering city and within it, like a pearl hidden in a shell, he sensed his anchor, the reason he had come to this world. The pull had grown in intensity over the past few months, and now the anchor's presence was like a beacon for Lysistratos. The previous night he had felt a strange throbbing, as if somebody had slung a chain around his heart. A chain to bind him forever. The anchor was finally born. Lysistratos felt a joy he had never thought possible. Finally his presence on Ana-Darasa made sense. He had found his reason for being.

Even though the anchor was exceptionally strong—a fact that pleased Lysistratos—his mind was still blurred, for he was so young. The Emperor of the Storms did not care. Now that he had encountered his own purpose in this world, the passing of time no longer affected him. He could wait.

"I'M STILL furious." Canubis crashed his fist down on the wooden table around which the Emeris were gathered. "It just can't be that a bunch of heathens march into the Valley like it's an open market and come this close"—he held up his thumb and forefinger, indicating a hair's breadth—"to destroying us all. This was planned thoroughly and executed almost perfectly. We were lucky this time, but I won't rely on luck alone to keep us safe. It's high time to remind the followers of the Good Mother that their false goddess has no place on Ana-Darasa. They dared to reach for my brother's heart with their filthy hands!"

As if on cue, all gazes turned to Casto, who sat at the table next to his mate. He was slowly getting used to being treated like an especially valuable possession, which, according to the prophecies, he somehow was. Now that Ana-Isara had officially recognized him as Renaldo's heart, the divine brothers were only waiting for the arrival of the last Emeris before they would conquer this world for good.

Casto's place in the hierarchy had changed considerably, and he was still busy assessing and analyzing the resulting consequences.

His relationship with Canubis and Renaldo was indisputable. He owed them obedience, period. Even though he resented it, his scope regarding those two was narrow, and he was in no hurry to test its limits. Hulda, Noemi, and Cornelia were out of the equation. They were very intelligent, immensely powerful ladies he would always treat with the greatest of respect, since he was neither a barbarian nor stupid. Aegid and Kalad were almost like friends, even though he still felt unsettled by Aegid's intense personality. Wolfstan and Bantu were level, reserved characters, but you did not become a member of this elite circle without a will of steel and special talents.

In Ummana, Casto had learned that it always paid not to neglect the silent ones. If you did, you could very well die. Noran, on the other hand, was his enemy. He was torturing Casto's best friend, did it on purpose to hurt Casto as well, and he would be damned if he did not make the master smith pay for his sins one day.

"Therefore, Renaldo and I have decided to attack and destroy Medelina."

Canubis's voice pried Casto from his musings.

"It's one of the cells where the Good Mother is strongest, and according to the traitors we tortured, Assani and Damon were schooled there. I want that city down in the dust."

The amber eyes lit up dangerously; there was no doubt about Canubis's determination and anger. It was a terrifying display of his dominance. Kalad was the first who dared to voice some doubt.

"I do understand your fury, Canubis, and please believe me when I tell you that I share it wholeheartedly, but Medelina is incredibly fortified. The city is one of the few that still have something akin to a standing army, so they're not defenseless. Even with forces like ours, it's questionable whether the city will fall."

"I agree with my brother." Aegid's voice was level, as always, but it carried weight because of that. "Attacking Medelina is madness. It will cost us many fighters, and we can't be sure about the outcome."

As usual in such situations, Renaldo's face was frozen into an impenetrable mask. His brother, on the other hand, showed his agitation openly.

"We can't let them get away with this. We have to set an example."

Now Bantu spoke as well. "I do understand, Canubis, but the question is…."

Casto studied the map pinned to the wall behind the Wolf of War. There was a truly simple solution to this problem, even though he had hoped to have left this part of his life behind for good. Just thinking about it made his head ache, but he was a member of the Pack, mate to a god. He owed it to all of them to neglect his own well-being for the greater good, especially when the alternative meant losing so many skilled warriors. *It's also your chance to get your revenge!* the voice in the back of his head whispered persistently. It was too good an opportunity to pass on.

He cleared his throat.

"I agree with Aegid and Kalad. Attacking Medelina would be a calculated waste of lives. Besides, it doesn't make sense to go against a city you can easily control with other means."

Canubis glared at him. He had anticipated that his plans would not meet with immediate approval, but he did not like how his brother's mate not only opposed him, but also spoke in riddles.

"Explain yourself, Casto. I don't have time for one of your games."

For a moment anger bloomed in the noble features of the prince, but after a sidelong glance at Renaldo, who looked at his mate with a clear warning written all over his face, Casto held back. Nevertheless, he could not keep himself from speaking with exaggerated patience, as if his audience were a slightly slow child.

"All I'm saying is that Medelina is a member of the Confederation of the Plains. The mistress of this alliance is Ummana. The Twin Cities are superior to all other members."

"And?"

Canubis, like the other Emeris, did not see where Casto was going. Even Renaldo seemed confused. Casto sighed.

"The key is Ummana. And it so happens that I know from reliable sources that the rightful king of Ummana was married to a barbarian god from the North only a week ago. According to the laws in the Valley, Ummana is yours and your brother's."

Silence. They all stared at Casto as if seeing him for the first time. The young man rolled his eyes.

"What do you think 'Your Highness' means? It's not an empty phrase. I'm the firstborn. This summer I turn twenty-two, which means I'm of age and can claim the throne for myself. It could be that the Council won't accept my marriage because Renaldo is male and thus the continuation of the line is in danger, but they can't deny my claim to the throne. You're going to rule through me."

Kalad started laughing.

"That's brilliant! Crazy, but brilliant."

As if these words had lifted a ban, they all started talking at once, all enthusiastic about the idea. Only Canubis watched Casto with a questioning look in his eyes. Renaldo silenced the Emeris with a gesture. Canubis took over again.

"I like your plan, Casto. It's elegant and effective. But it has a catch. I know you have terrible memories of Ummana. It was hell for you, not home. You're my brother's heart, a part of my family. Nobody, not even me, has the right to ask something of you that can hurt you so deeply."

While his brother spoke, Renaldo got up and embraced Casto protectively. This gesture, in connection with the concern from Canubis, stunned Casto into silence. No human being had ever cared for him like that before, and until now he had been sure not to need this kind of love. Deeply moved, Casto felt tears pooling in his eyes and swiped them away with a fierce gesture.

"It's true that I'd rather have Renaldo whip me in public again than ever go back there, but for the sake of my brothers-in-arms I'm willing to do it—as long as you don't send me alone."

"Alone? I'd never let that happen, my own." Renaldo's voice was stern. Kalad slapped Casto's back.

"Seems as if your royal ancestry finally comes in handy."

"I can't wait to see you in your natural habitat." Hulda's voice was teasing but carried a serious undertone. Her expression showed how much she was aware of the difficulty of the situation. One after another, the Emeris confirmed their support for Casto. Canubis bowed slightly to the prince, a wolfish grin on his lips.

"It seems, Your Highness, as if you're going to claim the throne of Ummana with the deadliest personal guard in the world at your side."

FOUR TIRING hours of tactics talk later, Casto entered the stables for the first time since the wedding. The first three days, he and Renaldo had spent in seclusion, and Casto felt himself blush just thinking about what they had done. The time where the newlywed couple could concentrate solely on each other had been terrifying in its intensity. Casto had discovered sides to the Barbarian he had never thought existed. He, too, had opened to his mate in a way that had first filled him with fear, and then, when Renaldo had gently pushed him further, with surprised happiness. It was just like Ana-Isara had predicted. He could trust Renaldo. Of course, Casto was aware of the irony. The first person he'd ever relied on had to be divine. And yet his trust hadn't breached the final border; the horrors hidden deep within his soul were something Casto wouldn't let his mate and god see. He was too afraid of what could only be a hideous monster in the clear light of day.

After seclusion had ended, the congratulants had come. And because he was not only the mate, but also officially the heart of the Barbarian, it had taken almost four days to receive all the presents and well-wishes from the members of the Pack.

Today was the first day on which something vaguely resembling routine took place—at least the kind of routine that would from now on rule his life.

Lys welcomed him with a whinny, and Casto just had to smile.

"My brother! I missed you!"

In silence they stood, their foreheads pressed together, enjoying the other's presence without disturbing it with something as mundane as words. Lys was the same as always, the one constant that never changed. Casto caressed his brother's muscular neck.

"They dressed you up pretty nicely for the ceremony."

The stallion snorted, and Casto started laughing.

"Of course it's fitting. You *are* a king, my brother." Then he turned serious. "I'm sorry I could never give you anything like this. All you ever knew with me was lies, loneliness, and hardships. I'm glad you're finally getting the appreciation you deserve."

Gently but firmly, Lys bit down on Casto's hand. Casto closed his eyes when Lys's emotions flooded his senses. The love this powerful being felt for him was almost more than he could bear. Lysistratos didn't give a damn about appearances. All he wanted was Casto's love.

"And you'll have that till the end of time, my brother."

The stallion snorted, then he nudged Casto out of his stall. Casto turned and saw Sic waiting shyly at some distance until his friend would notice him. Casto beamed at the slave.

"Sic! It's nice to see you again! Did everything go well while I was gone?"

Sic averted his eyes; his voice trembled. "Yes, Master."

Casto furrowed his brows.

"I thought we talked about this, Sic. You're my friend. I'm expecting you to use my name."

"How can I dare that, now that it's obvious who you are?"

Casto's lips thinned.

"Don't remind me. Please, Sic, this is important to me. Don't start treating me like a fragile glass egg. I'm getting enough of this from the Barbarian."

Sic was having a tumultuous inner debate and it showed clearly on his face, but in the end he squared his shoulders and stretched out his chin.

"Fine, Casto. I'll try to ignore your noble lineage. But please, don't be mad at me when I can't do it all the time."

"It's enough for me that you're trying. So, what happened while I was gone?"

"Nothing interesting. The other slaves weren't happy that you left me in charge, but after Lord Canubis announced that you're indeed his brother's heart, they all were hell-bent not to provoke your anger. Many of them are afraid you could make them pay for their previous behavior. The horses are fine, your plans for training have been followed through, so you can start where you left off. Before you do that, there's something I want you to have."

Clumsily, Sic placed a small bundle in his friend's palm.

"My best wishes for your wedding, Casto."

Deeply moved, Casto hugged the young man.

"That's very friendly of you, Sic. I thank you."

Casto ripped the present open and froze in admiration.

"Holy Mothers! This is perfect!"

"You like it?" Sic sounded surprised.

"Do I like it? I love it!"

Reverently Casto held the miniature of Lysistratos in his hands. Sic had managed to carve a perfect likeness of the proud stallion, starting with the arrogant gaze and the elegantly set neck, and ending with the perfectly muscled body. Set into the thick mane was a small eyelet with a thin leather band. Casto held out the breathtaking work of art.

"Can you put it on me, please? But make sure the knot is tight. I simply can't lose this."

Sic was happy to lend his friend a hand and followed him when he went looking for a mirror to admire himself.

"It's simply gorgeous. You're truly talented, Sic."

The young man blushed in joy. "Thank you, Casto. It's nothing big."

"Sic, out of all the presents I've gotten till today, this one is by far the best. And you know why? Because it's from a true friend who knows me well enough to give me something of personal value. Any idiot can give an expensive present and then boast about their generosity, but to find something I truly treasure—only you have managed to accomplish that. You have my gratitude."

Now it seemed as if the sun was rising in Sic's face. Beaming, he hugged Casto. Joy made his voice sound as young as he truly was, and a shadow of his former optimism bloomed.

"I'm honored."

"Now that we've talked this through, let's get to work. Otherwise your efforts to stick to my plans have been in vain."

3. REMISSION

"You took your time in the stables."

Faced with this not exactly heartwarming welcome, Casto cocked an eyebrow at his mate.

"I was gone for six days. There was a lot to do."

"Has the traitor messed up?" Renaldo's voice was stern. Sic was still a red rag for him, and the servants in the stables hadn't been the only ones who had resented the young man getting so much responsibility. Casto had to restrain himself from snapping at Renaldo.

"Sic has done a great job substituting for me. But there are always some decisions I have to make myself, no matter how good my people are."

"Are you getting angry?"

"Not yet, but if you don't cut it out, I will. I had different plans for tonight than to rehash old fights."

Renaldo grinned.

"Come here and I promise we'll rehash entirely different things."

Casto complied without hesitation, eager to get into bed with the Barbarian as soon as possible. Ever since he had allowed Renaldo to take him without restraint, their love games had reached heights that made him crave more. The bed was the one place where he had no problem letting Renaldo take the reins.

Renaldo was fumbling with Casto's clothes, helping him out of his boots and all the layers of clothes he wore as protection against the biting cold. Suddenly he paused.

"Where did you get that? It's beautiful!" He dangled the pendant Sic had given to Casto from his fingers. "You can clearly see it's Lys. Whoever made this is a gifted artist."

Casto evaded his mate's gaze. "It was a present for our wedding."

"A more than fitting present. Tell me, who gave it to you?"

"A friend."

Renaldo took Casto's face in both hands. "In case you haven't noticed, my own, even though I'm a barbarian, I'm not stupid. I do realize when you're trying to dodge me."

Casto sighed. He didn't want to have a fight with Renaldo tonight, but it was inevitable once the topic was about Sic. Mentally preparing for the oncoming argument, he answered in measured tones. "It's from Sic. He made it."

Casto tensed in anticipation of the outburst that would follow his words, but nothing happened. Instead Renaldo stared at the wooden figurine, lost in thought.

"He's gifting my heart, but not his god?"

Casto answered without thinking. "Because he thinks his god has left him. He's too terrified of his wrath and won't risk getting close to him."

Renaldo looked up. For a long time, his gray eyes bored into the impenetrable, seemingly innocent blue ones of his lover. When he finally spoke, his voice was hesitant.

"He means a lot to you, am I right?"

"Yes."

Casto found it easier to admit the truth than to start playing tactical games again.

"And it seems as if you mean a lot to him as well."

"He's my friend."

Again Renaldo lost himself in the perfect pendant. Never before had he seen such a vivid, gorgeous work. It was a pity that hands as talented as these were kept busy in the pits. Fortunately this was something he could change. He leaned forward to kiss his heart.

"Somebody able to create something so beautiful can't be bad, can he?"

"Sic is a good person. I've told you before."

"I know. Tomorrow I'm going to have a talk with your friend, and then we'll see how generous I am."

"My lord, are you serious?"

Casto stared at Renaldo wide-eyed. He had not expected that the Barbarian would ever budge when it came to this topic.

Gently the Angel of Death caressed Casto's hair.

"I may seem insensitive sometimes, but I do realize when something is bothering you, and I know how much you like Sic. I'm not blind either. This pendant"—again he let the miniature glide through his fingers—"is the most intimate and considerate present you've gotten for our wedding. Including my own gifts for you. Sic must really love you to have put so much effort into it."

The sheer joy in Casto's face filled Renaldo with happiness.

"I can't promise anything, but I'll deal with him openly and then we'll see what I can do."

"Can you take him away from Noran?"

Sadly Renaldo shook his head. He understood why Casto wanted to get his friend away from Noran. Renaldo himself considered Noran's actions against Sic despicable. Unfortunately the laws of the Pack were in favor of the master smith.

"I'm afraid not. I can only try buying him from Noran, but I doubt my brother-in-arms will give his consent. He is too caught up in his revenge. Nevertheless, I can see to it that Sic doesn't have to work in the pits anymore and that Noran shows some restraint."

Filled with gratitude, Casto nestled against Renaldo's chest.

"You're truly generous, Barbarian. How can I thank you?"

"I'm your god. I don't want you to think my grace can be bought with certain—favors. But since you're asking, I like it when you get physical."

As a reaction to the teasing tone in Renaldo's words, Casto fluttered his long lashes coquettishly. His right hand started fondling well-defined abdominal muscles while his left swept a loose strand of hair out of his face.

"I'm an obedient servant to my god. Never would I even think of trying to buy your grace. I'm fully satisfied being at your beck and call. Tell me, Barbarian, how do you want me?"

The hunger dominating Renaldo's face was almost more than Casto could bear.

"In every way possible, my gorgeous prince."

SIC FEARED the worst when one of the overseers came to escort him from the pit he was working in. And to think the day had not been too bad until now. During his morning punishment, he hadn't lost count even once, and Noran had been so busy, he had only raped him quickly. Sic did know his criteria for a good day were in stark contrast to what most people would have defined as acceptable, but since his treason, every morning he did not bleed was a good morning. Unfortunately this seemed about to change now. There were only three men who could summon him from the pit: his master and his gods. Sic had no inclination to meet any of them.

His heart fell when he saw Lord Renaldo waiting for him in the small, well-heated room of the overseers. Already mentally prepared for the pain his god would surely give him at any moment, he sank to his knees, his gaze demurely cast down. Lord Renaldo rose from the chair he had been sitting in. Threatening like death itself, he towered over Sic, who dreaded the moments to come.

"Get up, Sic."

The lord's voice was surprisingly soft. Trembling, the young man did as he was told.

"Look at me."

Again Sic obeyed, simply because disobedience was unthinkable in front of his god. Renaldo could have ordered him to ram a dagger into his heart and Sic would have done what was asked of him without hesitation. His green-blue eyes stared in terror at the regal face that was, against all odds, not filled with rage. When Lord Renaldo spoke, there was even some warmth in his voice.

"Yesterday you made Casto very happy, Sic. Your present has pleased him."

Since he didn't know what was expected of him, Sic kept his mouth shut.

"When my heart is happy, I'm happy as well. Casto wants me to forgive you. Before I do that, I want to know what you want."

"I don't understand, Master."

Sic wanted to look down again, but Lord Renaldo put his forefinger under his chin and forced him to keep gazing into the impenetrable stare of his god.

"I want to know what you want."

Sic swallowed hard, unsure what he should do. Then he suddenly realized that nothing he did could make his fate worse. Determined, he stuck out his chin.

"I want to forget that I was able to betray my friend, my god, and my master. I don't ever want to think about the fact again that I was too stupid to see Damon's threats for what they really were, empty shells. I want to go to sleep at night without hating myself for what I've done. I want to face Casto without being reminded that I don't deserve his friendship, and I want to be able to face my god without fearing his hatred and knowing at the same time that no matter what he's going to do to me, I'll still get away lightly.

Trembling, Sic took a deep breath, overwhelmed by his own outburst.

"But I can't have any of these, because I have sinned against everything I held dear. All that's left for me is to want what you want and to find the strength to bear what you deem fit as my punishment."

For a long time, the gray eyes penetrated Sic's desperate gaze without blinking. When Lord Renaldo finally spoke, his voice was raw.

"I have lived for a long time, and I've seen my share of traitors. Most of them regret their actions one day, usually when they have to pay for their sins. Still, I've never met anybody who accepted their fate as completely as you do. I forgive you."

Sic stared at Lord Renaldo wide-eyed, waiting for a cruel punch line and half expecting to be woken from this bizarre dream at any moment, but when nothing of that sort happened, he collapsed on the ground with desperate sobs.

"Master."

It was this one word, full of happiness but also filled with utter regret about everything that had happened, that convinced Renaldo of the justness of his decision. He picked the young man up and pressed a gentle kiss to his forehead.

"It's true. I forgive you."

Still sobbing, Sic reached for his god's palms and kissed them reverently.

"I swear to you, Master, I will never disappoint you again. Ever."

"I know, Sic, I know. But I want you to promise me something else. Should you ever be forced to choose again, you will protect Casto, do you understand?"

Renaldo saw realization dawning on the face of the smith. What he was asking of Sic was nothing less than living his life for Casto from now on. It was a price Sic was more than willing to pay, since this meant his existence would have some reason again. Not to mention that Casto would surely appreciate him more than Noran had ever done. He nodded, tears streaming down his face.

"Yes, Master, I promise."

"That's all I'm asking of you. And now come with me. I have better tasks for you than ruining your talented hands in the pits. From now on you'll be working for Casto the whole day. He has orders to leave you enough time to create such masterpieces as the miniature of Lys."

Sic looked down. His hands twisted nervously for a moment while he tried to make up his mind; then he reached into his torn tunic and produced a small package that he offered Renaldo with shaking hands.

"My best wishes for your wedding, Lord Renaldo."

Renaldo opened the rough piece of cloth, and pure astonishment conquered his features.

"Sic, this is perfect." He was holding a wooden bust of Casto, about the size of a child's fist, but so lifelike he almost expected it to start talking any minute.

"You are truly talented, Sic." Then Renaldo furrowed his brow. "Why are you giving me this only now?"

Sic stared intently at the ground. "I didn't dare to bother you with such a trifle. My fear was too great."

Again Renaldo forced Sic to meet his eyes. "You don't have to fear me anymore, slave. I forgave you. As far as I'm concerned, you're part of the Pack again, and I will give you my protection." He hesitated a moment, and when he carried on, genuine regret colored his voice.

"You're my brother-in-arms's property and at the moment, there's nothing I can do to change that. You'll have to bear with what he imposes on you. But I will take care of it, this I promise."

Sic smiled wistfully at his god. "It's fine, Lord Renaldo. Since I do deserve punishment. I'm already thrilled you forgave me. Perhaps, one day, my master will find it in his heart as well."

The hope permeating Sic's voice made Renaldo cringe. He could not bring himself to tell the young man the truth—that among all the warriors in the Pack, Noran was the most unforgiving and merciless. It would sooner happen that the Good Mother left this world voluntarily before Noran forgave Sic.

Renaldo sent Sic to Casto before he went to see Noran to negotiate his slave's future.

NORAN REGARDED Renaldo coldly when he entered the smithy. Ever since Noran's affair with Arja, their relationship had taken a turn for the worse. It had hurt Renaldo too much that his brother-in-arms and former lover had indeed been willing to leave them all for a beautiful face, and Noran had been too proud to ask his god for forgiveness. After Casto had forced Noran to spare Sic's life, he had stopped covering his animosity with politeness. If it went on like this, Renaldo would have to punish him, something he'd rather not do since people could get the impression that the Emeris and their demigods were not as closely knit as they had to be in order to defeat the Good Mother.

"Renaldo, what brings you here?"

No joke, no friendly bickering, not even a few set phrases. Noran did not seem to care anymore what his god thought about him. Renaldo didn't mind, though, since at the end of the day, he was still Noran's lord and god, and like everybody else, the smith would bow to his will.

"I'm here because of a rather complicated matter. You've been sharing a slave with Casto for some time."

Noran glared at him. "The traitor, yes. You know that."

"Indeed I do. I want Sic to stop going to the pits and instead work for Casto all the time. He is satisfied with Sic's performance and says he could make good use of him."

Noran's features hardened even more when the meaning behind Renaldo's words sunk in. His voice was vitriolic. "Don't tell me you forgave that dirty little traitor. I'd have never thought your wedding would make you so weak."

Now Renaldo had enough. It was one thing when Noran was grumpy and dismissive, but another when he was impertinent. Renaldo stared at the smith with all his authority until Noran lowered his gaze and knelt. Only after Noran had shown his respect did Renaldo start to talk.

"For your own good, I'll pretend you never said this, *brother*. But I'm warning you, should you ever imply again that Casto is no good for me, you'll get to know a side of me you surely won't enjoy.

"Sic is going to work for Casto, and I expect him to be physically able to do so, understood? I'm aware your thirst for revenge hasn't been sated yet, and in accordance with our laws, I will respect your claim of ownership for now. But I do advise you to make peace with yourself, because when our campaign in Ummana is over, you are going to sell Sic to me. At a reasonable price, of course. Have I made myself clear, Noran?"

Grimly, Noran stared at the ground. "Yes, my lord."

Renaldo nodded. "Then it's fine."

He turned around and left the smithy, left Noran seething with anger and suppressing the impulse to run after his lord and god and raise his hand against him. Neither Canubis nor Renaldo had ever talked to him in such a degrading manner. It was humiliating to be reminded of his place in the Pack like he was nothing more than a slave. And it was all the traitor's fault. He must have somehow managed to get on Renaldo's good side again, but he wouldn't benefit from it. Once the campaign was over, Noran would sell a broken puppet to his god, a toy that only worked for Noran. The traitor would be either destroyed or enthralled by Noran, once he was done with him. Then Renaldo could see whether he was still worth his attention.

"WAS THAT wise, brother?"

Canubis let the wine swish around in his cup, his amber eyes trained on Renaldo, who had just told him about his skirmish with Noran. Renaldo poured him some more of the bloodred liquid.

"It was necessary. Ever since the incident with Arja, Noran has changed profoundly. He's no longer the man I knew. I doubt he'd still be a chosen of the Mothers now. He's become cold and cruel."

"Like us."

"Definitely not like us. We don't take pleasure from it. Noran enjoys hurting Sic."

Canubis sighed. "I agree with you. He has changed for the worse. But our laws protect him. He can do to and with Sic whatever he pleases." He took a long sip from his cup. "What made you forgive the traitor? I didn't know you had a soft spot for him."

Renaldo smiled dreamily. "The present he gave to Casto. And Casto himself. He loves Sic, and I could no longer bear watching him worry about his well-being."

"Does Sic deserve forgiveness?"

Instead of an answer, Renaldo got up, rummaged for the bust of Casto, and showed it to his brother. Canubis stared at the piece of art in awe.

"It's his present for my wedding. He made it although he knew I wanted him dead, although he was so terrified of me he didn't even dare give the present to Casto to pass on to me. Yes, he deserves my forgiveness—like nobody did before."

Canubis's fingertips traced Casto's wooden likeness. He sounded distant when he spoke. "It looks as if he'd start laughing any moment. One can feel how much Sic loves and admires Casto. For that alone he has indeed earned condonation."

The brothers were silent for a moment. It was a comfortable, intimate silence in which each of them could ponder his own thoughts without disturbing or excluding the other. It was Canubis who finally spoke again.

"Have you talked to Casto about the Spring Ceremony?"

His brother's face froze.

"Yes, I have."

"I take it he's not ecstatic?"

"His exact words were 'Over my dead body.'"

Canubis felt a pang of sympathy for his little brother. "I know it's a bad moment to mention this, but I've told you so. You forced him and now you're paying the price."

Miffed, Renaldo emptied his cup in one go. "I know. It was a mistake, but last year I simply didn't know what to do. He was so unbelievably stubborn."

Canubis grinned. "Unlike now that he's the personification of obedience."

"Shut it. He's irresistible when he's opposing me."

"Nevertheless, you'll be joining the feast without him. You know you can't wriggle out of it."

Morosely Renaldo nodded. There was indeed no way for him to be excused from the festivities. Even though Casto refused to accompany him, he had to fulfill his duty. Under these special circumstances, it was legitimate to sleep with others, but the thought alone made shivers run down his spine. The idea of kissing somebody other than his heart, touching them intimately or even taking them, was so absurd he couldn't help wonder when he would wake from this nightmare.

"I'm sure Casto will have a change of heart come next year. He just needs time to get used to the situation." Canubis tried to be as gentle as he could since he wanted to encourage his brother. But Renaldo wasn't in the mood right now. Snorting derisively, he poured some more wine.

"I thought you'd know my heart by now. He doesn't have to get used to anything. This is a matter of principle for him. He'd rather bear me sleeping with others before he participates in a ceremony that is, in his opinion, humiliating him. Damn, Canubis, you were there when he had me brand him."

"A vicious move indeed."

Canubis still didn't know what to make of that coup. On one hand, he was amused how easily Casto had gotten the better of his brother and himself. On the other hand, he couldn't help but wonder how far Casto was willing to go when he thought something was to his advantage. Casto had proven how ruthless he could be against himself and when he was willing to subordinate his own well-being so easily to reach his goals, Canubis couldn't help but wonder what Casto would do to and with the people around him. A man like Casto could be a blessing as well as a curse for the Pack.

Even his idea to take the throne of Ummana and thus ensure his mate's and brother-in-law's dominance on the Plains without any bloodshed showed his readiness to sacrifice everything to a higher goal. Where this would lead, nobody could predict. The one thing Canubis was able to foresee was that his brother would not enjoy this year's Spring Ceremony.

To get Renaldo's mind off the sore topic, he started talking tactics about Ummana, something that filled them both with happy anticipation. Casto had given them detailed information about the power structures within the Twin Cities. Despite the fact that his knowledge about the people ruling the city was five years old—and therefore probably outdated—they had been able to get an idea about the mechanisms on which politics there operated.

According to Casto, the city was a snake pit controlled by the Council of Elders, which consisted of eleven members who were appointed by the richest families every five years, and the representatives of the guilds, who had the combined power of all their members to back them up. They were usually elected every three years, and the shortened period made their tactical decisions unpredictable sometimes. Except for the guilds of merchants and slave traders, whose people usually came from a wealthy background, most of them had mainly commoners as members. Of course, this did not keep them from meddling successfully in the affairs of the state. That the different institutions were intertwined socially and politically, like a barn full of unthreaded balls of wool, didn't help matters at all.

As long as a strong sovereign held the throne, as had been the case under Queen Isiris, the cumulative power of the Council, the guilds, and the families was concentrated on increasing the wealth and influence of Ummana.

If the king was too weak, the Council, the guilds, and everybody with enough money to join the skirmish tended to tear each other apart. There were no laws or codices of honor binding everybody equally. Money could buy everything and everybody, alliances were forged and broken as the participants pleased, and at the end of the day, the only thing that counted was who had managed to survive and gain even greater riches in the process.

To make things even worse—or more interesting, depending on one's point of view—the members of the Confederation of the Plains happily joined the schemes, always eager to gain an advantage over the others or even force a bigger chunk out of the delicious cake that was Ummana. Medelina, Kre, and Sravrana were monarchies and ruled by tightly knit royal clans. Alemba and Eppirat were governed by the military and naturally the most able-bodied among the cities. Wa'na Atoka was kind of exotic, for its citizens elected a tyrant every five years. Among the members of the Confederation, Medelina was the most powerful after Ummana. King Erac was a shrewd, merciless politician who had the goal to make Medelina equal to Ummana.

Every member of the Confederation had an embassy in the Twin Cities, as well as an army of spies to make use of even the smallest display of weakness the ruling class in Ummana showed, thus constantly increasing the confusion in the city.

If Casto's evaluation was right, then his five years of absence had been enough to destabilize the Twin Cities enough to be of advantage to them. They would conquer a vacuum needing to be filled. What would happen once Casto had seized the throne was an entirely different story. There was no way to tell how everybody, from the members of the Council down to the citizens, would react.

Canubis and Renaldo had never bothered much with the Twin Cities; they were too far away to be of great interest to them, although they were the center of trade on the continent. In their early days, before they had started to hole up in the Valley every winter, they had conquered and destroyed the Twin Cities twice or thrice, but those times were long gone and of course things had changed drastically since then. They were about to venture into unknown territory, and the thrill of possible gain was slightly diminished by worries about all the things that could go wrong.

"We will have to be extremely cautious. Since we have to move fast, we'll only take the best of our warriors, but as backup we should have the wolves come with us."

Canubis watched his brother intently.

"Will you be able to keep your thirst for revenge in check until we've gained a safe position?"

Renaldo's face turned into a mask. Whenever he thought about what his precious heart had had to endure in Ummana, his blood boiled. He didn't plan on risking their lives for the sake of getting even with Casto's enemies, but there was no way he would let them go unpunished either.

"It'll be up to Casto. If it bothers him too much, I can't guarantee anything."

Canubis nodded. He knew this was all the concession he would get from his dangerous, fire-wielding brother. Then again, he did not need more. If push came to shove, they could always cause a bloodbath and kill everybody who dared to oppose them. In many ways this would be more satisfying than losing themselves in tactical games. Either way, Canubis was looking forward to this campaign.

"We're riding one week after the ceremony. May the Mothers bless us."

4. SPRING CEREMONY

THE NIGHT before the Spring Ceremony, Casto was tossing and turning in his bed, unable to find any rest. Next to him Renaldo was sleeping soundly, seemingly unfazed by the fact his husband wouldn't accompany him to the most important feast of the year. When Renaldo had asked him, Casto's first reaction had been disgusted resistance. The thought of being paraded around naked, adorned like a cheap tavern whore, in front of all the drunk, lusty mercenaries, only to fall prey to the Barbarian's lust for the entire night, watched by all those hungry eyes, made him break out in cold sweat. There was no way he would ever be humiliated like that again. The memory of the previous year was still vivid in his mind and made bile rise in his mouth whenever he thought about it.

On the other hand, he knew exactly how important the Spring Ceremony was for Renaldo and how much he wanted Casto to be by his side. Despite his own wishes, Renaldo had forgone forcing Casto and had been uncharacteristically accepting of his husband's decision. Casto was conflicted. His instinct demanded he spend the following day—and especially the night—with Lys at the stables. His love for Renaldo—which still felt raw and new—compelled him to overcome his repulsion and bow to his mate's wishes. Restless, Casto weighed both options, as well as the possible outcomes, until he finally managed to fall into a nervous sleep. He woke a short time later without having found any rest. Renaldo was tight-lipped; it seemed as if only his sleep had been unperturbed by Casto's refusal. The tension between them was so unbearable that Casto made haste to excuse himself.

"I wish you a nice day, Barbarian, and enjoy the feast."

Genuine pain flashed across Renaldo's face, but he quickly composed himself again.

"I thank you, Casto. I assume I'll be seeing you tomorrow?"

Casto gave his consent with a bow before he rushed out of the chambers. He panted heavily in the cold spring air. Renaldo's pain was like a knife in his chest.

Casto cursed under his breath. Of course he was going to participate in the feast; how could he have ever thought differently? He had pledged his eternal love and fealty to Renaldo, not to mention the obedience he had compelled himself to. Even though Renaldo had not asked it of him directly, it was nevertheless clear what his will was.

Still torn but also determined, Casto went to the buildings where the sauna and baths were located. In one of the smaller rooms he found Frankus, who couldn't believe his eyes.

"Casto, what are you doing here? I'd have never thought to see you today, of all days."

Casto made a face. "Believe me, Frankus, I wouldn't have thought it either. It seems I'm a more obedient servant to the Barbarian than we all thought."

"Does Renaldo know you're here?"

Casto shook his head. "No. I might bow to his will, but that doesn't mean I'm not going to let him suffer for forcing me last year."

Frankus laughed. "You're definitely not an obedient servant, Prince! On the contrary, you're refreshingly mean. I like it."

Casto bowed to Frankus in mockery. "I'm glad to have your approval, Frankus. Do you think you can make me presentable for tonight?"

"But of course. It'll be my pleasure. I will deal with you personally, my gorgeous lord."

Still filled with warring emotions, Casto succumbed to Frankus's experienced touch. He already knew the procedures from last year, but this time he felt them more intensely, because he was no longer blinded by rage. Casto realized that every single step was subordinated to a higher purpose, namely preparing him for the strain of the night.

Bit by bit Casto changed from an individual into a recipient vessel ready to serve Renaldo's lust. First of all, his body hair was removed with a mixture of honey and sugar, just like the year before. His velvet-smooth skin should please the Barbarian. Then came the sauna sessions, which left him relaxed and eager. When Frankus started washing him with scented soaps in the pool, Casto was already reduced to his purpose of the evening. His personality was gradually drowned in a haze of lust. The nerula oil, massaged into his skin by two slaves, changed him into a creature solely driven by instinct. All he could think about was that he would soon be allowed to serve Renaldo, that his god would take him until the morning came. The thought was so erotic, Casto came more than once before the massage was done.

Then Frankus came back and brought with him a brush and a box full of gold dust, ready to start the tiring task of turning Casto into a living statue. After more than two hours, he stepped back and admired his work.

"You look breathtaking, my beauty. Even if I say so myself, you're a masterpiece."

Casto managed to smile despite the fire burning his blood and the mixed emotions turning his thoughts into chaos.

"I was prepared by the best of all."

"Now you're flattering me. Come, I'll take you to the waiting chamber."

WHILE CASTO was prepared for his mate, Renaldo paced his chambers like a caged animal, drank wine, and cursed his own stupidity. Why on earth had he assumed it would be without consequence when he forced his recalcitrant slave to do something he resented? Now he paid a cruelly high price for this miscalculation. The only thing he could do, considering this unpleasant situation, was get over it with some dignity. Despite his repugnance, he put on his best clothes, not wishing to give the impression he didn't pay the feast due respect.

When his brother came to get him, Renaldo looked as breathtaking as ever. Canubis patted his shoulder.

"I'll never get used to your unearthly beauty. If we weren't brothers, I'd be jealous of you."

"There's no reason to be. Unlike you, I'll be celebrating the feast without my heart. So my beauty is quite useless."

"Don't be so downcast. Despite your married status, you can have some serious fun tonight."

Irritably Renaldo cast his brother aside.

"I had 'serious fun,' as you call it, my entire life. I was looking forward to enjoying the peace of a steady relationship."

"And I won't get tired of telling you that I warned you."

"Shut up and get going."

They made their way to the sauna in oppressive silence. Still quiet, they entered the room where Noemi was waiting for them. The snake witch was naked, covered in gold dust, and wearing an alluring smile. She knew how stunning she was and enjoyed playing with the status of a slave girl. Canubis bowed to his wife.

"My jewel, you're gorgeous as always."

"And you, my lord, are generous, as always."

Noemi's voice was soft. If Renaldo hadn't known her so well, he could have thought she was indeed only a slave girl. Now his brother put the golden collar with the black diamonds around her neck, fastened the golden chain to the eyelet, and turned to leave. Renaldo had his hand on the door when he suddenly felt the familiar tingling that betrayed Casto's presence. A cool, mocking voice reached his ears from the far side of the chamber.

"You want to leave without me, Barbarian? After Frankus has taken so many pains to make me presentable for you?"

Renaldo spun around as fast as he could and froze.

On the day of their wedding, Renaldo had thought his lover couldn't look any better. He had to revise this assumption, because the creature he was facing now surpassed everything he had ever seen, was more than he could ever wish for. The long, well-defined muscles were highlighted and enhanced by the gold dust, like the play of shadows on a superb statue. The mesmerizing blue eyes were made even more dazzling by the black kohl that surrounded them, and the wheat-blond hair was tamed by a band of dark blue leather, the ends dipped in gold dust, just like at their wedding.

It wasn't just Casto's looks that overwhelmed Renaldo's senses, but also his fire, which had never burned with more intensity than at this moment. Casto's inner strife, his disgust concerning the feast, were as tangible as his love for Renaldo, and culminated in a powerful blaze surrounding them both like a coat.

Renaldo had always known his fire was irresistible, that it seared everybody who came too close. It was the burden he carried. Casto burned with the same intensity, destroyed everything he touched, always restlessly searching for the one as terrifying and dreadful as itself, looking for the counterpart that had tasted the same loneliness as he. In this cramped room, the flame that had been parted such a long time ago flared up in all-consuming power, showing its true face, the lethal force it contained. The air started to boil. No human being could have survived in this heat, and even the Wolf of War and his witch wife retreated a few steps from the Angel of Death and the prince.

It was an intimate moment when the fire engulfed them both, proof of their unity. Renaldo closed the gap between them, his hand extended, and his fingertips traced Casto's cheeks ever so lightly, his voice full of awe. It almost seemed that he understood only now what it truly meant to find his heart.

"You're like me. We're one."

The fire blazed again and then retreated, not extinguished, but tamed for the moment. Renaldo's hands trembled from the sheer force he experienced. From birth he had been the master of fire, but it had taken him centuries to gain control of his abilities. He had always known he would be able to completely tame the flames once he was back to being a fully-fledged god and that everything he did until then had to be carefully thought over. What Casto offered him now was almost more than he could handle.

Canubis placed a hand on his brother's shoulder. He was more than pleased with what had just happened.

"It seems as if Casto is fueling you even more than we had hoped. I just felt as if I were standing on top of a hill during a thunderstorm and lightning was crashing all around me."

"It was almost terrifying." Noemi's voice was thin. "If I didn't know you both so well…." She stopped, regarding the two men reverently.

Casto tried to assure her with one of his most charming smiles. "Whatever happened just now, my lady, I can assure you it wasn't for the purpose of upsetting you."

"It's fine, Casto. People don't call me a witch for nothing. Have you been able to control it?"

The prince shook his head, then turned to his mate, who was still caught in loving awe.

"I probably would have been able to control it, but that wasn't necessary. It was just a harbinger and a last validation that we truly are one."

Renaldo's fingers stroked Casto's hair gently. "If you hadn't decided to give me this present, we probably would have had to wait some time longer for this. What made you toss your principles to the wind?"

Casto pressed a soft kiss on his mate's hand.

"In case you haven't noticed, Barbarian, I love you. Moreover, I recalled the countless times when you spared or forgave me against better judgment. I owed you one."

"At the risk of you changing your mind again, I have to tell you that you're wrong. Sparing and forgiving you was my decision alone. You're my heart. What I'm doing for you, I do because I love you. You don't have to pay a bill and I don't expect any favors from you—at least not too many." The Angel of Death grinned suggestively. If Casto hadn't been covered in gold dust all over, Renaldo would have been able to see him blush from head to toe.

"I'd better get the collar. I'm sure our followers are impatiently waiting for us." Canubis bowed to his wife once more, then went for the door. "My jewel, I'll be back in a heartbeat."

"I'll be waiting for you, my lord."

"When she says it, it sounds genuine." Renaldo looked at his lover reproachfully. Casto only shrugged.

"I'm standing naked, covered in gold dust, in front of you, willing to let you have me the entire evening in front of an audience although I deeply resent it and don't have to. You should be grateful, *my lord*."

At those last words, Casto's voice rose in mockery, his eyes glinting.

"I am grateful, don't get me wrong. I just wanted to give you a hint what else you could do to please me."

Before Casto could make up his mind whether to be angry about the teasing, Canubis returned with the golden collar. Suddenly dead serious again, Renaldo put the precious jewelry around the prince's neck. The blue diamonds sparkled in the candlelight like little suns. When the clasp closed with an audible click and the Barbarian fastened the thin golden chain to the eyelet, Casto had to swallow hard.

He had chosen his destiny, had bound himself to Renaldo once and for all. Casto felt peace growing inside. Truth be told, he had decided a long time ago, and now he had to stand by it.

Canubis smiled warmly at his wife, his brother, and his brother-in-law.

"Today is a special night. It's the first time we both have our hearts with us on the Spring Ceremony. The Mothers are favoring us."

"Not like our followers, who must be really impatient by now. We took our sweet time."

Renaldo slung the chain that connected him to Casto around his wrist. "Let's go."

CASTO FOLLOWED his mate reluctantly into the night. Although spring had finally returned to the Valley, the cold was still prominent. Not to mention the snow, which hadn't even begun to melt. The prince was glad about the short distance between the sauna and the great hall; otherwise he would have surely frozen to death.

When Canubis opened the broad doors, applause broke out. With their hearts on their chains, the divine brothers proceeded through the middle lane toward their places at the table. Casto concentrated on keeping his gaze trained on Renaldo's back, but out of the corner of his eye he still saw more than was good for his peace of mind. The faces of all people present were blushing in happy anticipation; the stares directed at his body seemed to spear him. There was no malice, no contempt; instead he felt a hunger, a lust he couldn't cope with. All of a sudden, Casto realized the Barbarian had not forced him last year solely because he wanted to humiliate him. It had also been a demonstration of his own power and Casto's standing. Letting him take part in the feast in such an exclusive position sent a message louder than words. Casto was precious and highly valuable; he was loved and respected by his owner, which made it inevitable that everybody else had to treat him the same way. The prince felt his cheeks burn when he thought about how viciously he had cursed the Barbarian the previous year, how much hatred he had thrown his way. Silently he begged for forgiveness, determined to make up for his crass miscalculation.

Their little parade had now reached the far end of the table, and the two demigods turned to their assembled underlings, the cups with wine held high.

"*Blod an Ana-Darasa!*"

"Blood for Ana-Darasa!"

The warriors repeated the ancient chant, and after they all had sacrificed some of their blood, the feast began. Casto stepped around his mate's chair to refill his cup. Renaldo grabbed his wrist, pulled him onto his lap, and offered him the wine.

"Drink, my own."

The red liquid flowed like lava down Casto's throat and kindled his lust until only ashes remained of his will. He no longer minded the Angel of Death's hand on his penis or the hot, deep kiss he was receiving from his lover. All he wanted was to belong to Renaldo, to yield to his will.

"My beautiful, precious darling. I promise, you won't forget this night in a hurry."

Groaning, Casto arched his back and succumbed to the demigod's power.

GHOSTS OF THE PAST

1. UMMANA

THE GROUP of riders stopped their horses on a rise and gazed down into the plains where the Umman River drifted lazily. The city bearing its name sparkled and gleamed on both banks in the bright sunlight like an exotic gem. The name of the Twin Cities was well earned. They were like mirror images connected by countless bridges over the river that had made them so unbelievably rich. From the seaside, majestic trade ships glided toward the city, escorted by countless heavily armed frigates that protected the cargo from pirates with the ferocity of a pack of wild dogs.

The harbor was formed like a half circle where the ships dropped anchor, discharged their cargo, and got repaired in the dockyards before they were loaded with new merchandise and started their journey back to the cities along the coastline of the Eastern Kingdoms. The cargo was then sent either by caravan or on smaller boats on the river into the continent to make its owners even richer than they already were.

The merchandise coming from the heart of the continent was sent out over the sea. Ummana was the biggest collecting point for merchandise of all kinds in the whole world. Like an especially fat spider, it sat on the lifeline of international trade, and her citizens were well versed in securing themselves a good part of the riches flowing through their hands.

Even from the distance, the travelers from the North could see that the city was overflowing with life. It wasn't only the ships and boats practically clogging the river, but also the countless caravans flocking toward the center of all trade from every direction.

"Ummana."

With awkward movements that lacked his usual grace, Casto slid down from Lys's back. Renaldo was regarding his mate with worry. The closer they had gotten to Casto's former home, the more anxious and withdrawn he had become. He barely spoke anymore, and even Sic was no longer able to draw him out. During the night he was again tortured by bad dreams. Now that Renaldo was able to understand what Casto was screaming, he was even more determined to punish everybody who had even the slightest complicity in his heart's suffering as brutally as possible.

To prepare them for their mission in the Twin Cities, Casto had not only given them detailed information about his life in Ummana, he had also taught them the language so they could communicate without the aid of a translator. During the course of the last days, though, Renaldo had realized that his lover had kept his darkest memories to himself. It hurt him deeply that all he could do to help Casto was pull him close during the night when he startled from his sleep, bathed in sweat. Seeing the proud young man so vulnerable only deepened Renaldo's hatred for the city.

Renaldo dismounted his horse and put an arm around Casto.

"Is everything all right, my own?"

An insecure smile flashed across the sensual lips. It almost broke Renaldo's heart to see Casto so shaken.

"I underestimated the power of my memories." He buried his face in Renaldo's chest. "I'm afraid to disappoint you, Barbarian. What if I'm not strong enough? What if I'm leading us all into perdition?"

Instead of Renaldo, Canubis answered, his voice as unshakable as his personality.

"You definitely are strong enough, Casto. There's no doubt about it. You're the heart of a god. And in case you've forgotten," the powerful Wolf of War added with a broad grin, "I'd love to remind you that you're the only one able to put up with my dear brother for any length of time. I'm surprised you even know the meaning of insecurity."

Good-humored laughter broke out around them. Renaldo shot his brother a vicious glance, and Casto looked up. His leader's amber eyes elated him. The prince straightened up.

"You're right, Lord Canubis. I'm a prince—no, since yesterday I'm a king, mate to a god. It's time to act like one."

The Wolf of War patted Casto's shoulder.

"Well said, Your Majesty. We'll take a break here, get something to eat, dress ourselves up, and then we'll conquer the richest city in the world."

TENO, THE guard on duty at the western gate, reared up from contemplating the state of his fingernails when he heard hoofbeats heralding a large group of riders. When he realized how elevated the group was, his surprise deepened.

For the next few days, no delegations from other cities were expected. This week their king would have come of age and ascended to the throne, if he hadn't gone missing some five years ago.

It was a painful time, for the cities had been gradually sliding into chaos ever since Prince Castolus had vanished so suddenly. So far only the citizens had realized this. On the surface business was still thriving, but because of the unsteady political situation, important investments were kept on hold and necessary reforms were delayed. The other cities of the Confederation were gathering like hungry vultures around a carcass, ready to rip Ummana to pieces. It was still four years until Princess Anesha would be old enough to claim the throne, provided she survived till then. Rumors were flying that she had only narrowly escaped an attempted murder.

The Council of Elders, Aran, the father of Anesha and Casto, and some of the most influential heads of the guilds were engaged in a merciless battle for supremacy in the city. The outcome of that battle was becoming more and more uncertain. All citizens of Ummana were praying to the gods of profit that this precarious situation would end soon.

The foreign group had now come close enough for him to distinguish its members clearly. It seemed as if the visitors had come a long way; most of them were obviously from the North, even though there were some desert dwellers and people from the Eastern Kingdoms among them. Three men were in the lead, two of them grim warriors who escorted a slender, arrogant-looking young man sitting on a decidedly noble warhorse. The young man's wheat-blond hair sparkled in the sun like a crown, and the blue eyes were so bright, Teno had to avert his gaze. Once he had known a look like this very well, when Queen Isiris was still alive.

It took a moment, in which the guard was listening to his own thoughts as if they were strangers in his head; then he went down on his knees while the young man and his entourage reined in their horses.

"Your Highness!"

At this time of day, the western gate was always swamped with people, and Teno's strange behavior kindled their curiosity. Fevered whispering set in and quickly developed into loud cheering when more and more citizens recognized the beautiful stranger as their king. The news of his return spread like wildfire through the city. Renaldo tensed while more and more people started to rush toward the gate, toward Casto. Happy anticipation vibrated in the air, and the cheers rang in the ears of the demigods and their warriors.

They had not expected this. Neither that Casto would be immediately recognized, nor that he would be welcomed in such an overwhelming manner. Unsure of what to do, the Angel of Death shot his brother a questioning look, but the Wolf of War was, for once, at a loss himself.

Casto, on the other hand, seemed to be unperturbed by the commotion. Like a statue he sat on Lys's back, his mesmerizing blue eyes scanning the crowd in a benign manner. Every sign of insecurity was gone, and he basked in the welcome his people were giving him.

Another glance between Canubis and Renaldo confirmed how utterly grateful they both were to have this strong, proud king at their side. It was definitely better than being his enemy. Now Casto raised his hand, and the masses fell silent. Like one person they knelt, paying their king due respect. Casto's voice echoed through the streets.

"I have to thank you, citizens of Ummana, for this warm welcome. I have come back to claim what is rightfully mine. Now let me through."

Casto's companions held their breath, half anticipating that the people would crush them in their excitement, and ready to forge their way into the city with blunt force. But again they had underestimated Casto's authority. Silently the crowd parted, lined up in reverential rows that led them along the streets to the gates of the palace. When Casto started to move, the cheers broke out again, accompanying them through the city, heralding their arrival to the leaders of the city long before they actually met them.

Despite the positive reaction from the people, the warriors were tense. They feared an assassin might mingle in the crowd, ready to go after Casto's life. To prevent this they clustered around him, ready to kill anybody trying to get close. On guard, the mercenaries were unable to appreciate the beauty of the place they had entered.

Sic and Daran, on the other hand, who were both riding in the middle of the baggage, the traditional place for the slaves, didn't know where to look first. The buildings lining the main street were all high and slim, like elegant racing dogs, and their walls were plastered with chalk, making it hard to gaze at them directly in the glaring sun. Their horses' hooves stomped on solid, evenly laid stones the color of young leaves. Neither of the two young men had ever seen a stone like this, and later they would discover that all the main streets had pavement in a different shade. The people they passed were mostly well-dressed, in short tunics that ended midthigh and were cinched at the waist with belts of leather or linen. Sticking out like flowers in a field of grass were those who obviously didn't have to care about money in the least. Men and women alike wore silk so fine it was almost see-through, dyed in vivid colors ranging from light red to orange and yellow. Their belts were made of gold, and the jewelry they wore was almost as blinding as the walls of the houses. Everything in Ummana seemed to be too much, too rich, too vibrant, and Daran wondered how Casto could have come to resent a place as charming as this.

When they reached the gates leading into the palace, the Angel of Death, as well as the other warriors, were able to relax a little bit. The citizens had not followed them here, so there weren't as many people they had to keep an eye on.

The palace of Ummana was also the center of the Twin Cities, virtually and literally. Before it united with the sea, the Umman divided into two rivulets that embraced between them a small island on which the palace had been built. All roads led to this one building that presented its marble-tiled front to the plains, whereas the back looked out on the sea like a silent, threatening guardian. It was almost like a small city in itself, with blooming gardens, exclusive shops, and small but unbelievably expensive houses cowering in its shadow. Inside it resembled a beehive without a clear concept of indoors and outdoors. Floors could lead into small gardens with fountains as well as into great halls or exclusive chambers.

The mercenaries' attention was focused on the broad steps leading into the palace building itself, where quite another crowd had gathered. They did not cheer. There were three groups, and all of them showed the same suspicion in their eyes, ready to take Casto prisoner and accuse him of fraud. The biggest group was made up of eleven men and women in floor-length dark red robes, whom the Angel of Death identified as members of the Council of Elders. Standing at the foot of the stairs, they stared with open hostility at this most unwelcome disturbance of their daily affairs.

A few feet behind them, three men and two women wearing elaborate clothes with the insignia of the most influential guilds had positioned themselves. It was obvious how displeased they were with Casto's sudden appearance, but unlike the members of the Council, they seemed to be willing to accept this turn of events more readily in case it could guarantee them an advantage.

At the top of the stairs, close to one of the marble columns, Renaldo spied two men he recognized instinctively as the most heinous and despicable he had ever met. They, too, were dressed expensively, showing off their wealth carelessly and in rather bad taste. The bigger one of them stared at Casto with a mixture of fear and hatred; his slightly slanted eyes were shadowed by the column and almost seemed to glow. From the way the man moved, Renaldo knew he had to be Casto's father, although there was no facial resemblance. The King of Ummana definitely took after his mother.

The tension in the air was almost palpable, and everybody was waiting for another to make the first move, to show weakness. From the disappointment in the noble people's faces, the Angel of Death knew they had realized Casto was indeed their king. Lys was standing in front of the Council members with his neck held proudly; his rider examined his old enemies coldly.

Casto's appearance was so regal, Renaldo felt his chest swelling with pride. There was no telling what Casto was thinking at that moment. If he was afraid, he was hiding it well. The place was silent like the grave; only the challenging snort of the Emperor of the Storms echoed across the square as a declaration of war. Like a statue Casto was sitting on his stallion's back, every span a king who had come to claim what was rightfully his. Silently the two parties stared at each other, waiting for the other to give in.

The Council of Elders broke first.

With a grand gesture, the leader of the Council, an elderly man in his sixties whom Renaldo identified as Nambuno, according to his mate's description, bent his knee in front of Casto. As if this had broken a dam, the others followed, somewhat glad that the oppressive atmosphere was at least slightly disturbed. Seemingly oblivious of the trial of strength he had just lost, Nambuno's voice resounded unctuously in the square.

"Your Highness! We are so glad to have you back unharmed. By now we had lost all hope."

The king smiled coldly, a gesture that made more than one of the assembled nobles break out in cold sweat. They remembered clearly where they had last seen a smile like that and what had happened when that person had been displeased.

"I am sure you were hoping for the best, though. I could almost feel your good intentions, especially yesterday, on my birthday. My, my, my, how your prayers were with me all the time…."

The threat in those words was so thinly veiled it made the men and women shudder in fear. This was no longer the shy, obedient boy they had known. This was their king, who had no reason to be lenient toward any of them. Nambuno managed to hide his insecurity even though his voice lost a good part of its former grandeur.

"How can we be of service, Your Highness?"

Casto's voice and expression were as arrogant as Renaldo remembered them from their first time together.

"I want the royal wing prepared for me and my entourage. Clear the entire building so that we have some privacy. Our slaves will instruct your servants about what is needed. Come tonight, I don't want any other slaves but my own in this part of the palace.

"It is also my will that you send messengers to confirm my return to the entire city. I'm planning to have a big feast in celebration of my ascending the throne. The citizens can look forward to that. For tonight you will organize an intimate dinner, only the most important people in the city. That's it for now."

With a careless gesture, the king dismissed the people who only an hour ago had been the most influential and powerful in Ummana as if they were nothing but a bunch of slaves receiving their orders. Lys turned around on his hind legs and paraded away from the square. Canubis grinned like a fool when he followed Casto.

"You truly are a king, Casto. I'm very proud of you!"

Not a muscle moved in the young man's face when he turned to his leader.

"Strictly speaking, I'm far more than just a simple king, Lord Canubis. I'm the heart of a god, after all."

Renaldo started to guffaw, and everybody who had heard Casto's answer joined him.

"Well said, my own. But let me repeat my brother's praise. You were outstanding! Where are you taking us?"

"To the stables. I want to see how the horses are accommodated. Plus this way the servants have time to prepare the rooms without us getting under their feet, and you can become acquainted with the palace."

"THE QUEEN is dead!"

"Queen Isiris has died!"

The words were carried through the palace like a soft rustling that would soon turn into a gale. First it was only a whisper behind raised hands, but it grew in volume until the terror behind the news had gained enough power to reach over the palace's walls and into the city. On this night death was an unexpected and truly unwelcome guest. He had taken the queen with him and left the city without a ruler at a crucial time.

The small boy in the elaborate chambers heard the words as well; they crept viciously into his heavily guarded world, seeped like poison through his ears toward his heart, and rendered him paralyzed. He was still too small to fully comprehend what consequences his mother's death would have, but with the instincts his family had honed to perfection throughout the centuries, he knew he was facing hard times. Too young to escape, he would have to brave the storm gathering over the city.

WHILE THE king inspected the stables, the Council of Elders met in a chamber in the southern wing of the palace. They were babbling excitedly, like chickens suddenly attacked by a hawk. Nambuno had some trouble restoring order.

"Please, sisters and brothers, calm down. I know this day has turned out quite differently from what we could have wanted, but it's definitely too early to start panicking."

"Panicking? You think the king's sudden return is a reason for panicking?"

The speaker's voice was shrill, but not due to her emotions. Unfortunately, Amicia had been cursed at birth with a voice that reminded one of a flock of seagulls haggling for the dead fish in the harbor. It did not diminish her standing in the city, though, since she was the head of one of the richest families in Ummana and used to getting her will.

"I'd rather call it a catastrophe. Everything we've gained so far is now lost, and we have to assume that Castolus is still under his father's thrall. I wouldn't put it beyond Aran to have plotted this from the very beginning. Or am I the only one suspecting it's no coincidence that the prince has arrived exactly one day after his birthday, when we have no chance whatsoever to oppose his claim?"

The other members of the Council nodded their agreement. They all were nervous, like sheep who had just heard wolves howling, since Castolus's return meant all their plans had evaporated into thin air. More than ten years' worth of scheming had gone down the drain in one painful moment. Driven by despair about their bleak prospects, one of them even went so far as to voice the unthinkable.

"What if the king meets with an accident? Things like these happen on a regular basis. Of course we would be disconsolate, but what's done is done."

"Shut your mouth, imbecile!" Nambuno hissed like an alley cat. "Haven't you heard how the people have welcomed him? If he dies now, we'll undoubtedly have to deal with riots, and the whole situation is complicated enough already."

Embarrassed, the young man fell silent. He hadn't been a member of the Council for long, and the sharp rebuke tore at his ego.

"What about his entourage? They're obviously barbarians, so it shouldn't be hard to play them." A woman who had been a member of the Council for five years made this suggestion. Her voice was seemingly calm, but those who knew her could tell how agitated she was—she hadn't stopped cracking her knuckles since she entered the room. This time it was Amicia who rolled her eyes. There was nothing she abhorred more than blind politicking without due consideration.

"The king's men are unknown persons to us. How often have I told you we don't play with the unknown? They look rich and powerful, and they're armed to their teeth. Even if we manage to use them for our purposes, they could still cause a bloodbath. No, as hard as it is, we have to lie low and try to find out more about them. It would also be nice to know what kind of relationship Castolus and his father have now."

"Why don't you just ask him?"

The woman talking now was breathtaking. Her clear blue eyes sparkled angrily; her wheat-blonde hair was arranged in a complicated coiffure and glowed whenever it was hit by the sun's rays filtering into the chamber through a high window. Princess Anesha was the mirror image of her older brother.

"I hear you blabbering about tactics and politics, when all we should think about is how to soothe the king's wrath. We have betrayed him, have left him defenseless in front of his enemies. Damn it, *we* were his enemies. Now he's back, and the people have welcomed him with open arms. I'm surprised you can only think about how to get out on top.

"I'm telling you, anything that doesn't cost us all our lives would be miracle. Castolus has the right to condemn us for high treason, something we shouldn't take lightly. Discuss as much as you want, but in the end, we'll all pay the price for our crimes against the king."

Anesha left the room with a flourish, barely able to suppress a condescending snicker until she was alone. *These idiots!* The older she got, the easier she found it to play with them, as if they were mere puppets on strings. Granted, the new situation was dangerous in more than one respect, but if she played her cards right—and she intended to do so—her victory was only a question of time. The princess was sure she would be able to deal with Castolus; he was her brother, after all, and from what she had seen so far, he was exactly like her. Getting on his good side might prove difficult, but what worth had a victory when you didn't have to work for it? Not too long from now, the Council would pay for trying to reduce her to nothing but a figurehead while they kept all the real power to themselves.

Inside the chamber, the members of the Council were staring at each other in silence. Anesha had voiced their deepest fear, that their lives were forfeit. Finally Amicia spoke again.

"Anesha is right. The king has no reason to be fond of us. But as much as he may want to subject us to his revenge, he still needs us to govern the city. We should try to show him how irreplaceable we are. My suggestion is, we all get our documents in order so we can give the king all the answers he needs."

The men and women voiced their agreement but kept on wondering silently how they could make the most out of this new development.

IN THE still of the night, Lysistratos tried to cope with the pain and the fear the anchor emitted. A few months ago, something major had happened, something that changed everything. The mother of the anchor had died. Since then he had been subjected to the "care" of his father, a most unpleasant man Lysistratos would have loved to kill. Although he was by now able to see through the anchor's eyes and feel his emotions, they still had no conscious bond. The anchor was aware of Lysistratos's presence on a feral level, but he was too young and too preoccupied with his drastically changing life to acknowledge their connection. All Lysistratos could do at the moment was absorb the boy's pain and fear, his utter terror and raging fury, and thus help him through these difficult times.

IN YET another part of the palace, a similar discussion took place, but the content and conclusion were a lot less amiable than those of the Council.

Aran was prowling on the expensive carpet in his office, his hands behind his back, his eyes dark with rage.

"That worthless midget! Why couldn't he just die?"

"I don't know what your problem is. This scenario is perfect for us." Voltara was slouching in a chair, his feet on Aran's desk, his voice as bored as his body language suggested.

"What do you mean, 'perfect'? Don't you get it, you idiot? My son is back, and since yesterday he has an official claim to the throne. All trumps we may have had are gone. The cards are shuffled anew."

"Who cares about the trumps when you can control the joker? Your son is ours, Aran; we both have seen to that. He may look all high and mighty now, but I'm sure he hasn't forgotten who his masters are."

"Are you sure about that, Voltara? Because I've been doubting for some time if we managed to break Casto. He's his mother's spitting image, and Isiris was a gifted actor when she had to be. Where would my son have found the courage to flee if he was completely enthralled by us? I suspect he played us, waiting for the right moment to escape."

"Courage born of despair." The torturer made a dismissive gesture. "Give me half an hour alone with him, and you'll see how he starts begging to do your bidding."

"What about his companions? They don't look as if they could take a joke."

Again the torturer showed his contempt openly. "What about them? They're barbarians. Nobody's going to miss them."

AND IN a house far from the palace, a man was kneeling in front of an elderly woman, his voice ripe with anticipation.

"It all happened, mistress! Just as you've predicted! They've all come, the two bastards, their hearts, the Emeris."

On the woman's face, a smile appeared, as cold and cruel as a sudden chill freezing the buds in spring.

"The Good Mother has enlightened me, blessed be her power! Now listen well, because today is the last day you see me. Two days from now, I'm going through the ritual to create the poison. My servant will bring it to you. You have one week to smuggle it into the palace. Be careful! You can't be delayed, for the effect diminishes with every day. If you can't manage to give it to the king, one of the Emeris is fine as well. As long as the barbarians have to mourn at least one death. Don't try it with the bastards or the witch. It wouldn't have any effect on the brothers, and the witch is too strong. That wretched snake is protecting her. Do you understand?"

The man nodded eagerly.

"Yes, mistress. Everything will happen the way you want it to."

The woman extended a hand whose fingers looked like claws.

"Be blessed. If you manage to succeed, the Good Mother will reward you richly."

His eyes bulging in religious ecstasy and with his body still bent subserviently, the man left the room.

The priestess of the Good Mother shook her hand as if she had touched something filthy. Her personal servant appeared silently, like a shadow, with a bowl of water. The hag caressed her hair.

"In two days I'll be leaving you, my child. You will hand that scum the poison and then monitor him. I don't want this to be a failure."

"Yes, my mistress." The young woman hesitated for a moment; then she took the priestess's hand and kissed it reverently.

"When am I allowed to follow you, mistress?"

"As soon as the attempt is successful. I'll be waiting for you, slave."

The girl's eyes lit with happiness. "You are too generous, mistress. Everything will go as planned."

Daran was sitting on a trunk in the middle of the chambers the desert brothers had taken as theirs, trying to calm his thoughts. Ummana had stirred him up in ways he wasn't able to comprehend yet. Too much had happened in those few hours since they had entered the city, and Daran couldn't shake the uneasy feeling that the trouble had only just begun.

"You know, no matter how long you stare at the wall, no hole will appear. Neither will the trunks miraculously unpack themselves."

Kalad's mocking voice jolted Daran from his bemused state. He bolted upright and apologized. Because even though the desert brothers spoiled him like crazy, they were still his masters and expected him to fulfill his duties. Daran was meticulous about doing their bidding, since this was the only way he could convey his gratitude to them.

"I'm sorry, master. I was just thinking."

"That much I could tell. Now stop worrying and start working. Aegid and I still have some things to do, but when we're back, we'd like to take a bath with you."

Daran lowered his gaze to hide the happy anticipation blooming in his face. Taking a bath was only the prelude to more carnal acts between them.

Kalad chuckled. "You're way too adorable, little thief!"

He pressed a gentle kiss to Daran's temple and was off again.

In the chambers right next to those of the desert brothers, Wolfstan watched as his darling wife patrolled the rooms, memorizing every corner and developing different escape routes in case of an emergency. When she was finally satisfied, Hulda stopped in the center of the main room, her voice slightly condescending.

"It will do."

The armorer tried to suppress his smile and failed. Like everybody else in their group, Hulda had been deeply impressed by this place Casto called home. It was just like her to hide her awe behind some snarky comments. Of course, the telltale twitching of his lips hadn't escaped her. One perfectly curved eyebrow shot skywards.

"What?"

"It's nothing, my dear. Just me being happy."

Hulda huffed but approached him nevertheless, now with barely concealed lust illuminating her features. Wolfstan was glad their slaves were already done unpacking and had left them alone.

Noemi Amerasu was staring at the walls just like Daran had, but nobody dared to disturb her. Even Canubis waited patiently until his heart was done with whatever had been going on in that complicated mind of hers and relaxed her stiff shoulders, which was his cue to sling his arms around her. A sigh escaped from her lips.

"What is it, my precious jewel?"

Slender fingers closed on his arms, and the Wolf of War could feel his wife channeling some of his strength into herself. It worried him deeply, since she only resorted to this when she was desperate. Her voice was ragged, as if she had just woken from a deep sleep.

"This place is no good. It's rotten through and through. I can feel the poison seeping into us. If we're not careful, we are all in danger. It terrifies me."

Canubis hugged her closer, willing more of his power into her, trying to comfort her with his strength.

"I won't tell you to relax, since we both know how accurate your senses are, but I'm telling you to trust the Mothers. They're with us. Always."

"I know. And still…. It's Casto we have to worry about the most. He's wearing this place like a second skin. But that skin has the potential to choke him to death. He's already reaching his limit, and the dance has only begun."

Her husband rested his chin on her shoulder.

"Casto is no longer alone. He has my brother. He has us. He will persevere."

Noemi closed her eyes once more. When she finally managed to answer, she couldn't tell whether it was her gift or hope speaking.

"He will. He must. But what will become of him?"

IN THE royal chambers, Renaldo was worrying about his heart. Since the confrontation on the stairs, Casto had hardly spoken. Now he was holed up in the bathroom, and the Angel of Death knew better than to force himself on his lover now. He had known it would be difficult from the start. During their journey south, he had begun to understand that "hard" was too friendly a term to describe what they were getting themselves into. But only now did he fully comprehend how naïve he had been. Ummana had been a nightmarish prison for Casto, one he had barely managed to survive. Conceited as he was, Renaldo had assumed his presence and their marriage had been enough to free the young man from his past, to shield him from the dark memories bound to haunt him once they got there. The realization of how little he still knew about his heart had come to him too late and as a shock. All he could do now was to try to keep the worst from Casto, although he did not know how to protect him from himself.

TOGETHER WITH the members of the Council of Elders, the leaders of the guilds, the most influential heads of the families and, of course, her sorry excuse for a sire, Anesha was waiting for her brother and king to make his entry in the private dining hall of the royal family. The tables were groaning under the weight of the finest china, glasses, and golden cutlery to be found in Ummana. Castolus's sudden return had the same impact on the kitchen as if somebody had thrown a stone into a bee's nest. The main cook hadn't missed the chance to air out the most valuable tableware under her care. The hall hadn't seen such splendor since the death of the queen.

Oblivious to the small miracle the kitchen staff had performed within only one afternoon, the assembled citizens clustered in small groups, conversing in hushed tones, their tension tangible. Fear of the unknown, of what their king might do next, was written on their faces. Anesha couldn't suppress an amused smile. It was fitting how those who had put her brother through eleven years of hell were now squirming like worms on a hook.

A fanfare announced the king's arrival. Everybody hurried to their seats to greet the new ruler of the Twin Cities. Anesha's eyes were glued on her brother when he entered through the broad double doors. She had not been present during his arrival in front of the palace and was now curious how the years away from home had changed him.

Castolus had undoubtedly become an intimidating man. A man who hadn't forgotten that the larger part of politics in Ummana was grounded on ostentation and surprise. The king, as well as his entourage, outshone the assembled nobles with their pompous attire. Her brother was leading the train with the natural air of a born leader. His blond hair, so much like her own, flowed down his shoulders openly, held only by a golden headband in the form of two wings embracing a blue diamond between them. His regal features didn't betray any of his emotions, yet his eyes glinted so coldly, it made Anesha shiver. A tunic made of dark blue silk hugged his tall, slender body, enhancing the muscular arms and long, shapely legs. Around Casto's waist, a belt made of black leather held a sword, and his wrists and upper arms were decorated with golden bands that sparkled in the flickering light of all the candles in the hall.

As breathtaking as her brother might have been, the man walking next to him managed to outshine him without an effort—just as he outdid every male Anesha had ever seen. He was definitely a barbarian from the North. His dark brown hair fell in slight waves down to his shoulders, and his facial features were so disturbingly perfect, he seemed like one of the palace's idealized marble statues. The barbarian was wearing a dark blue tunic as well, the cloth caressing his skin like most of the women in the hall undoubtedly wanted to do with their bodies. Where her brother emitted graceful elegance, this warrior radiated danger. He seemed like a sleeping tiger, ready to strike out and kill its prey without warning. The way he was scanning the crowd worried Anesha. There was a cold determination in his eyes that was a harbinger of death. She had to be careful if she wanted to stay ahead of the game.

Behind her brother and his perfect companion came a man who was even more intimidating. As tall as the first barbarian but with more mass, he reminded Anesha more of a bear than a cat of prey. Nevertheless he, too, moved with the lethal grace of an experienced killer. His amber eyes seemed to analyze and categorize everybody in the hall according to the threat they could pose.

When their eyes met, he cocked an eyebrow before looking on. He was dressed completely in black; only the golden wristbands he wore lent some splendor to his appearance. In light of the pure dominance he was emitting, he didn't have to dress up any further.

And anyway, the female next to him was trumpery enough. She was more than two heads shorter than her escort, and her hair cascaded down to her calves in a stream of fiery red. It was held back by a golden tiara formed like a snake. Her harmonious but rather plain features were made irresistible to any onlooker by the sparkling, emerald-green eyes that seemed to see right through the impenetrable fog that was Ummanian politics. Anesha knew instinctively that this slim, barefoot female was in many respects more dangerous than the fierce warriors Castolus had brought with him.

Behind this remarkable pair followed a woman the princess immediately wanted to bow to, so stunning and regal was she. Her golden hair was plaited in complicated braids on the back of her head, with some loose strands falling down to her hips. Her unblemished face—with full, sensual lips, big, expressive eyes, and high cheekbones—was crowned by a gold-and-silver coronet.

It was obvious at first glance how incredibly old the jewelry was, fitting attire for such a majestic woman. The voluptuous curves of the beauty, who was only about a hand smaller than the barbarians in front of her, were accentuated by a lavender-colored dress with cap sleeves and a golden belt around her hips.

Next to her walked a man who, unlike the rest of the warriors, emanated serenity. He was as tall as the queen treading beside him, and his hair was a light chestnut color with the first streaks of white in it. Of all the people the king had in his entourage, he seemed to be the most composed.

Three desert warriors preceded the end of the procession. Two of them were even taller than the Northerners at the front. One was of sturdy build and a sour face; the other one was more slender but almost as muscular, with snow-white hair, pale blue eyes, and so many tattoos covering his body—including his face—it was impossible for Anesha to distinguish individual motifs. The third one was smaller, about the height of the majestic female, with hair hanging down to his shoulders in countless braids. Lively brown eyes dominated his youthful features, and in his eyes, Anesha could glimpse the sins of the angels. She was sure this man had never said no to any offer presented to him.

The desert warriors were followed by twenty heavily armed mercenaries who took position along the walls of the hall when Castolus and his entourage took their seats at the head of the table. Offended and intimidated by this silent but very open threat, the assembled nobles started to murmur excitedly.

Casto raised his hand and asked for silence, his face an impenetrable mask when he started to speak.

"My dear Council of Elders, masters of the guilds, Father, and, of course, my precious sister, Anesha, I do have to apologize for my sudden disappearance as well as for my surely surprising return. As you all know very well, I did not have much choice."

The eyes of the king were as hard as the blue diamond on his forehead.

"I am also aware that I haven't introduced my company yet, an omission I'm going to correct now."

He turned to the perfect barbarian, and his voice was a little softer when he made the introductions.

"This is Lord Renaldo, Angel of Death for the Mothers, god of the North, and my husband."

Everywhere in the hall, people held their breath in panic. Terrified glances darted around the room, but before anybody was able to get over their shock, Castolus proceeded, seemingly unfazed by the commotion he had caused.

"This is his brother, Lord Canubis, Wolf of War for the Mothers, god of the North and lord of the Valley. His wife, Noemi Amerasu, the snake witch. Lady Hulda, Mother Superior of the Sisters of the Night, and her husband, Lord Wolfstan, armorer of the Pack."

Her brother introduced the other men as well, but Anesha was too shocked to do more than register it unconsciously. Castolus had truly managed to stun them all. Not only had he unexpectedly returned, he had also brought with him the leaders of the most dangerous army in the world. If anybody had doubted whether the young man was fit to become leader in the Twin Cities, they had their answer now. It was clear that Castolus was determined to rule, and he had gotten himself some truly fearsome allies. While she was still musing about this shocking revelation, another piece of what her brother had said prodded her brain, until it finally managed to get her full, horrified attention. Frowning, she stared at Casto.

"Please excuse my rudeness, brother, but did I hear you right? Have you just called Lord Renaldo your husband?"

The joyous smile illuminating the king's face was answer enough. He glanced at the barbarian, full of love, his voice soft. "It's true, Anesha. Lord

Renaldo was generous enough to take me as his mate even though I was only a slave to him."

Anesha felt tears welling up inside when she thought about the shocking story behind those few words. Even though she wasn't a sympathetic person to begin with, and life in Ummana had hardened her to the point where even she thought of herself as ice-cold, she did feel sorry for what her brother had to endure after he managed to escape from the Twin Cities. Before she could answer, though, Nambuno got up, his voice so full of righteous indignation he sounded like a pig just before the butcher sliced its throat.

"Impossible! The leader of Ummana is obligated to the throne! That includes the question of succession. Whatever you have with this barbarian, the Council will never approve! You have to annul this affair immediately."

Deadly silence ensued after these words. The faces of the warriors were frozen. Castolus started to say something, but next to him the Angel of Death slowly rose, his countenance a mask of boundless fury. Suddenly Anesha got the feeling that the candles in the hall started to burn more fiercely. The air around Renaldo seemed to flicker, and the majestic woman, Hulda, who was sitting next to the Angel of Death, moved away to escape the heat radiating from the god.

"How can you even think about questioning my marriage with Casto? Ana-Isara herself has blessed my heart, and no human can break what she has forged. You dared to betray my lover, your future king. For years you looked the other way while he was humiliated and beaten. The only reason you're still alive is that I haven't thought of a fitting punishment for you yet. But rest assured, I'm going to deal with you, and I can promise, you won't like it in the least."

His eyes were burning with rage and possessiveness when the Angel of Death turned to the king. Castolus's hair flew up in the heat his mate emanated, but apart from that he stayed unperturbed. He closed his eyes and smiled when Renaldo placed an ostentatious kiss on his mouth before he turned back to the nobles.

"Casto is mine alone, and none of you should ever dare doubt our union again."

The Wolf of War rose as well. "I assent to my brother's words. Any one of you who tries to go against us or who so much as contemplates questioning Renaldo's marriage with Casto will be eliminated. As well as anybody who thinks an assault on my brother-in-law would be an acceptable solution to this rather difficult political situation." Canubis was standing next to his brother without minding the heat around them one bit. He wasn't too happy about how things had turned out, since the plan had been to lie low for the time being before they decided what their next steps would be, but then again, it was always better to have things out in the open. Now people knew where they stood. The divine brothers shared a look behind the king's back that made it clear to everybody just who was calling the shots in the city from now on.

As if this terrifying demonstration of raw, barbaric power had never taken place, the king gave a signal and the servants started bringing the food and wine. Nambuno, pale as linen and trembling all over, sat down as well. He had spoken up on a whim, because he did not like how the whole situation had slipped from his control, and now he regretted it deeply. Losing his composure was not befitting for the leader of the Council, and baring his weakness was stupid. Unfortunately the damage was done, and so he tried to regain some of his dignity by acting as if nothing had happened. Still, he was unable to enjoy the feast, and more than once did he glance in the direction of the Angel of Death—who chose to ignore him.

DURING ONE of the breaks in the feast, Anesha got up to greet her brother personally. Like everybody else in the hall, she had no clue about Castolus's plans, but she was determined to change that. The suspense added a certain thrill to the matter and made her blood sing. Unerring instincts, honed over centuries within her family, were on high alert, making her eager to use even the tiniest advantage she could find.

Gracefully she bowed to Castolus. "Welcome back home, my brother. And my best wishes on your marriage. You have found yourself a most splendid mate, if I may say so."

The young man she hadn't seen in years smiled openly, and Anesha was unable to find any deception in it.

"I was very lucky indeed. I thank you, Anesha."

A serious expression shadowed the princess's face.

"I'm so sorry, Casto. In all those years, I was unable to be your ally. You must have been terribly lonely."

She was almost expecting Casto to ignore her half-assed apology, as would have been understandable, but he did not make such a beginner's mistake. On the contrary. Once again did he manage to surprise her when he got up and hugged her fiercely.

"You were nothing but a child, Anesha. What could you have done? And look at me—everything has turned out just fine."

"No thanks to me, brother." Anesha just couldn't resist probing some more. Castolus wanted something, and she would be damned if she allowed him to get the better of her.

"Let's not talk about unnecessary things. I wish to introduce my mate to you."

She briefly admired how skillfully Casto had evaded her as the Angel of Death rose from his seat and took Anesha's hand to place a gentle kiss on the back that made her fantasize about how the warrior would look naked in her bed. She managed to fight back the blush both Lord Renaldo's presence and her anger were causing and to focus on what the handsome barbarian was saying.

"I'm pleased to meet my heart's sister. You're charming, Princess."

"And you're very generous, Lord Renaldo. May I compliment you on how well you've mastered our language?"

A smile like a thousand suns illuminated the disturbingly beautiful features.

"I have the best teacher, princess. Casto has taught me well."

"One of the few occasions where you actually needed me."

It was only a soft murmur, and Anesha was not sure whether she had heard right and if those words had been meant for her ears, but she stashed them in a corner of her complicated brain for later inspection. Something sparked in the warlord's gray eyes, something Anesha was unable to interpret except that it seemed to please her brother in a perverted way.

"It doesn't fit you well to be so disrespectful towards your mate, Your Highness."

Despite the soft rebuke, the tone was gentle. Casto's breath hitched visibly enough for Anesha to notice.

"I've only stated a fact, my lord."

Renaldo leaned over to his heart, and his lips moved close to the king's ear, causing him to blush deeply. With a satisfied smile, the Angel of Death turned back to the princess.

"I'm so happy to have made your acquaintance. We'll surely have many chances for some idle chitchat in the days to come."

Shuddering slightly from the underlying threat in those words, the princess bowed to the most desirable man she had ever met. She felt a pang of regret. The way the Angel of Death was devouring her brother with his eyes stated clearer than words that this perfect specimen was lost to anybody except Castolus.

"I'd be more than pleased. Lord Renaldo. Castolus."

Her brother hugged her again, and this time he gave her the opening she was looking for.

"Come to my chambers after this is over. We need to talk."

It wasn't an invitation, it was an order, but she finally saw her chance.

"Of course, Your Highness. I know the way."

SLIGHTLY LOST, the boy looked around the chamber that would be his home from now on. Right after the pompous funeral for his mother, the queen, his father had come and taken him away. He hardly knew the man. Except for a few official occasions where a meeting was unavoidable, his mother had seen to it that he had no contact with this stranger with the exotic eyes. Now that he'd gotten to know him better, he could understand his mother. Lord Aran was dangerous. Deep inside him, ambition burned so hot it clouded his judgment and influenced his actions in a way best described as fatal.

It was this man who had pried him from his normal surroundings to take him into this far-off stinking chamber under the pretense of turning him into a good, strong king. The boy was still small enough to want to believe his father's words, although he already knew better. Not long after, everything remotely childish would be lost to him forever.

2. TACTICS

After the banquet, Anesha avoided talking to the members of the Council, although Amicia had made her wish to parley clear. When she got the chance, the princess slipped away from the rattled Council. Before she dealt with those hyenas, she needed to get a better grasp of the situation. In her own chambers, she changed from her formal attire into a lighter, more comfortable dress and undid the complicated coiffure that had been giving her a headache the entire evening. Then she went to the royal wing. The guard at the first door let her through immediately and offered to show her the way, but she declined with a smile.

"Thanks, but I do know where I'm headed."

In the long hallway lined with expensive paintings and exquisite statues that depicted her ancestors in the most flattering way possible, she met a young man who was carrying a bottle of wine. If Anesha hadn't already seen this evening that the barbarians from the North brought forth the most handsome men, she would have been surprised to stumble upon this gem.

The slave was only slightly taller than she, with long, black hair hanging down his back in a wrist-thick braid and beautiful eyes that shone lively in a face dominated by a friendly, slightly mischievous smile. Since the slave was wearing nothing except a dark green leather collar and a small loincloth of the same color, not one part of his anatomy was left to imagination. For the second time this day, Anesha had to fight a blush while she imagined having this delicious tidbit in her bed.

Now he bowed to her graciously. His voice had a soft, husky tone. "My lady, welcome. May I be of help?"

He righted himself and the muscles under his skin moved as smoothly as if they were oiled. Anesha had to concentrate to ban erotic images from her head.

"I want to visit my brother, King Castolus. I assume he's in his chambers?"

The beautiful slave nodded. "Indeed he is. But I don't think you want to enter right now." His eyes glinted wickedly. "The king is busy."

"Busy? With what? He himself has… oh."

The young man's grin spread even more when he sensed her distress. "I'm sure he'll be done soon, my lady. Do you want to take a seat? May I offer you some refreshment?"

He led her to one of the lounges grouped around the fountain in the middle of the royal wing. From here, the chambers of the leader and his family members were placed radially. When her mother died, Anesha had still been a toddler, and since she had from then on lived under the care of the Krapati family, her memories of the rooms were hazy. What she did remember was that she had loved the view of the garden she had from her chamber. She wondered who of the barbarians had taken that place.

Anesha was just about to sit when a strict voice resounded from one of the rooms.

"Daran! What's taking you so long? Did you fall asleep on your way back?"

The speaker used one of the dialects of the desert and the princess did not understand every word, but the message was clear. Her good-looking companion answered in the same dialect, his voice still amused. He did not seem to fear the unknown speaker, despite the gruff tone.

"No, Master. But I did meet a guest."

"Who could that be?" The smallest of the three desert warriors Anesha had seen at the banquet stepped outside. His brown eyes regarded her in surprise; then he lowered his head ever so slightly. It was obvious he did not view Anesha as an equal and was just trying to be polite.

"The lady wants to see her brother, but I've informed her that he's—indisposed—at the moment."

Kalad's eyes wandered from Anesha to Daran and back before he raised his voice.

"Aegid? Can you come for a moment?"

The giant with the white hair appeared in the doorway, shooting his fellow warrior a questioning look. Kalad had already turned his attention back to the princess; a threatening undertone accompanied his next words.

"Princess, I do apologize for my slave's abominable behavior. He's obviously badly trained."

He shot a poisonous look at Daran, who stared at the ground with a guilty expression.

"I hope he has not offended you, but if so, please speak freely and be assured he will regret his foolish actions."

The tattooed man placed a heavy hand on the young man's nape, a gesture that filled Anesha with fear. She herself was not squeamish when it came to punishing rebellious slaves, but the silent threat Aegid radiated made her feel pity for the slave, who looked so very vulnerable next to the muscular warrior. Somehow she had expected Daran to protest his innocence or to plead for mercy, which would have been understandable given his masters' anger, but he remained silent, his gaze kept down. He either knew from previous experience how useless it was to beg or he was petrified. Either way, it still struck Anesha as strange how this until now lively slave should give in to his fate just like that. She hadn't had the impression that his masters kept him on a tight leash or that he was afraid of them—quite the contrary, in fact. The princess suspected something deeper going on and smiled as politely as possible.

"Daran hasn't offended me. I think it was very chivalrous of him to accompany me here. And he has informed me that my brother is giving in to his carnal instincts in a very diplomatic way, without being vulgar. I can't find any fault in his behavior."

Kalad regarded his slave with narrowed eyes. "Do you have anything to say?"

Anesha didn't know what she had expected, but surely not that the young man would incriminate himself.

"The lady is very friendly, but I've to admit I behaved shamefully. I was cheeky and provocative."

"As I thought." Kalad sighed. "Leave. We'll talk later."

Aegid let go of Daran, and the slave scurried into his masters' chambers without making a sound. Still confused by the scene she had just witnessed, Anesha decided to defend Daran once more.

"I think he's misjudging himself. I really couldn't find any fault in his behavior. You don't have to punish him on my behalf."

The giant answered with a friendliness she wouldn't have thought possible, considering his anger about the slave and his frightening appearance.

"It's very friendly of you to defend the scoundrel, but he's familiar with our rules and knows when he's done something wrong."

"I have to admit, I'm surprised that he told the truth so willingly. Especially since he seems to know what kind of punishment he's facing."

"He's badly trained, not abominably. There are few things we abhor more than lies. Daran is aware of that."

Kalad offered her a bowl with fruit. Anesha chose some grapes and her next words carefully. Perhaps there was a chance to make this juicy piece of flesh her possession.

"Please forgive my curiosity, but your slave is fascinating to me. He's alluring in many ways and very well-behaved, although you seem to think differently. I've never met a slave with so many assets as Daran has. He must be very… valuable."

The warriors shared a look that took Anesha a moment to recognize. Pure jealousy mixed with irrational possessiveness was written in the men's faces, although they weren't even aware of it. Anesha realized she had just crossed a line the mercenaries did not even perceive as one. Her instincts had been spot-on; there was a lot going on between these three men, and most of it was unconscious. Wise people kept out of relationships that had more layers than could probably be healthy.

An uncomfortable silence started to grow. While the princess was still musing whether she should break it or not, her brother came out of the royal chambers, looking slightly flushed.

"Anesha! What a pleasant surprise! I hope I didn't make you wait? If so, I have to apologize, but I can see you were in good company."

The princess got up to greet her brother. Aegid and Kalad bid her a short good-bye. They entered their own chambers with determined expressions.

"I hope I haven't gotten Daran into trouble."

"Daran?" Casto sounded suspicious.

"I may have mentioned how appealing I think he is. They didn't like it."

Her brother started laughing.

"Don't worry, you're not the first one to make that mistake. When their precious thief is concerned, the two tend to be tetchy. And about Daran, he's always in trouble, but not the kind you seem to fear."

"Oh. Are you referring to the kind of trouble you've just been in?"

To Anesha's delight, her brother blushed a deep red. She herself was no prude, since she had found out at an early age that a sense of shame was more often a hurdle than helpful. Being able to embarrass Castolus delighted her. It gave her back some of the control he had taken so completely by summoning her into his territory.

"Something like that. Although you can't compare the two, of course."

"Of course. I'd never dream of it!"

Anesha took a step backward to regard her brother critically. The king was only wearing blue trousers made of silk that sat low on his hips. Anesha had free range of vision on his muscular, beautifully sculpted torso with its razor-sharp abdominal muscles. Frowning, she pointed at the two black runes over his heart.

"What's this?"

Her brother smiled softly. If those tattoos carried any unpleasant memories, he did not show it.

"Those are the signs of Ana-Isara and her sister. They signify that I'm part of their family."

Casto could tell from his sister's body language how unhappy she was to see her brother scarred like this. It had nothing to do with sisterly love, but with pride in their royal ancestry that forbade such a degradation usually reserved for slaves. Before she could voice her distress, he turned around to show her his back.

"This sign is from her as well. I know how it looks, but I can assure you, everything's fine."

"How can this be fine, Castolus? This is humiliating! And I don't even dare to imagine what kind of pain you had to endure while these—signs were burnt into your flesh."

Casto turned and took his sister's hands in his own, trying to make her understand something he had resented from the bottom of his soul not too long ago—and, truth be told, had not come entirely to terms with yet.

"I admit, the pain was brutal, but I welcomed it, for it was the ultimate proof that I'm Lord Renaldo's heart. It made me happy."

"Castolus! What on Ana-Darasa have you gone through?"

For a moment Casto was inclined to believe his sister's feelings. Not that he would have been so stupid as to actually fall for her act, but her consternation seemed genuine, and the idea of someone from his family actually caring for his well-being had a strange allure. Because of that he answered her truthfully, with only a small, well-concealed threat in his words.

"I was in hell, sister, but I managed to survive and to escape."

Anesha sighed. She clearly understood the subtext and decided to move on to less dangerous territory, or so she hoped. Her gaze fell on the studs in Casto's nipples.

"Are those from your goddess as well?"

"No, those are signs of my husband's grace."

"They suit you. Although I think the glass stones are a tiny bit over the top."

Her brother grinned broadly.

"That's no glass, sister mine. Those are real diamonds. As I said, the studs are signs of grace, and the Angel of Death doesn't bother with trifles."

"I've kind of guessed *that* already." Anesha's voice was dry. Her brother offered her his arm.

"Let's go into my chambers and chat. I'm sure there's a lot we have to talk about."

LIKE HIS mate, the Angel of Death was wearing only linen trousers, and he moved with the naturalness of a man who was utterly comfortable in his skin. There was not the slightest hint of shame in his behavior, and the princess just knew she wouldn't be able to embarrass him as easily as her brother. He greeted Anesha with a slight nod and then led her to a group of lounges situated in the arcade leading to the balcony. Casto left for a moment and returned shortly after with Canubis and his wife.

Gracefully her brother filled a cup of wine for his mate and each of his guests before he sat down next to Renaldo. Anesha did not like seeing her brother acting like a servant so nonchalantly but avoided commenting. As if he had read her thoughts, Casto treated her to a reassuring smile.

"I've already told you, sister. Even though I'm a king, Lord Renaldo is my mate and god. It's appropriate for me to serve him."

Renaldo guffawed as if the king had just told a hilarious joke. "Be assured, Princess, your brother only acts so demurely because he wants to make a good impression. I've never owned a worse slave than him. He can be as stubborn as a donkey."

Against her will Anesha had to laugh as well. The warrior's open tone relaxed her a little. Even if Castolus was already plotting, his mate seemed to be approachable. So she decided to keep up the small talk.

"This sounds more like the brother I knew. I've trouble imagining you as a slave."

Her brother shrugged dismissively. "I had an official collar and everything."

"That might have been the case, but you never once addressed me as 'master.' If I recall correctly, your usual title for me was 'Barbarian.' You still call me that."

Anesha stared at Casto in disbelief.

"You affronted the Angel of Death, the most feared warrior in the world? Mother has indeed bequeathed you with more guts than brains."

"I like your sister, Casto. Such an intelligent young woman. And so much wiser than you, obviously."

Casto made a sour face, but before he could voice his distress, the Wolf of War ended their little skirmish.

"As much as I love listening to your bickering, I think we're here for an entirely different reason?"

Immediately they all turned serious. Casto nodded at his sister.

"What happened while I was gone?"

The princess had suspected right from the beginning that her brother was primarily interested in information, and if she played her cards right, she'd have a foot in the door.

"Many things, brother, and there's hardly anything you're going to like."

Anesha saw the king draw a deep breath; then she had his full attention—or almost. While she started to report, she couldn't help but notice how her brother and the snake witch conformed to their mates. Both reacted to the slightest movement of their lords like fine-tuned instruments did to an experienced musician. And the hands of the warriors never let go of their spouses. Canubis's right hand was resting on his wife's thigh, his long fingers stroking her ceaselessly, as if he was afraid she could vanish should he break contact with her skin. Renaldo's hand was placed firmly on his lover's nape, a gesture that reminded Anesha of Daran and his masters. She realized it was a mixture of dominance and protective instinct on behalf of the Angel of Death, but to her, it still was humiliating, as if a father scolded a rebellious child. Her brother did not seem to mind being treated in such a patronizing manner. The princess decided to ignore the finer details of her brother's relationship with this intimidating warrior for the moment and got on with her report.

"YOUR ESCAPE caused quite a commotion in the city. When Father finally realized he wouldn't be able to get you back on his own, he offered an irresistibly high reward for the person who found and retrieved his poor kidnapped boy. For almost a year, the city was swamped with bounty hunters. If you threw a stone, you could be sure to hit one of them. The Council, of course, was not nearly as devastated as Aran. The members tried to get him out of the palace with all their might, but they had underestimated him. He has stable alliances with some of the most powerful families in Ummana. His influence is so great, the Council had to be careful not to get into trouble themselves. And as long as you weren't declared dead, we were all caught in the power vacuum." She shifted a bit in her seat, trying to stay focused on the information she was about to reveal and not get distracted by the way Renaldo and Canubis were hovering over their mates.

"On one side you have Aran, who has the backing of the families. On the other you have the Council, who can also count on some rich allies, not to mention their own financial prowess. The heads of the guilds form their own group and enjoy tipping the scales. They don't like that Aran's doing business with people who are planning to diminish the power of the guilds, but they like it even less that the Council is seriously thinking about cutting tax benefits for resident craftspeople in order to strengthen competition." Anesha took a sip from her wine.

"During the few votes we had, they always went with the side that promised them the highest profits. And although some leaders of the guilds are also members of the most financially potent families, you can't count on them staying loyal. They're hot on being reelected to their posts. The merchants, slave traders, cloth makers, and mariners choose their new leaders next year. None of those holding the posts now will risk taking a set position until then, and afterwards it won't get any easier. The influence of the guilds is growing. They've never been this strong, which would have never happened with a dominant king or queen. And of course they're trying to use this new power. Your sudden appearance has probably alarmed them even more than the Council. They see their hopes dashed, so be careful, brother." Casto's face had darkened, a fact that surprised Anesha, because showing emotion was weakness and in Ummana, weakness equaled death, either politically or literally. Perhaps Casto wasn't as well-prepared to take over the throne as it had seemed. Then again, with allies like the Wolf of War and the Angel of Death at his side, he probably didn't have to be. Anesha had little doubt that the barbarians, should things not go according to their wishes, would revert to violence without hesitation. She had to tread carefully if she wanted to stay on top of this game.

"The personal guard has remained neutral until now. Neither Father nor the Council have been stupid enough to go after their privileges and pay, although they're almost hysterically looking for new sources of income. Revenues have been decreasing dramatically during the last two years, although sales have increased. The main problem is that they're all so busy going for each other's throats, they don't see anything else. I don't have to tell you how bad this is for business. And about half a year ago, the personal guard was stirred up as well. There are too many political assassinations at the moment, those targeting me included."

"Assassinations? Plural?"

"Yes. Two, to be correct. Within the last six months. I'm the last legitimate heir, which makes the guard touchy. You know Aktan. He's a levelheaded man who isn't keen on getting involved in silly politics, but now he's decided to take the initiative. He's been meeting in secret with me and representatives of the Council, and we didn't talk about next month's timetable for the guard. I'm almost sure he's going to take my—pardon—your side to restore balance."

"Did you find out who was responsible for the assassination attempts?"

Casto was all business now. Anesha could practically see his brain working.

"I do have a suspicion, but I wasn't able to find out anything substantial despite having the best spies working for me. About two years ago, followers of the Good Mother started coming into the city. They're spending money like crazy and they're missionizing. Until now, neither Father nor the Council have taken any measures against them. My guess is, they're being paid."

"Why should the leaders do anything against a religious group?" Noemi's voice betrayed her curiosity. Casto's face was grim.

"Because it's forbidden to missionize inside the walls of Ummana. Our ancestors had some very distinct ideas about successful trade, and they realized early on that religion is an impediment to making money. For that reason you won't find any temples in Ummana. We have absolute freedom of religion as long as people keep it to themselves. The moment somebody tries to missionize, the state intervenes. In bad cases, missionizing can lead to execution. The only god we truly worship here is the god of trade. Everything that nets you more money is good. Anything leading to losses is bad. Religion inevitably leads to losses, which is why it's unwanted."

"I'm not sure whether I like your attitude. I mean, we *are* gods." Canubis and Renaldo shared a long look.

Noemi grinned. "We're going to worship you in the privacy of our chambers only. That should keep us out of trouble. I don't think you have to be afraid of being chased out of town with swords and fire."

When she heard those cheeky words, Anesha involuntarily tensed up and waited for the reaction of the warriors. After everything she'd seen so far, she was expecting the Wolf of War to put his wife firmly in her place. Instead the warlord merely leaned in to kiss her, his eyes glowing in amusement. Anesha realized the barbarians were a lot more complicated than she had thought. And she wondered what surprises—pleasant and unpleasant—were still waiting for her.

Casto returned to the topic at hand.

"So we have three main groups, of which one is undecided, as well as the personal guard and a religious splinter group we know nothing substantial about. That's not ideal but still better than I dared to hope. Now that I'm claiming the throne, the guilds are going to contact me soon. If I play my cards right, they're going to be on my side. The personal guard will follow their example, since Aktan favors clear circumstances. The Council and Father may pose problems, but none I can't deal with."

Anesha nodded. This, at least, was what she had expected. Her brother was going to claim not only the throne but absolute power over Ummana, and she was right there to secure her piece of the cake.

"I haven't told you the good news yet, brother." Now the princess was openly malicious. "Despite their desperate attempts, neither the Council nor Father have succeeded in getting their hands on your and Mother's private property. As I've already mentioned, business has been good the last years, and the private investments have brought hefty dividends. You haven't been there to spend any money, which means all your revenues are on the plus side. If I'm not completely mistaken, you already hold the majority in the Council. And if you include my own not-too-meager riches, they don't stand a chance."

The siblings both looked like cats who had just devoured the proverbial bowl of cream.

"What are you talking about?" Renaldo had a questioning look on his face. He had followed the dialogue intently and was proud to have understood most of it, but the last exchange had evaded him.

Anesha treated him to her most charming smile. "Ummana is a city of traders. We have different laws than the rest of the world, as you may have noticed by now. Although it would be more accurate to call them guidelines, because nothing you can buy with money is cast in stone—except for those rules protecting the riches of Ummana, of course. Our ancestors had a deep understanding of human nature, and to keep precious funding money from being wasted on bribes, they ruled that the power of a family within the Council is measured by its financial prowess. The richer you are, the more worth your vote has. For that reason you won't find poor people in the Council. It doesn't make sense to raise your voice without money to back up your opinion. This way we ensure that only the interests of the most productive members of society are at the focus of attention, and decisions are always made in favor of business. The system also includes the ruler, whose power is measured by his capital. And your husband is an absolute ruler."

Renaldo stared at his heart, who was sitting next to him with a smug expression.

"How much money are we talking about, Your *Highness*?"

Casto pretended to be thinking about it.

"Without knowing the correct numbers, I'd just say it like this: should we get married again tomorrow, I'd be the one receiving the branding iron."

LYSISTRATOS WAS running with a storm. He had to let off some steam in order not to destroy the entire city of Ummana. His anchor was eight years old now and trapped in a never-ending nightmare. During the day he was subjected to the drill of various teachers who had the order to turn him into a perfect king. The morning was reserved for lessons in history, politics, mathematics, and languages, where each of his mistakes was punished physically. In the afternoon the anchor's body was hardened by riding and fighting training, where his sadistic instructors pushed him beyond his limits on a daily basis. Exhausted both mentally and physically, the anchor was only able to make it through each day out of sheer stubbornness. And the trial did not end in the evening. Once the teachers let him out of their claws, the anchor then had to deal with the torturer, a man so despicable, Lysistratos seriously wondered why the earth had not yet opened up to swallow him. This human scum delighted in playing with the anchor, trying to break him in every possible way. The physical pain was something the anchor had learned to deal with. The mental strain, on the other hand, was slowly getting to him. He was terrified of the ghosts the torturer had woken with his stories, unable to distinguish dream and reality anymore. When the night came, the anchor was caught in a void of deepest despair. Lysistratos tried to get through to him, to help him, but the mortal fear the anchor felt, combined with his unwavering stubbornness, created an almost impenetrable shield. Lysistratos did not want to use force to get through to the anchor, knowing this would only complicate things. He had to be patient, although he longed to be with the anchor on a conscious level. Torn by fury and despair, the Emperor of the Storms let out his frustration by fueling the storm.

AT THE same time Anesha reported to Casto, Daran was kneeling demurely in front of the broad bed in his masters' chambers, waiting for their verdict. They were looking at him sternly, since his behavior had discredited them.

It was Kalad who broke the silence.

"I really don't know what we should do with you, Daran. Every time I get hopes you've finally understood what serving us means, you make a mistake like this one. I could almost get the impression that you're doing it on purpose."

In alarm the thief looked up, his brown eyes pleading.

"No! I'd never dare to do that! Please, Masters!"

Aegid grinned.

"Don't worry. We won't tell anybody. And as long as you're such a disgrace, we can't sell you either."

"Who'd want the likes of me?"

Kalad's fingertips played with Daran's coal-black hair. "Well, the princess was really hot on getting her hands on you. And determined enough to pay any price. So you better behave, little thief. If you overdo it, it would be easy for us to get rid of you."

"I doubt that." Daran's words were full of confidence and just a faint trace of mockery.

Aegid stepped behind him, his big hands resting heavily on the thief's shoulders.

"How come, prey?"

Gracefully Daran turned on his knees until his face was level with the warrior's crotch. He opened Aegid's belt with practiced ease.

"Because you took great pains training me the way you want me to be. And though it may sound conceited, I do know I'm the best thing that's happened to you in decades."

By now Daran had freed his master's penis and started licking it. Aegid closed his eyes to enjoy while Kalad opened the thief's loincloth, his eyes burning with lust. He knelt between the invitingly spread legs of their slave and entered him with one long, vigorous thrust. Daran groaned contentedly but kept concentrating on his other owner's orgasm. As usual, the desert warriors reached climax at the same time. After more than eight hundred years spent together, it wasn't really surprising. And Daran loved it when the two let their guard down like this, since it was proof that he was part of their unity. When their first hunger was sated, the warriors retreated from their slave's body, and Aegid helped him up.

"You're right. You're the best thing that's ever happened to us."

His face turned serious.

"Still, your behavior toward Casto's sister was cheeky. We'll have to punish you for it."

Daran's heartbeat sped up. He'd known the desert warriors long enough to know what his punishment would be. Without much hope he tried to propitiate them.

"Please, I'm begging you! I promise to be obedient from now on, but please, show me some mercy!"

Kalad grinned saucily. "It's too late for begging, little thief. And believe me, you deserve what we're planning."

"Master! Please! You've promised to show me around the palace tomorrow!"

Aegid picked Daran up and carried him to the bed. "And we will, slave. We do keep our promises."

The young man made one last, desperate attempt. "How can I accompany you when I'm unable to walk?"

"You should've thought about that before you were so insolent."

Kalad sealed Daran's lips with a kiss while Aegid started stroking his member. Groaning, the thief gave up.

A FEW exciting hours later, Kalad sat in an armchair, watching his slave's sleeping face, and drank some bloodred wine. Aegid approached him, his voice no more than a whisper.

"Brother."

Kalad looked up. His usually bright eyes were darkened by fury, his fingers curled around the cup so tightly the knuckles shone white.

"She wanted to buy him."

The sentence was hissed so angrily, Aegid was only able to understand it because they had known each other for so long. He sighed.

"She's not the first."

"Have you seen how she has undressed him with her eyes? The slut."

When he remembered the hungry looks Anesha had bestowed on their thief, Aegid felt his own blood boiling.

"He wasn't wearing a lot. But I can understand you. The thought alone…."

He, too, regarded the sleeping Daran possessively.

"Don't forget, Kalad, he's ours alone. And he knows it."

"Are you sure about that?"

"Of course. And even if I weren't, do you think he could serve us like he does if he weren't committed wholeheartedly?"

Kalad got up.

"Probably not. But I don't like it. I'm contemplating locking him away while we're here."

Aegid had to admit that the idea had a certain appeal, but he did not want to restrict Daran like that.

"That wouldn't be very nice of us. And besides"—now Aegid's eyes lit up in unbridled anticipation—"it's an interesting game. Plus, Daran is intuitive enough to pick up on it and please us even more. Let's make the best of this interest others might have in him and turn our sex in a slightly more feral direction."

At the prospect of even more intense intercourse, Kalad didn't hesitate.

"I like your idea, brother. And if we do it right, Daran won't have many chances to leave the chambers anyway."

Satisfied and at one with the world, the warriors joined their remarkable slave in bed.

3. NIGHTMARE

Since there wasn't any more to talk about before the first Council meeting where Casto would declare himself king, Anesha left her brother, as did Canubis and his wife. Casto and Renaldo were alone.

"Can we trust her?" Renaldo's voice was stern. He had trouble reading Anesha. Like her brother, she was an enigma.

Casto rolled his eyes in feigned consternation. "She'd be shocked if I did. Here in Ummana, different rules than those you're used to from the Valley apply. Anesha is my sister, yes, but first and foremost she's my mother's daughter, a calculating, highly intelligent and ruthless politician who commands great resources. She's gone through her options and knows her best chances lie with me—at the moment. As long as I can offer her an advantage nobody else can, she'll be loyal to us. My guess is she wants to get back at the Council—another reason for her to stick with us. But I'm not making the mistake of relying on her loyalty. She has her own agenda, whatever that is. At the moment we need each other, so everything's fine."

Repulsed by this prosaic perspective, Renaldo made a face. Deep down he was a man of the sword; the subtleties of shady politics disgusted him. He regarded it as more honest to kill an opponent with a weapon than to outmaneuver him until he had nowhere left to hide. The self-confidence with which his heart seemed to adapt to these hostile surroundings made him anxious.

"I already abhor this city. Considering how you grew up, I'm surprised you have even one decent bone in your body."

Renaldo felt guilty before he ended the sentence and wished he could take it back. He had spoken what was on top of his mind, completely ignoring his mate's feelings. Now he regretted it deeply, knowing it was too late to back out.

And, sure enough, Casto's eyes took on that dark, stormy quality that spoke of a fight to come. Casto's anger was reflected in his tone. "Are you doubting me?"

Renaldo had had enough fights with Casto to realize that lying would only make things worse, so he followed his initial train of thought.

"I'm just saying, you're moving through this snake pit as if you'd know exactly what vipers are a danger to you."

"And that makes me what? A coward? Unworthy of your grace?"

Somehow Casto's tone lacked the usual fire, which was more alarming than an outburst.

"Please, Casto. That's not how I meant it and you know it."

Casto looked at him with eyes that had turned from stormy to sad. The gathering rage was replaced by deep exhaustion that spoke louder than words about Casto's current state. Renaldo tried to remember when his husband had last slept an entire night. It must have been before they left the Valley.

"I don't know what you mean. I don't seem to know anything at all."

"My own, please. Come here. I don't want to fight."

"I'm sorry, Barbarian, but I can't. I want to be alone right now."

Without waiting for his mate's reaction, Casto turned on his heel and retreated into the sleeping chamber. For a brief moment, Renaldo toyed with the idea of following him but decided against it. He knew he had only escaped a major fight just now because Casto was too tired to press the matter. Not respecting the boundaries he had set meant playing with fire—in the literal sense.

The Angel of Death poured himself a cup of wine, took one of the lounges from outside their chamber onto the big balcony that looked out into the royal garden, got comfortable, and stared into the night sky. Ummana annoyed him like no city before; he even disliked the sunny climate, the oppressing heat that was suffocating during the day and barely tolerable at night. Perhaps it was the unfamiliar situation. Under normal circumstances they would be camped out in front of the city gates, making strategies about how to breach the walls. There were no walls to breach here, only sleek, repellent politicians fighting tooth and nail with weapons Renaldo neither liked nor understood. He had been worried the strain could be too much for Casto, but now that he thought more about it, he was wondering whether he had misjudged his heart completely.

Casto moved with suspicious confidence on the slippery parquet of schemes and treason Ummana presented to them, and for Renaldo's taste, it had been too easy to establish the king's power. So far nobody had protested Casto's right to claim the throne, at least not openly, and Casto himself had shown no inclination to punish those who had made him suffer so terribly. He was either petrified by fear—which was highly unlikely—or he had anticipated how things would play out, which could only mean he was not as shaken as he pretended to be. The tense atmosphere in which everybody waited for somebody else to make a mistake, to show weakness, grated on the demigod's nerves. If this were the Valley, matters would have already been resolved. The enemies would be adequately punished, and the wolves would be sated and content.

While Renaldo was pondering these treacherous thoughts, anger started to bloom inside him. This was Casto's home. According to his own statements, he had had almost seventeen years' time to learn every trick he needed to survive. And Renaldo knew next to nothing about the people—their enemies—here or what exactly Casto had survived. The things he had done. From what Renaldo had seen so far, his heart had been a snake among snakes, as poisonous as the worst of them. Renaldo had known from the start that Casto was keeping secrets from him, and for some time he had let it go, because the mystery had tickled him. Those times were gone, though. He'd almost lost Casto because of those secrets, and after that fateful night in the small inn where Casto had finally confided in him, Renaldo had thought the secrets were part of the past. Now it seemed as if Casto had very carefully weighed his words and decided on his own definition of complete honesty. But if Casto was not completely open to him, Renaldo could not protect him effectively. The idea of losing his heart made ice-cold fear tighten its grip around his guts. And just feeling fear made him angry. He was a god of war, for the Mothers' sake! Fury flared inside him, an overwhelming flame that burned every sensible thought and left nothing but the wish to destroy. With a clash the goblet fell to the ground. The wine soiled the white stones like freshly spilled blood, glinting in the moonlight as a bad omen of impending danger.

Renaldo got off the lounge in a flash. He would teach his property to keep things from him. If Casto had seriously thought he could do this all on his own and keep Renaldo out, he would show him differently. It was high time for Casto to learn what it meant to belong to the Angel of Death. Renaldo stormed into the chambers, ready to give his heart a thorough beating in order to get some sense into him.

He stopped dead in his tracks when he heard the sobbing. Casto was curled up on the gigantic bed, his face buried in the cushions so nobody could hear him cry. His shoulders were trembling, and the tattooed wings on his back seemed to move in the flickering light of the lonely candle burning in the room. Deeply worried, Renaldo reached out for the young man. His anger had completely dissipated.

"Casto, what's the matter?"

"Please, Barbarian, leave me alone. I don't want you to see me like this."

"Damn, I'm not a complete bastard. Do you really think I could leave you alone when you're in such a distressed state?"

A raw sob was the answer; then Casto tried to turn his back on him. Vigorously Renaldo grabbed Casto's shoulders, pulled the young man close, and started rocking him gently, as if he were a child.

"Shh, my own. Everything's fine. I'm here, I'm going to protect you."

Choking, Casto snuggled up to his mate. "I'm sorry, Barbarian."

"What for, my own? That I'm an insensitive idiot? That I've insulted the one person I love more than my life? You don't have to be sorry about anything, my own, my heart. I'm the one who behaved horribly."

"I'd never betray you, Barbarian, never."

Guilt made the demigod's heart constrict and twinge when his lover seemed to read his thoughts.

"I know that. As I said, I'm an idiot sometimes, and this whole campaign is getting on my nerves. Can you forgive me?"

Casto kept his gaze down and embraced his mate even harder before he answered with a voice raw from the tears he had cried. "If you're going to hold me a little longer, then yes. I forgive you."

In silence Renaldo kept on rocking the young man until Casto's even breath told him he had finally fallen asleep. Gently he laid Casto down on the cushions, stretched next to him, and watched him sleep. He had to be cautious not to let this damn city get to his head and make him blind to reality. The idea that Casto could betray him seemed absurd, now that they were lying so close to each other. The king had vowed eternal fidelity to him; there was no reason to doubt him. And if he needed more time to fully confide in Renaldo, then he would grant Casto that time.

Lovingly Renaldo caressed the king's cheek and was just about to close his own eyes when Casto started to whimper. His hands shot up in defense, and his head darted left and right as if he wanted to escape from something. With a high-pitched, childlike voice he started to beg in Ummanian.

"Elem, a-vi ries! Re ulnar amer! Re rellin! Elem, re amial nuto, sami!"

"Please, don't do this! I promise, I'll be good! I'll be obedient. Please, I'm begging you, Master!"

Cautiously the Angel of Death shook his lover's shoulder.

"Casto, it's fine. You're having a nightmare. Everything's fine."

Casto's eyes flew open, but the mesmerizing blue was empty, staring into nothing. Again he started to beg.

"Elem, re tomol! Ni nuto nareal sindi allil…. Elem, a-vi ries! Le-ro!"

"Please, I swear! If you could give me one more chance…. Please, don't do this! No!"

Renaldo had enough. He grabbed Casto by both shoulders, jerked him up, and slapped him hard.

"Damn it, Casto! Wake up! You're dreaming!"

Slowly the king's gaze cleared, and his eyes homed in on the Angel of Death.

"Barbarian."

He lowered his head, embarrassed that he had shown weakness.

"Just leave me alone. It was only a dream."

"Only a dream? Surely you jest. You've been dreaming like that every night since we've left the Valley, and it's getting worse. I had to slap you to get you out of this one!" Renaldo's voice took on a soothing tone. "Don't you think it's time to introduce me to your demons? It would be my pleasure to slay them for you."

Casto stayed silent for so long, the Angel of Death feared he wouldn't get an answer. Then the young man's head shot up, his jaw tense with defiance.

"Perhaps you're right. It's time to share my humiliation with you."

Again Casto fell silent, but after a few deep breaths, he started to talk in an almost absent monotone. "I was still small. Mother hadn't been dead for more than a year. My father had already started molding me the way he wished when Voltara came to court. Father hired him immediately. I think those two had been destined for each other at birth. Until that day, my father had settled on hitting me for punishment every night, but Voltara showed him a bunch of new possibilities, including how to effectively use a leather strap. Finally it was decided that it would be best if Voltara had free rein over me. From that day on, I didn't spend a single night in my own bed. Depending on my behavior, I was either brought to the cellars or to the royal tomb. Voltara chained me to my mother's sarcophagus in a way that I could only lie down and sleep when I rested against it. All the time he told me horrible stories about dead people rising from their graves to terrify me even more." Casto shuddered and snuggled against Renaldo's chest, a sure sign that he was upset.

"He managed to push me so far that I was willing to do anything if it meant I didn't have to sleep in the tomb. Voltara is a cruel sadist—pain arouses him as well as submissiveness. If I wanted to get out of the tomb, I had to beg him on my knees to hit me with the strap. When it was over, I had to thank him for the lesson and then...."

Casto stopped. His breathing was hitched, tears were streaming down his cheeks, and he was trembling all over. The memory was like a smoldering knife forcing its way into his body and soul, hurting him brutally over and over again without ever letting the wound heal. Renaldo held him tight, caressing his back. If it hadn't been for Casto's agitation, Renaldo would have left the chambers right then to have his revenge on the man who had dared to hurt his precious lover so badly.

"Take your time, my own. I'm here with you. Take your time."

Again the young man took a deep breath, then resumed his story. His voice was so low, the Angel of Death had to strain to understand him.

"I was always naked when he punished me. When it was over, I had to lie down on the ground. Then he towered above me and—sullied me. He never touched me, at least not in a sexual way, but he jerked off on a regular basis after hitting me. Sometimes he came back in the middle of the night, woke me, and did it all again.

"During that time, I learned to fear the dark. Darkness brought sleep and when I was asleep, I couldn't hear him coming. I always knew he would come, but never when. That was almost the worst, waiting for him, dreading his appearance. He knew this and used it against me. Do you know what the worst was? That I was almost glad when he finally did come, because then, at least, the waiting was over.

"Only when I met Lys was I able to overcome my fear of the dark. He showed me that the gloom is a friend, not the enemy. Ever since we decided to come back to Ummana, I've started to remember. I feel like an eight-year-old again, and I'm frozen inside by fear, but I can't show it to anybody because if I do, we're all in danger. The Council, the guilds, my father, Anesha—they're all waiting for me to display signs of weakness. Once they detect it, they're going to act without mercy."

Shocked more deeply by his heart's confession than he would have ever thought possible, the Angel of Death stroked Casto's nape. He had always known it was bad, that the things the young man kept from him were indescribable, but he would have never guessed how brutal the truth actually was. It made his respect and awe for Casto grow even more, but it also heightened his worry. The pressure Casto had to endure now would have broken a weaker man. Considering how long Casto had been withstanding the emotional strain, it was a wonder he was still functioning so flawlessly.

"Don't worry about useless things, my own. You're a god's mate and I swear to you, they all will regret deeply what they've done to you. Once I'm through with this city, it will curse the day your father first laid hands on you. I've promised you protection, doubly so, as your warlord and mate. Be assured, I won't let anything bad happen to you ever again."

Not saying anything, Casto snuggled up to his husband, for once willing to let himself be consoled. His breathing evened and his thoughts, which had been in constant uproar since their arrival in the city, calmed down. He knew all too well how difficult things were going to be. Everything that had happened so far was no more than preliminary skirmishing before the true battle began, but he was still grateful for Renaldo's words. They gave him the strength to keep on going.

"I thank you, Barbarian. And I entrust myself to you."

"My own, my precious, beautiful own. Everything's going to be all right. I promise."

The king's blond head rested heavily against Renaldo's chest.

"I'm so tired."

"Then sleep, my own. I'll be guarding you."

Gently the Angel of Death caressed his lover's silken strands until he fell asleep again. Talking about his worst memories and fears seemed to have banished the nightmares, at least for now, because the king slept through the night without startling even once.

LYSISTRATOS WAS bursting with pride. Another year had passed, a year during which the anchor had not wavered nor bent even though he had to face hardships no ordinary human would be able to endure. Tonight, for the first time, Lysistratos had managed to breach the shields the anchor had built around himself. It was a moment of triumph and bliss, to be finally connected with the anchor, even though it had only been briefly. Suspicious as he was, the anchor had greeted Lysistratos with so much open hostility, it made the demon shudder with joy. This one was indeed strong. Strong enough to be a king. Strong enough to be the brother of a demon.

Casto shivered. There it came again, the strange presence of a creature he did not know. It was no ghost and definitely no human either. For the better part of a month, this thing had haunted him, made his nights even worse than they had already been. He was afraid he would lose his sanity for real if this went on any longer. Casto closed his eyes. There was only one way to deal with this, and it frightened him to the core. Then again, what did he have to lose? His life had already hit rock bottom, so why was he still afraid? Casto opened his eyes again.

Lysistratos could not believe it. For months he had tried to reach the anchor, only to be thrown out most violently time and again, and now, all of a sudden, the anchor let him in! He was defiant, of course, and still guarded, but nevertheless. Carefully, as not to spook the anchor, Lysistratos opened up to him, showed him who he was, offered him his love and friendship, two things the anchor had not known in his life so far. Reluctant and wary and too tired to keep on fighting, the anchor accepted what the Emperor of the Storms offered.

Once their connection was established, they both reveled in the warmth of the other. The chain binding them turned from a burden into a blessing.

4. ASSAULT

Lost in thought, Casto stood in front of the mirror and adjusted the golden clasps that fastened the black velvet cape to the white tunic with the coat of arms of his family stitched into the area right above his heart. It was his third day back in Ummana and probably the most crucial one—today he would take on the crown and officially become the king of the Twin Cities. It was an act he dreaded almost as much as he longed for it. The moment he accepted the throne, the fight would be on. Casto had no illusions about what he was getting himself into. Even before he set foot in Ummana, he had started scheming, trying to anticipate every move his opponents might make. That he did not have the latest information about what was going on in Ummana was a serious drawback—one he had already started taking care of. The day before, he had contacted three of the spies whose services he had often used before he left. Since he had more than enough money to pay handsome fees, they had been eager to fill him in on everything that had been going on during his absence. To Casto's relief, most of the politicians he had encountered back in the day were still in the game. It meant he was going to deal with people he had already studied intensively. At the moment, that was his biggest advantage—that he knew them, but they couldn't imagine what he had become. With a little luck, this could provoke them to make mistakes.

Casto sighed. He had a nagging feeling that the Ummanian politicians were the least of his problems. During the banquet, Renaldo had demonstrated how unfit he was in dealing with the finer points of diplomacy. Not that Casto resented what his mate had said and done; on the contrary, he had enjoyed the terrified looks on the faces of the nobles, especially Nambuno, that fat old toad. Unfortunately, Casto was going to need the Council to govern Ummana and the Confederation, so for the time being, Nambuno was safe. Of course the old man knew that, which was probably part of the reason he had dared to speak up in front of everybody during the banquet. Keeping Renaldo from killing everybody he deemed a threat was the most important task until Casto managed to establish a new status quo.

Casto already regretted his decision to come back to this place where he had only known misery. It was too late now, though. If he focused on his thirst for revenge, he was able to bear the suffocating memories and the pressure coming not only from his opponents but also from his allies. Casto extended his chin defiantly, a determined expression on his face. He *was* the king of Ummana, and it was time to show them all.

ON HIS way from the royal wing to the throne room, Casto was accompanied by members of the royal guard, four of the mercenaries, and two wolves. Since it was the custom that the future leader of the Twin Cities entered the throne room alone, Renaldo had not wished to take any chances and for once, Casto had agreed with him. Walking through the palace unguarded would have been beyond foolish.

When they arrived at the heavy wooden doors with the golden inlays, Casto's guard stepped back. He drew one last, deep breath; then his hands closed around the massive loop-shaped handles, and he pulled. The doors opened slowly, gradually allowing Casto to see the crowd gathered inside the throne room. It was about thirteen paces long and ten paces broad, with five windows at each side that reached from the floor up to the ceiling. At the far end, the throne stood on a pedestal, flanked by four golden columns, onto which a black baldachin with golden embroidery was fastened. Right and left of the throne, the Angel of Death and the Wolf of War had taken position, something that was unheard of. Usually the new leader was all alone on the pedestal, to show his supremacy. Casto had to concentrate to hide his grin. He had pondered the wisdom of breaking with tradition in such a blatant manner for half a day before he decided to do it. As it turned out, his wager had paid off. There was not one Ummanian noble whose face did not show a mixture of consternation and fear, an emotional state that made it easy for Casto to play with. According to their rank, the nobles were lined along the walls, with the members of the Council and Aran closest to the pedestal.

With measured steps, Casto passed the political elite of Ummana, his gaze never leaving the crown resting upon a cushion on the seat of the throne. The closer he got to his goal, the more familiar he became with the people watching him. From the corner of his eye, he recognized Lady Sellin, head of the guild of merchants; Lord Rabnar, leader of the slave traders; Lady Sephrina and Lord Ammean, the heads of the Sylves and Ereat families. Then came his father, Lord Aran, still as repulsive as Casto remembered him. Casto wondered briefly why Aran had not tried to contact him yet but did not ponder the thought further. Thinking about his sire woke emotions Casto was not willing to deal with, especially at a moment like this. Lord Nambuno and Lady Amicia, the heads of the Krapati and Donai and unofficial leaders of the Council, stared daggers at him. They were more than a little displeased that Casto had refused to grant them an audience before the crowning ceremony. This, too, had been a well-calculated move to rattle them even more. Casto needed time to get reacquainted with the realities of Ummanian politics. While he did so, he preferred his opponents to be in a state of confusion. It also kept interaction between the nobles and the barbarians at a minimum and was therefore desirable.

Now Casto reached the throne. He bowed to the crown before lifting it from the black cushion. It felt surprisingly light for a symbol of such great power. Of course, it was made of a mixture of gold and silver, a hammered headband about half a hand high and encrusted with pearls, diamonds, emeralds, and rubies. Subtlety had never been his family's strong point, and the main purpose of the crown was to show off the immense wealth Ummana generated, a wealth that was synonymous with power and influence, two things the Twin Cities had in abundance. Slowly Casto turned around to face the crowd. Everybody, including Renaldo and Canubis, was staring at him, waiting for him to claim the responsibility and open the battle. Casto held the crown up high while he glared at the assembled nobles. His voice was firm and carried through the hall like the sound of a bell.

"Rie, Ma'ho Castolus ka Ummana, ta'lo ka Re'ha Isiris ka Ummana tani ewonda ka dra'vana, la tosi Re'haro ka malatok'na tani haro da Kre'wonn."

"I, Prince Castolus of Ummana, firstborn to Queen Isiris of Ummana and rightful heir to her throne, declare myself king of the Twin Cities and leader of the Confederation."

Lady Vespia, the ambassador from Medelina, flinched slightly at this choice of words, like many other politicians in the hall. Expressly mentioning the Confederation in his speech was yet another none-too-subtle way to make his position clear. None of the politicians liked what they heard, especially since Casto had spoken in ancient Ummanian, which heightened his intention of becoming an absolute ruler. The way he had stressed his rightful claim was a clear warning to those who thought of opposing him. A warning that was even more impressive because of the two barbarian warlords whose impassive gazes were almost as unnerving as Casto's calm authority. Now he put the crown on his head with a firm gesture. The moment the cold gold touched his skin, Canubis and Renaldo raised their ceremonial swords high in the air. Their voices boomed through the throne room and were joined by the citizens who had gathered outside in front of the palace.

"Hail to King Castolus! Long live the king!"

While he gracefully accepted his people's cheers, Casto studied his enemies closely. The members of the Council had some difficulty not showing their animosity but managed to retain neutral expressions. Anesha bowed to him with a broad smile on her lips. For her, things were progressing well and so, until something more lucrative came up for her, she would stay loyal to him. The ambassadors of Sravrana and Wa'na Atoka seemed to be genuinely pleased with Casto's ascent to the throne while the others, especially Lady Vespia, looked as if they had just been asked to swallow a toad alive. Subduing them was going to be interesting. Judging from their forced smiles, the guilds had decided to remain neutral for the time being. Casto felt an ominous chill running down his spine. Except for Renaldo and Canubis, he had no true allies in this room, and he did not trust even them completely. Renaldo might own his heart and soul, but there was still a tiny part of Casto that resented being the god's servant. If push came to shove, Casto knew Renaldo would overrule his will, and that was reason enough for him to maintain some distance, small as it might be. He was alone among enemies, as he had been all his life. The crown that had seemed to be so light was suddenly more than he could bear. Only Casto's will of iron prevented him from taking it off and running away.

As if he sensed his mate's distress, Renaldo moved closer and placed his hand briefly on Casto's lower back. The short contact was enough to jolt Casto out of his moment of self-pity. He straightened his back and sat down on his throne, waiting for his subjects to come forward and swear their loyalty to him. This part of the ceremony was purely for show, since even the smallest children in Ummana knew that true loyalty did not exist and that the other kind had to be bought at a worthy price. After this tedious and superfluous process, the royal guard came into the throne room to escort Casto to the balcony facing the front of the palace, where the citizens had gathered to greet their new king.

"WHAT A farce."

Nambuno emptied an entire cup of wine in one go. Amicia watched him closely. She had known Nambuno all her life and respected him as a politician as well as one of her closest allies. Seeing him fall apart worried her deeply, since he was one of the few people in Ummana who had the means to oppose

King Castolus successfully. Amicia had no illusions about her current situation. Within only three days, the Council had lost almost everything. Their fight for dominance with Aran had suddenly turned into a desperate struggle for survival. Of course, Castolus would not go against them as long as he needed their help, but once he had established his own alliances, he would take his revenge—if the barbarians did not preempt him. Getting on the king's good side was not an option—not after everything that had been done to him. Their only chance was to corner him politically and thus gain the upper hand again, a feat not entirely impossible but highly improbable. Castolus's barbarian allies alone were intimidating enough to call for careful action. The way the young king had handled the coronation added to Amicia's nervousness. She had seen a man who knew exactly what he was doing and, more importantly, what he wanted. To get the better of him, she needed Nambuno.

"So what do we do now, Nambuno?"

He put down the cup with a clink and a determined expression on his face. The moment of weakness was gone, and the seasoned politician had taken over again. Amicia breathed a sigh of relief.

"We have to go through our options first. Aktan and the royal guard will stick with Castolus. They never liked the chaos of the recent years. Anesha could perhaps be persuaded to join our side again, but only when the king is seriously weakened. The guilds—well, nobody can predict their actions, and I don't want to rely on any of them when elections are so close. At the moment, our best bet is Aran, as much as I hate to admit it."

Amicia made a face. She had come to the same conclusion and liked it even less than Nambuno. It was bad enough having Aran as an enemy; joining forces with the irascible man was not something Amicia would have contemplated only five days ago. Unfortunately they had no choice. Castolus had cornered them so completely, they had to be grateful for still having any options at all.

"So be it. We approach Aran. He should be inclined to listen since he has even more to lose than we do."

Nambuno nodded gravely.

"Let's see what he has to offer. We have to tread very carefully, though. I don't trust those barbarians in the least. So let's not rush unduly and arouse their suspicion."

Amicia shuddered. Just remembering the cold glint in the eyes of the Angel of Death when Nambuno had questioned his relationship with Castolus made her blood freeze.

"So much for your grand hypothesis that Castolus is still under our control."

Aran glared at Voltara, who was pacing the small room where they had met. The torturer was worried. He had honestly believed it would be easy to get past the barbarians and reclaim the king as his toy. During the crowning ceremony, it had finally dawned on him that reality was different from what he wanted it to be. This could become unpleasant for him quite quickly if he did not play his cards right. If he wanted to escape unscathed, he had to throw the king a bone that would distract him while Voltara left the Twin Cities. Luckily enough, a very juicy bone was right in front of him, waiting to be sacrificed. Aran was so caught up in his ambitions that even now his greatest fear was not losing his life but seeing the throne slip away from him. Voltara smiled. He had enjoyed playing with the gullible Lord Aran, yet the time had come to sever their ties for good. While he started to reassure Aran with soothing words, the torturer already plotted his downfall in the back of his mind.

In the royal chambers, Casto enjoyed a shoulder rub from Renaldo. He groaned when the warrior found another knotted muscle and smoothed it out.

"You're all tensed up. Try to relax a little bit."

Renaldo did his best to keep the worry from his voice. Since they had set foot in Ummana, Casto had started to change profoundly. The nightmares and growing uneasiness had been bad enough to make Renaldo doubt the wisdom of their decision. At the banquet and later, during the discussion with Anesha, Renaldo had started to realize what kind of person Casto could be when he had to, and he didn't like what he had seen. The coronation had only served to heighten his worries. The man who had crowned himself and claimed not only supremacy over an entire city but also over the Confederation had only vaguely resembled the man he had married some three months ago. The walls Renaldo had thought breached had risen again, and he had problems approaching his husband. Even when he was touching him like he did now, Casto seemed distant. Renaldo leaned in to nibble the young man's earlobe.

"What's going on in that complicated brain of yours, my own?"

With an impatient gesture, Casto shook his husband off.

"Nothing I can put into words yet. Thanks for the massage."

Made speechless by the dismissive tone, Renaldo watched as Casto got up and vanished into the bathroom. He felt anger welling inside but reined it in quickly. The last thing they needed now was a fight about something petty. As much as it annoyed him, patience was mandatory at the moment.

THE MAN touched the small vial hidden safely in his worn tunic with loving care. Yesterday, during the king's coronation, his mistress's slave had entrusted him with the poison, and since then he had been looking for a way to smuggle it into the king's food. But the servants of the barbarians were vigilant; they did not allow any strangers close to the food designated for the demigods and the Emeris. Time was running out. He could almost feel the power draining from the vial, making the poison ineffective. He had to hurry, otherwise the mistress's plan would fail and his own destiny would be cruelly sealed.

Anxiously his gaze darted through the kitchen and stopped dead at one of the stoves. Slaves were just preparing a tray with bread, soup, and fruit to be brought to the royal chambers. He prayed to the Good Mother for help in this dangerous situation, and his pleas were answered. An apprentice tripped and knocked over a cauldron with boiling oil that spilled like a current on the stone floor. Everybody jumped hastily to safety; some tried to help the boy, who was badly burned and rolling on the ground, screaming. In all this chaos, the man tightened his grip around the handle of his mop, made an innocent face, and started to wipe up the oil. He managed to get close enough to the tray to empty the entire vial into the soup without anybody noticing it. After staying long enough to make sure the food had really been brought to the king, he left the kitchen. In a small alleyway, his mistress's slave was waiting for him. A happy smile contorted his features.

"The poison has been placed. Not long and the walls of the palace will resound with lamentations."

The slave's ordinary face lit up in satisfaction.

"You did well. The mistress is pleased."

"What about the reward she promised me?"

A soothing smile reassured him. "But of course. You shall get your reward. Come here."

The man was so full of anticipation, so excited, he didn't even see the knife that cut his heart. When the corpse landed heavily at her feet, the slave made a disgusted face.

"This is the reward granted by the Good Mother for those loyal to her. I hope you're satisfied."

Then she turned around and vanished in the shadows.

SIC KNEW immediately that he was in trouble when Noran yanked the door open. His bad mood was like a thundercloud darkening the entire room. Ever since Renaldo had forgiven Sic, Noran had become even more brutal and crueler than he had been before. He still played games with Sic's feelings of guilt, but he had also increased the physical punishment. It was as if Noran was losing all restraint. On their journey to Ummana, he had held back, mainly because the tent didn't provide enough privacy to punish the traitor as he saw fitting, but he hadn't refrained from taking him every evening just to remind him of his place in the Pack. As soon as they had reached Ummana and he had once again the seclusion of a brick-built room at his leisure, Noran started to reimburse himself for the reserve he'd had to exert before. There was no night in which Sic did not cry himself to sleep in despair, and today wouldn't be any different. Frightened, he knelt in front of his furious master, who kicked him viciously.

"Get up, you worthless piece of shit! I'm hungry, so get going and bring me some food."

Sic rose as fast as possible.

"Yes, Master."

He hurried to leave the room, knowing Noran would sanction tardiness with a beating or worse. In front of the fountain he met Casto, who was just taking a full tray from a servant.

"Sic, where are you hurrying to?"

"My master is hungry and in a bad mood."

Casto frowned. He was aware how Noran was making his friend's life as hard as possible, and he was longing for the day he could take his revenge. Until then he did everything in his power to protect Sic from the master smith's wrath.

"Here, take this. I don't have time to eat anyway."

Sic shook his head.

"You have to eat. I know how hard this is for you. I'm fine."

"Don't be stupid. I can see he's beaten you again. Take it—that's an order. A royal one."

Grateful, Sic took the tray. Casto shot him an encouraging smile before Sic returned to his master's chambers. Noran looked cranky.

"That was fast, slave."

With his head bowed low and his hands trembling, Sic served his owner the soup.

"A servant had just come up."

"Lucky you."

Noran's tone implied clearly how displeased he was. He tried to find a way to turn Sic's quick fulfilment of his will against him but couldn't come up with anything. While he was eating, he watched the young man cowering at his feet, waiting for his next demand.

"Get up and undress. Once I'm done, I want some dessert."

Satisfied, Noran observed how the little traitor started trembling all over, but he still got up obediently and stripped off his shabby tunic and the thin trousers he'd been wearing.

"Stay like that."

Hushed, Sic complied, trying to brace himself against the pain in his heart he would be enduring soon and which, although he should have been used to it by now, still surprised him with its brutality. Way too soon, the master smith ended his meal. His eyes regarded his naked slave with hunger.

"Kneel down in front of the lounge."

Sic did as he was told. He rested his upper body on the padded lounge and spread his legs without his master telling him to. With some luck, his servile obedience would soothe Noran's wrath enough to let the torture end quickly. Ever since Noran had implied that he might forgive Sic if he served him sexually, Sic had started applying oil to his hole three times a day to always be ready for his master's needs. He was starting to doubt that servicing Noran would earn him the master smith's forgiveness, but a last spark of hope kept Sic hanging on. Sic heard the warrior's belt sliding open, and his muscles tensed. He waited for his master's hands to grab him mercilessly to prevent him from escaping, as they always did.

But nothing happened. Instead, Sic heard Noran make a choked sound, followed by a crash. Unsure, Sic turned around, half expecting a cruel trick to punish him even more brutally.

Noran lay motionless on his belly; his breath was so faint it barely moved his upper body. Hesitatingly, Sic reached out to him.

"Master? Are you all right?"

When he got no reaction, the young man dared to shake his master. Again Noran didn't move. With difficulty Sic rolled the heavy body around. Noran was as bulky as a dead ox. His eyes were rolled up so high only the white was still visible, and bloody foam clustered at the corners of his mouth. In alarm Sic bolted up and out of the door. He ran directly into Kalad, who was on his way to his chambers.

"Whoa! Slow down, slave! I can't imagine what could be so pressing to run down an Emeris for it."

"Please, Master, help me. Something's wrong with Lord Noran. He lost consciousness. Please, hurry!"

Without waiting for Kalad's reaction or regard to manners, Sic grabbed the desert warrior's arm and dragged him to Noran. Kalad only glanced at his fallen brother-in-arms briefly before he acted.

"Aegid! Get Noemi, right now! Daran, come here! Hurry!"

A few heartbeats later Daran appeared in the entrance, his friendly face filled with worry.

"Master! What's happened?"

"I don't know yet. Take care of Sic. He's shaken and needs looking after."

Kindly, Daran took Sic's hands in his and led him to a chair, a stream of soothing words pouring from his lips. He made Sic drink a cup of water, helped him dress, and kept his arm slung around Sic's shoulder while they both watched as Lady Noemi came running into the room. She knelt next to Noran's motionless body; her healing hands touched his face. When the witch attempted curing the master smith, her features tensed. Only a few moments later she let go of him, worry blooming in her shining green eyes.

"Kalad, Aegid, help me get him on the lounge. Then go and tell Canubis and Renaldo. This is serious."

A short time later, the demigods were standing in front of Noemi; Casto and the other Emeris waited behind them. All of them had concern and disbelief plainly written on their faces.

"He was poisoned." Noemi sounded desperate. "It's a very potent poison, and it was magically enhanced. I can't heal it. Whoever created it knew what they were doing and was aware of the limits of my power."

"You're telling me he's going to die?" Canubis's voice was gloomy, since they all knew what it meant if they lost an Emeris.

"Yes, my lord. In its natural state, the poison attacks something in the blood until the victim suffocates. The magic has changed it so that it now feeds on the part of Noran that is Emeris. If he weren't so young compared to the others, he'd already be dead."

"I always thought we can't die?" Aegid was clearly shaken.

Noemi looked at him sadly.

"Not by a human's hand or by time. The kiss of the Mothers protects us from these things. The older we get, the more potent the protection. You could say the divine spark is growing inside us. But this poison was made with magic—very old, powerful magic. Creating a weapon like this requires great determination because the price is the spell caster's life."

"I don't understand. Why, of all people, Noran? Why not Casto or one of us?"

Canubis's gaze was glued to his dying Emeris.

"Bad luck. The poison was meant for me." Casto's voice was constricted. "I had asked for something from the kitchen, but then I had no time to eat, and Noran had just sent Sic to get him a meal. It should be me lying there, not him."

Renaldo hastened to sling his arms around the king.

"Stop talking nonsense, my own. We don't even know whether the poisoner knew whom the tray was meant for. It could have been any of us."

"Whoever it was knew about the special powers of the Emeris." Noemi's shoulders slumped. "All we can do is make his last hours on Ana-Darasa as comfortable as possible, although I doubt he'll notice."

"Do you mean to tell me I have to watch our brother-in-arms die?" Aegid was thunderstruck. Canubis glared at his wife.

"Is there nothing you can do, Noemi?"

Noemi dodged the Wolf of War's gaze. "There is a tiny chance, but it's not really a possibility."

"If my Emeris can be saved, I want to know about it, Noemi."

"I'm sorry, my lord. But the price is too high."

"Look at me, woman!" thundered the Wolf of War. Reluctantly the snake witch obeyed. "Tell me right now how Noran's life can be saved!"

Noemi whimpered in despair, trying desperately to escape from this situation. When she found no way out, she submitted to her master's will. At that moment, there was nothing left of the loving husband who always treated her with the utmost gentleness. Now he was talking to her as her god, who would not tolerate any back talk or defiance. It was impossible to disobey him.

"The poison feeds on the divine spark. If I induce normal life energy into it, it will burn out. But the price is a life, my lord. Whoever is the donor will probably die. And before you ask, it has to be a human. Neither you nor any of the Emeris can do it."

Muted by horror, they all stared at each other. The implication was clear. Canubis had to choose a sacrifice to die in place of his Emeris. And Noemi would be the one to kill that sacrifice.

THE AWKWARD silence was shattered by Sic's voice, thin and full of sorrow. "I'll do it. I'm human through and through. I only hope my energy is enough."

"Sic, no! You've heard what Noemi said. I don't want to lose you!" Casto had rushed to his friend's side and was shaking him like a rag doll. "Don't do this to me, please!"

Sic smiled, full of affection. He was grateful to have Casto as his friend.

"You're very kind, Casto, but I've been dead for almost a year now. I died the day I betrayed you and my master. Your grace has granted me a respite, for which I will be eternally thankful to you, but my destiny was decided the moment I sinned."

"No!" Casto's voice was a desperate whimper. He could not lose Sic, not like this, not for Noran, of all people. Everything inside him revolted against it.

"It's fine, Casto, really. And who knows, perhaps my master will grant me his forgiveness one day."

For an eternity, Casto's gaze was glued to Sic's determined face. Then he hugged his friend vehemently, his tears wetting Sic's cheeks. Casto had known from the very start that his return to Ummana would come with a hefty price, but he would have never thought Sic would be the one to pay it. All he could do now was keep up a dignified front to honor his brave friend.

"It's my pleasure to call you my friend, and I swear to you, I won't forget you till the end of all time."

Sic hugged the king back and when he let go of him, he kissed his hands.

"Thank you, Casto. That means a lot to me."

With a barely concealed sob, Casto turned away from him. Renaldo pulled his heart close, his right hand extended toward the smith.

"I align myself with Casto. We will never forget your name and what you have done for us. Your sin is forgotten as if it had never existed."

Canubis placed his hand on Sic's shoulder. He was relieved that the situation would resolve itself so easily. To him, Sic was still a traitor, somebody whose life didn't have any worth for the Pack. That Sic would give up his life to save Noran redeemed him in Canubis's eyes and also spared him the difficult decision of whom he should sacrifice. For the Wolf of War, everything had played out smoothly.

"I promise you, the spirits of our enemies will soon follow you into the Green Lands, and they will serve you as slaves there."

Having granted Sic his forgiveness with those threatening words, the Wolf of War straightened himself, his amber eyes glowing ominously.

"It's time to alert the wolves. Let's go hunting."

Like a fever, the words rushed through the warriors. Their faces turned from sorrowful to lethal, their bodies tensed in a subtle way, and the lust for blood was apparent in their eyes. Canubis turned to his wife.

"Noemi, you save my brother-in-arms. Hulda, you stay with my wife."

The killer nodded coldly. When the Emeris left the chamber, Sic felt something akin to pity for those who dared to oppose the divine brothers. Whoever was responsible for the assault on Noran would curse the day they first had the idea.

With the aid of Daran, Hulda positioned a second lounge next to the one with the dying Noran. Daran left with a bow; his further attendance wasn't needed. After he closed the door, Hulda positioned herself in front of it with a grim expression on her face. Anybody dumb enough to try getting in without permission would die a fast, brutal death.

Noemi took Sic's hand and led him to the lounge, her face smeared with tears. While she helped him to lie down, she talked with a firm, only slightly shaken voice.

"I promise you, Sic, you won't feel any pain. You'll become very tired and then you'll fall asleep. Perhaps you'll dream a bit, but it won't be nightmares, of that I can assure you. I'm so sorry!"

She placed a gentle kiss on his forehead.

"It's fine, my lady, really. I'm ready."

Still crying, the snake witch knelt between the two lounges. She knew what she was doing was necessary, but it went against her very nature to end a life, even if it meant saving another one. And Sic's willingness to give up his own life made it even harder for her. His self-sacrifice was like a festering wound that wouldn't heal for a long time.

She placed her right hand on Sic's chest, the other one on Noran's. Silence fell. For an eternity nothing seemed to happen. Then Sic started feeling tired, as if he had worked in the smithy all day. The smithy! He would miss the place, even though it had been more of a prison than a home the last few months. Slowly Sic slid into sleep, glad that he could finally rest.

5. LUKSARI

IN THE emptiness that was the world between, Noemi Amerasu stared in plain horror at the body of the slave she had known as Sic. The realization of what he was hit her like a punch to the gut, and if it had been possible, she would have stopped the process and let Noran die.

Sic was pure. His body was made of blinding light, like Noemi had never seen before in a human. She knew the legends about the Luksari, creatures who were born human and filled with light. They had always been rare and hard to recognize, but it was said that meeting a Luksari meant great luck. And Noran was indeed lucky, although in a perverted way. Noemi cried like a child. The young smith, who had been branded by her husband and brother-in-law and had been so cruelly tortured by Noran, was completely innocent. She gagged when she beheld amidst the blaze the wounds he had endured at the hands of his gods and master. This was wrong, absolutely wrong! Sic should have been treated with awe and affection by them, but—with the exception of Casto's friendship—all he had ever encountered in the Valley was pain and humiliation. There was no way they could make up for this sacrilege. Desperate, Noemi looked for a way out, for a chance to at least partially wipe the slate clean, but she felt this was not in her power.

A hissing sound made her turn around. The snake was here, as grand and beautiful as Noemi had ever seen her. Like always, the unblinking black eyes stared directly into the core of her soul, something she would never get used to. After an agonizing amount of time during which Noemi wished from the bottom of her heart for things to be different, one of the most powerful bearers of ancient magic slid past her and approached the blinding light that was Sic. With her neck shield wide open, the snake hovered over the young man. The split tongue darted back and forth nervously; then the flat snout touched the smith's forehead. For a moment the light shone so brightly, Noemi had to avert her gaze. When she dared to look again, her soulmate was gone without sparing her another glance. Sic's body was pure and unmarred; the snake had taken the memory of his wounds with her.

The witch knew that the scars Sic had to endure were too old to be healed in the real world, but here, in the space between, the only place that mattered in the end, he was whole again. It was a double-edged gift the snake had bestowed on her. It made Noemi's task to exchange Sic's life for that of Noran a lot easier, but as soon as it was over, the memory of that present would gnaw on her conscience like a rat on a fresh corpse.

HULDA WATCHED the three motionless bodies in front of her out of narrowed eyes. She could feel life and death joining hands in their eternal dance. As the mother superior of an order of assassins, she not only knew about death; she was also painfully aware of the worth of life. In addition she had developed a fine sense for the streams of energy surrounding all living things at all times, which remained a mystery for most other people. Right at the moment, a fierce battle was going on, the streams in turmoil like belligerent bulls during mating season. The air was thick and heavy, as if a thunderstorm was coming. Among this aggressive chaos, her sister's energy was like a breeze that slowly but surely restored order. The fierceness retreated, the storm calmed down, the battle was won, but a bitter aftertaste remained.

Groaning, Noemi lifted her head, her green eyes full of guilt and pain like Hulda had never seen before. Next to her, Noran stirred. His legs twitched and then he sat up. His gaze strayed through the room and stayed glued on Sic.

"What's happened?" His voice was full of suspicion. "Why's the traitor lying here, resting?"

"The traitor has a name. It's Sic, and Sic is busy dying in your place, you ignorant, cruel monster!"

Noemi's voice was sharp, her whole body tense.

"Hulda, help Noran get off the lounge and then remove him from my sight. I won't allow him to sully Sic's deathbed with his presence."

Without another word the killer did as she was told. She knew her sister well enough to realize something was horribly wrong, but she also knew she would find out soon enough. Noran shot puzzled glances from her to Noemi while Hulda led him out of the chambers.

"What's happened, Hulda?"

"You were poisoned. Noemi healed you using your slave's life energy. Obviously she has found out what you've been doing to him during the past few months. My advice is to keep your distance from her for the time being, unless, of course, you still wish to die."

The guilt flashing across Noran's features told Hulda louder than words that her suspicions regarding Sic had been on the mark, a fact that made her furious. In front of the fountain, she pushed Noran away.

"How could you behave so abominably? I thought I knew you, but during the last months you've turned into a stranger, and one I don't want anything to do with. If you couldn't find it in your heart to forgive the poor boy, why didn't you sell him? Or kill him? Did you have to torture him so brutally?"

Noran's shoulders slumped. In quiet moments he had asked himself the very same question, and the answer had been so ugly he hadn't been able to accept it. When faced with Hulda's wrath, he had no other choice, though.

"I couldn't help myself. Every time I looked at him, I was reminded of Arja. Of what she did to me. And Sic accepted his punishment so readily. I simply couldn't stop. It was so easy to vent it on him, to make him suffer."

"Arja's been dead for a hundred years, Noran. I know she used and hurt you, that she gave you wounds that are almost impossible to heal, but it's high time for you to wake up and stop pitying yourself.

"You let her fool you. You were willing to betray your family, your gods for her. Face the truth, accept your sins, and perhaps one day you'll get a chance to make up for it."

Deeply shocked, Noran stared at Hulda. He could not remember a time when she had ever used words as direct as these. Usually the mother superior preferred a more subtle approach.

"Why are you so agitated, Hulda?"

"You're asking why I'm agitated? We almost lost you, you idiot! And then I had to stand by and watch while a helpless human, a slave, offered you the help none of us could give you. To top it off, it was a slave who had no reason to do anything for you. I'm deeply ashamed, especially since I know none of us will ever be able to repay this debt. Sic is going to die, and absolutely nothing can absolve us of this sin."

Suddenly Noran understood what he had been denying all this time.

He was going to lose Sic.

The pain started in his stomach and swamped his entire body, made him lose all feeling while the revelation echoed endlessly in his empty brain. Groaning, he sank to his knees. He felt tears streaming down his cheeks while regret—terrible, futile regret—burned his soul until he thought he could no longer bear the pain. Helplessly he reached out for Hulda.

"It can't be, Hulda. Please tell me this is not true. I can't lose him. No."

Sadly, the killer caressed his hair, her voice so soft he almost couldn't hear it. "Face the truth, Noran. The love of your life is about to leave Ana-Darasa. I wish I could help you. I wish I had spoken up sooner, but I had hoped you'd see reason yourself. I will never forgive myself."

Then the beautiful woman sat down next to him, slung her arm around his shoulders, and together they kept watch throughout the night.

6. REGRET

IN THE early morning hours, the Emeris returned triumphantly. They had a prisoner with them, a young woman who was struggling desperately in Aegid's grip while a stream of the most profane slurs against the divine brothers left her lips. Her clothes were dirty and torn, and on her right cheek a bruise was forming. She had obviously fought back, although in vain. Everybody was thrilled to see Noran up and about, but Hulda didn't hesitate to dampen the good mood.

"Noemi is still with Sic. She didn't want to leave him alone."

Pointedly ignoring Noran, Casto disappeared into the smith's chambers. Noemi looked up when he entered. Her eyes were red from crying, dark circles had formed under her eyes, her voice was nothing but a hoarse whisper, and she looked exhausted.

"He's taking his time. But I didn't want him to be alone. Not after…."

"Not after everything Noran did to him."

"You know?"

Casto's face was grim. "I'm sure he hasn't told me everything, but I know enough. It was very kind of you to stay with him. Now you should get some rest. You look like I feel."

The snake witch managed a weak smile.

"Not very charming, Your Majesty."

"I know. And I'll make up for it."

"Forget it. I know how much you're suffering. I'll take a nap and then I'll come back."

Gently she pressed a kiss on Casto's forehead before she left the room. She was worried about Casto. It was not only the physical exhaustion that was getting to him, but the emotional distress to have returned to the place of his worst memories. In order to protect himself, he'd reinforced the shell around his heart and was transforming into a lifeless statue right in front of her eyes. Noemi was afraid that losing Sic would be more than the king could bear. If he got truly lost, not even Renaldo would be able to call him back.

In front of the door, her husband looked questioningly at her. The Emeris were assembled around him and their faces, too, betrayed their worry and dismay.

"He's still alive, but the end is near."

Again she started to cry, a hysterical sobbing that forced its way out of her throat. Carefully her master and god took her in his arms.

"Come, my jewel. Let me take care of you."

He picked up his crying wife, his amber eyes fixed on his underlings.

"See to our prisoner's safe housing, then get some rest as well. We meet again at noon."

The warriors returned to their chambers, the flush of the successful hunt swept away by the tragic events.

KALAD AND Aegid locked the prisoner in, and two wolves stayed back as guard. Daran was waiting for them with wine and refreshments, but the young man was jittery and nervous. His eyes were red, as if he had cried a lot. Kalad pulled him close.

"It's fine, little thief. It's been a long night."

The slave buried his face against his master's chest.

"It's not only the assault, master. It's Sic. What he has done…. Giving his life just like this, for a man he must have hated. I'm wondering whether I could do the same for you, putting my life on the line."

Gently Aegid stroked Daran's naked back.

"Could you?"

A sob was the answer.

"I'd love to say I'd do it without a second thought. I really wish I could say that. But if I'm honest, I don't know. And I'm deeply ashamed. You're so good to me. You've never hurt me or punished me roughly. Sic, on the other hand…."

Daran fell silent, thought for a moment, and started anew.

"We all have our suspicions what he's had to endure the last months. And when I helped him get dressed, I saw what Lord Noran has done to him. He was embarrassed. And yet he was willing to die for this man. I'm afraid what it says about me that I'm not even sure whether I could make the same sacrifice for you."

"First of all, Sic has always been different. None of us has understood why he loved Noran so much, since he's known him only as the brutal shell you have seen. Sic is his own person, just like you, and the two of you don't have a lot of things in common. You're levelheaded and cool. You'd never jump into a situation headfirst, which is one of the things we love about you. So you being doubtful about your reaction only shows how honest and analytical you are. If in doubt, I'm sure you'd do what is right for you."

Aegid's voice was calm; he knew what kind of tone would soothe Daran. Kalad pushed him a little away, and his hands cupped Daran's face.

"We're very pleased with you, Daran. And now stop worrying your pretty head over such trivial matters. Your masters are filthy and aroused from the hunt. It would be splendid if you could take care of both problems."

A last sob, then Daran pulled himself together to serve his owners' needs.

"I'M SO sorry, Sic. So unbelievably sorry. I should have done more to get you away from Noran. I had so many plans for us. I wanted Lys to ride with you through a storm. That's such a great feeling—you'd have loved it.

"I'd already made plans how we would build your own smithy and how incredibly famous you'd become for your talent. As soon as Renaldo bought you, I'd have freed you, of course. We would have been equal. I never wanted things to turn out like this."

Casto's voice was raw and full of despair. It filled the room like a lament, remembering things they had shared, full of hope for a future that had ceased to exist, and regretting the cruel present.

It was this voice that woke Sic from his slumber. Still dazed from sleep, he looked around. Empty, dark space surrounded him, only bearable because of the light dancing around the edge of his vision. Like a golden thread, Casto's voice twisted through the void, enticing him, showing him the path back into the world. Without thinking, he wanted to give in to the allure, since it was Casto calling for him, but a hiss stopped him dead in his tracks.

Slowly he turned around. A gigantic snake was coiling before him, its black eyes regarding him calmly. The frill was spread, and the diamond-shaped pattern on the massive body shone in vivid hues of green and yellow. Although the beast was heading directly toward him, Sic didn't feel afraid. His instincts told him that the creature was not there to harm him. He thought he remembered a cold kiss, but his mind was blurry.

Again the snake hissed and this time, Sic understood what it was telling him. Like the tinkling of silver bells, the words resounded in his mind.

"I greet you, young smith."

"Am I dead?"

Sic knew the question was stupid. What else could he be? But he wanted to confirm it. Something like laughter echoed in the void and made the light around him dance.

"Not yet. My witch took a lot of your energy, and a human would be dead by now. But you are different, shining one."

"I'm as ordinary as dirt. How can I be different?"

"You're not human, for a start."

There was mockery in the silver bells, but Sic didn't have time to react to it. He had other worries.

"My master? If I'm not human…."

Again a ripple of condescending laughter.

"Don't worry. The dark one is fine. Even though your energy isn't human, it was more than sufficient to save his life. Which brings us back to you. You're a Luksari, a creature of magic so old even I seem young in comparison. It's been a long time since I last met one of your kind. You do tend to pop up in the most unexpected of places."

Sic wasn't sure if he had heard right. The snake surely meant somebody else, not him. He was only a slave, and an unworthy one at that. Still the strange creature kept on addressing him with this outlandish title.

"Luksari do not die. At least, not if they don't choose to. And that's why I'm here, to tell you about your possibilities, since you seem to be confused."

"Possibilities?"

"As I said, Luksari don't die. You can do whatever you want, go wherever you please. You can even choose to enter the Green Lands. I know Ana-Aruna would be thrilled to welcome you there. It's entirely up to you."

Sic smiled crookedly. The irony of the situation did not escape him. For the first time in his life, he was told to do what he wanted—when all he could want was to fulfill the oath he had sworn to his god.

"I think we both know what I'm going to do. Casto needs me, so I'm going back to him."

The unblinking gaze of the snake held his own without showing the slightest emotion.

"Then you also return to the dark one."

Sic shuddered, knowing this was the sacrifice he had to make.

"I know. That's the price I'll pay."

Determined, he turned toward Casto's voice before the snake could make him hesitate any more. His friend was desperate, and it was time to ease his mind. Without turning away or protecting itself otherwise, the snake bore the blinding light flaming around the Luksari. It had been eons, on another world, in a different time, since it had last encountered such purity and power. It only hoped it wasn't the last time it had the honor of talking to a Luksari.

The light faded, and out of the darkness Ana-Isara appeared next to the snake, her white hair flowing in a breeze that couldn't reach the realm in which they were meeting.

"Thank you" was all the goddess said before she vanished again.

SIC'S EYELIDS fluttered; then he opened his eyes. His gaze met Casto's disbelieving face. He grinned weakly.

"Why are you staring at me like that? I mean, you're the one who called me back."

"Sic!"

Casto hugged his friend so vehemently he had trouble breathing.

"Please, Casto. I'm back, but I do need air!"

"Forgive me. It's just—I'm so glad! Are you hungry? Thirsty? Wait, let me help you. You surely want to sit up, don't you?"

"Casto, calm down, please."

"Noemi! I have to tell Noemi! You stay here and don't move, understood?"

This said, the king was gone. Sic sat upright and gazed around the familiar room. Whether it had been a good idea to come back was yet to be seen, but he really didn't have a choice. He had abandoned Casto once; it wouldn't happen a second time.

He looked up when his friend and Noemi came bolting into the chamber. The snake witch was crying again, but this time out of relief.

"Sic, I'm so glad! How do you feel?" With a scrutinizing glare, she placed her cool hands on his shoulders. Sic could sense her examining his body with her gift, down to the last nook and cranny. He felt shame rise inside.

"Please, my lady. I'm fine. It's not necessary for you to…." He lowered his gaze. *"For you to see my disgrace,"* he had wanted to say, but the words were stuck in his throat. The witch caressed him gently.

"It's okay, Sic. I don't want you to be ashamed of something that's not your fault. Your scars are my disgrace, mine and the other Emeris, even of our gods, but they are not yours, do you understand?"

Insecure, Sic nodded. He didn't understand anything but would never admit it.

Noemi turned to Casto.

"He's fine, more or less, but he needs all the rest he can get. His life energy has been almost completely consumed. I'm still surprised he's made it back. It will take some time until he has recovered. I'm going to send you some food and inform Canubis and Renaldo. See to it that he doesn't overexert himself. I'll be back soon."

Casto nodded. His face showed his grave determination when he turned back to his friend.

Sic sighed. "I guess the offer with Lys is off the table for now?"

SAVAGE POLITICS

1. ATTACK

THE TWO demigods were more than happy when they heard about Sic's recovery. Now that the mood was more relaxed than before, Renaldo dared to ask his sister-in-law why she had been so upset about the young man's sacrifice. Noemi turned serious again.

"Because we've made a terrible mistake. Sic is a Luksari. Completely innocent. His corporeal body was the most beautiful thing I've ever seen—apart from the wounds you and Noran have inflicted on him."

Shocked, the brothers shared a look. Luksari were so rare, neither of them had ever seen one. Ana-Aruna had told them about the race, which was one of her most favorite, but even she had only met a few. The Luksari hadn't been made like all the other races, but had simply come into being unbidden. Most probably they were a byproduct of the process when the wild magic had been tamed. They were fairy-tale creatures who brought great luck to those treating them well. Under these circumstances, Sic's suffering was even worse. Torturing a Luksari as they had done was a sin they could never hope to redeem. Noemi's further words did not help to soothe the brothers.

"Shaa-Azar has healed him, at least in the realm between. I'll try to treat his scars here, if he allows me to. He's deeply embarrassed about his blemished body. And the pain some of the scars still give him is a constant reminder of what he had to endure. I really can't tell whether he'll ever get over this trauma."

"There's no way Casto's going to leave his friend at the moment."

Renaldo didn't have any illusions in this regard. After everything that had happened, it would be stupid to separate his heart and the smith. Canubis exchanged a long, thoughtful glance with his brother. They were both worried about the current state of affairs in Ummana and about the impact it had on Casto. Until now they had held back to get a feel for the people, and this had been a grave mistake. It had almost cost them one of their Emeris. It was time to set things straight.

"Perhaps it's for the best. Gives us the opportunity to clear up a few things. To establish a certain order before matters get out of hand. Let's call for this princess, Anesha. I want her to be there when we question the prisoner."

Renaldo nodded in agreement. He knew exactly what his brother wanted.

"It surely can't hurt to have a few words with the Council as well, without the king."

Both men sounded distracted, as if they were merely toying with some thoughts that had just occurred to them. Noemi shook her head. She had learned to read the signs and knew her husband and brother-in-law were up to no good.

"Do whatever you think is necessary, but try to avoid any undue excitement for Casto. He's not doing well, and the situation with Sic has almost tipped him over the edge. I'm still worried it could have been too much. We should thank the Mothers on our knees that the young smith has survived."

Guilt sparked in the eyes of the Angel of Death, but his brother shook his head.

"Don't start overthinking it. Casto is your heart. He's strong. It was his idea to come here. We made this decision together."

"Of course you're right. But it hurts, seeing how he's suffering."

"Rest assured, Renaldo, at the moment he's more than happy. He's so glad Sic is still alive, he's even forgotten how tired he is." Noemi smiled softly. "I hope the two will find some rest together."

Her face hardened. "I'm going to have a word with a certain smith. Noran has a lot of explaining to do."

Canubis pressed a loving kiss on her face. He was glad things had taken a turn for the better. Even though he acted the part of indisputable master, it had hurt him deeply to force his wife to do his will. He was capable of doing it when he had no choice, but his weakness was that he could barely stand it. In addition, Noemi was a strong-willed, powerful woman who could make his life difficult if she chose to. Because of this, he was glad she would vent her anger on somebody who deserved it.

"I leave it to you, my jewel. We'll give the order to leave Casto and Sic alone. Renaldo, what do you think? Should we show this city what it means to challenge the wrath of the gods?"

The Angel of Death answered with a smile that would have turned any other face into a hideous grimace, but his perfect features only gained another, more terrible facet. It was a death mask, terrifying yet alluring, like the shimmering waves of the sea hiding the deadly rocks on which ships slit their bellies.

Together the brothers left the chambers. Noemi went to find Noran. Her anger toward the smith had been slightly dampened by the joy at

Sic's recovery, but now it reached new heights. Normally she had a calm personality and failed to see the point in giving in to unproductive emotions like fury or hatred, which made her all the more dangerous when she did give in. In this case, Noran would be at the center of the storm.

The master smith had moved in with Hulda and Wolfstan. He was sitting in a chair and looked at her with sad puppy eyes. That look made Noemi even angrier.

"Is he dead?"

"No. Sic is alive. He woke up about an hour ago."

Noran jolted up as if he had been hit by an electric charge. Hope bloomed in his face like a flower in spring. "Sic is alive?"

The snake witch regarded him coldly. She could see that Noran had finally realized what his apprentice meant to him, but she wasn't in the mood to forgive him because of it.

"Yes, but not for you, you cruel monster of a man. I'm here to tell you that you will keep your distance from him in the future. You will give him his freedom, and then you'll stay away from him. Have I made myself clear?"

Noran was clearly unhappy about her words. A last spark of his old arrogance sprang to life. "The slave is mine. I decide what happens to him."

"No, you don't. Not anymore. Sic saved your life, so you'll do what honor dictates in such a case. And before you make so much as a peep, I want to remind you of who I am and what I'm capable of. When I bargained Sic's life for yours, I could see what you've done to him. You should be ashamed. It's one thing to punish a traitor; you might even use sex to subdue him, even though this is against everything the Mothers stand for, but to use his love to manipulate him is downright contemptible. I'd even say unforgivable.

"In the Mothers' name, Noran, he's barely twenty, still a child compared to you. He had no chance to survive your little psycho games unscathed. You've hurt him in ways I can't even begin to describe. You should get down on your knees and thank the Mothers that you didn't manage to break him.

"So my advice is to do what I say, because otherwise, I swear to you, you're going to get to know me in ways you can't imagine in your worst nightmares."

Beaten, the once conceited and overbearing smith lowered his head.

"I hear you, Noemi."

"Fine."

With a last, condescending glare, the snake witch left the master smith.

"YOU MAY torture me as long as you wish, bastards. I'll never talk!"

Without reacting to this challenge, the Wolf of War gave the prisoner a vicious kick to the ribs. Automatically, Anesha rubbed the same place on her body. She could almost feel the female's pain. Insecure, she glanced at Captain Aktan, the leader of the royal guard. He was pale but otherwise unperturbed. The princess had been surprised when the brothers asked her and Aktan to come to the royal wing, but by now she was sure about their motive. The unbridled violence with which the warriors were questioning their prisoner was a thinly veiled threat directed at her, showing that the barbarians had no qualms hurting a female.

But their victim showed endurance. For an hour she had been resisting the brothers' attempts to get detailed information about the assault against the king. The Wolf of War was starting to lose his patience when his brother spoke for the first time since they had all entered the narrow room.

"Let me do this for you, brother."

Canubis's eyes narrowed. He didn't like what Renaldo was suggesting.

"You think you can control it?"

"Yes. It has grown in strength, but it's always been a part of me."

The Wolf of War weighed his options for a moment and decided to take the risk. If Renaldo was wrong and his control of the fiery monster inside him hadn't become absolute since he'd taken Casto as his mate, Ummana would face a fire it had never seen before. If things went really wrong, everybody except the Emeris would be burnt to a cinder. But if things went right…. He took a step backward.

"She's all yours, brother mine."

With a flourish he indicated the bound woman. Then he turned to Anesha and Aktan, his face a frozen mask.

"You may want to take a step back. This could be—uncomfortable."

Her heart beating like a war drum, the princess obeyed, her gaze fixed on the broad back of the Angel of Death.

Renaldo started caressing the prisoner's cheeks, while she was throwing the worst insults she could think of at his beautiful face.

"Shh. It's not right for such sensual lips to utter such profanities. I can see you're a good servant to your mistress. She has taught you well, hasn't she?"

The young woman spit bloody slime on the blue tunic of the demigod. "She has taught me to withstand the insinuations of false gods, even when they come with a pleasing face and unbearable pain. There's nothing you can do to me, barbarian, that my mistress hasn't taught me to endure."

"Oh, I'm sure she has shown you a lot. I'm wondering if she's ever told you about how to walk through fire?"

For a split second, fear flashed in the gaze of the woman, but she caught herself.

"You can burn me at the stake and I still won't tell you anything. Come on, bastard, do whatever you deem fit. I won't say a word."

Again the Angel of Death stroked the woman's cheek. His voice was soft and friendly, which made him even more threatening.

"Who on Ana-Darasa has made you think I'd be interested in the pain I can inflict on your body? That's my brother's forte. No, I'm going to do you a favor. In just a few moments, you'll know whether you're truly worthy of servicing your mistress."

The two torches in the windowless room flickered and started to burn with a long flame, as if a sudden breeze had fanned them. The air around the Angel of Death began to shimmer, like on the first night during the banquet. Heat wafted through the room, so intense and uncomfortable that Anesha, who—like everybody growing up in the Twin Cities—was used to high temperatures, staggered to the door. Aktan remained in his spot, but his discomfort showed openly.

Their unease was nothing compared to what the prisoner had to endure. She screamed in despair, high and shrill like an animal close to death. Anesha couldn't see what the Angel of Death was doing to her; he didn't even seem to touch the writhing body, but whatever it was, it had to be terrible. It didn't take long until the female broke.

"Please, stop it. I'll tell you everything you wish to know, everything. Just stop. I can't take it."

The Angel of Death retreated a step. His voice was unperturbed.

"Who knew about the assault?"

"Only my mistress, me, and the man who brought the poison to the palace."

"Who was the target?"

"My mistress wanted the king to die, because that would have the greatest impact on you, but as long as there was a death to mourn, she wasn't picky."

"She's dead, isn't she?"

Genuine sorrow marred the bloodied face. "Yes. It took all her energy to create the poison."

Renaldo turned to his brother. They shared a long look, which, as Anesha had learned, was akin to a lively discussion. Then the Angel of Death concentrated on his victim again.

"Who did you pay to be able to move freely in the city?"

"The king's father, the Council, the leaders of the guilds of merchants and mariners."

"In other words, the rich and influential." Canubis's voice was grim.

"We had to make sure not to be disturbed."

"How did you know we would come? You seem to have been planning this even before I knew that Casto is my heart."

The young woman smiled snidely. "My mistress was a powerful seer. The Good Mother had shown her in a vision that she should come here, in case the priest in the Valley didn't manage to kill the Angel of Death's heart."

"I tend to forget how methodical the Good Mother can be." Renaldo had been talking to himself, but the prisoner still reacted to his words.

"She's the Good Mother. She sees everything. She knows everything. In the end she'll win."

"I doubt that, bitch. This world is ours, not hers."

"And what are you going to do with it? You're nothing but some puny little gods of war who lead their followers into death. The Good Mother has different plans for us. She loves humankind."

"That may be the case, but in the end, she still asks the same price as we do. Which you're going to pay now, since I'm getting bored." The Angel of Death's hands embraced the young woman's face almost lovingly.

"You can only kill my body. I will be free and return to my mistress. It'll be my pleasure to witness your downfall from the other side." The female's eyes rolled up in religious ecstasy. A bloody smile turned her face into a mask of horror.

Renaldo, too, was smiling. He regarded the traitor with amusement.

"I hate being the bearer of bad news, but you're not going to meet your mistress ever again. You are going to burn for the rest of eternity."

The heat was like a wall, bulldozing through the small room and made even worse by the inhuman screams of the Good Mother's follower.

Anesha pressed herself against the wall, shivering all over. "What's he doing?" Full of panic, she stared at Canubis, who was glaring at her with his unnerving predator eyes.

"He's burning her soul. That's the punishment waiting for those who dare challenge us."

Without thinking consciously about it, Anesha lowered her gaze and curtsied deeply. She understood her brother now, realized why he did the barbarians' bidding so readily. There was no way around Canubis and Renaldo. They were the masters of this world, and you could either submit to them or pay the price for resistance. Knowing this also brought a certain relief. The fight was over. Anesha bowed to these men who could eliminate her in the blink of an eye.

Slowly the heat started to fade from the chamber. The prisoner's body hung lifeless in the chains. The Wolf of War offered Anesha his hand.

"Get up, Princess. It's time to call the Council."

She placed her elegant, small hand in the muscular paw of Canubis, fully aware that she was the demigod's property from now on.

"As you wish, Lord Canubis."

The powerful warrior smiled at her, his gaze saying louder than words that he too was conscious of how their relationship had changed.

ANGRILY THE boy attacked the dummy with his sword. Just now he had found out that his sister was living under the care of the family Krapati outside of Ummana. And not even today, on his birthday, was he allowed to see her. He was old enough to understand why that was the case, but it didn't soothe his fury. It made him crazy how powerless he was, how helpless against his enemies. All he could do at the moment was bear what was happening to him, turn his suffering into strength. He had to wait for the right moment to destroy his enemies, but it wouldn't be easy. There was no way he could find allies at court; everybody who so much as treated him in a friendly manner was banished from his side. He was so lonely, he sometimes feared he was going mad. All that was left to him was his pride; his unbreakable, indestructible pride.

"WHAT'S GOING on?"

"Why are we here?"

"This is unheard of!"

"I want this explained right now!"

"There was no meeting planned for today."

Like a flock of overexcited geese, the members of the Council were blabbering. When Aran and Voltara entered the throne room together with the leaders of the guilds of merchants and mariners, the unrest grew. The only one keeping her cool, at least in appearance, was Amicia, and she too was alarmed enough to go directly to Anesha.

"Princess, what has happened? Why has the king called this meeting?"

"It wasn't the king who summoned you here."

Renaldo's cold voice made everybody present jolt. Anesha had to admit that the brothers had staged their entrance perfectly. For barbarians who had no idea about the finer points of high politics, they acted surprisingly aloof. They entered the throne room with the two desert warriors, Aegid and Kalad, as well as ten of their mercenaries, who were followed by twenty members of the royal guard. The armed men swarmed out and took posts at all the possible exits so that nobody who might have thought of escape stood a chance. Then the two brothers marched to the end of the table, sat down on two chairs at the place reserved for the king, and asked the shocked politicians to sit as well.

Having so many armed warriors surrounding them lent the brother's words enough gravity to make the nobles sit down without any back talk. With cold and menacing glares, the demigods sized up everybody present until the leaders of the city started to squirm in their seats. They all were seasoned politicians who had fought countless battles, but none of them had prepared them for a confrontation with the Wolf of War and the Angel of Death.

It was Canubis who broke the silence. His voice was calm and didn't betray any emotions, which made it impossible to read his mood.

"Yesterday, there was an assault on the king."

The nobles shot nervous glances through the throne room; nobody dared to make eye contact. Political assassinations weren't uncommon in Ummana, but an assault on a member of the royal family or the sovereign was a rare exception. Such a deed could shatter the notoriously fragile balance in the city. On the other hand, they all had been alarmed by Castolus's sudden return and the intimidating allies he brought with him. Enough to contemplate the unthinkable. The only question was who had had the guts to take matters in hand.

Seemingly oblivious of the tension around him, the Wolf of War spoke on. "Casto is safe. He's resting right now. We've managed to find the one responsible for the assault and made her talk. You wouldn't believe what we found out."

The politicians all concentrated hard on their fingers, which suddenly seemed to hold a never-ending fascination. The silence grew heavy. Slowly they started to realize that they had stepped into a trap. Being at the Wolf of War's mercy made none of them happy.

Canubis smiled viciously. It didn't take much empathy to know what was going on in the heads of the disgusting, cowardly tacticians. He didn't try to hide his contempt anymore.

"As I told you on our first night here, anybody who dares to touch my brother-in-law is dead. Each one of you has accepted hush money from the Good Mother's bootlickers and thus made the assault possible. Therefore, you're all officially charged with treason."

At this, Captain Aktan and his men stepped forward. Without regard to their vehement protests, the nobles were all bound.

"In a few days, the king's going to speak your verdict. Until then you'll enjoy the hospitality of the palace dungeons. I'm sure you'll find your new accommodations… refreshing. Perhaps some of you may want to use the time to think about the sins of the past. If any of you feel the need for counseling, we're willing to listen. Of course, under the pledge of secrecy."

The Wolf of War sounded more than satisfied. Anesha thought he seemed like a sated, fat cat rolling in a warm spot after having devoured a juicy mouse.

"You have no right to do this!" Again it was Nambuno who was made reckless by indignation. "This is Ummana, a free city! We have laws and rules. You're just a bunch of filthy barbarians. How can you dare treat us in such an underhanded manner?"

The Angel of Death stepped forward until he was face-to-face with the old man, his gray eyes narrowing down to angry slits. The assault on Casto had shaken him more than he had thought possible. At the moment his anger was still controlling the fear in his heart, but it was only a question of time until the impact of what had happened hit him—and then not even the goddesses would be able to protect those who got in his way. Nambuno got a first taste of what was still to come.

"We dare because we are stronger. Because we are gods. And, yes, we dare because of the laws governing this city. You've taken on more sins than is good for a single human, and now you're paying the price for your hubris."

Nambuno's stomach turned to ice, but he hadn't become one of the leading politicians in Ummana because he was easily intimidated. "I wish to talk to the king. Does he even know what you're doing?"

Despite being impressed by the old man's courage, Renaldo still silenced him harshly.

"The king sanctions everything I do. He's mine."

After that the royal guard took the indignant prisoners away. Only the divine brothers, Anesha, and Captain Aktan stayed behind.

"You've just imprisoned this city's entire government. Who do you think is going to step in until my brother has spoken his verdict?" Anesha's voice trembled slightly. Until the end she had doubted whether it would be that easy to strike right at the core of Ummana's power. Now that it was done, the resulting responsibilities besieged her mind like a horde of starving beggars.

The Wolf of War's answer did nothing to ease her mind.

"I'm sure there are dozens of talented young men and women waiting for a chance like this. You only have to find and install them."

"I was afraid you'd say something like that. I'd better start working."

With a curtsey, the princess left the two warriors. Her thoughts were already occupied with whom she should choose for the new council. The leading families wouldn't make the task any easier.

Meanwhile, Renaldo instructed Aktan.

"They all stay in the dungeons, no matter who comes to get them. And Voltara is mine."

The captain felt the hair on his neck rise when the warrior's unbridled fury hit him directly. Even if it hadn't been tradition for the royal guard to stay at the ruler's side, he still would have chosen Castolus. Too intimidating was the presence of Canubis and Renaldo, and too great the similarity of their true personalities to all the stories he had heard. Only a fool would challenge such superior forces, and Aktan was anything but.

"I've given orders to put him in a single cell. You can do to him whatever you please."

IN THE almost impenetrable darkness of a moonless night, Casto and Lysistratos enjoyed the freedom of running. Once Casto had accepted Lysistratos as his brother, his fear of being chained in the royal tomb was gone. As soon as Voltara had realized this change, he had stopped sending Casto there for the night. Instead, he increased the physical punishment in order to gain back the authority he had lost. Casto still was not allowed to sleep in a bed, though.

Every night, Voltara brought him to the cellars and locked him in a tiny, rat-infested, stinking chamber without any windows. He meant to break Casto's resistance this way, to wear him down both mentally and physically. Casto never struggled when he had to go down into the darkness, nor did he plead for better treatment. He just silently stepped inside the small room and waited patiently until the torturer was gone. Then he removed one of the old, battered bricks in the wall, got the key out, and opened the door. It had not been easy to get his hands on that special key, but it had been worth the trouble. Now Casto could move around as he pleased, at least during the night, and it pleased him to meet Lysistratos then.

The Emperor of the Storms could easily sneak into the city and the palace once the shadows were thick enough to be harbingers of the approaching night. In the beginning the two of them had mainly enjoyed the other's presence and the soothing knowledge that they were no longer alone. When Casto had mounted Lysistratos's back for the first time, it had been like an epiphany. The prince had been a gifted rider to begin with, but with Lys, he quickly turned into a master without equal. With the Emperor of the Storms, Casto experienced freedom for the first time in his life.

BEFORE THE Angel of Death went for the torturer, he decided to look for Casto. It was already past noon when he entered Noran's rooms. Silence greeted him, and for a moment the worst possible images flitted through his mind, until he glimpsed his heart and the young smith on one of the lounges, fast asleep. They were lying with their faces toward each other, their foreheads touching, and their hands intertwined. It was a picture of peace and intimacy. Renaldo felt jealousy chewing on him with sharp teeth. It took some effort to regain his composure. He knew the two young men were only friends and that Casto was his alone.

Still, the thought of his stunning mate bestowing even a shard of affection on somebody else was hard to bear, especially if that somebody was a Luksari. Sic was able to give the king something Renaldo couldn't: friendship. Pure, unadulterated friendship. The Angel of Death had Casto's love, his loyalty, his trust and obedience. But they would never be friends; for that the age difference and the power gap were too great. At the end of the day, he would always be Casto's master and god, no matter how close they might be. Sic, on the other hand, could meet Casto on the same level. They were close in age, and despite the differences in background and education, closer than the god and his heart. Yet the Angel of Death knew it was right to be happy for his mate and Sic, since both deserved the joys of true friendship.

Renaldo made a face. He hated it when common sense reared its ugly head. But he would act like a mature adult and vent his anger on somebody who had earned it. With a last glance at the sleeping men, the demigod retreated, determined to make the torturer pay for his crimes.

THE DUNGEONS of Ummana were a lot friendlier than those in the Valley, even though their current inhabitants surely held a different opinion. Renaldo did not waste time checking whether the members of the Council were safely locked away, but went straight for the door behind which his heart's worst nightmare was waiting.

The torturer blinked in the light of the torches that filtered into the cell behind the Angel of Death and surrounded him like a halo. For the first time, Renaldo studied the sadist thoroughly. Until now he had avoided doing so, mainly because Casto had desperately tried to keep his distance from the man who had made his life in Ummana a never-ending martyrdom.

Voltara was a small man, perhaps seven spans and with a slim build. Nevertheless, he was no weakling, for there were well-defined muscles showing under his silken shirt. His short ash-blond hair showed the first streaks of gray and was thinning at the sides. The eyes in the common face were small; they reminded Renaldo of a rat and were constantly darting around, never focused on a person or object and unable to hold another's gaze. If it hadn't been for the overwhelming sense of cruelty surrounding him, the Angel of Death would have thought the man was a pitiable lunatic without any social competence.

Now the vermin eyes darted from the door to Renaldo and back, clearly looking for a chance to get out. For a man, Voltara's voice was too high and reminded the Angel of Death of a fingernail scratching over a piece of glass.

"I'm wondering why the king's husband is visiting me in my cell?"

Full of contempt, Renaldo sized up the cowering worm at his feet. "I think you know the reason only too well, Voltara."

Renaldo could almost see the man's brain racking itself for all the possible outcomes of their meeting. This scum really thought he had a chance to get the better of Renaldo, to escape the dungeons unscathed. It was plain disgusting. And so the Angel of Death refrained from playing any games, partly because he was simply too furious to stall any longer, partly because he did not want to spend more time in the presence of this rat than was absolutely necessary. He couldn't believe a despicable piece of trash like Voltara had dared to lay his hands on Casto.

"Admittedly, it took some time, but in the end, Casto told me everything. I know in vivid detail what you, a worthless waste of air, have done to him. You've tortured a god's heart, and for that you'll still be paying when this world has long turned back to dust."

Like most sadists Renaldo had met during the course of his long life, Voltara was a coward deep within. He enjoyed bullying those weaker than himself, but when he had to face the smallest hardship, he turned into a spineless, whining creature.

Renaldo faced with deepest contempt the trembling man who was begging for mercy in a high, squealing voice. He had planned to make this human trash pay for Casto's suffering a hundredfold before he sent his soul to the Mothers, but when faced with such cowardice, the Angel of Death decided to let the torturer follow the servant of the Good Mother.

He felt the fire blazing inside him, the same flame he had thought was the curse of his life before he finally met Casto. Casto, who had changed everything. The fire that had burned so many until the wayward king came along was no longer a burden but a terrible weapon, a most welcome, indispensable part of himself.

Heat radiated from his body. The straw in the cell started smoldering, burst into flames, and was ashes before it could seriously hurt the screaming man at his feet. Renaldo leaned down, grabbed the torturer, and let all his anger fuel the flames that were now consuming his prey. The screams reached his ears from faraway, a balm to his enraged mind. He slowly allowed the fire to burn with more intensity, until it had separated Voltara's soul from his body. Without any mercy, the Angel of Death sent what was left of his enemy into the realm between, condemned to burn for eternity, for the flames would only go out when their master ordered them to.

DEEPLY CONCERNED, Lysistratos blew his warm breath into Casto's nape. The prince had his arm in a sling and was trying valiantly to hide the pain he was feeling. Casto was fifteen now, on the verge of becoming a man. His father and the torturer were aware of it as well and even more determined to keep him subjugated. Perhaps they could sense that Casto was slipping through their fingers, that he was becoming more and more independent despite their cruelty and sadistic schemes.

That day, Casto had made a mistake. He had underestimated his father's ruthlessness and paid a high price for it. Lysistratos flattened his ears when he remembered the crunching sound Casto's elbow bone made when it broke under the brutal grip of one of the guards. For hours Lord Aran had made his son kneel in front of him without treating the fracture. First Casto had clung to his stubborn pride, thinking not even his father would allow the future king of Ummana to become crippled. When he realized how utterly wrong this assumption was, he swallowed his pride and started begging just as Lord Aran wanted. Humiliating himself like that was not easy for Casto, and it hardened his heart even more, made him less human and more like a monster every day. He could feel the change, and he truly hated it. It was a triumph he did not want his father to have. With a tired gesture, he leaned his head against Lysistratos's warm neck, too worn out to hide his despair. The stallion whinnied softly in an attempt to take Casto's mind off the events of the day.

2. FREEDOM

FOUR DAYS after his selfless sacrifice, Noemi decided that Sic had recovered enough to leave the bed and, more importantly, the chamber. Happily, Sic put on the light tunic Casto had brought him the night before. He watched the sun rise over the palace gardens, eagerly anticipating the warm rays on his naked skin. Casto had promised to get him in the morning and show him where he had grown up. Sic heard the door opening behind him. Still fascinated by the spectacle the morning sun was giving, and full of joy, Sic greeted his friend without turning.

"Good morning, Casto! Isn't the sunrise glorious? I can't wait to get out of this stifling room and breathe some fresh air."

"It is indeed a nice morning."

Sic froze. He turned around slowly. With his gaze cast down, he knelt. "Master."

Noran clenched his fists when he heard all happiness vanish from his slave's voice. He knew it was his fault alone, but he had not anticipated how much it would hurt. The worst torture was nothing compared to the pain he felt at that moment.

"Please, Sic. Get up."

Still staring at the ground, the young man obeyed. His hands trembled when he opened his tunic without Noran ordering him. With a soft rustle, the cloth glided down and Sic was standing in front of his master naked, waiting for him to reclaim his possession.

Guilt overcame Noran, attacked him like a hungry predator when he glimpsed the terrible proof of his own cruelty on Sic's skin. His marks, forever engraved into Sic's skin, were a silent accusation; the scars marring the young man's torso in broad, angry red streaks seemed to mock him. He could never hope to make up for this sin.

"Sic, please. It's fine. This is not what I came here to do. Please, get dressed again."

Hesitantly, Sic obeyed. It was obvious that he didn't trust his master's words, that he was expecting to be deceived like so many times before.

When he was dressed, Noran took a step toward him. Sic tensed in fear. He thought his apprehension had come true, and he was waiting for his owner to hit him. The master smith raised his hands in a soothing gesture.

"Don't be afraid. I'm not going to hurt you. I only want to take off the collar."

With shaking hands Noran opened the iron around his slave's neck. Underneath he saw raw, deeply wounded skin that had formed thick scars because of the constant friction of the metal. The master had to suppress the trembling in his hands. He felt the urge to send the one who had done this to his love to the Mothers, but there was no way he could kill himself. Disgusted, he threw the iron away. His voice shook.

"I'm giving you your freedom, Sic. I abjure all claims I might still hold over you, and I swear to give you all the help you need to live freely. Whatever you want, you just have to tell me."

In absolute silence, Sic stood in front of him. His chest was heaving. To believe what his master had just told him was impossible for Sic; Noran's words had come too much as a surprise. Slowly, hesitantly, he looked up. Finally he found the courage to ask a question.

"Why are you doing this, Master? You said yourself I don't deserve feeling the smallest scrap of happiness." Sic chewed his lip, afraid he had said too much.

Noran gulped. He chose his next words carefully, knowing well he couldn't expect to be forgiven by Sic, and yet full of hope that his words could mend what his deeds had broken.

"I was wrong. You're a good person, Sic. You saved my life although you had no reason to do anything for me. You deserve your freedom."

"Do I really?" Insecurity tainted the young man's voice. Sic himself couldn't believe he deserved forgiveness.

"You betrayed me, nothing can change that. But you did it to protect me, and I was too blind to see it. All that mattered to me was that I couldn't trust you, just like Arja back then. But you're not her, I know that now. Anyway, it's too late, isn't it? What I've done is as unforgivable as it is unspeakable. All I can do now is tell you how sorry I am, how much I regret what I did. And hope you'll be able to forgive me one day."

Suddenly Sic felt anger welling up inside. He did not know how this emotion managed to overcome his fear of Noran, but it did, took control over him, and made him say things he wouldn't have dared to think only a few days ago.

"Would you have forgiven me? If none of this had happened, if you had never been poisoned, would you have forgiven me?"

Noran regarded Sic full of despair, because he knew he would lose the young smith now, but he was still determined to tell the truth.

"No. I'd have probably never forgiven you. Renaldo had planned to buy you this autumn to save you. But to defy my god, I decided to destroy you so completely that nothing but an empty shell remained. I wanted to eliminate you."

Shuddering, Sic listened to the fate his master had been planning for him. Deep down he had suspected it already. Noran had been too brutal and cruel after Lord Renaldo had bestowed the mercy of his forgiveness on Sic. But hearing it straight from his master, getting the confirmation that he had been willing to give his life for such an inhuman monster, still came as a shock. A shock that made it possible for him to say the next words with absolute conviction.

"I saved your life because you did the same for me when you bought me from Dalwon. Regarding this, we're even. Concerning my betrayal—I regret what I did, that I went behind your back and didn't find the courage to trust you enough. I blame myself for destroying whatever relationship we had, although I doubt it was more than the one-sided infatuation I felt for you. I'm not sorry for the time I spent with you. I was content being your property, even though my admiration and love never reached you. Up until a few months ago, you were a strict but fair master, and I had nothing to complain about. And when you allowed me to live after my betrayal, I was even grateful. I had hoped to win your trust back somehow, and I had been willing to do everything to achieve this goal.

"But then you used my love to punish me, to hurt me in ways I'm sure you'll never be able to comprehend. The scars on my skin are nothing in comparison to the wounds still bleeding in my soul. And that I can't forgive. You shattered my heart, and I'm still not sure whether I'll ever be able to find all the pieces."

Sic almost felt pity when he saw the spark of hope dying in his former master's eyes. He didn't say anything, didn't try to defend his actions; he just turned around and staggered out of the chamber like a man who had just been dealt a deadly blow. Sic could only stare at the spot where his master had been standing. The center of his world was gone, thrown out by his own hands. His time with Noran seemed like a dream now, one he was slowly waking from. There was no going back. For the first time in his life, Sic was free in every sense of the word. His emotions fluttered like a flag in the storm of his impossible deed.

When Casto found him only a short time later, he was still staring into nothing.

"Sic, what's happened? Are you unwell?"

Sic looked up, tears in his eyes, his lips spreading in a wide smile. "I'm fine, my friend. Noran was here."

The mesmerizing blue eyes of the king lit up in alarm. "What did he want? Where is he now?"

"He's given me my freedom and, to be frank, I don't care what he's doing now. I'm free, Casto. Free!"

Sic started giggling hysterically. He still couldn't believe what had just happened.

Casto hugged him happily; his voice trembled with joy. "That's wonderful, Sic. You can't imagine how much I've been hoping for this." The king took a step backward, his face serious, but his eyes were full of mischief. "Well, then, my free friend. What do you want to do now?"

Sic didn't have to think long; the words left his mouth without using the detour via his brain.

"I want to feel the sun on my skin. I want to go wherever my feet carry me without a master directing my steps. I just want to enjoy the fact that I have nothing to do. And you've promised to show me the palace."

"You mean the stables and gardens. There are no happy memories tied to the palace."

This one dry sentence was enough to jerk Sic from his happy state of mind. He knew how much Casto was bothered by their stay in Ummana, and he cursed his stupidity for not showing more consideration.

"Casto, are you really okay? I can feel how much you hate being here."

A tired smile was the answer. "It's gotten better already. Especially now that you have survived. I don't have nightmares anymore, but my sleep isn't relaxing either. I'll thank the Mothers on my knees once we're back home again."

"Is there anything I can do for you?"

Casto's features brightened.

"You can indeed. Let's get out of here! I want to be gone before the Barbarian remembers any urgent governing he needs me for. We both have earned a break."

Quickly and silently the two friends left the royal wing. A short time later, Sic was wandering in awe through the voluptuous jungle that was the garden of the kings. In the high trees, exotic birds with vividly colored feathers sang the sweetest songs he had ever heard. On the perfectly raked paths, lizards and snakes fled from their steps, and soft-eyed stags with blinding white fur allowed them to stroke their necks. The air was filled with the sweet scent of thousands of flowers growing in abundance everywhere.

Sic was so charmed by all this beauty, he couldn't decide which wonder to run to first. With a child's curiosity, he drew Casto's attention to even the most mundane things in this miracle world. The king followed him with a smile through all the canopies, wherever Sic's feet carried him. After two hours they chose one of the countless fountains to get some rest. While their naked feet splashed in the cool water, Sic beamed at his friend.

"It's beautiful here, Casto. A true paradise."

A shadow darkened the king's face.

"At first glance, surely. I'm glad you like it."

"Casto, I'm sorry! All this beauty made me forget how terrible it must have been for you, growing up in a place like this."

"It was bearable here. But I was rarely allowed to visit the gardens. It always made me angry, knowing that there was such perfection in close proximity, but I couldn't be a part of it because my own life was so—sullied. Today is the first time I can see the gardens for what they really are. A place where life is celebrated. I owe this to you."

The sorrow in his friend's voice touched Sic's heart.

"Is there anything I can do for you? No matter what."

"No, not really. You can pray with me that we won't be staying here much longer. That we'll get to go home before this place takes my soul away again."

Casto forced some cheerfulness in his voice to distract Sic. This was his first day of freedom, and Casto wanted his friend to be happy. "Let's stop pondering such gloomy thoughts. This is your day, and we're here to enjoy it. If I remember correctly, I've promised you a ride on Lys."

Sic was full of nervous anticipation.

"You were serious?"

"Of course. Let's go."

ON THEIR way to the stables, they passed one of the patios that permeated the palace like combs in a beehive. A music even sweeter than the one from the birds reached Sic's ears. It was the monotonous hammering of steel on steel, the hiss when gleaming metal was dipped into cold water, the higher, more exquisite sounds when petite hammers met gold and turned it into art.

Without thinking Sic followed this siren's song and finally reached the royal smithy located in the patio. In the cooling shade of twelve archways, forges and anvils were placed radially around a fountain that provided the water for cooling the metal. There was buzzing activity all around them, and Sic didn't know where to look first. It was all so familiar and comforting, he could not help but go there as if pulled by invisible strings.

A tall, muscular man blocked their way. He had a friendly, open face with lively hazelnut eyes that regarded the two young men with a hint of suspicion. His voice was deep and warm.

"My name is Jago. I'm the master of the royal smithy. What can I do for you?"

First, Casto and Sic bowed their heads in respect, as was befitting in front of a master. Then the king spoke, since Sic was still too busy being enchanted.

"My friend's a smith and would like to work here. You don't happen to have a vacant anvil?"

Jago scrutinized the two visitors suspiciously. The one talking was remarkably beautiful and knew how to phrase his sentences. His friend only made short eye contact before he stared down at the ground. Both were dressed well, like the rich nobles in the city, but the silent one had scars on his neck, wrists, and arms. Jago didn't need a lot of imagination to know what the rest of his body looked like or how he had gotten those scars. The two were a very contradictory pair, and whomever they might be, he decided to be careful.

"What's your name, boy?"

"Sic, master. My name is Sic."

"And what's your rank?"

"I'm an apprentice, master."

"Well, an apprentice, you say."

"He's really talented, I can assure you of that." Again it was the blond who spoke. His voice was insistent, with a pleading undertone. "Please, give him a chance."

Jago thought about it. He had too much work for too few men. Even if Sic should prove himself clumsy or inept, he could still use him for odd jobs.

"Fine. You can work on probation for today. If I'm satisfied with your performance, we can talk about a lasting arrangement. But I've to warn you,

you'd earn more down in the city. My budget is limited and, strictly speaking, already drained."

The young man beamed. His bad financial prospects didn't seem to bother him in the least.

"It doesn't matter, master. I'd be honored to work here."

The good-looking blond furrowed his brows.

"What do you mean, limited budget? This is the royal smithy. Your business should be thriving."

His tone was so sharp, Jago unconsciously matched it and answered in the same manner.

"And what would a child know about it? Since the death of Queen Isiris, things have changed a lot. The council has cut the royal smithy's rights in order to snatch more money for themselves. Instead of the usual share in the revenue, my men and I are working for laughable wages. I had to let good smiths go, and the ones who still stay work at their limit for practically nothing. They stay out of loyalty to me, but I can't tell how long that will continue."

Sic looked at his companion.

"Can you do something about it, Casto?"

The blond sighed. "Of course. One more point to my list. I wish you fun, Sic. I'd better get back to Renaldo and start working."

The men hugged each other; then the blond nodded toward Jago. "It was my honor to meet you, Master Jago. Please look after my friend. He's been through hard times."

Suspiciously, Jago's gaze followed the young man. He had a nagging feeling that he should be familiar with him, but he didn't know where to place the exquisite face. He turned to Sic, who once more lowered his gaze respectfully to the ground.

"Who was that? He mentioned the Angel of Death. Is he a servant of the barbarians?"

"We all are. But Casto is his lover as well."

Jago's mouth gaped and cold fear grew in his heart. "*That* was King Castolus?"

"Yes, master. Didn't you recognize him?"

"What do you think? If I had, I surely wouldn't have talked to him like I did."

Sic hesitated for a moment before he dared to speak. "You don't have to worry, master. It's a good thing he knows about your problem. He's going to take care of it."

Jago gave up. "Whatever he's going to do, we don't have time to wait for it. I've got a mountain of repairs—nothing complicated, but it all should have been done yesterday. You can take this anvil and share the forge with me. If you're done with a piece, you take it to Igo over there. He'll cross it out on the list and see to it that it gets back to its owner. Let's get to work."

Beaming, Sic slung a leather apron round his hips, chose one of the repairs from the truly intimidating mountain in front of him, and started to work. In his joy he didn't realize that Jago watched him like a falcon to find out what this apprentice was capable of. Strictly speaking the young man was too old to still have that rank, which meant he had either started late learning the skill or, what seemed more probable, that he wasn't suited for it.

He looked closely while Sic skillfully repaired a weapon belt and started wondering what was wrong with the young man. The way Sic worked and moved around in the smithy made clear that he definitely was not an apprentice. To test him further, Jago handed him a tiara from a rich customer. Two diamonds had fallen out of their setting. The piece was cheaply made and surely not from one of the smithies in Ummana, but because it had been a present, the owner wanted it to be restored at all costs.

Sic examined the tiara intently, his disgust about the bad work only showing briefly on his face. Then he started to repair it. Full of awe, Jago bore witness as this newcomer turned the piece of trash into quite respectable jewelry with apparent ease. *Not an apprentice*, he thought, *and definitely no fellow either. I'm facing a young master.*

He approached Sic and took the hammer from his hand. Insecure, the young man evaded his gaze.

"Why didn't you tell me how good you are?"

Sic stayed silent, his eyes glued to the hammer the master was holding.

Jago sighed. "Look at me, Sic. I don't understand why you haven't told me the truth. This"—he dangled the tiara in his fingers—"is the work of a master, not an apprentice."

"I didn't want to lie, master, you have to believe me! The man I served before you, he said I'd never be good enough to become a fellow. I'm sloppy and hasty. I can be grateful if I'm allowed to even come near an anvil. He said I wasn't even fit to clean up properly."

Jago felt anger rising inside. Without knowing anything else about Sic's former master, he realized what kind of game the man had been playing with his apprentice. It made him furious that a talented man like Sic was not aware of his own worth and felt ashamed of his work because he thought it wasn't good enough. Jago's voice was firm.

"Whoever your master may be, he's an idiot. This work is fantastic! I couldn't have done better myself, and I bet if I let you do the commissioned work, you'll be more successful than me. You've got talent, Sic, exceptional talent."

Jago watched as the green-blue eyes in Sic's open face widened in surprise.

"As far as I've understood, you'll be here for some time, until the king gets everything in order. Am I right?"

A shy nod.

"Splendid. I'll see to it that you can take the master exams as soon as possible. Then you're officially a master smith, and you can get appropriately paid for your high-quality work. What do you think? Isn't this a great idea?"

Sic smiled timidly. He was completely overwhelmed by the turn of events.

"It's a brilliant idea, master. I thank you. You're very generous."

"THAT WAS kind of a short trip." Renaldo pressed a kiss on Casto's cheek in greeting.

"We took a stroll in the gardens, and then we found the royal smithy. As you can imagine, it was impossible to pry Sic from it. He's standing behind an anvil now and is happy."

"Good for him. And good for me that you're back so early. We have a lot to do."

With a sigh Casto flopped down on one of the chairs. Of course there was a lot to do, especially now, while the members of the Council were rotting in their cells. The Angel of Death and his brother had called a trial for the following day, although the actual verdict had already been decided. It was a matter of appearances and tactics, of intimidating the enemy as much as possible.

Casto didn't know why, but Anesha was helping the divine brothers with frightening zeal. Slowly the suspicion was dawning inside him that he might have underestimated her hunger for revenge and power—a mistake he'd better not repeat, for too much was at stake.

Initially jurisdiction in Ummana lay with the ruler and was transferred to the person he or she chose as a representative. The decision was entirely up to the king, which meant Ummana had already seen all facets of jurisdiction in the course of the centuries. Some of Casto's ancestors had judged even the smallest cases themselves, others had surrendered control completely. It was an entirely subjective decision that had led to great problems in the past.

There had been a lengthy discussion whether it was a wise move to appoint Renaldo as a judge. Anesha and Renaldo had voted for it, while Casto, Canubis, and Noemi thought it more intimidating when the king himself presided. They all agreed that the prisoners would not be granted a private audience, as was customary with citizens of such high standing. Casto felt no inclination to spend more time than strictly necessary with the people who had sacrificed him so easily, and he agreed with Anesha that it sent a strong signal to all those who might think about protesting against his decision. Which was the second reason the trial would be public, to be a foreshadowing of the future course of politics in the city.

"It'll show that the time for secret agreements is over, that you're determined to rule with an iron fist. It'll bring stability for the people, and business will thrive when the merchants get a demonstration of your resolve."

Anesha had used business as her last and strongest argument to convince her brother, who had been reluctant to let the public witness the trial. Renaldo was aware of his lover's hesitation, as well as of the reasons for it, and therefore insisted on reviewing the procedures for the coming day.

"I don't want you to make the slightest mistake. We woke the serpents with the arrest, and I don't want to be bitten a second time."

Casto sighed again. Not that he hadn't warned them of exactly this.

"I'm aware, Barbarian. And I've already explained to you numerous times and in great detail why I think your way of dealing with the council isn't wise, to say the least. Some of the snakes you've angered produce quite effective poisons."

"A tooth we'll pull tomorrow. The royal guard is on our side, so we've enough men to nip an uprising in the bud."

Casto nodded in surrender. Renaldo would never understand the rules on which Ummana ran. For an old god, he was remarkably naive when it came to understanding the human soul. Not that he was stupid—the Barbarian was really good at seeing through people—but he came from a world where his will—and that of his brother—were the law. The unbending rules governing life in the Valley didn't go well with the constantly shifting tides of politics in Ummana. Money was the ultimate motive for everybody, and a man you viewed as an enemy today could become your best friend the next, provided business went accordingly. Hatred or revenge had to take second place behind the overriding imperative of maximum profit.

Canubis and Renaldo, on the other hand, took everything personally and were unforgiving in their anger. Casto, too, was furious with Nambuno and everybody else who had left him to his father, but he also knew how much he needed competent help to govern the city, to keep the money flowing, and to maximize profits—not to mention dealing with the Confederation, especially Medelina, for which the divine brothers had special plans. Plans he was supposed to put into action. Dead, the members of the Council were useless to him, at least for the time being. The only person profiting from that rash move was Anesha, because now the Council consisted solely of people indebted to her. In their anger and haste, Canubis and Renaldo had managed to isolate Casto politically, and they refused to acknowledge the damage they had done. It made Casto furious whenever he thought about it. He felt reminded of the time when he had still been a boy and completely at the mercy of others.

Of course, his worries had fallen on deaf ears. Renaldo had treated him to the "unbending glare," as Casto had labeled it in the privacy of his head, which meant he wouldn't budge. Anesha and Canubis had backed Renaldo and because of that, Casto would be sentencing his father and the entire Council to death come the next day.

"Casto, are you even listening?"

Renaldo's voice interrupted the king's musings.

"I don't want you to hesitate for even the blink of an eye tomorrow. Don't show the slightest weakness. Those damn bastards are getting away lightly, considering what they've done to you. If it were up to me, I'd torture them for the next two months without taking a break. Losing their heads is a mercy they don't really deserve."

The Angel of Death had talked himself into a frenzy. His gray eyes were sparking, and his inner fire made the air around him flare. Casto felt his own fire waking in answer to his mate's flame. He still wasn't able to control it, but he enjoyed feeling the sheer power racing through his veins.

His loins pulsing, he got up from the chair and started undressing. What he needed right now was a distraction from the problems piling up in front of him. Growling, Renaldo pulled him close. They had found out quickly that the fire made their intercourse even more intense and fueled the rush. Like wild animals they attacked each other, stripped of all control, a fact that, as Casto well knew, aroused the Barbarian even more. His whole life, the Angel of Death had been forced to hold himself back in order not to hurt or even kill his partners. With Casto, consideration wasn't necessary; on the contrary, the young king enjoyed it when Renaldo went wild. The warrior's hands were holding Casto in an iron grip while he pressed him against the wall. Spreading his lover's legs with his knee, Renaldo entered him in one long, brutal stroke.

"You're mine, Casto. My property. It makes me go crazy knowing you're in danger."

The Barbarian's teeth ripped Casto's nape. The king sighed when he felt his blood starting to flow. Renaldo was quenching his thirst while riding Casto with hard thrusts. Renaldo's despair, as much as the resulting anger that fueled both their passions, reminded Casto that they had barely seen each other since the assault. He had spent most of his time with Sic, and the Angel of Death had been busy bringing terror to the leading families of Ummana. They hadn't yet talked about the consequences of the attempt. It was a blunder he was now paying for with athletic, brutal sex—which was fine with Casto, since it helped him relax. He felt the first dark wave of an overwhelming orgasm coming and welcomed the wonderful feeling of drowning in pure lust.

Renaldo was still drinking; his tongue licked over the wound he had given his mate, bathed in the blood that seemed to boil from the fire. Again he started thrusting into Casto, lifted him up, carried him to the bed, and kept on taking him there. Casto was willing and he reacted obediently to every one of Renaldo's demands, a sure sign that he too had been shocked by the events of the past few days. They finally desisted when the simmering heat of the afternoon was banished by the more soothing breeze of the oncoming night.

In the bathroom, the Angel of Death inspected the wound he had inflicted on his lover.

"It isn't bleeding anymore. But you'd better drink some more. I took more than usual."

Although Casto was exhausted and quite unsteady on his feet, he couldn't suppress an acid retort. "You did? Totally accidentally, I presume, since you always know how to keep your cool and hold back."

"Sarcasm doesn't suit you, Your Majesty. Haven't I told you before?"

"Countless times, but I don't think the problem is my sarcasm but your inaptitude to deal with it. Plus I'm right and you know it."

"And here I was sorry for drinking so much."

Casto turned serious. "You shouldn't be, Barbarian. We both needed it, and it's not like I didn't enjoy it."

Slightly worried, Renaldo touched Casto's still-hot skin.

"My own. It troubles me when you're so levelheaded and subservient. If I had done the same back in the Valley, I'd be busy making it up to you for at least three weeks. This city is getting to us."

A calculated smile was the answer.

"A little making up doesn't sound half bad, my dear husband. But you're right, Ummana is grating on my nerves. I only hope we can leave this cursed place as soon as possible."

Lovingly, the Angel of Death put his arms around Casto.

"Canubis and I might have found a solution. It's still a bit hazy, but if everything goes right, we can go back home soon. Anesha is still busy checking the details."

Casto looked up in alarm. He didn't like not being privy to Renaldo's plans, but he had resigned himself to the demigod's unique way of dealing with things. Consulting with Anesha was an entirely different thing, though. Casto doubted that Renaldo realized how dangerous she was. He also had trouble not letting his jealousy show in his voice.

"What did you do to my sister? It's uncharacteristic of her to be this helpful."

Renaldo smiled knowingly. Casto's anger hadn't evaded him.

"The princess was there when I questioned and punished the servant of the Good Mother. Witnessing the power of a true god seemed to have a healing impact on her attitude. She still is a snake, but now she's using her poison for us."

Casto was rendered speechless. How could one single person be so incredibly stupid? He did not even try to keep the derision from his voice.

"And you believe her act?"

Renaldo didn't like what his mate was implying, so his reply was equally acidic. "Why shouldn't I? I have looked into her eyes. She was truly terrified. Since then she has been very helpful."

"Of course she's been helpful! Everything you have asked of her has strengthened her position! Her influence is growing steadily. As for her being terrified—do you think I'm afraid of you, Barbarian?"

Renaldo furrowed his brows. "No. It's one of the things I love about you."

"Then what makes you think my *sister* is afraid of you? All your little demonstration of power has done was make her more careful. She's going to work her way around you, and naïve as you are, you won't even realize whenever she takes a big chunk out of you."

"Is that what you are doing, King? Working around me?"

Casto glared at Renaldo in open threat.

"What do you think, Barbarian?"

Renaldo felt his fire blazing again. He was furious about his mate's stubbornness. Knowing that what Casto had said was true did not help his temper. "I think you're getting in too deep. You're so caught up in how things are supposed to work in Ummana, you've completely forgotten that you're no longer part of this game. You belong to me now, to the Pack, and we follow our own rules. So Anesha is gaining more power? Let her bask in her petty victory over the stupid barbarians. If push comes to shove, her blood has the same color as everybody else's—and we are the ones who'll spill it. Besides, we're not here for you to sit on that throne permanently. We're here to teach Medelina a lesson and then return back home. Let your sister have this city she so desires. I dare say you already have something a lot better."

For a moment the fire between them blazed before it went out completely. Casto stared at Renaldo with an expression the Angel of Death had never seen on him before. It was a mixture of sadness and defeat, as if Casto had just realized something truly devastating.

"You're right. I have lost my focus." Casto looked away. "I'll never be your equal, will I? I'll never be good enough."

The sudden shift in emotions startled Renaldo. Casto wasn't the kind of man to belittle himself. He usually had a healthy attitude toward his strengths and weaknesses, and it was unsettling when he started to lose his grip. Ummana was indeed a dangerous place.

"Now you're talking nonsense, my own. You might be young, which excuses a lot, but for me you're an enigma. You keep me constantly guessing and hanging with your tantrums, your unpredictability, and your bright mind. I can assure you, I haven't felt bored for even a second since we met. Quite the contrary, in fact.

"And before you drown in self-loathing, keep in mind that nobody besides Canubis is like me. You're making me happy and, more importantly, you bear with me. All my life I've been waiting for somebody strong enough to withstand my flame. You're my heart. Please accept that."

To choke off any further discussion, the Angel of Death took the king's beautiful face in both hands and kissed him passionately.

"Ready for a second round?"

For a moment it seemed as if Casto wanted to decline, but then a challenging smile blossomed on his sensuous lips.

"That kind of depends on you, Barbarian. Do you think you're up to it?"

Growling, Renaldo pounced on Casto, relieved to be able to distract the king from his musings for the time being.

3. NEW FRIENDS

THE EVENING sun cast its last rays over the royal smithy and reminded the apprentices and fellows to wrap up their work. One after another the men left the place, until only Sic and Jago remained. Jago turned to Sic, who was standing in front of him like a lost lamb.

"You did splendidly on your first day here. I'd be honored if you decided to start working for me."

A beaming smile full of true gratitude brightened Sic's features. "You're very friendly, master. It's my honor."

Jago couldn't suppress a smile either. Sic's genuine joy reminded him of why he had chosen to be a smith. "Shall I escort you back? The palace is a labyrinth, and I have a feeling I'd get into trouble with the king if you don't return to him safely."

Awkwardly, Sic stared down. "To be honest, I wanted to ask if it's all right to spend the night here? I really don't want to go back to the royal wing, and I'm sure Casto doesn't mind me staying at the smithy."

"But I mind!" Jago shook his head indignantly. "There's no way I'd let a talented young man like you sleep on the floor. If you don't want to go to the royal wing, you'll come with me."

Sic felt crimson invading his cheeks and kept his gaze trained on the ground. He had no intention whatsoever of spending the night with this man, but he had been free for only just a few hours and wasn't yet used to voicing his will. Being Noran's possession for so many years had drilled something else into the marrow of his bones: obey the wishes of the master. And so he acquiesced to Jago's suggestion, although he didn't like it.

"As you wish, master."

Jago's brow furrowed. He could sense something was amiss, that Sic was feeling uncomfortable all of a sudden. Jago was an honest man who rarely made bones about anything. Since he had no idea why things had soured so unexpectedly, he asked directly.

"I've a feeling as if I were missing a ton of context here. Sic, what's the matter?"

Insecure, Sic stared at his shoes. He was wishing from the bottom of his heart that the earth would open up and swallow him before things became even more embarrassing than they already were. Of course, his silent pleas were ignored. He wrung his hands.

"It's nothing, master. I didn't want to appear recusant or ungrateful. I promise I'll be obedient."

Jago started to suspect Sic's strange behavior had reasons he didn't want to know anything about, but he just couldn't leave things the way they were.

"What will you be obedient for? No matter what the apprentices may have told you, my wife is a passable cook and does know how to take care of a guest. You don't have to be afraid of being forced to do the dishes."

Bewildered, Sic looked up. "You do not wish to share a bed with me?"

Sic's genuine surprise made Jago's heart constrict. He realized what the young man had been afraid of, and the thought that the scars on his wrists and neck weren't the only ones made him furious. To soothe Sic, he tried to downplay the situation with a joke.

"What? No! Despite the fact that you're so not my type, Cassia would skin me alive. She's pregnant and as irritable as a merchant whose caravan is late." He stared intently at Sic. "I don't really want to know why you thought I wanted you in my bed, do I?"

Sic was still wringing his hands so desperately the joints were cracking.

"No, you really don't want to know. I'm sorry, I read the situation wrongly. I didn't want to bother you. It would be my pleasure to accept your hospitality for tonight—if I'm still welcome."

Relieved they were back to calmer waters so quickly, Jago patted his new employee on the shoulder.

"Of course. I really want to get to know you better."

Side by side they strolled through the labyrinth that was the palace, enjoying the soft evening breeze until they reached the section where those working in the palace had their homes. Since Jago was a master smith, he called a rather large accommodation with a neatly cropped garden his own. The heavy wooden door with ornamental iron fittings was ajar, and from inside came such a beautiful singing voice, Sic couldn't help but think of Cornelia, the Emeris in the Valley. Jago beamed with pride.

"My wife is an excellent singer. She usually works as a midwife, but since her time is so near, she has to slacken off a bit. This isn't to her liking and makes her quite irritable, so please forgive if she's impolite. She can't help it at the moment."

"Jago, is that you? I can hear you ranting out there! You do know talking to yourself is a first sign of becoming senile, don't you?"

From the shadows, a belly appeared that seemed to fill the entire world. Attached to it was a petite woman with the aura of a giant. Cassia was tiny, probably even smaller than Lady Noemi, and Jago towered over her like a mountain over a hut. The child growing inside her seemed to take after its father and made it look as if Cassia would explode at any moment. Apart from her protruding belly, she was a good-looking woman with soft black locks she had pinned at the back of her head. Her dark brown eyes were lively and reminded Sic of a singing bird. The rather wide and full lips turned up in a friendly smile when she realized her husband had brought a visitor.

"Please forgive my quirkiness. I hadn't expected Jago to come back with a guest. I'm Cassia."

Sic bowed politely to the pregnant woman. "My name is Sic, my lady."

"Sic stumbled into my smithy today, looking for work. And lucky guy that I am, he's the biggest talent I've ever met."

Embarrassed, Sic stared down. He wasn't used to being praised and didn't know how to react. But the couple took all decisions from him.

Jago turned to his wife. "Can you see to it that Sic gets himself cleaned? And give him some of my clothes. I'm going to send a messenger to the king to let him know where his friend is spending the night."

"You're a friend of the king?"

Sic evaded Cassia's gaze. "Yes, my lady. But the lowest. I'm just a servant."

Impatiently the midwife clucked her tongue.

"Firstly, I doubt that, and secondly, I must tell you I'll butcher you with my own hands if you dare call me 'my lady' one more time. My name is Cassia. Everything else makes me feel a thousand years old—despite being shapeless like a whale."

Involuntarily, Sic had to laugh. He was used to being surrounded by strong, unbending women, and Cassia was as indomitable as the ladies Noemi and Hulda.

"As you wish, Cassia. But be assured, you don't look old. I'm surprised you're old enough to be married."

Tiny but strong hands patted his cheeks.

"You're really cute. But sweet talk won't save you from taking a bath." She sniffed with ostentation. "Even without getting closer, I can tell you're in dire need of one. Come on, get going."

With shooing motions, as if she wanted to drive a flock of hens back into the henhouse, she ushered him through the entrance door. Inside it was cool and dusky. The house was even bigger than it had seemed from the outside, with a roomy kitchen that also served as a living space, and three chambers along the hallway. At the end of the corridor was a huge bathroom with a tub in the ground, two washbowls, and a mirror the size of a round shield. It wasn't as luxurious as the chambers in the royal wing and definitely not as spacious as the housing of the Emeris in the Valley, but it was more than enough. Cassia got two big towels from a wardrobe and handed him a piece of soap and a small jug with oil.

"Here, you can start already. I'm going to get you some clothes."

When she was gone, Sic closed the door carefully before he took off his tunic. Feeling a pang of regret, he let the silken cloth fall down. Half a day of hard work had not been good for the material. Sic doubted whether it could be saved. He entered the tub and started washing with quick, determined movements. He had always enjoyed rinsing the sweat off after a day's work, but he had never understood how some people, namely Daran, could spend hours in the water. Dripping, Sic left the tub and started to oil his skin, a blessing he had been missing for several months now. He was just about to reseal the jug again when Cassia entered the bathroom with a bundle of clothes.

She stopped dead in her tracks. Her eyes widened in shock when she realized what she was seeing. Sic squirmed under her scrutiny. In his high spirits, he had almost forgotten what a gruesome sight his scarred body was. Hastily he grabbed one of the towels to cover himself, but Cassia deterred him with a forceful motion of her hand. Her voice was trembling with rage.

"Who did this, Sic? Tell me, so I can have a word with them!"

She approached Sic, and her small hands glided soothingly over the scars as she talked absently to herself.

"Somebody has started treating it, but way too late. I'm asking you again, who did this?"

Sic couldn't face the midwife; he was too humiliated, both by what had been done to him and why it had been done to him.

"My god and my master. It was punishment for misbehavior."

Cassia's gaze was glued to the scars on Sic's torso. She couldn't suppress the trembling of her body.

"What kind of misbehavior justifies tearing your skin to shreds? And in such a ragged way, to top it off."

"I betrayed my god, Cassia. Normally death is the punishment for such a grave sin. Seen like this, I'm grateful to be still alive."

The midwife made a sound between a grunt and a snort, showing openly what she thought about this view.

"When did the treatment of the scars start?"

"Three days ago."

"And when were you hurt?"

"About eight months ago."

Expertly, Cassia examined his body.

"Whoever is taking care of you knows what they're doing. I assume you have a special salve to make the skin smooth?"

"Yes, Lady Noemi made it for me."

"Lady Noemi? Is she your healer?"

"She's taking care of me. She's Lord Canubis's wife."

Cassia's eyes widened.

"The famous snake witch is treating you? That's good news. Wait a minute." The midwife's eyes narrowed to slits. "Why isn't she healing you with her gift?"

"The wounds are too old. She can't change the tissue once it's healed."

Lost in thought, Cassia caressed a broad scar on Sic's chest. "It makes sense. As soon as scar formation is completed, it's no longer a wound."

She turned away abruptly, and Sic was grateful for it. Being examined so closely by a complete stranger made him uneasy in more than one way. He was glad Cassia was giving him some breathing space to regain his composure.

"I have a salve very similar to the one Lady Noemi has given to you. Its purpose is the same. When we're getting your stuff tomorrow, I'll have a talk with her to find out how she was planning to treat you further."

Sic could only stare at the tiny woman, unable to understand or comprehend the turn events had taken this day.

"Why are you doing this, Cassia? I'm a complete stranger to you, and you're taking care of me as if I were part of your family."

"I don't know where you've been growing up, little barbarian, but where I come from, people help each other. Apart from that, I'm really good at reading people. You're a good person, Sic, I can feel it. No." She held up her hands in a dismissive gesture when her guest wanted to interject. "This discussion ends here. And now keep still so I can look after your scars."

DINNER WITH Jago and Cassia felt like paradise for Sic, who had never before sat at a table with a family. He was so happy, he completely forgot to eat. Jago grinned at him broadly.

"I guess Cassia's cooking is worse than I said. You've hardly eaten anything."

Absentmindedly, the midwife hit her husband with a spoon. Sic got the impression that this scene played out on a regular basis. The intimacy between the spouses was like a warm hug that included him, although he didn't know why they would accept him so readily. After dinner Sic helped clear the table and insisted on doing the dishes despite Jago's heated protest. Cassia ended the discussion by propping herself in a chair. With a sigh, she put her feet on the table.

"I declare the dish washing to be a man's job. And if you give it your best shot, it surely won't take long. I quit for today."

Working together, they were indeed done in no time at all. They just were about to sit down in the garden when Lady Noemi appeared with two servants and the messenger Jago had sent.

Sic bowed low. "My lady."

"Good evening, Sic. Master Jago, Cassia. I'm pleased to meet you. I've brought some of your stuff, Sic. Mainly clothes and medicine. I assume you prefer staying here over returning to the royal wing?"

The snake witch's green eyes regarded Sic with sympathy.

He blushed. "It depends on how long I can try Master Jago's hospitality."

"As long as you wish. I thought that was clear." Cassia's voice was determined. She shared a look with Noemi that was only too familiar to Sic. He knew he would have no say in what was going to happen to him from now on.

"Of course, Sic can return to us any time he wishes to. He can also take his own lodgings or—and this option is surely favored by the king— stay with you."

"Then we have a deal. He's living with us. I saw that you've started treating him, Lady Noemi. Perhaps you can tell me what you're planning to do next."

"Please, Cassia, my name is Noemi, especially for a colleague. I've only heard the best about your abilities."

"At least before I was a stranded whale."

"I know, the last weeks are the worst. I hope you'll allow me to assist you when the time comes."

"It'd be my pleasure. Please, come in. Do you want some tea?"

"That would be nice."

Before Noemi followed Cassia into the kitchen, she turned to Sic.

"Casto has been busy since his return at noon. Renaldo has finally realized how close he was to losing his heart again and is watching him like a hawk. I'll tell him where you are and how you're doing. He's probably going to visit you tomorrow, after the trial."

Sic nodded silently. Noemi's voice was serious. "He's going to need you. He's not doing well and to be honest, I don't know how long he'll be able to bear the emotional tension."

"I'll be there for him, Mistress. I always am."

A warm, radiant smile was his reward.

"I know."

Noemi and Cassia disappeared into the kitchen. Jago indicated the chair beside him.

"Sit down. It seems the two of us are on our own while the women are busy planning your life."

"Are you really fine with me staying here, master? You were awfully quiet."

Jago snickered. "Experience, my friend. Once my wife has decided on something, there's no point trying to talk her out of it. She's going to do what she wants, no matter the hurdles. And she has decided that you need her help. So she's going to help. Apart from this, I agree with her. Stop fretting and enjoy the evening. Can I offer you more wine?"

IN THE kitchen, the midwife and the healer were sitting quietly at the table, both staring into their tea mugs, unsure how to begin their conversation. It was Noemi who finally spoke up.

"Again, thank you for taking Sic in. He has endured hard times and needs stable surroundings."

"Don't mention it. He deserves it. About his wounds...."

"I can imagine what you're about to say. And I'm not going to justify what has happened to him. It was a mistake, a very bad one. If it's any consolation to you, we're all worked up over it."

Cassia stared at the healer for a long time. Then she took a sip of her tea, made a face when she realized she had forgotten to add the honey, and corrected this mistake while speaking.

"I'm not going to talk to you about the responsibilities of a healer. I can see you know them well and how much it pains you to have forfeited them. But I'm furious, and I'm going to need some explaining. Sic is a gentle soul, any idiot can see as much. What on Ana-Darasa has he done to merit such a brutal punishment?"

Noemi closed her eyes for a moment. It was nice talking to another healer, somebody who shared her values, but it was also hard to explain an entire life philosophy to a total stranger. Still, Cassia deserved a truthful and thorough answer, especially since she was going to take care of Sic. And so the snake witch tried to make the midwife understand something that had taken her almost a century to comprehend.

"You're aware who Canubis and Renaldo are? I know this city isn't exactly hospitable towards religions and belief, but I'm sure you've heard stories."

Cassia nodded. "We all have. Let's say I'm not entirely convinced about their divine nature, but willing to believe in their savage personalities."

Noemi flinched slightly. The midwife sure didn't mince words. But then, if she had been in her place, she wouldn't have either.

"Well, everything you've heard about them is true and probably underestimated. They're worse than anything you can imagine. Their wrath knows no mercy, and anybody who breaks the rules they have set has to pay the price. To an outsider it must seem strange that so many people follow them, but once you get to know their ways, things become clearer. I'm not saying they're always right, most certainly not, but they've been walking this world for so long, they never act without reason."

Cassia mulled these words over for some time. She could sense how important the topic Noemi was talking about was. Understanding such a complicated matter was never easy, and the midwife hated jumping to conclusions—although in this case, it had a certain appeal.

"How long do I have to live to really get them?"

Noemi chuckled.

"At least a century. Probably more. As I said, they're ancient. They rarely make sense to me." She paused. "So you're not hopping mad anymore?"

"Not at you. Being a healer can be difficult. I've lived in this city for almost ten years now and know this better than anybody. But I still resent those who did this to him. It was beyond barbaric."

"I agree. Which is why I'm trying really hard to make it better for Sic. His physical wounds, the scars on his body, they're bad, but not as bad as his mental state. Although he's so young, he's already hit rock bottom more than once. What he needs now is a loving, stable environment that helps him to find out what normalcy means. It's the first time he's been free, so he'll be reluctant to speak up. A lifetime of obedience can't be taken away as easily as a collar, as you probably know. I want him to get used to his new status, to find out what he's worth. I want him to become self-confident enough to follow his own dreams."

Cassia's eyes narrowed. She was no fool and was pretty sure Noemi wanted her to understand something she was merely implying.

"Do I sense a certain plan here? A plan that is not necessarily at one with the gods' will?"

The snake witch met her gaze fully. There was a hint of steel in those emerald-green eyes that made Cassia reconsider her opinion of the young woman—if she was young.

"You sense right. As I already said, what has happened to Sic is partly my fault, which I'm trying to make up for. My husband and his brother would love to have him go back with us to the Valley—for reasons too complicated to discuss now. And Sic most probably will comply—that is, if he's given a direct order, or if he's still a slave in his head. The direct order I'm going to take care of, but his mind is a different matter. I'm going to need your help."

"You really think he'd be better off in a city like Ummana?"

"Not on his own. But with a family to back him…. Of course, I'd take care of his expenses until he can earn some money on his own. I don't expect you to help out a stranger for free."

"Cut it out, Noemi. You know damn well I'll help whom I choose. And I already have chosen Sic. So there's no need for you to bribe me. Just tell me honestly, how high are the odds of seriously pissing your gods off?"

Noemi couldn't help but laugh. Cassia was the type of woman she liked from the bottom of her heart.

"At the moment, they're still too shaken to get pissed, so you're safe, although I know this is not what you want to hear. Once they have time to think about it, they might realize they've been played, but then I'll be the one to take the blame. Chances are you'll already be dust by then. They can be pretty slow."

"But they will be annoyed?"

"Most certainly."

"Then I'm in. Helping Sic and thwarting his torturers' plans in one go is an offer I can't resist."

The females looked at each other in gleeful companionship. With a wicked grin, they held up their teacups in a mocking toast. Then Noemi leaned back.

"Now that we've talked about the business part, let's get to more pleasant topics. Tell me, how is midwifing going in this city?"

Cassia laughed dryly.

"I thought you wanted to talk about something pleasant? Well, let me see…."

On and on their discussion went, until Jago and Sic finally came in to end their fun. With the promise of meeting again the next day, the two women embraced each other, and then Lady Noemi went back to Canubis while Sic enjoyed his first night in freedom.

As CAREFULLY as possible, Casto sneaked out of Renaldo's embrace, put on his tunic, and left the chamber. He knew Renaldo wouldn't approve of what he was planning to do, to say the least of it, but he had no choice. If he ever wanted to get rid of the ghosts of the past, he had to face them while they were still alive. Tomorrow at this time, his father and the Council—those who had betrayed him so cruelly—would have left this world, condemned by an angry god, convicted by their king. Ever since he had returned to the city of his childhood, he had felt smothered by an irresistible undertow of fear and despair. Driven by his overdeveloped protective instincts, Renaldo had kept Casto away from everything and everybody he viewed as a threat to his heart. But Casto was not a child anymore. He was a man, a warrior, and a king, lover to a god. If he wasn't able to take care of his own business, what right did he have to stay with Renaldo?

The guard down in the dungeons was surprised to see him but let him pass without fuss. With his mouth dry and his breath heaving, Casto entered the cell in which his father was awaiting his destiny. The light of the torch blinded him, so Aran turned his head, a cynical smile on his lips.

"My one and only son. I was wondering when you'd find your way down here. You've been evading me ever since your return to the city."

"Are you surprised, considering the circumstances when I left?"

"I think you've always misunderstood me, son. I only wanted your best."

"I know. My power."

Aran growled, showing for a brief moment his true, unsightly face. "It was my damn right! That dirty slut you call mother never showed me the respect I deserve. It's all her fault."

Casto felt cold shivers running down his spine when his father displayed his contempt so openly. Aran had always had considerable problems hiding his feelings, which was one reason he had never made it to the top. He was too easily figured out.

"Is that why you hate me so much?"

The chained man shrugged, as if the question itself was too stupid to merit an answer.

"Whoever said I hated you? Do I hate the hammer with which I hit the nail? Or the coins I use to buy a new pair of shoes? No. Of course not. You've always been a means to an end for me. I do admit I felt a certain thrill at hurting you, especially when you began to resemble your mother more and more, but first and foremost I was interested in utilizing you as a tool. You were my ticket to the big game. That's all there was to it."

Hurt more deeply by those words than he had thought possible, Casto extended his chin in defiance.

"I think Mother saw through you from the start. She knew what kind of creature you are, although I don't understand why she kept you around after you had fulfilled your task of producing Anesha and me."

A cruel smile contorted the features already marred by age and a life spent in greediness.

"She had no choice. Our marriage was purely political and was arranged for two reasons: producing legitimate heirs and gaining a stable alliance with Sravrana, which in return would acknowledge the Twin Cities as the ruler of the Confederation and thus keep Medelina at arm's length. Getting rid of me was no option. What do you think has kept the Council from acting against me all that time?"

Unconsciously Casto touched his throat. He had always known his suffering hadn't been for personal but purely political reasons. It still didn't make it easier to accept the fact that in the eyes of the Council and his father, his life had no value at all. With the unerring instincts of a sadist, Aran sensed an opening and turned the proverbial knife without hesitation.

"You don't really believe your precious Angel of Death has married you out of love, do you? Believe me, he knew what he was doing. It seems, my son, as if you're damned to be nothing but a pawn."

"You're lying! My master loves me!"

Even in his own ears, the sentence sounded hollow. To top it off, he had referred to the Barbarian as his master, something Casto usually tried to avoid at all costs. The situation was throwing him more and more off-balance, and the king felt tears wet his eyes.

Aran chuckled coldly. "You call him master and think he loves you? Open your eyes, son. He's a barbarian, and you're nothing but a valuable toy he's using for his own gain. You are, and always will be, a nobody."

Anger welled up inside Casto. His blue eyes sparkled like stars in the night sky as he regarded the chained figure of his father. The man who had made his life hell. The same man who had driven him into Renaldo's arms. Suddenly he smiled. Objectively, Aran was nothing but a pathetic coward. He had used a helpless child to secure his claim on the throne, an action that was beyond pathetic. And he hadn't even managed to reach his goals. Aran had used Voltara to tame Casto because he was too inept to do it himself, and now he was sitting here, bound in a stinking cell, and didn't possess the strength to leave this world with dignity. Casto wondered what he had been afraid of all the time.

"Yes, I do call him master. Unlike Voltara or you, he has earned the title. And before you drip more of your venom, I'd like to remind you who is going to speak your death sentence tomorrow. When the headsman chops off your head, wallow in the knowledge that you're dying because of a pawn's will."

Casto turned his back on his father and left the cell. The door closed with an ominous bang, but Casto was aware that his problems wouldn't be buried with his father. They were still there, still real, but for the first time in years he had the feeling the burden was getting lighter. One day Aran would be nothing but a fading memory, dissolving like the fog on a sunny morning in the Valley. For the first time since he had returned to Ummana, Casto felt something like relief budding in his heart. He still dreaded the coming day, when he would sentence so many powerful politicians to death and challenge the wrath of their families, but now he was determined to win the battle.

WHEN HE slipped back into his chambers, Renaldo was waiting for him. He held a cup of wine and was propped up in a heap of cushions on the floor.

"You were faster than I anticipated."

"You knew what I was doing?"

The Angel of Death got up, his left brow quirking in mockery.

"I always know where you are, my heart."

Casto approached him with a pleading look.

"You're angry."

It wasn't a question, but a statement.

"I'm aware you had to do this for peace of mind, and I don't deny you the right to do so. But I'm furious that you sneaked away like a thief in the night without telling me anything. You don't trust me."

Casto lowered his gaze in consternation. He was too shaken to argue with the Barbarian.

"I'm sorry."

"It's too late for that now. The only concession I'm giving you is that you can decide whether you want to be punished now or later."

Casto leaned his forehead against the warm, soft skin of Renaldo. "Now."

Wordlessly Renaldo picked him up. His fire's heat engulfed them both, and Casto closed his eyes complacently when he felt the soothing embrace of the flames that were lethal to anybody but him. He did not care what kind of punishment Renaldo had planned for him, as long as he didn't let go of him for the rest of the night.

4. EXECUTION

UNNOTICED BY the crowd, Raglan's hands delved into the pockets of the man in front of him. Carefully he removed the wallet from the hidden slot a talented tailor had integrated in the light cape. True craftsmanship indeed. The wallet had a promising weight, and Raglan estimated the contents at fifty gold coins. It was a perfect start to a day that favored pickpockets.

The news that King Castolus had accused all members of the Council of Elders of treason and would be giving them a public trial had stirred up the entire city. Even those who usually kept their distance from the patricians because of their noble ancestry did not want to miss the spectacle. As a result, the far-reaching plaza in front of the palace was overflowing with people who were competing with each other by spreading the most adventurous rumors about the king, the defendants, and the entire situation.

The last public trial in Ummana had taken place about a hundred years ago, and the indictment had been corruption. The defendant had been cleared of all charges, because he had offered the judge nominated by the king the opportunity to invest quite a large sum in his enterprise. After this last, and certainly not most spectacular, misuse of magistracy, the tradition of trial had ended. It was simply too difficult to find people honest enough to be solely interested in the truth.

Since then, conflicts were usually solved by either a more-or-less neutral facilitator, money, or when all else failed, the members of the guard—then often terminally. The system wasn't better or worse than the one before, and thus gained the status of a tradition in no time at all. In theory the ruler still had jurisdiction and also the right to appoint a representative, but this hadn't happened for so long, nobody seriously deemed it a possibility anymore.

King Castolus would break with all those traditions today when he personally sat in judgment. Rumor had it the convicts couldn't hope for a reprieve either. The king had flatly refused to grant the members of the convicts' families an audience so they could offer consolation money, nor had he spoken to the traitors directly and given them a chance to defend themselves. As if he had lost his mind, he insisted on this open confrontation, which would make some of the most powerful families in the city turn against him.

Of course, there were many others who couldn't be happier about this redistribution of power and who were willing to help him along, but it was a dangerous situation. Should Castolus break under the strain, Ummana would tumble into chaos. After the last rather meager years, this was not a desirable option. The king was taking a high risk, and the prosperity of Ummana and its citizens were his pledge. Many admired him for his guts, but there were also those who feared the worst. It was obvious how much the king had changed during the years of his absence, and there was no telling what he had become.

The young man who had disappeared so suddenly five years ago and returned only a few days before didn't seem to fear the wrath of the elite. Considering who his allies were, his unyielding attitude did not come as a surprise. Raglan hadn't seen the barbarians himself yet, but everybody knew the stories about the two warrior brothers from the North and their invincible army. Apparently Renaldo and Canubis were immortal, even gods. The men riding with them were demigods and they, too, couldn't be killed by humans. Even if it was all just stories, the fact remained that the brothers commanded the most lethal army in the world, and Castolus had bound the Angel of Death by marriage. He could afford to ignore the unspoken laws and conventions in the city.

A FANFARE announced the king's arrival, and the murmuring in the plaza died down. The silence while the royal guard took position in front of the gallery where the trial would be held was almost deafening. The guard was followed by twenty warriors from the army of the divine brothers. Raglan had first thought it was a joke when people told him the mercenaries had come to the city with so few fighters, but when he now saw the fully armored men, he realized half of them would still have been enough. Their equipment was utilitarian, without jewelry or ornaments, but in perfect condition as was rarely seen. Raglan had no doubts that each of these warriors was able to handle at least five opponents simultaneously, and there were the divine brothers and the Emeris as well. Only a complete madman would dare go against a culmination of such deadly precision.

The fighters formed a semicircle behind the chairs that were placed at the back of the podium. Again a fanfare was blown, and the king entered the stage.

Castolus was wearing a dark blue silken tunic fastened with golden pins on his shoulders. On his forehead rested a blue diamond, embraced by a pair of golden wings. For Ummanian standards, this was practically humble—until one estimated the worth of the egg-sized diamond. Raglan felt a shiver running down his spine when confronted with such riches. If only he could get close to the king for a moment…. But then he caught a glimpse of the beautiful mask that was the face of the Angel of Death, and he unconsciously retreated a few steps. Lord Renaldo was the kind of man better avoided, unless one had a profound death wish.

His brother, Lord Canubis, radiated the same wild, unrelenting danger, and Raglan wondered what it was like to spend one's life with such intimidating men. The king didn't seem to be bothered by his companions' lethal aura; if anything, his features were even more impenetrable than those of the Angel of Death.

After the three men had taken their seats, the convicts were brought before them by members of the royal guard. Time hadn't been kind to the once proud members of the council. They hadn't been allowed to refresh themselves before the trial or to change clothes. Wearing the same dress as on the day of their arrest, the men and women had lost most of their former grandeur. The fine clothes were covered in spots and creases, and their wearers looked tired and desperate. Seeing the formerly arrogant leaders of the city in such a debased state came as a shock to the assembled audience. A well-calculated shock, if Raglan interpreted the satisfied grin flashing across the Wolf of War's lips correctly. The new rulers of the city showed blatantly what they thought about the established powers.

They were now kneeling on a wooden bench, one next to the other, their backs facing the crowd, their eyes cast down. Even the father of the king, normally always ready with a quick retort or some cynical remarks, was unaccustomedly tame, as if all his energy had been drained at once.

All those who had still hoped for a conciliatory ending had to face the bitter truth. It was as if reality had struck them with claws of steel. The mood among the assembled people was chastened; everybody felt anxious about what their inscrutable king would do next.

Silence descended. The audience was waiting almost impatiently for what was going to happen now. Raglan realized that he, too, had been so fascinated he'd almost forgotten to keep on working. He pulled himself together, and just when his fingers delved into the next pocket, the king started to talk in his clear, melodic voice.

"My dear fellow Ummanians. It has only been a few days since I've returned to our beloved city, and I'm appalled by the changes that have taken place during my absence. Important reforms have been sacrificed to the political whims of the Council and the guilds, our allies in the Confederation are sensing an opening and try to rebel, and business has dramatically decreased. All I can say is, I'm deeply shaken by these developments. And I'm grateful to our citizens who have bravely stayed without turning their backs on our precious Ummana. I promise here and now that all crimes, schemes, and secret agreements will come to an end today."

The king made a short pause, intended to increase the dramatic effect of what he had just said. The whole world seemed to hold its breath; all eyes were glued to him. Castolus was a master at playing a crowd.

"I accuse all members of the Council, as well as Lord Aran and the leaders of the guilds of merchants and slave traders, of treason."

Again there was a moment's silence in which the accusation, which everybody knew had to come although nobody had believed it would until now, sank in. Then the king resumed his speech before anybody was able to voice a protest, because all the onlookers were still stunned. This time he did it with a steely undertone that made clear how serious he was.

"Not only did they try to break me, the future King of Ummana, the rightful heir of Queen Isiris; no, they even allowed a religious belief to grow in the streets of Ummana like a poisonous cancer, and they watched as business went down by more than twenty percent without taking any action."

This time the king allowed the information to sink in for a couple of heartbeats before he ended his speech.

"These are the crimes they are charged with. I know there are many who would wish to speak today, most of them in favor of the convicts, but I've decided to hear only the most distinguished witnesses—my sister, Princess Anesha, and Captain Aktan, Commander of the Royal Guard."

When Castolus mentioned business losses, a consenting murmur had rippled through the crowd. Neither the conscious sacrifice of the future king nor the impending danger of a religious invasion upset the citizens as much as the prospect of losing money. Ummana's residents might be without honor and principles, but their loyalty toward profit was as unbreakable as the mountains in the North.

Watched by the impenetrable eyes of the barbarian brothers, first Captain Aktan and then Anesha testified against the Council. Every attempt by the family members of the convicts to be heard during this show trial was brutally prohibited by the guard. In the end the king spoke his verdict without allowing the convicts to utter even one word in their defense. Showing no emotion at all, Castolus sentenced the entire Council and his own father to death. The only mercy he bestowed on his enemies was to order the sentence to be carried out away from the prying eyes of the crowd.

Escorted by his mate and brother-in-law, the king left the podium. Those who had been subjected to his wrath were taken to justice by the members of the royal guard. The crowd started to scatter, now that the show was over. Raglan, too, went on his way back to his hideout, where he counted the day's booty with shining eyes.

Although he had never gone to school or experienced any apprenticeship, the instincts honed by a life on the streets told him the city and its inhabitants were going to face interesting times. With his merciless verdict, the king had declared war on some of the most influential and powerful families of Ummana. A war that would only be won when one of the opponents went down.

After the events of the day, Raglan was inclined to wager his money on the king. Castolus might have been half child when he fled, but he had returned as a shrewd, seasoned politician and warrior.

"I THINK we don't have a choice but to leave, my brother."

Casto rested his forehead against Lys's blaze. Since the incident with his broken arm, Lord Aran and the torturer had become even stricter and crueler than before. Now that Casto had turned sixteen, the verbal and physical abuse reached new heights. If he did not want to be destroyed by those two men, Casto had to escape them. At court he had no allies and no financial resources to speak of, since he was still considered underage, with no claim on his mother's legacy. No matter how much he resented it, his prospects in Ummana were bleak. If he wanted to defeat his enemies and get his revenge, he had to withdraw, gather new strength, and come up with a foolproof plan. Once Casto had made the decision, there was only one minor problem to overcome. How he could get away from Ummana without Lord Aran's spies and henchmen bringing him back immediately?

Lys nudged Casto gently, giving him to understand that he would take care of the details of their escape. All Casto had to do was wait for Lys to pick him up.

Casto could not believe it. When Lys told him he would call a storm to cover their escape, Casto had thought his brother was trying to make a fool of him. Now here they stood, ready to ride out into the worst thunderstorm Casto had ever seen. He felt his heart race with fearful excitement, knowing this was the point of no return. Without looking back at the palace even once, Casto got into the saddle. He bent low over Lys's neck, patting the black fur to reassure them both. Lys listened to the howling, screeching winds for a moment before he started to run, eager to reach the center of the storm where they would be safely hidden from all their enemies.

SIC WAS busy hardening a sword slug in the cold water of the fountain when Casto, still wearing his ornate clothes and the diamond on his forehead, approached him. The young smith only had to glance at his friend to realize how close he was to a breakdown. His normally mesmerizing blue eyes were lusterless and had sunk deep into their sockets, the bronze tone of Casto's skin seemed sallow, and he was very pale. Sic grabbed Casto's arm, led him to an alcove, and offered him some water. For a long time, they sat in silence next to each other. Casto was staring blankly ahead, his fingers playing nervously with his drink. When he started to talk, his tone was hoarse.

"I did it. I sentenced the Council and my own father to death. I've taken a handful of stones and thrown them into a wasps' nest, and all I can do now is hope nobody I love has to pay the price for my reckless deed."

"You did what your god, your mate, was asking of you."

Sadly, Casto looked at Sic.

"It's still my doing. I should have opposed him more. Everything that's going to happen now is my responsibility. I should have never made the suggestion to come here."

"If you hadn't done it, the army would now be running against the walls of Medelina, Lord Canubis and Lord Renaldo would lose countless warriors, and I would still be in my master's grasp. To be frank, I prefer the situation as it is now."

"Damn, Sic. I'm afraid I'm not strong enough. I can't take it anymore. All I want is to leave this city and the schemes that are choking me. I'm not worthy of being a god's heart."

"You're an idiot. You've survived eleven years all alone in this snake pit. You've managed to tie a man to you the entire world is terrified of, yet you treat him like an amusing obstacle. You've defied a god and not only did you survive, but you also managed to win said god's love. You've forgiven a pitiful traitor although he almost killed you. You had the strength to make me your friend when you had every reason and right to hate me. And you really think you're not worth being loved by the Angel of Death? This is not the Casto I know."

Tears were raining from the sky-blue eyes now.

"I don't know, Sic. I don't know anything anymore. And I'm so unbelievably tired."

Sic caressed Casto's wet cheeks gently. Even though he still shied away from any physical contact with others, feeling Casto's warm skin under his fingertips was one of the few things he did not fear but crave. It gave him an anchor in this world that had treated him so cruelly until now.

"You never cease to amaze me. I've always admired you for your courage, for the arrogance with which you treat Lord Renaldo. But most of it is just façade, isn't it? When will you accept that you belong to a god?"

Defiance reared to life in Casto's regal face. This was about the core of his being.

"How can I, when all my life I've been striving to be free?"

Sic breathed a heavy sigh. It was the old song again. The main problem was that it was exactly Casto's stubbornness that made him so perfect for the Angel of Death in the first place.

"You swore fealty to him. Why do you have such a hard time submitting to him, entrusting him with your life?"

The king thought so long about this question, Sic was sure he would not get an answer. But in the end, Casto started to speak. His voice was low and soft, as if he was still pondering all the possible answers in his head.

"I've been asking myself the same thing countless times. I've always been puzzled by how naturally you accept your fate. How serenely you bore whatever your master did to you. But I think it's because you don't know better. You've always been a slave, but I was born a king."

Despite the rather degrading words, Sic had to smile. He knew Casto didn't mean what he had said in a belittling manner, and he was glad his friend had started talking about his emotions. Once he did that, he was on his way back to normal.

"I hate proving you wrong, my friend, but I, too, wanted to be free. Every slave does, the only exception probably being Daran, but I think we can agree that he doesn't count. My master saved my life when he bought me from Dalwon, and it was a debt I thought I'd never be able to repay. I was willing to serve Noran for the rest of my life, since it was thanks to him that I was alive at all."

Sic paused for a moment. He suspected his next words wouldn't be welcome.

"The way I see it, you and Lord Renaldo are the same. In Ummana you were a prisoner, then a fugitive, haunted by ghosts of the past and some very real and unpleasant humans. Your god has made you a king, has accepted you as his heart. What else could you desire?"

Indignantly, Casto stuck his chin out. He didn't like what Sic was telling him in the least, especially since it was so close to the truth.

"I want to be the master of my own fate. I want to get on Lys's back and ride wherever his legs may carry us without thinking about a jealous god who might view this as a personal insult. Nothing I do is without consequences, and I'm getting tired of having to think about everything."

"Oh, Casto!" Sic slung his arms around his friend and pressed his forehead against that of the king. "I hate being the bearer of bad news, but you *are* special. Do you really think your life would be different if your mother was still alive and you had stayed in Ummana? Nobody is truly free, not even Lord Canubis and Lord Renaldo. Even they have to obey the whims of fate. If you really want to be stripped of all responsibility, you'll have to retreat into the wild and live on your own. But you don't want that, do you? You love your god too much."

Casto made a whimpering sound. Accepting the truth was hard; in his emotionally depleted state, it was almost enough to break him.

"Did I ever tell you what it's like to beat the storm? When we fled from Ummana, Lys showed me for the first time the extent of his power. To escape my father's henchmen, he called a terrible storm. It was unbelievable! There was so much raw force, so wild and untamed, all around us. We were at the center of the storm, of all the chaos Lys had unleashed. And although I could have died, I felt entirely safe. I knew Lys would carry me through unscathed. We were so happy, so ecstatic about being free. Unfortunately it didn't last. Sometimes I curse the day Renaldo caught me."

"But you love him!"

"Of course I love him. More than I'll ever be able to express in words or deeds. But this love is also my prison. It's the bars that keep me trapped."

Sic felt a bitter smile playing around his lips. Before he knew what he was saying, he had already started talking.

"At least your love is reciprocated. The man I love tried to destroy me."

Casto stared at Sic in surprise. "You still love him? After everything he's done?"

"Of course. I hate myself for it, but I can't change it either. I have resigned myself to loving Noran till my last breath. Be grateful you have somebody to share your prison. I'm all alone."

Again they sat in silence, each of them caught in his own personal misery. Casto took Sic's hand, and the warmth seeping through that touch consoled them both. When Casto resumed talking, his voice was determined again. He had made a decision.

"It seems as if we were both fooled by fate. But this doesn't mean we're helpless. We're going to take matters into our own hands."

Sic grinned. "That's the Casto I know. Defiant and stubborn to the end. I'm glad you're back."

"I just needed a short break. Thank you, Sic, for listening and setting me straight again."

"What are you going to do now?"

"I'll pay Lys a short visit, then I'll go back to Renaldo and submit to my god."

Sic shook his head. "I never know whether you're joking or serious. Please, don't do anything rash. I have no intention of sharing my bed at Jago's house with you because you've had a fight."

"Idiot." Casto punched Sic's upper arm playfully. "I always know what I'm doing, so there won't be a problem."

WHILE CASTO was busy setting his thoughts straight with the aid of Sic, Renaldo had returned to their chambers. He had felt his mate's tension but could not do anything to improve it since, strictly speaking, he was responsible for it. Because of this, he had allowed Casto to meet Sic. To be on the safe side, he had sent two wolves to guard the king inconspicuously. If Casto found out about this secret guard, there would, without any doubt, be a major fight, but the Angel of Death didn't trust anybody in this damn city, and the thought that somebody could try to harm his heart again made him furious.

To soothe his raging mind, he poured himself a cup of wine, a truly delicious year that teased his throat with the bittersweet flavors of a summer that had lasted too long. After he had tasted the different wines offered in Ummana, he had started to understand why Casto was so snobbish when it came to drinking and why he preferred water over a wine that was only average. Before he had met Casto, Renaldo couldn't have cared less how his food and wine tasted. When he and Canubis had still been gods, there had been no need for sustaining their bodies. And after Ana-Isara had taken their hearts, they had been too devastated to care about anything at all. All of a sudden there had been a need to provide fuel to their systems in order to keep them going, and they had done so in a pragmatic manner.

After all, what did taste matter when you had no heart to appreciate it? Now that he had this essential part of himself back, Renaldo noticed a growing interest in what he—and especially Casto—consumed. The concept of a favorite dish still remained a mystery to him, but he was now able to understand why his mate was so picky about what he ate.

His musings were interrupted by relentless knocking. With a sigh Renaldo put the wine down. He only hoped it wasn't some pressing political business that could not be conducted without him and his brother again. He would have never thought how difficult it could be to rule over a city. Back home in the Valley, everything was easier. People there knew his will and submitted without back talk or unnecessary questions. Those who defied him were punished according to the severity of their crime, and that was it.

In Ummana everything was different. Nothing was cast in stone; an agreement made today could be worthless tomorrow. Even he and Canubis had trouble dealing with the ever-changing circumstances in this town. It was high time for them to return to the Valley, but not before they had put the followers of the Good Mother in their place. Their plans regarding this goal were a little stuck at the moment, though. A lot depended on the reaction of the ambassadors to the public trial and how Casto managed to play them to his advantage. Since they were aiming for a lasting solution, namely keeping the followers of the Good Mother out of the Confederation, they couldn't just kill everybody in their way, a fact that made the Angel of Death cranky even though he understood the necessity of holding back.

Renaldo opened the door and found himself nose-to-nose with Noran. Since the assault they hadn't talked even once, but it hardly mattered because their conversations before had been superficial at best. It was a development Renaldo had pitied in the beginning, but now it only made him angry. He would have never thought it possible to grow so far apart from a man he had enjoyed in his bed. Noran was no longer who he used to be. He had transformed into a creature Renaldo hardly recognized as his former friend. Too much had happened between them, too many things had gone unspoken, to simply return to their old ways. Noran was looking at him with insecurity written all over his face, but Renaldo didn't feel merciful and had no inclination of making it easier for him.

"What do you want?"

Renaldo was aware how gruff he sounded, but like Noran, he had given up pretending for the sake of something that was gone for good.

His former friend and lover answered with a thin, slightly trembling voice. "May I enter, my lord?"

Thrown off guard by the unaccustomedly polite tone, Renaldo cocked an eyebrow before he gestured his brother-in-arms to enter. Noran turned around in the middle of the room, his brown eyes filled with regret.

"So, what do you want?" Renaldo did nothing to hide his irritation.

Staring fixedly at his god, the master smith knelt down.

"I wish to apologize to you, my lord. And ask your forgiveness. I'm aware how late I am, but I hope you will listen to me nevertheless."

Renaldo was so surprised, he allowed Noran to talk with a nod of the head. He wasn't sure what he had expected, but a submissive Noran hadn't been on the list. Suddenly interested, Renaldo regarded the master more carefully. Noran looked tired; deep lines had formed around his eyes and at the corners of his lips, and his cheeks were hollow, as if he hadn't eaten properly in weeks. Cruelty and bitterness, which had consumed him so relentlessly during the past few months—and decades—were gone, leaving behind only regret and despair.

Although he was still a giant of a man, at least double the mass of Renaldo, he seemed shrunken. It appeared as if the events of the last days had left quite an impact on him. The shell Noran had been building around himself since Arja's betrayal, and that had grown in thickness after Sic's conviction, was showing its first cracks. Beneath it a deeply wounded soul emerged, a soul that felt the weight of its deeds growing heavier with each passing day and that was now desperately trying to gain at least some forgiveness, although it was clear such an act of mercy was not justified in this case. Hesitantly, the master smith started talking, as if he did not know how to phrase his cause.

"I never apologized to you for having been willing to betray you for Arja. She pretended to be concerned about me, and that made me blind. I'm sorry I even considered choosing her over my family, my gods. I still don't understand why you've never punished me for it, but be assured, I will accept anything you deem appropriate as expiation."

Speechless, Renaldo stared at Noran. He couldn't believe what he had just heard.

"That's it? Now, over a hundred years after Arja's death, you crawl up to me and ask my forgiveness? Don't you think you're a little late? And presumptuous? If this is all you have to tell me, then get up and leave. I'd like to end it before I get really angry."

Noran gulped. He had known it wouldn't be easy, and the pain he was feeling when his god rejected him so bluntly was nothing compared to what he had inflicted, but he still felt as if Renaldo had rammed a knife into his guts and then slowly twisted it.

"No, that's not all. I also want to apologize for my despicable behavior toward your heart, my lord. I used Sic to hurt Casto. I'm really sorry."

Renaldo could feel his anger fanning the flame inside him.

"What do you expect from me, Noran? Forgiveness? Punishment? Let me tell you something. I'd have forgiven you the business with Arja if you'd come to me immediately. I was angry and hurt, because you had shared my bed before. But I would have forgiven you because you were my friend and because I could understand you, up to a certain point. What I cannot forgive is you hurting Casto. He's my heart. I feel his pain as if it were my own. You can be proud of yourself. You've managed to strike him at his most vulnerable point.

"Luckily for you, you're an Emeris and part of the family. At the moment this is the only protection you have against my wrath. But even if I could punish you the way I want, I could not imagine what I'd have to do to you in order to amend Casto's suffering. I don't think physical pain can avenge what you've done to my heart."

Filled with remorse, Noran lowered his gaze. Blinded by hatred, he had not only almost killed the most important person in his life and hurt him in an unforgivable manner; he had also made his god's heart suffer. Now that he was seeing clearly again, he finally understood what kind of blasphemy he had committed.

"Concerning this, you can rest assured, my lord. Whatever I've done to your heart, I'm receiving payback a thousandfold now. And you're right, no physical pain can come close to the agony I have to bear every second of the day because I've tortured the love of my life. I've destroyed the one thing most precious to me. Ever since I realized this, every breath I take is pure anguish and life has lost its shine. I've damned myself."

The perfect features of the Angel of Death froze in an angry mask.

"Is that why you're here? Because you're hoping to ease your burden when I forgive you?"

"No. Nobody can take this burden from me. I'm here because I know I've made a grave mistake, and I wanted you to know I'm aware of it and that I regret it deeply."

Now Renaldo was definitely furious. He stared coldly at the kneeling man in front of him. "Fine, you've told me you're sorry. I know what you're feeling. But I don't feel pity for you, Noran, because you've rejected my friendship out of pride. You betrayed me, plagued my heart, and struck at the very core of what we're fighting for. You're no longer the man I once knew, and your new face makes me despise you. From now on you and I will have the same relationship I have with all our mercenaries. You're a warrior in my army and I'll protect you, but that's it. And if you ever dare come close to Casto or Sic again, I'll show you that the pain you're feeling now is nothing compared to what I can do to you! Did I make myself clear?"

"Yes, my lord."

"Then leave now. Get out of my sight!"

Still staring fixedly at the ground so Renaldo wouldn't see his tears, Noran obeyed his god. He had known it wouldn't be easy getting back the Angel of Death's trust, but he had not anticipated such a dismissive reaction. It seemed as if gaining Renaldo's forgiveness would be even harder than he had feared.

When the door closed behind Noran, Renaldo exhaled loudly. A heat wave rolled through the chamber and made the floor-length curtains billow as if they had been caught in a breeze. It had cost all his self-control not to let Noran burn. How could he dare grovel and whine for forgiveness after all this time? Renaldo was seriously wondering what he had seen in the man. But when they had met for the first time, Noran had been a different person. Difficult, yes, but not as inexpiable and filled with hatred as he was now. Arja, that cursed bitch, had turned an open, friendly man looking for love into an introverted monster Renaldo hardly recognized as his friend anymore. Perhaps the Noran from back then would return someday, but until that happened, Renaldo would do everything in his power to keep him away from his heart and Sic.

Just thinking that Noran could trouble Casto with his newfound remorse, Renaldo shuddered. The king had enough sorrows of his own without caring for the emotions of a man who had brought him nothing but hardship.

5. FIRE

As if he had read his thoughts, Casto entered the royal chambers. Smiling happily, Renaldo turned to his lover, who had just taken the diamond off from his forehead. The anger he felt about Noran turned into lust. He imagined how Casto would open the pins on his tunic and let the cloth slide to the ground, caressing his naked skin. To Renaldo's surprise, Casto did exactly this, his hungry gaze trained on his mate. Gloriously naked, he approached Renaldo, stroking his lengthening member with his right hand while his left caressed his abdominal muscles the same way Renaldo used to do. Hypnotized by this alluring spectacle, Renaldo fantasized about what would happen next, how Casto would open his arms in a silent invitation to grab and subdue him. He wanted to hear Casto begging to be taken hard by him. When Renaldo reached for his mate's wrists, Casto parted his sensuous lips imploringly.

"Please, Barbarian. Please—"

The sentence was cut short. Casto's gaze darted through the room as if he had just woken from a bad dream, his fingers trembling. When the mesmerizing blue finally focused on Renaldo, it was tainted in a foreboding black, a sure sign that Casto was only a breath away from exploding.

"Get away from me!" he hissed. "Leave my chambers, right now!"

Confused, Renaldo tried to pull him close. He didn't understand the sudden change in attitude and was inclined to ignore it. "I don't understand, Casto. What's going on?"

"I've just given you an order, Barbarian. Take your hands off me and get out of my sight."

Heat wafted between them. Renaldo hated it when Casto called him "Barbarian" in such a dismissive tone and reacted accordingly. "Watch your tongue, slave. I don't know what your problem is, but I expect you to apologize this instant. Your behavior is unacceptable. What's gotten into you?"

Casto was almost hysterical now. His shoulders were trembling and his entire body was tense, like a snake before striking.

"I don't want to apologize! I want you gone! Leave me alone, now!"

"Calm down, Casto. Since when do you act as if you were the one in command here?"

With cheeks burning from fury, Casto tore away from his husband. The heat in the room had become unbearable, but neither of them registered it.

"Since I've become king. Since I've to deal with all the schemes in this damn city. Since you've made me speak a death sentence I didn't want to impose. I'm the damn king of Ummana, and I'm telling you for the last time: get out!"

Casto's breath was labored, and his hair flew in the heat emanating from his body. His almost black eyes stared at Renaldo, backed by authority gained from centuries of royal dignity. The Angel of Death realized he could either obey his heart's command or break his stubborn neck. After a few moments of heated internal debate, he chose the first.

"Damn it, Casto. The last word on this hasn't been spoken!"

After this open threat, Renaldo dashed out of the room. Casto sank to his knees, exhausted, dumbfounded, and shaken to the core. He couldn't believe what had just happened, refused to assume the Barbarian hadn't realized he had been controlling him. After his talk with Sic, Casto had been determined to face his fear of Renaldo's dominance, and in the beginning, things had gone well. It was always easy for him to submit to his mate in bed.

But then he had suddenly noticed that the lust he felt, the things he was doing, were not directed by his own will. He could feel Renaldo's presence making him dance like a puppet on the strings of his thoughts. And without realizing what he was doing! As if tearing down Casto's last bastion of free will was nothing but a game for the demigod. Sic might have a point, but right at the moment, Casto would have given his right arm not to be in love. He was convinced being alone was far better than being the toy of a man who didn't even know what he was doing.

Shivering, Casto curled himself into a ball on the ground, trying to get over the shock his husband's behavior had inflicted on him.

TREMBLING WITH rage, Renaldo stormed out on the broad balcony that extended into the royal gardens and was laden with lavishly blossoming potted plants, marble statues, and small, intricately sculpted columns. With clenched hands he started cursing in the language of the Ancients, using the most horrible curses he could think of. The heat of his fury was like a wave he sent crushing into the dusk. All he wanted was to destroy something. He wanted—no, he needed—to find an outlet for his rage, or he would go back and do things to his heart he would surely regret later.

How could Casto dare talk to him in such an insolent manner, to defy him so blatantly, after everything they had gone through? It almost seemed as if time had been reversed to when Casto had been a stubborn slave bending to no one and nothing.

A grating sound tore Renaldo from his boiling emotions. A beautiful pot of about one and a half ells in diameter, with a small tree growing inside, burst into shards in front of him. The sight cooled the Angel of Death in an instant. Thinking straight again, he gazed around the balcony and registered with growing horror the damage he had caused. It almost seemed as if a hostile army had raged there.

The pots were all broken, the massive marble statues looked as if they had been repeatedly smashed to the ground, the columns showed deep cracks, and from some of them long, thick splinters had chipped. The plants were all dried up, as if they hadn't gotten any water for months. In an uncontrolled fit of temper, he had destroyed everything fair and alive on the balcony.

"What bug has bitten you?"

Hulda sounded amused when she emerged from the shadows of an alcove. She continued before Renaldo had a chance to answer her. "Let me guess, you had a fight with Casto. I can't imagine what else could manage to rile you up like that."

Still irritated but also a little embarrassed, Renaldo barked at Hulda. "If you already know the answer, why bother asking?"

Completely unfazed by this demonstration of divine rage, Hulda shrugged. "Politeness, I guess. Or the desire to let you taste my superiority. Your choice."

"Just leave me alone, Hulda. I've no time for one of your little games."

"Tsk, tsk, tsk. You really overdid it this time, didn't you? But you're lucky I'm not easily offended." Hulda's eyes shone with malicious glee. "I'm absolutely content witnessing what Noemi is going to do to you once she finds out what you've done to the place."

Again Renaldo started to curse. His sister-in-law loved this balcony, especially the flowers he had just burned. The prospect of the lecture he was going to get for his thoughtless deed did nothing to lift his spirits.

"Don't tell me this was unintentional?" Disbelief resounded in Hulda's voice.

The Angel of Death made a face. "It was. I was angry with Casto and in order not to hurt him, I came here. But I didn't want to go so far."

"It's not really surprising. You and Canubis, you're gaining more power every day. Nevertheless, it would be wonderful if you could learn how to control your powers. If a human had been here, he or she would be dead now, and you probably wouldn't have noticed it."

Contritely Renaldo eyed the destruction he had caused.

"I'd better start tidying up."

"Good idea. Noemi is still with Cassia, but she'll be back soon. It would be better if things looked a little nicer then. Not that it's going to save you, but perhaps she'll feel merciful."

"You could help me." Renaldo tried to sound as pleading as possible. It was a scheme that sometimes was successful. Thoughtfully, the Mother Superior of the Sisters of the Night watched him, then her long lashes fluttered coquettishly.

"I could do that, but it would take the fun out of it. No, you created this mess, and you will set it straight. Perhaps you'll be more careful next time."

Renaldo's eyes narrowed. "Be careful, Hulda. I'm your god, not a little boy."

The killer patted his cheek lovingly. "Somehow you're both to me. And you know I'm right. I always am." She turned away from her god and disappeared between the columns, her hips swinging in a way that made every man's blood boil. Renaldo sent some scorching curses her way, untouched by the allure of her body. Since he had met Casto, he found it easy to withstand temptation even if it came in such perfect guise.

Renaldo started cleaning up the chaos he had caused. It was too late to save the burned plants and the pulverized statues, but he could at least sweep up the stone splinters and the dry earth and take it away. The only good thing about this tedious work was that he could lose himself in thought. Now that his anger had dissipated, he tried to analyze why Casto had transformed from a willing vessel into a hissing, spitting alley cat in less than a dozen heartbeats. As far as he was concerned, everything had been fine. Better than fine, in fact. He had been looking forward to the sex, and he was sure he had shown it to his lover. So why the sudden tantrum?

Renaldo leaned heavily on the broom he was using to clean up. Casto's mood swings were something he had learned to live with by now, and he even prided himself in being able to discern how seriously he had to take them. This one had been grave. When Casto was just angry, Renaldo could soothe him with sex easily. Being rejected meant that the young man was not just angry but also upset and riled up, always a dangerous combination. If he wanted this situation resolved anytime soon, he had to take the first step. Involuntarily Renaldo had to chuckle. Before he'd met Casto, he wouldn't even have contemplated giving in during a fight, let alone apologizing to the other party. His mate had changed him profoundly. Taking a deep breath, he entered the chambers.

Casto was huddled on the floor, his arms slung protectively around his knees. His voice was hoarse.

"I thought I told you to leave me alone?"

Renaldo cursed himself from the bottom of his heart. This was even worse than he had anticipated. Casto was not just angry or upset, he was shaken. And instead of being his support, Renaldo had added to his confusion. Sometimes he seriously wondered whether he would ever be able to read his mate correctly.

"You did. I'm here to apologize to you. I shouldn't have yelled at you like I did. I'm truly sorry."

His capricious, stunning husband looked at him with trembling lips. He was obviously still contemplating whether he should throw another tantrum or accept this peace offering. To Renaldo's relief, he chose the second option.

"I accept your apology. I may have overreacted a little bit."

Glad that things had calmed down so quickly, Renaldo reached out to caress Casto's cheek.

"My own! Thank you. And please, don't get mad at me again, but I'd really like to know what just happened. You don't lose your composure like that for nothing."

A deep crimson crept into Casto's cheeks. He avoided Renaldo's gaze.

"You were in my thoughts, Barbarian. Everything I did before I lost it was your will. I was your puppet."

When Renaldo finally realized what Casto had just told him, he felt a surge of satisfaction followed closely by guilt. He *was* able to control Casto. He had forced him against his will. Gently, he brushed his lover's face. "I'm sorry, Casto. I didn't know I was doing it. I was just thrilled that you seemed to have read my thoughts. Please forgive me."

The young man sighed. "It's okay. It was just too intense. I'm horrified by the idea of belonging to you so completely."

Not showing how much this statement hurt him, Renaldo decided to try a different approach. "Do you trust me?"

The question was loaded. It contained their entire relationship and all the problems they were having. For Casto, trust was a multilayered thing he did not easily bestow and if he did, only partially. Renaldo, on the other hand, viewed trust as a thing that was either given wholly or not at all. These two very different points of view clashed on a regular basis and were responsible for many of their fights. Even now, Casto wasn't willing to submit to his mate's paradigm. Slowly he looked up. Even though there was a certain amount of defiance in his voice, he was clearly still shaken.

"Yes, I do."

The Angel of Death decided to accept what Casto was offering. This was not the time to pressure him even more. "Then get up and close your eyes. I'm going to show you how much you mean to me."

Much to Renaldo's surprise, Casto complied. Renaldo stroked his mate's cheeks with his fingertips. Then he leaned in, gently touching his lips to Casto's eyelids. He travelled farther down, leaving a trail of feathery pecks on Casto's face, and finally settled reverently on his lips. Carefully, Renaldo opened Casto's mouth with his tongue to give him a long, intense kiss. Only when Casto gave up resistance did Renaldo allow his hands to wander farther down, to caress Casto's back and to take away his trousers. The young man groaned, intoxicated by lust, and his member pressed hard against his mate's skilled hands. Renaldo imagined, this time deliberately, how Casto snuggled against him, how his nails left burning traces on his back.

Whimpering, Casto obeyed the thought command, submitting to the demigod's will with only a hint of defiance left. Renaldo picked Casto up, carried him to the bed, and held him down with his weight. His kiss became more demanding, more carnal, while his right hand grabbed Casto's erection imperiously. Helpless and consumed by lust, the young man undulated beneath his lover, begging to be taken. A smile full of love brightened Renaldo's features. He pictured Casto down on his knees, his legs slightly spread and ready to welcome his mate. Again Casto obeyed, shivering as Renaldo applied some oil to ease the way and screaming his consent when Renaldo entered him in one long, powerful thrust.

Renaldo allowed Casto to orgasm once; then he leaned in, his lips close to his moaning mate's ear.

"Do you know why I'm so pleased when you submit to me? Because you're mine alone in these moments. I know then that you're absolutely safe, that nobody can harm you. I have absolute control over you and needn't fear losing you."

He straightened up again. His grip on Casto's hips tightened, and with a few measured strokes, he fanned the flames of lust into a gale. While he was thrusting steadily, he kept on talking as if he were having a philosophical debate with himself.

"I love you so much, I would very much like to bind you to my bed with golden chains. If I weren't sure you'd react with extreme defiance, I'd already have done it. It makes me go crazy, not knowing where you are, dreading what you're doing and what's happening to you. The thought alone of you getting hurt, of somebody laying their hands on you, makes my blood freeze. Every time I allow you to leave my sight is preceded by a long internal struggle, and we both know I don't always win."

Casto whimpered softly, whether in answer to Renaldo's monologue or as a reaction to the sensual assault remaining unclear. Again the Angel of Death formed a picture in his head. This time Casto reacted without hesitation. With a muffled scream, he rested his upper body on the bed. His ass came up invitingly and tightened when the angle changed. Teeth clenched in an effort not to spill immediately, Renaldo started talking again.

"You give me lust I've never experienced before. Kissing you is more intense than any sexual encounter I had before you. Touching you, inhaling your scent, all these things require all the self-control I possess, otherwise I'd subjugate you nonstop. You're a present given to me by fate. You're mine, not because I'm your god, but because I love you so much it gives me physical pain. Nobody will ever love you the way I do, so it's only right for me to mold you the way I like."

Renaldo felt Casto tense at these words, ready to defy him, but he had anticipated it and held on to the young man without mercy, taking him relentlessly, giving him unspeakable pleasure while at the same time subjugating him. Shortly before Casto reached another peak, Renaldo stopped and retreated. Casto made a protesting sound.

"Lie on your back."

Groaning, Casto did as he was told. Renaldo towered over him, sliding slowly back into the heavenly, tight opening. His gaze was lost in the mesmerizing blue of Casto's eyes.

"You already do everything I ask of you in bed. Why is it such a big deal when I no longer convey my will with words?" He thrust hard a few times to lend his words more weight. "You've sworn fealty and obedience to me. And I know you love me. When will you start trusting me as well? What do I have to do to make you understand that I'm neither your father nor a member of the Council? When will you let go and allow me to make you as happy as I am?"

Renaldo thrust two more times before he allowed Casto to come. Crying, Casto averted his gaze, his shoulders trembling. Renaldo pulled him close, his voice gentle again.

"I swear to you, Casto, I won't ever use this power unless I have your explicit permission to do so. I won't do anything that frightens or repels you. You have my word."

Casto's shaking hands touched Renaldo's firm torso. "I'm not afraid of you, Barbarian. I'm afraid of myself. All my life I've had to be wary. The only person I could ever trust was myself. Things have changed, but I have a hard time accepting it. It would be so easy to let everything go, to relinquish control. But what's going to happen to me then? It would be treason to the child who went through hell with the only goal survival no matter the cost. I would give up the boy who gathered the courage to leave the city with his stallion although he didn't know what would become of him. And the man who survived as a mercenary for almost a year? Where will he end up once I allow you to possess me entirely?"

Gently Renaldo kissed Casto's forehead. "Sometimes you're really dumb, my own. They're all here. I've fallen in love with each and every one of them, and none of them is so weak as to be obliterated by me. You'll neither betray nor lose them, I can assure you. They're a part of you, but it's time for you to accept that I'm a part of you as well. I'm not some random stranger you have to keep at a distance."

"I've never seen you as that, Barbarian, I can assure you. But you're so many things to me—my lover, my master, my lord and god. And I'm just a human serving you. Sometimes I just don't know who you are. And I don't like it."

"Casto, my own, my heart. First and foremost, I'm the man who loves you more than anything else in this world. Everything else is incidental. The most important thing is the love I have for you."

Renaldo could see how his words reassured Casto. He embraced him, more in an attempt to soothe than anything else, but again his heart managed to surprise him.

"Then do it. Show me how you want me to be."

"Casto!"

It was the last word Renaldo spoke that night.

"HE REALLY did it! I simply can't believe it! No king has ever dared to go against the leading families in such a blatant manner."

"No king has ever had the backing of the most powerful warriors in the world. Castolus can afford to break with tradition."

Doran, son of Amicia and, since her undignified end, new leader of the Krapati family, made a clucking sound. He was a man in his thirties who had already acquired an ever-growing potbelly and an impressive double chin. He was also a successful merchant and seasoned politician. The shoals of Ummanian politics were nothing new to him, but since the king had let the wolves free, Doran found it difficult to recognize the playing field, especially since it was now drenched in blood. Not that he was in principle against a strategic murder; no, he himself had ordered his share of eliminations and had been the target of assassins as well. That was not the point. What had unsettled him deeply was the open demonstration of barbarian cruelty. It was dangerous to act against somebody who could—and would—change the rules on a whim.

He regarded Silva, the daughter of Nambuno, who had become, just like Doran, head of her family after her father lost his head in such a spectacular manner. She was a few years older than him, with children at the right age to marry. He respected her as a shrewd businesswoman and cold-blooded politician. Of all families in Ummana, the Krapati and Donai had the closest relationship. They did business together so often and had arranged so many lucrative marriages between each other, they almost counted as one family. Silva got up and paced Doran's office with long strides as was her habit when she was going through her options. The hem of her elaborate silken dress whispered on the heavy brocade carpets covering the ground.

"The main question is what the king wants. I can't imagine those barbarians staying here for good. As far as I know, they live in a valley far up in the North. All their life is about war, which they bring to the continent almost every year. I'd be surprised if they'd exchange their strategic fortress for our vulnerable city."

"But what else could they want here? Did Castolus just want to get his revenge? I hardly think so."

Silva cursed. Her language was quite colorful and made Doran blush.

"We simply don't know enough about them, and it's driving me mad! How can we act sensibly when we don't even know their motives?

Regarding the king—I'm afraid we've underestimated him gravely. He must have already plotted his ascent to the throne when he was still in court. There's no other reasonable explanation for his behavior."

"Perhaps it's time to get more deeply acquainted with Anesha. She seems to be surprisingly close to her brother and the barbarians. And she has installed the new members of the Council. The king has accepted her proposal. Knowing her, she's trying to secure her position and broaden her influence. Since Castolus is bound to the barbarian, the continuation of the family lies with her. She's going to use that."

Silva nodded. She had always known that the king's little sister was a dangerous wild card. Although she herself had been very young when Isiris died, she could remember the queen well. Anesha was her spitting image in every respect.

Devious, unrelenting, and intelligent enough to make the best of her assets.

"Anesha is no fool. She knows her best chances lie in an alliance with her brother. Their combined financial power is more than impressive. She's hardly going to help us."

Doran stared musingly out the window over the busy city. Every business transaction, no matter if it took place on the street, in the counting houses, or in the big warehouses, was like a small heartbeat keeping the gigantic trading machine alive and thriving, lending it the dynamic that made Ummana the most powerful city on the continent. Trade was what kept all of them going, and it did not sit well with the views of some barbarian warriors from the North. Executing the Council had caused an earthquake among the citizens, and it was impossible to say how things would turn out in the long run. It was possible that business would thrive because the deadlock paralyzing the executive organs was gone now. But there could as well be a drop since the new situation was so uncertain. No matter how you looked at it, it was time to act.

"As much as I resent it, Anesha is our only option at the moment. Regarding what's happened the past few days, I'd say it's unwise to confront the barbarians directly. They had no qualms killing the entire Council, so a family leader wouldn't pose a problem to them. Our way back in is via Anesha. And who knows," he added weakly, "perhaps we're in for a pleasant surprise."

Silva rolled her eyes. She obviously didn't share his optimism, but neither could she ignore the severity of their situation. The new members of the Council had been handpicked, and most of them came from smaller families and were indebted to Anesha one way or another. Ties to the big families and the guilds were almost nonexistent; there were no common interests, no points of leverage that would allow Silva, Doran, or the other big families to get back into the game—at least not yet. With the unusual new cast, the princess had deftly outmaneuvered them, an affirmation to Silva that her assessment of Anesha had been right. If it was about the preservation and expansion of her power, the princess was absolutely ruthless.

"I will arrange a meeting with Anesha. Just the three of us. There's no need to involve the others just yet."

Doran smiled knowingly.

"I agree. We don't want to wake sleeping dogs."

NEW BEGINNINGS

1. MASTER EXAM

"And how did it go?"

Expectantly Casto and Cassia eyed Sic, who was slinking down the stairs from the house of the guild of smiths with drooping shoulders. He looked exhausted, which didn't come as a surprise after more than eight hours of both theoretical and practical exams. He managed a grimace that could be interpreted as a smile, if the onlooker was feeling generous.

"To be frank, I don't have a clue. The written part was okay, thanks to you."

He bowed to Cassia, who patted his arm reassuringly. She had spent the last two weeks teaching Sic neat handwriting and the right structure of answers in order to impress his auditors right from the start. Even though Sic had learned to read and write, his reading skills were much better than his writing, simply because there had rarely been a need for him to write things down. He was grateful to Cassia for working so hard with him.

"Whether they liked my masterpiece, I can't tell. They made lots of notes and asked me what felt like a thousand questions. After this interrogation, I had to work on a dagger and make a draft for a commissioned work. All the time they pestered me with questions. I was hardly able to concentrate. I'm not used to so much attention."

Tired, Sic sat down on the bench between his friends in front of the guild house. Casto handed him a bottle of wine.

"Drink. I thought you might want something strong."

Sic took the bottle slowly.

"On an empty stomach? I haven't eaten since this morning."

"Could be interesting."

When he glimpsed Sic's sour face, Casto pulled out a linen bag. "Just joking. I was sure they wouldn't feed you, which is why I brought this. Bread, baked by Hulda herself and with her best regards."

Sic grabbed the loaf eagerly. Nothing was better than the taste of the bread Hulda made. Except when you smeared it with butter and honey, but that was bordering on decadence. Cassia watched the two young men questioningly.

"It's bread. What's so special about it?"

Sic didn't bother to answer. Instead he broke off two pieces and gave them to the midwife and Casto.

Cassia took a bite. Her eyes went wide and a grin spread across her face. "Heavenly!"

Sic and Casto nodded knowingly. They both remembered taking the first bite of this special bread. It was like an epiphany, feeling the mild spiciness and pleasant sourness of the dough on your tongue. The sensation was instantly addicting.

Cassia's teeth worked hard, then she reached for the loaf. "I'm pregnant. Hand it over!"

Sighing, Sic obeyed the tiny female in front of him. During the last week, the midwife had become crankier by the minute. According to Noemi, this was a sure sign that she was due soon. It also meant Jago and Sic had to fight for every bit of food against a tiger hell-bent on getting it all and using her condition shamelessly to boss the two men around. He managed to secure himself another piece before his usually charming hostess pressed the loaf to her swollen body like a greedy three-year-old.

"I can get more." Casto was helpfulness personified.

Cassia's eyes lit up. "More is good. I'm starving here."

Before one of them could react to this exaggeration, Jago approached them. He, too, looked tired, since he had been present the entire time while the other masters tested Sic. It was the law that a master who introduced an examinee wasn't allowed to take part but had to be there. Expectantly, the two young men faced him while his wife was still busy devouring the bread.

It had been more difficult to nominate Sic for the exam than Jago had anticipated. Because he wasn't a citizen of Ummana and hadn't been taught by a master from the city, the guild had first wanted him to work under a local master for a year before admitting him to the exam. Only after hours of encouragement and the hint that Sic was a close friend of the king was Jago able to talk his colleagues into granting his protégé a chance. But the mood had been heavy with resistance, since the members of the guild didn't like being forced into something, and certainly not by a king who had appeared out of nowhere and destroyed order in the city. Only a few had backed up Jago, the others had been determined to make the young man fail no matter the cost.

Until Sic had presented his masterpiece.

Even Jago hadn't seen it before, since Sic hadn't wanted him to help. They all had been rendered speechless. The young smith had crafted a belt from pure gold. It was almost one and a half ells long and made of thousands of miniscule eyelets that were interwoven like a cloth, which made the belt as flexible as a silken one. On both ends a single emerald was fitted into the very tip, looking like a dewdrop falling down. The wearer could decide whether to sling the belt twice or thrice around their body and where to close it. It was a masterpiece none of the smiths had ever seen before, let alone created themselves.

Sic had been buried under an avalanche of questions but remained surprisingly calm. Even when he had to work on a dagger and then make a draft under the prying eyes of his examiners, he stayed calm. After he had fulfilled all his tasks, they had sent him outside. Inside the smithy, silence ruled. Finally Aries, the head of the guild, started to talk. He had been strictly opposed to letting Sic take the exam, and Jago was almost sure he would find a way of denying the young man his title. But Aries surprised them all.

"I thank you, Jago, for insisting on taking Sic on as an examinee, although I was against it. I'd have never forgiven you if this gifted young man had been acknowledged by any other guild than ours. He already is an adornment to our craft, and I only hope he'll open shop here in the city to add to the guild's fame."

Applause and approval came from the assembled masters. Aries patted Jago's shoulder.

"You can tell him he has passed."

JAGO BEAMED at Sic with genuine happiness.

"You've passed. Not only passed, but with the highest score an examinee has ever reached. Aries and the others are so excited, they're going to have a banquet for you next week in order to introduce you to the other guilds. Your belt will be exhibited in a special room so everybody can see how unbelievably talented you are. Congratulations!"

Sic was thunderstruck. So many emotions were assaulting him, he did not know which he should give in to. Happiness, relief, joy. But there was also melancholy, because Noran wasn't here to share this moment with him. And anger, because Noran had convinced him he was unworthy and incapable.

Casto hugged him violently, prying him from musings that had no place at such a moment. "Congratulations! I knew it. You're the best! I can't tell you how happy I am for you!"

Sic reciprocated the hug, clinging almost desperately to his friend. Then Jago came, also full of joy. The master punched him hard on the back, which was his special way to show appreciation.

"Move it, you big bear! I want to congratulate Sic as well!"

Cassia had finally managed to get to her feet. Sic leaned down so she could hug him. Her lips graced his cheek in a gentle kiss.

"Best wishes, Sic. You've really earned this."

At the same moment Sic started to answer her, Cassia's face contorted into a pained grimace, and her small hands dug like claws of steel into Sic's nape. Automatically he got a tighter grip on her back, preventing her from falling down.

"Sweetie, what's the matter?" Jago helped his wife, worry clouding his features.

"What do you think, numbnuts? The child is coming!" Cassia hissed, but her tirade was cut short by another contraction. Groaning, she fell onto the bench.

"It's too fast. Our offspring seems to be in a hurry. Get me back home and call for Noemi. And do it now!"

Then she started concentrating on her breathing, as if the chaos her words had invoked wasn't of any significance. Casto took over without hesitation. He turned to the two personal guards who followed him like shadows whenever he left the palace.

"You two, run and get Lady Noemi. Tell her Cassia's time has come. Hurry!"

The men wavered. Renaldo had threatened them with an exceptionally painful death should they lose sight of his lover for even a second. But their god's heart had his own special brand of authority.

"Get going! I'm not alone—there are still the wolves."

At that moment Cassia let out a high-pitched scream and lent Casto's words additional weight. The men started to run. Casto snorted and turned to Sic.

"You'll take care of Jago. Give him some of the wine and get him home in one piece. He looks as if he's about to keel over any minute. I'll look after Cassia."

While Casto lifted up the tiny, groaning woman, Sic grabbed his mentor's arm.

"Come with me, Jago. We have to get you home so you can welcome your baby."

The big man stared into nothing. It looked like he had just received a deafening blow.

"She's in pain. My sweet one is suffering."

"Yes, I know. But Cassia is strong. She's going to pull through. She needs you now. Come!"

Jago shook his head like a cat that had gotten wet. A determined line appeared around his mouth. He followed Casto with long strides through the streets of Ummana. Luckily the houses of the guilds were not far from the palace. When they reached Jago's home, Noemi was already there, accompanied by Renaldo himself. The snake witch only glanced briefly at Cassia, then took over.

"Casto, carry her to the sleeping chamber. Renaldo, make it warm. We don't want the baby to freeze."

She regarded Jago. "Do you want to come?"

The master stared at his groaning, whimpering wife.

Cassia still had enough energy to roll her eyes derisively. "He won't be of any help, Noemi. And we already talked about it. I don't want him there, in case things get—complicated."

The snake witch nodded. "Sic, take care of Jago. I'll call when we're done. Casto, I need clean towels and warm water. And some cushions. Renaldo, warmer, please."

Unquestioningly the men followed Noemi's instructions. Sic brought Jago to the garden and offered him the wine. Jago took a deep pull from the bottle.

"I'm sorry your big moment ended so abruptly."

"Are you kidding? Firstly, I didn't know how to react anyway and secondly, what could be better than Cassia giving birth now?" Sic hesitated for a moment. "I really like you a lot. I'll never be able to thank you and your wife for making me part of your family."

Jago placed a hand on Sic's shoulder. "It's fine. We like you a lot as well. For Cassia you're the little brother she never had, and I'm just glad I found a new friend."

He took another pull. "This wine is really good. And heady. I don't want to welcome my child drunk. Please take care of me, yes?"

"Of course. That's what friends are for."

IN THE sleeping chamber, Cassia clung screaming to Renaldo, her entire body as tense as a bowstring. Calmly Noemi worked the different spots on the midwife's skin that would give her at least some release.

"The contractions are coming very fast. That's good, because things are progressing faster, but it's also more tiring. You're doing well, Cassia. Your cervix has already opened up a good deal."

The midwife made a grunting noise. "I only hope this monster fits through my pelvis, otherwise all the trouble was for nothing."

"We talked about this. Everything's going to be fine, I promise." Noemi grinned impishly. "You're having your baby in the presence of a god. What can go wrong?"

"To be honest, I prefer the presence of a snake witch over that of a god of war. Nothing personal, Lord Renaldo."

"Don't worry. I do feel a little diminished, but if I were in your place, I'd prefer Noemi as well."

He made a face when Cassia's fingers dug into his arm again.

"How long is this going to take, Noemi?"

The witch looked at him reproachfully. "Get your act together. You're a god of war, not a wimp. If Cassia can bear the labor pain, you should be able to deal with a few blue spots on your arm."

Then she concentrated on her patient again. Casto cooled Cassia's heated face with a wet cloth.

"You're doing great. It won't take much longer, I'm sure."

The midwife shot him a crooked smile. "This is your first birth, isn't it?"

Since Casto had become a regular guest in her home, she had gotten used to leaving out the polite talk. The beautiful young man with the intense blue eyes smiled briefly.

"Is it that obvious?"

"No, I was just guessing. You're doing well—for a king."

A grin spread over Casto's entire face and made him look like a careless boy, a rare and therefore precious sight. Cassia didn't know much about the years Casto had spent far away from Ummana, but like all citizens of the Twin Cities did, she suspected something about what he had endured here. It was akin to wonder that he had survived, and an even greater wonder that he hadn't turned into a killer without any emotions. She could understand why Casto had bound himself to the Angel of Death, and it had nothing to do with a wish for revenge or a longing for power.

Lord Renaldo was like a tower of strength, a bastion against which no attack could be led. He and his brother might seem cold and cruel, but they were also steady, something a lost child like Casto would deem comforting.

A new contraction overwhelmed her and buried all thoughts under a wave of pain. Cassia could feel Noemi's cool hands on her belly. It was soothing to know the snake witch was there. The redhead's voice cut through the agony.

"I'm afraid our worries prove to be true. Your child is too big, Cassia. We'll have to deliver it in a different way. I'm getting everything ready."

Cassia nodded weakly. Considering the difference in height between her and Jago, it would have been a miracle if the child could be born the normal way. She had slit open the bellies of expectant mothers before, but it was never nice. There was no sedative strong enough to numb the mother effectively and at the same time keep the baby unharmed. Getting your belly sliced open was not on Cassia's list of enjoyable things to try, but it was a reliable method to save both the mother and the child.

She watched intently as Noemi prepared everything for the operation. First she gave Cassia a potion that stopped the contractions. While they waited for the herbs to work, the witch turned to Renaldo. She had a sharp scalpel in her hands.

"It has to be clean."

The god nodded. He concentrated on the steel, and a burst of heat made her sweaty hair fly up. Fascinated, the midwife watched as the steel started to glow an angry red. Satisfied, Noemi put the scalpel in a clean bowl and gave Casto some instructions.

"It's going to be pretty bloody. I want you to hand me exactly what I'm saying, understood? And keep the bucket ready."

Casto and Renaldo nodded. Both men seemed to have lost their speech when confronted with the severity of the situation. Still, they were doing remarkably well. Cassia had often witnessed how men who were oozing testosterone made fools of themselves as soon as blood was introduced in a sickbed or during a birth. But the king and his mate kept their composure. Noemi looked at each of them.

"Are you ready?"

Then her bloody work began.

Out in the garden, Sic and Jago heard Cassia screeching like a demon from the other world. Jago was already up, wanting to rush to his wife's side, but Sic held him back.

"Stay. They're going to get us when everything is over. Believe me, you don't want to disturb Noemi during her work."

Jago stared at his friend with beady eyes. "But she's in pain."

"I assure you, Cassia is in the best hands. Noemi is a very experienced healer and a snake witch. Your wife and child are safe with her."

Frustrated, Jago sank to the ground. "I hate it. Just sitting there, unable to do anything! I'm so useless! I wish I could be in Cassia's place."

"I know, I know. And Cassia would probably agree. But it's her task to have your baby safely and yours to protect it once it's here."

Soothingly, Sic rubbed the master's shoulders and back. He couldn't help but feel regret, for he would never be loved like Cassia was worshipped by Jago. Or Casto by Renaldo. Having somebody who was willing to face the greatest agony, even death, to protect what was dearest to them—it had to be wonderful to invoke such feelings.

He kept on whispering encouraging words into Jago's ear while they were waiting for the night to end. Cassia's wails suddenly stopped, and they heard another kind of scream, the angry, always slightly indignant mewling of a newborn.

Sic shoved Jago. "Seems to me like you're a father now."

A blissful grin spread on the smith's face. Only moments later, Casto and Renaldo entered the garden. Renaldo nodded at the two men.

"You can see them now."

Jago was gone in an instant, but Sic fell back. Casto hugged him briefly.

"Everything's fine. They're both well."

"I'm so glad! And relieved. How bad was it?"

Casto's features twisted. "Let me say it like this. I thanked the Mothers more than once that I'm not a woman. Having a child is no task for cowards."

"I agree with you."

Renaldo had approached the two young men. Sic bowed respectfully. "My lord."

Renaldo grabbed his arms. "Casto has told me congratulations are in order. You're a master now. I'm hardly surprised, talented as you are. As soon as you have some time, I'll have a few commissions to make."

"I thank you, my lord. You're very kind."

The Angel of Death smiled, and Sic felt as if the sun was rising.

"I think you should go in now. Cassia has been very clear about that."

After bowing again, Sic got on his way.

Renaldo watched him musingly. "He's still afraid of me."

"What did you expect, Barbarian? You threatened to kill him should he challenge your wrath again."

"I admit I was kind of drastic, but at the time it was appropriate. I guess I'll have to be patient."

The Angel of Death turned toward Casto. "Which leads us directly to you. I haven't given you those guards for the sheer fun of it. They're not your personal messengers. How dare you send them away just like that?"

"Cassia was in pain. Somebody had to get Noemi."

"You could have sent just one of them. Don't think I haven't noticed."

Casto lowered his gaze. It had been foolish to think he could deceive the Angel of Death with such a halfhearted argument.

"The wolves were still there," he murmured defiantly.

Strong hands grabbed his wrists and heat ruffled Casto's hair in an angry reprimand, but Renaldo's voice was surprisingly gentle.

"I understand that you feel trapped, but we agreed this is for the best. I don't have to worry constantly, and you can still move around. But if I can't trust you, it doesn't work."

Slowly Casto looked up again, carefully rearranging his features into an expressionless mask. He hated it when Renaldo was so obviously right.

"I'm sorry, Barbarian. It was stupid of me. I promise to keep our agreement from now on."

The gray eyes lit up triumphantly. Renaldo pulled his heart close with a fierce motion and kissed him hard.

"Then I'm at ease. Still, I won't let you get away with it so easily. You're coming with me now, and then we'll have a long talk about obedience to your lord and master."

Casto groaned in protest, and the Angel of Death grinned broadly. Teasing Casto was one of his favorite pastimes, although it was akin to riding the proverbial tiger.

"Really? It's late—or early, depending on how you see it. And the night wasn't exactly pleasant. I promise to be good, really! If only you'd let me sleep."

"Mmmmh. There might be a chance to convince me, but you're going to need a strong argument in your favor."

At these words, Casto's body language changed in subtle ways. His standing leg kinked slightly at the hip, his eyes clouded over into the deep, dark blue that always betrayed his lust, and his lips opened wide enough to show his white teeth. Nervously his tongue darted across the soft skin on his lips.

"Shall I convince you right here?"

"No, let's get into our chambers. The sun's rising, and I don't plan on sharing what you're offering me with anybody."

With laughter spilling from his mouth, Casto took Renaldo's hand, and together they left the garden.

In front of Cassia's sleeping chamber, Noemi greeted the flustered Sic.

"Calm down. She and her daughter are fine. Come on now, you can enter."

She gave him a friendly push toward the door before she gathered her things and left. When Sic stepped through the door, Cassia and Jago beamed at him from the bed. The master had sat down next to his small wife. His heavily muscled arm was slung around Cassia's shoulders, and his gaze was resting, full of love, on the tiny bundle in her arms. Slowly Sic approached. He felt like an intruder on this peaceful scene.

Cassia must have sensed his hesitation because her brow furrowed. "Don't even think about it, Sic. You're a part of this family, and I want you to welcome our latest addition."

She held out the bundle to him. Trembling, Sic took the baby in his arms. The golden eyes of the little girl glared at him with such intensity, he immediately fell in love. A broad grin split his lips while hot and cold shudders ran down his spine.

"Hello, little lady. I'm Sic, your uncle. I promise, I'm going to take good care of you."

"Her name's Heljia." Jago's voice was feeble; he was obviously still overwhelmed.

"Heljia. What a beautiful name for a beautiful young lady. I've got a present for you, Heljia, and I hope you like it."

Sic handed the baby back to Cassia before he took out the small box he had filled only a few days before. He opened the lid, unfolded the silken cloth protecting the contents, and took out the pendant. In the rays of the rising sun, the diamond sparkled like a star. Before Sic could place his gift around Heljia's neck, Jago reached for it. He held the jewelry against the light and examined it closely. Sic had taken a blue diamond the size of an almond and put it in a frame of tiny golden blossoms that narrowed to a loop through which a small golden chain with a clasp made of blue steel was threaded. The work was so delicate, it was as if a spider's thin webs had acted as the model for it.

"It's magnificent!" Jago eyed Sic. "And way too valuable! The material alone, not to mention the time you spent working on it…. We can't accept this. You could get a fortune for this in the city."

Sic shook his head vigorously. "It's my present for Heljia. I made it for her alone. I could never sell this to anyone. Concerning the material— Casto says you should see it as a thank-you for making me so happy." He grinned broadly. "Of course, he's going to bring other presents as well, but we agreed this one should be her first."

Cassia touched the work reverently. "You know you owe us nothing?" She sounded suspicious.

"Yes, I know. You're simply two good-hearted people. Still Casto, Lord Renaldo, and I think your kindness should be rewarded. May I give her the pendant?"

Jago smiled. "Of course."

Sic leaned forward to put the necklace on Heljia, and Cassia suddenly shot him a scorching look.

"How did you know I was going to have a girl?"

Sic averted his gaze guiltily. "It could be that Noemi might have mentioned something like that." He glanced at the couple, but surprisingly the midwife was grinning broadly.

"And you didn't say a word!"

"Lady Noemi threatened the living daylights out of me should I make even one peep. She can be very persuasive."

"The sweet doll! I'm so glad she was there."

Unconsciously Cassia touched her belly, which had been healed by the snake witch after she had gotten Heljia out. Unlike her own patients, she would not have to deal with the consequences of such a difficult delivery. Her body was as unmarred as before the pregnancy.

"This would have been very uncomfortable if she hadn't helped me."

Jago kissed his wife, full of love. "You should get some sleep, my sweet one. Sic and I are going to take care of everything."

Cassia yawned. "You're okay?"

"Of course. We're big boys."

Mother and child were fast asleep before the two men had reached the door.

2. CELEBRATIONS

"Sɪᴄ, I'ᴍ angered!"

Startled, the young smith looked up from his work. The Angel of Death was towering over him with glinting eyes. The smithy had fallen silent, and the fellows and apprentices stared in mute horror at the enraged warrior. Renaldo's presence alone was awe-inspiring, and they all had heard rumors about what he was capable of when he got carried away.

To soothe the demigod, Sic knelt, his gaze demurely on the ground. "My lord, whatever I've done, I'm truly sorry. Please forgive me."

"It's not that easy!" Renaldo hissed like an angry cat. "For three days I've been fighting with Casto, and it's all your fault!"

Frantically Sic searched his memory for what he had done to incur Renaldo's wrath, but he couldn't think of anything. His god kept on scolding him in a more and more threatening manner.

"You've invited him to your banquet, but he flatly refuses to go there with his personal guard. He claims it's your big moment, and he doesn't want to ruin it. There's no way I'll allow him to go into town without protection. This is your fault alone, and I expect you to talk some sense into him, understood?"

Sic shuddered when he realized how bad the problem was. He had invited Casto as a friend without thinking twice about the consequences. "If he doesn't listen to you, why should he do what I say? Master, you know what Casto is like. If he's gotten it into his head to go without his personal guard, there's nothing I can do about it."

An angry growl resounded, accompanied by a gust of hot air that swept through the smithy like a miniature desert storm.

"Then I'm sorry. He won't take part in your feast."

Sic swallowed hard. He didn't want to imagine the battle that would ensue when Renaldo told his short-tempered husband his decision. And somehow Sic had gotten between the lines. He started thinking fast and finally came up with a suggestion that he hoped Lord Renaldo wouldn't deny right away.

"What if you accompanied him, Master? I'm sure he can't say anything against that."

"I've already pondered this idea as well, but I'm not invited."

The Angel of Death sounded insulted. Whimpering, Sic pressed his forehead to the ground. His stomach felt like it was frozen. He had never thought his god might want to take part in something as trivial as the banquet.

"Please forgive me, my lord. I didn't dare invite you. I didn't think you'd waste your precious time on something as unimportant as that. I'm truly sorry!"

"Damn it, Sic." The Angel of Death picked the young master up, and his gray eyes bored into the green-blue gaze of the smith. "Haven't I told you more than once you no longer have to fear me? You're a free man, member of the Pack and, most importantly, you're Casto's best friend. Of course I wish to be there when you're officially introduced and recognized as a master. It's probably the most important day in your life!"

Shaken, Sic lowered his gaze. "I'm sorry, my lord. It would be my honor if you'd come. I had wished for it but didn't dare to expect it."

"You idiot!" Renaldo's voice had gotten a lot gentler. One of the good things about the Angel of Death was that his anger was as quickly gone as it brewed.

"Promise me in the future you'll ponder less and come straight to me if something bothers you. If I deem your behavior recusant, I'll tell you so without punishing you. I swear. I'm your god, Sic. You can trust me."

"I know, my lord. But I haven't gotten used to it yet. The last time you held me like that, I was in pain for the rest of the day."

Renaldo let go of Sic as if he had burned himself. There was a hint of regret in his voice.

"We've talked about that as well, Sic. I'm not going to hurt you again. After all, you're a free man. You don't have to fear my hand anymore."

A shy smile stole onto Sic's features. "Then you'll come the day after tomorrow?"

"Of course. If Casto and I have made up by then."

Made bold by the now conciliatory mood, Sic decided to become a little more personal.

"I'm sure your heart is going to forgive you. Casto hates it when you're fighting."

"That's news to me. Until now I had the impression he loves to oppose me." The Angel of Death's eyes glittered with mockery. He winked at Sic and left the smithy as abruptly as he had entered it.

A sigh of relief escaped the assembled smiths. Igo was the first to break the stunned silence.

"I don't know about you, but I almost wet my pants when the Angel of Death came barging in. How you could stay so calm is a mystery to me!"

Sic grinned sheepishly. "That was just show. Inwardly I was frozen by fear. Lord Renaldo is a just but also very strict man. Displeasing him is always a bad idea."

"You don't have to tell me that. He's scary. When he says he's fighting with the king, he means it as a joke, doesn't he? Because I can't imagine anybody even thinking of defying him."

"Oh, the king does. A lot. He's not afraid of Lord Renaldo, something I've always admired. Then again, Casto is generally not afraid of anything. He's a very brave man."

Genuine admiration colored Sic's voice. He would never understand how Casto could so easily oppose a man who was feared throughout the continent.

"Well, he's not married to Cassia. Compared to her, even Lord Renaldo seems harmless." The mocking voice came from the fountain. Sic and the other smiths welcomed the newcomer, Janos, who had just returned from the city, with laughter. Sic shook the hand Janos offered him.

"Cassia is a wonderful person. It's not her fault Jago has fallen hopelessly in love with Heljia."

Again the air was filled with good-humored laughter. Since his daughter was born, the master smith hadn't come to work. He was too busy admiring Heljia while she was breathing. During his absence, Sic was officially responsible for everything, since he was now a master as well. But in reality Janos and Igo had taken over handling the daily affairs, because Sic was simply too inexperienced. The friendly camaraderie the fellows and apprentices were offering him was as new to Sic as the fact that nobody here was jealous of his talent. On the contrary, his new friends were proud of calling him master. It was an honesty he enjoyed deeply.

FROM THE shadows in an alcove, Noran looked down on the happy group at the fountain. His features twisted in pain when one of the young men slung an arm around Sic and said something that caused them all to guffaw loudly.

"I've never seen him laugh like that. So free and careless."

Hulda's hand came to rest on Noran's shoulder. "In the Valley he didn't have any reason to be careless."

"He looks so young. When I think of what I did to him…."

"Shh. I thought we agreed that you stop having such thoughts. Yes, you made a major mess and yes, you're going to pay for it, but it's important to look forward. Something like that must never happen again."

Noran sighed. "I know, Hulda. I just want him back so badly."

"Of course you do. But he's going to need time. This is perfect for him—it's normalcy. Sic must process everything that's happened to him before you can hope to ask his forgiveness. It'll take time, and perhaps it's never going to happen."

In desperate silence, Noran watched as two richly dressed merchants from the city approached the group. They addressed Sic directly and from his former slave's body language, Noran was able to deduce that he found the men's attention troubling. But before he could decide whether he should help Sic, two of the fellows had already taken over. One of them led the merchants to the room that served as an office-cum–warehouse, the other one took Sic aside and started talking to him in an urgent manner. The other smiths went back to work, and soon the regular blows of steel meeting steel filled the air again. With furrowed brows Noran watched as Sic reluctantly advanced on the visitors.

"What does this mean?"

Hulda beamed with pride.

"Sic is very popular. The guild has been exhibiting his master piece for three days now and since then, everybody wants him to make something for them. He's already a rich man, and as soon as his master title is official, he'll make a fortune. You have to give it to the Ummanians, they do have an eye for exceptional talent and nurture it accordingly. Pieces with the seal of Sic are almost unaffordable down in the city."

Noran felt pride swelling his chest. This, at least, was one positive thing about the way he had treated his slave. Sic had perfected his talent. It had been right to keep him under his thumb, to force him to work on himself all the time. Thanks to his strictness, a prodigy had become a master without an equal.

"Don't you think he could have become as good if you hadn't made him feel worthless?"

Hulda's voice was soft, with a hint of challenge. How she had been able to guess his thoughts yet again, Noran didn't want to know. He had gotten used to how Hulda could see through him and almost everybody else as if they were made of glass.

"I honestly don't know. I only know it worked quite well. Look at him, a master! I'm so proud of him!"

"And with good reason. But I still think you could have led him to success on a different route as well. Everything he ever accomplished in his life was to please you. Who knows, if you had encouraged him now and then, he might have gotten even better."

Noran threw Hulda a pained glance. "I thought I shouldn't be pondering the past anymore?"

Hulda chuckled warmly, thus taking the sharpness off her words. "You shouldn't. Just a thought, nothing more. Let's go."

With a last, longing glance at his love, Noran followed Hulda back to the royal wing.

"Well, to what do I owe the honor of this splendid meal?"

Anesha leaned back in her elaborate seat, her brows arched in mock question and the spoon with the last bite of the truly delicious dessert still in her hand. Doran and Silva exchanged a labored glance. They were aware the princess was playing with them, but the way things were at the moment, they had to put up with it.

"We had hoped to discuss the new situation at court, Princess. As you can imagine, we are a little concerned about the latest developments."

Silva had phrased her cause with utter politeness, yet hadn't managed to banish the irritation from her voice. Anesha treated her hosts to a beatific smile. From her point of view, the evening couldn't have gone any better.

"You're trying to hint at the restaffing of the Council, I presume?"

"Among other things."

Gracefully, Doran poured some more of the truly amazing wine into the princess's cup.

"It's no secret how unhappy we are about the new members. We don't deem it wise to hand over such difficult posts to the proxies of comparatively weak families."

Anesha's brows quivered in mockery.

"I can understand your worries. They mainly stem from the fact that your own influence is drastically decreasing. What is it, Doran? Are you afraid times could change?"

Silva was prepared with an angry retort, but the princess stopped her with a raised hand.

"I apologize for my bluntness. It wasn't very polite of me. My suggestion is we refrain from our usual tactics and talk openly. I know it's not the Ummanian way of doing things, but my brother and his companions have gotten under my skin. So what do you want?"

Again Silva and Doran exchanged a long glance. They waited with their response long enough to make Anesha edgy.

"Since you seem to have lost your speech, I'm going to tell you what you want. You need information about the king and his entourage to get back into the game. You're too afraid to confront Castolus directly—a wise decision, by the way—and therefore hope to get enough material from me to at least find a point of leverage. In addition, you want to know what my brother's planning for the future and how you can get the most out of it."

Silence ensued once more. Finally Silva broke it.

"And? What does this king, who appeared out of thin air, plan?"

A condescending smiled highlighted Anesha's gorgeous face. "Let me phrase it like this: if you decide to follow me, your chances of meddling once again in the big decisions in the near future will increase. My brother trusts me, a dangerous habit he seems to have caught while living with those barbarians. And I don't plan on passing on such a wonderful present."

Silva's heart started beating excitedly. As she had guessed, there was a way back to the top, and it would lead through Anesha. She was still angry about how the princess had used them, but she also knew the young woman would become a strong, shrewd queen capable of leading Ummana to new heights. With a smile that could be almost described as friendly, she toasted the future queen.

"I'm looking forward to working with you, my lady."

Nervously Doran held up his cup as well to join the two females, who were assessing each other like a pair of enraged king cobras, in their toast. Nobody had to spell out for him that Anesha was planning to snatch the throne from her brother, but considering the alternatives, he was willing to follow Isiris's daughter. They were playing with fire, especially since the barbarians were such serious opponents. Nevertheless, things couldn't stay the way they were. It was a risk, but the profit was simply too alluring.

Anesha leaned back in her chair triumphantly. If things kept on progressing like this, she would soon be the youngest queen on the throne of Ummana. And then…. She closed her eyes and called herself to order. First things first; her victory was only a few hands away from her.

WITH HIS eyes glittering happily, Daran wandered through the streets and alleyways of the Twin Cities, peeked into the shop windows, and enjoyed being part of this pulsating, vibrant bustle. After long, heated discussions with endless to-ing and fro-ing, the desert brothers had finally allowed him to explore Ummana on his own.

Of course, he had had to listen to an endless litany of orders and advice, but in the end, Aegid and Kalad had reluctantly let him go. Daran knew how hard it was for the two to have him out of their sight, and he was grateful to them for granting him this small piece of freedom. Even though the royal wing was spacious and offered countless diversions, it still was like a prison if you weren't allowed to leave it. Daran had held back as long as possible, especially after the assault on Lord Noran and Sic's noble sacrifice, but during the last days he had started to develop serious cabin fever. He had even become envious of Sic, a feeling he had suppressed with all his might, because if anybody had earned happiness, it was the young smith. His masters had sensed his inner turmoil, and since they were rarely able to deny him anything, he was finally allowed to go out into the city.

Not surprisingly, he had orders to stay on the main streets at all times and was strictly forbidden to even get close to any shady business, but that didn't faze him. He was just ecstatic to escape the chambers and glad to be able to prowl the streets of a real city again. Daran loved the Valley from the bottom of his heart, but compared to Ummana it was nothing but a tiny hut at the end of the world and devoid of all civilization.

Humming contently, he let himself drift with the flow of people, musing whether he should get his masters a present as a thank-you. At noon he visited one of the small inns that were common here and ordered some cold tea to refresh himself. He enjoyed trying all the different flavors of the refreshing beverage offered in the city. Just when he was contemplating whether he should get a second cup, a middle-aged woman with average build and short-cropped hair sat down at his table. She was dressed unobtrusively, neither poorly nor richly. Her light tunic was a washed-out blue, her sandals were made from leather, and the straps looked worn. Daran was slightly irritated because she had sat down without asking his permission first, but he decided to stay polite for the time being.

Now she smiled at him, a gesture meant to brighten the mood yet resulting in the opposite. Daran knew when somebody wanted to get the better of him, and her smile was restricted to the lips only without reaching the eyes. He was gesturing for the waiter so he could pay, when the stranger held him back with a gesture.

"Please, stay a moment, Daran. We have a lot to discuss."

Daran froze. "How do you know my name?"

The female chuckled in a condescending manner. "I trade information. It's my job to know as much as possible, even about the favorite toy of the lords Aegid and Kalad. My name's Asnari, by the way."

Daran tried desperately to keep his features neutral while going through his options. This situation was bad, and if he stayed any longer, he would get into serious trouble with Kalad and Aegid. On the other hand, there was definitely a reason this woman had approached him, and if he found out what it was all about, it would surely benefit his masters. Daran decided to stay and listen to Asnari's request.

"And what does a woman who deals in information want from a simple slave?"

Now the spy was beaming as if he had just shown an impressive trick.

"This city offers endless opportunities, even to a simple slave. If he acts with determination, he can quickly become a free man. A rich, free man."

Daran realized this sentence was the bait, and he wondered how stupid Asnari thought he was. He deduced from her body language that she had labeled him imbecile, something he could use to his advantage. He reciprocated her smile and tried to look as foolish as possible.

"I can be very determined, if I want to."

Asnari patted his hand like he was a dog that had obeyed a complicated command. "I thought so. And it's nothing bad I'm asking of you. My contractors are very powerful here in the city, and the new situation has made them—worried. They'd very much like to know what kind of person the king has become and what his plans for the future are."

"And if I tell you about it, you'll pay me?"

Greed colored Daran's voice and made Asnari nod with satisfaction.

"Yes. And I pay very well. Soon you'll be a rich slave."

"I don't know. I don't think my masters would be happy if I talked to you."

"They don't have to know. And it's not like I'm asking you to tell me secrets. I just want to know harmless things, like who calls the shots in your group besides Lord Canubis, and the structure of your hierarchy. That's hardly a secret."

Daran laughed with relief. "No, it's not. I can tell you everything about it. And you'll really pay for this?"

"Yes, you'll get paid. Gold to buy you pretty things." Asnari watched as her last words slowly sank into the simpleton's mind. She was ecstatic. The first attempt at recruiting had gone as smoothly as she wanted. Granted, Daran was an easy target. He was, of course, a sight for sore eyes, and she could imagine he had other qualities that made him interesting to his owners, but his sharp mind surely wasn't part of it. It did make her work a lot easier, and strictly speaking, a slave with his looks didn't have to be intelligent as well. Now the stunning yet witless features started to beam.

"Today I've seen many things I'd like, but they're expensive."

A greedy simpleton, the perfect mixture. Asnari swiped out her purse and counted five gold pieces into Daran's hand.

"With this you should be able to buy yourself a little something. Next time we meet, I'll have some questions for you, and if the answers satisfy me, you'll get more."

The elegant fingers closed hastily over the coins. "I can do with this whatever I want?"

"Of course. Tomorrow at the same time, we'll meet here. I'll be waiting at this table. Then we can talk."

"You're very friendly. So much gold! I have to go and get the pretty pin I saw before."

"Do that. I'll see you tomorrow! And don't worry about the tea. I'm buying."

A consenting nod, then the slave disappeared in the crowd. Asnari leaned back. Her client was going to be thrilled.

WHEN DARAN returned late that afternoon, his masters were already impatiently waiting for him. Kalad grabbed his arm before he had entered the room completely and pressed him against the wall.

"Do you have any idea how late it's gotten, slave? We may have given you permission to move around freely in the city, but I can't remember releasing you from your duties to us."

Daran's hands rested on Kalad's arms. He was glad to be back with his owners.

"I know, Master. And I didn't plan on staying so long, but something has happened."

Instantly the desert brothers' anger turned to worry. Kalad pulled Daran close while Aegid stroked his back.

"What's the matter, Daran? Are you hurt?"

"No, Master, I'm fine. But I had to make a decision, and I hope I didn't do anything wrong."

"Spill."

Kalad was tense. Daran leaned into Aegid's touch and started to report.

"I was approached by a woman named Asnari today. She wanted to recruit me as a spy and has offered lots of gold for information about all of you."

Kalad's face hardened, and Aegid's hands froze on their slave's back.

"What? I do hope you have turned her down! Anyway, this was your last venture into the city."

Daran lowered his gaze. "I accepted her offer."

Aegid's hold on him was now painful, and Kalad's fingers were twitching. He was only moments from beating his slave.

"First I wanted to turn her down, but then I remembered something Lord Casto said. That information is vital in Ummana. I thought this was too perfect a chance. I know I've no right to make such a decision on my own, but I was afraid she would get suspicious if I asked for a respite. She thinks I'm a spoiled, stupid lapdog she can manipulate as she pleases. That's good, isn't it?"

Insecure, Daran looked at the faces of his masters, who stared back at him as if they were seeing him for the first time. It was Aegid who broke the silence.

"Sometimes I wonder how we deserve you." He stared into thin air for a moment, then he sighed. "Casto needs to know this. We better go."

Kalad, too, sighed. "You're right. Let's go."

Together they entered the chambers the Angel of Death and his mate were occupying. After Kalad retold in short sentences what Daran had experienced, Casto jumped up, laughing happily, and hugged the thief.

"Daran, you're a genius! Good job! We won't be getting such a perfect opportunity anytime soon. You don't happen to know who the client is, do you?"

Daran flinched. He knew he was digging his own grave now.

"The client is Lady Vespia, the diplomat from Medelina. At least, that's what I think."

"And how do you know this?" Aegid glared at Daran in open threat.

"Because I followed Asnari after she recruited me."

"You stupid idiot!"

"My hero!"

Both exclamations came at the same time, although Daran didn't care much about Casto's approval. The only thing important to him was the fury his masters were emanating now. He knew he was facing some deep trouble this evening. Before Kalad could start scolding him, Casto slung his arms around the thief for the second time.

"Should you ever get tired of these two, you're always welcome to come to me, you gift from the Mothers."

"Ahem." Renaldo cleared his throat pointedly. Casto let go of Daran immediately.

"Never mind. Good job, Daran. When are you meeting her again?"

"Tomorrow."

"Then we don't have much time left. I'm going to discuss this with Renaldo and then tell you what you're going to feed Asnari."

The king turned to Kalad and Aegid.

"I know you're angry with him, but from where I stand, he did nothing wrong. Quite the contrary, in fact. If we're lucky, this is enough leverage to get our plans done. So please be lenient."

Aegid's face was grim. "We'll see how far our mercy reaches."

Daran shuddered but didn't protest when the desert brothers led him back to their chambers. As soon as they were inside, Aegid pushed him down on one of the lounges.

"What were you thinking, you idiot? Do you have the slightest idea how dangerous this is?"

"I know."

Daran looked down, his voice shaking. He was already regretting that he had accepted Asnari's offer. Now it was too late to change anything about it. Desperately he tried to convey to his masters the reason for his actions.

"I wanted to help. After everything that has happened, I feel so useless, and I don't want to be a mere toy, kept for its good looks. You're the best thing that's ever happened to me. Without you I'd be either dead or living a failed existence without any hope. I wish so badly to show you my gratitude, and when this woman approached me, I realized this was my chance and took it. I'm really sorry. I know I've disappointed you."

The brothers embraced him.

"You haven't disappointed us, Daran. Surely not. But we don't like the thought of you taking such a risk. Strictly speaking, this is not your fight, little thief, but ours. It's touching that you feel responsible, but it also increases the pressure on us. After all, you are in our care and we should be looking after you, not the other way round."

Aegid had spoken very calmly; still, it was obvious how hard it was for him to hold back. Insecure, Daran kissed his owners' hands. He could feel their tension, their anxiety and anger. Sometimes it spooked him how well he knew the desert brothers by now, how deeply they had gotten under his skin. Without them, he was sure, he would be nothing. Kalad had started to open the pins on his tunic. His hands glided gently over Daran's naked skin, leaving traces of fire that made his blood boil. The desert warrior pressed his lips to the thief's ear.

"Since you'll be pretty busy tomorrow, we can't punish you the way we'd want, but view what is happening now as a taste of the things to come after your mission. And don't even hope we'll listen to your pleas for mercy."

Daran groaned. Aegid had started to touch him as well, and his body was trembling in anticipation of all the deliciously agonizing things to come.

"I won't beg, Master. I know I deserve punishment."

"Good for you, slave."

"Sic, it was magnificent! A very nice banquet."

Casto hugged his friend endearingly. The new master patted the king's back with a tipsy smile.

"It wasn't my doing. Who'd have thought the guild is so good at celebrating? Although I suspect part of their troubles was because of your presence. And yours, of course, Lord Renaldo."

The Angel of Death beamed. "Somehow people always try to please me. A nice side effect to being a god. I can only recommend it."

Casto withdrew from his friend's embrace. "Arrogant as always. Your divine nature, dear husband mine, is, just like your beauty, a product of blind fate. Why you would be so proud about it, I'll never understand."

The eyes of the Angel of Death narrowed to slits. Sic could feel an uncomfortable heat spreading through Jago's front garden. Anxiously he retreated a few steps. Casto, on the other hand, was completely unruffled by this demonstration of divine wrath.

"You know I'm right, Barbarian."

Growling, the Angel of Death grabbed his lover's wrist and pulled him close. Casto fought back, but the demigod didn't even seem to notice. He flashed Sic a smile, the kind that could only be found on tigers before they crushed their prey.

"I thank you for letting me take part in your banquet, Sic. I'm very pleased. Unfortunately I have to part with you now. I know somebody who's in for some serious discipline tonight."

Shuddering, Sic bowed to his god. Just like with Casto, he never knew when Renaldo was joking and when he was serious. But judging from the hungry glow in both men's eyes, this was some kind of bizarre foreplay and not the harbinger of a fight. Still, the new master deemed it wise not to get involved in what could easily turn into a full-scale disaster, and so he bid his god and his best friend good-bye as respectfully as he could.

"I was honored to have you as my guest, my lord. I wish you a pleasant night. Casto."

The king had stopped fighting his mate's assault. His bright blue eyes gleamed in the beam of the torches like two ghost lights in the night. Half engulfed by the dancing shadows, Casto and the Angel of Death seemed like dangerously beautiful creatures born from dreams that had not blossomed into a nightmare yet.

"Sleep well, Sic. I'll see you tomorrow."

"I wouldn't be too sure about that, boldface!"

Giggling, and thus shattering the intimidating image Sic had just seen, the king tried once again to free himself from his lover's grip, but it was in vain. Adamantly, the Angel of Death dragged his heart away.

Lost in thought, Sic watched as the two left the quarters. The evening had been truly splendid. Even Cassia had come by with Heljia for an hour to witness as Sic was officially declared a master of his craft. Aries had held a very dignified ceremony, and in his speech he had expressed the hope Sic would stay in Ummana and augment the guild's reputation. The presence of the king and his mate, as well as the representatives of all the other guilds in the city, had added even more glamour to the feast. Jago had told Sic that even before the banquet had taken place, it had become a legend everybody wanted to be part of.

The only thing Sic knew, though, was that on that single night, his commission books had filled for the next two years. Jago had seen to it that he did not sell himself cheaply, making Sic a rich man before dessert had been served. The smith was still dumbfounded by how fast his life had taken a turn for the better. Not four weeks ago, he had been cowering before Noran's wrath, and now he was standing here, a free man, in front of the house of his family, had just become a master of his craft, and was a wealthy citizen of Ummana. He thanked the Mothers from the depths of his heart that he had found the courage to come back from the dead. He couldn't remember ever being so happy in his life before. The stars in the night sky were twinkling as if they shared his joy. Sic turned to the door, knowing Jago had left it ajar so he wouldn't disturb Heljia's sleep when he returned. From the door latch dangled a small package with his name written on it. He felt his heart constrict with love.

"You shouldn't have, Jago," he murmured to himself.

In his chamber, Sic lit a candle, got comfortable on the bed, and opened his present. When he saw what it contained, he went rigid. A chill overwhelmed his body as soon as he realized who must have given him this package.

With trembling fingers he picked up the golden amulet that had a blessing etched into the metal. It was new, the surface so meticulously polished the candlelight broke into countless beams when hitting it, but the beauty of the piece couldn't touch him, since he had seen the exact same one every day for the last eight years. It had been dangling right in front of his eyes on the rare occasions when Noran had taken him from the front. The master's disc, an award every fellow in the Valley was given when he was pronounced a master.

The memory made bile rise in Sic's mouth. Unconsciously his hand fumbled for the scars on his torso. Thanks to the intensive care of Cassia and Lady Noemi, the thick tissue had become a little softer and had ceased to remind him at every step of what he had gone through, but the two healers had also made it clear wounds like that could never be completely cured. He would be crippled and sullied for the rest of his life and had to be grateful things hadn't turned out worse.

A searing pain jolted him back to reality. He had grabbed the amulet so tightly, it had ripped open the skin on his palm. Blood trickled over the gold and down Sic's wrist.

And again he's hurting me. The thought shot through Sic's head like an arrow. It seemed as if this was all that was left between his master and him—pain. Sic felt tears streaming down his cheeks. Because of everything that had happened during the past weeks, especially the nerve-wracking preparations for the exam, he had almost forgotten the threatening, all-consuming void he still faced when thinking about his master. He knew this emotion kept him from facing reality but realized at the same time he couldn't keep going on like this.

It hadn't been enough to defy Noran; he had to deal with all the horrors that had happened to him, as well as with the love he still felt for his master. A love he considered to be a festering wound he couldn't get rid of, no matter how often he tried to purify it with fire. His affection was too tightly interwoven with his very being, since it was Noran who had formed him during most of his life. Never would he be able to escape this imprint, and the realization swallowed every last feeling of happiness.

His eyes clouded by tears, Sic stared at the bloodstained amulet, his right arm slung around his hips as if he wanted to protect himself against the assault from an invisible enemy. Like a stampede, his thoughts raced in his head and didn't quiet down till the early morning hours.

3. ERAC

"WELCOME TO Ummana, Your Majesty."

Stone-faced, Erac received the demonstration of respect from his official representative in the Twin Cities, Lady Vespia. He found himself in the uncomfortable situation of not knowing how to feel. When news about the sudden return of the rightful heir to Ummana had reached Medelina, he had felt anger. He, as well as the leaders of the other cities in the Confederation, had hoped the absence of a legitimate king would allow them to negotiate the contracts with Ummana anew. This hope was now gone, for a king on the throne meant the political strife in the Twin Cities had come to an end, at least for the time being.

That King Castolus had made the most powerful mercenaries on the continent his allies showed he had a hidden agenda. Erac had delayed meeting the young man on purpose, but when Castolus had sentenced the entire Council and his own father to death without batting an eyelash, he had realized it was high time to pay the mistress of the Confederation and her new king a visit.

Ummana had always been a difficult place, especially when compared to Medelina, which was led by a strong, widespread ruling family who saw to the keeping of the iron law. Of course, there were also some constants in Ummana one could rely on. The most important one was the greed of its citizens. A true Ummanian was willing to sacrifice his own flesh and blood for a healthy profit, not to mention such shady terms as honor or loyalty. A law that couldn't be bought and altered with money wasn't a law at all, but a friendly suggestion a true merchant was practically obliged to ignore. This was despicable, no doubt about it, but one could deal with it. In some respects the people in Ummana were more easily understood and manipulated because of it than the politicians in Medelina, who could cling to terms like honor and loyalty quite stubbornly.

The mercenaries from the North changed everything. Erac knew there was no way they could be bribed with money once they had chosen their prey, and their propensity to violence was legendary. Medelina had called upon the services of the Wolf of War once or twice, though never officially. Transactions had taken place through middlemen and had been deployed to bring politically unpleasant situations to a satisfying, quick, and above all, permanent end.

Erac didn't know how much of the ongoing politics in the plains the barbarians understood, but he was sure they were not as clueless as they chose to pretend. All his estimates were confirmed by Lady Vespia's report.

"It wasn't easy to gain access to the ranks of the mercenaries. Those warriors are unswervingly loyal to their leaders."

Discontented, Erac sipped from his wine. This was bad news. Not unexpected, but highly unwelcome.

"What happened?"

"The first one we approached killed the recruiter. I refrained from sending another one."

"But you were able to find somebody?"

"There were two candidates. First I wanted to try a freed slave named Sic. He's just been announced a master by the guild of smiths a few days ago. He's also close to the king and lives with Master Jago, head of the royal smithy. Theoretically he would be ideal, but I've gotten the impression Lord Renaldo would take it personally if something were to happen to him. I don't think he knows it, but he's under tight surveillance all the time. That's why we chose Daran. He's the lapdog of Lord Aegid and Lord Kalad, a spoiled, not-too-bright creature of luxury who has given in to Asnari's courtship without any troubles. It's easy to manipulate him, and the information is valuable. According to his reports, it's the Wolf of War and the Angel of Death who're ruling the city now, and they also influence the king's decisions."

Erac made a face. He was less than pleased about these meager insights. No doubt Vespia was trying to show her accomplishments in the best light possible, but he was too versed in the game not to realize she was bluffing with an empty hand.

"You're aware this isn't really groundbreaking news? What with the reputation of the brothers, I'd have been surprised if things were different. Your lapdog doesn't seem to be helpful at all."

Vespia tried to hide her irritation. She wasn't happy about Erac's sudden visit since it came at a highly inconvenient time. Having her king witness her failure to negotiating a better contract for Medelina was not the way forward in her career. Angering Erac fell into the same category, so she tried her best to stay respectful.

"Even though he's not the brightest candle in the chandelier, it still takes time to get him to reveal the interesting bits. And the lords are strict masters. Although they spoil him no end, he still fears their wrath. At least we know that the most dangerous threat after the brothers is definitely Lady Hulda. She's a spy and an assassin, and there are rumors that she's versed in magic as well."

"There's also the rumor that the Emeris are immortal. Gossip and fairy tales, Vespia."

"I wouldn't be so sure about that, Lord Erac. After everything I've found out and witnessed myself, I'm inclined to believe those rumors. And even if part of it should be proven a lie, they still are the most dangerous warriors in the world. Challenging them openly is simply not an option."

The king of Medelina brushed over the rim of his cup with his fingertips, causing a noise that made Vespia shudder.

"What do the barbarians from the North want down here? I doubt this is about revenge alone."

Vespia shrugged. She had been musing about the same question, but so far no plausible answer had presented itself. The barbarians were either even simpler than she had ever thought possible or, and this was the option she dreaded because she had a suspicion it might be true, a lot more complicated than she would ever be able to understand.

"According to the information I've received from Daran, it seems to be exactly this. He said the warriors don't plan on spending the winter in Ummana. Perhaps you'll have more success in finding out their motives. I've managed to arrange a private audience with King Castolus for you today."

Erac straightened himself up. If he didn't want to enter this meeting unprepared, he had to read Vespia's reports, even though he doubted the intelligence provided by this Daran person was even half as valuable as his representative wanted him to believe.

"Have the reports and a light snack brought to my rooms. There's not much time and a lot to do."

THE ROYAL wing had hardly changed since Erac's last visit. According to the reports of his predecessors, those chambers had remained the same for hundreds of years. The only difference from the good old times was the presence of so many warriors and of some truly intimidating wolves. The gray predators strode through the corridors like shadows that had a natural right to be there.

At the door leading to the private chambers of the king and his entourage, Princess Anesha was waiting for them. The young woman had grown into a real beauty, but Erac wasn't fooled by appearances. According to Vespia, the princess was a true daughter of her infamous mother: a cold, calculating politician who was not only willing to stop at nothing to get what she wanted but had already done so. Her alliance with the king was surprisingly stable, though, and she hadn't tried finding other allies until now.

Erac bowed elegantly before Anesha, who in return curtseyed.

"Your Majesty, I'm honored to welcome you to Ummana."

"I'm the honored one, Princess. May I compliment you on your truly stunning looks?"

Anesha laughed, and her unbelievably long lashes fluttered coquettishly.

"I gladly accept this compliment, but you should wait until you've met Lady Hulda. Then you'll know what true beauty is."

Erac pressed a reverent kiss on the back of Anesha's hand. He was a master of flirting and liked using this gift to his advantage.

"I can hardly imagine how your grace could be surpassed."

Again Anesha laughed, but then she turned serious. "Whatever you're trying to achieve by coming here, Your Majesty, I can only advise you to be careful. My brother is still angry about the Council's treason, and the barbarians—let's just say they're not familiar with the way we handle things here. They're very straightforward. Under no circumstances should you try to threaten Castolus. The Angel of Death is overly possessive, and he doesn't care whom he kills as long as his mate is safe."

Erac lifted a brow. For a moment he contemplated playing the clueless one but decided against it. Anesha had been uncharacteristically open, and it might pay to follow her example.

"I thank you for your warning. You seem to understand your brother's allies pretty well."

The princess shook her head. "Not really. But I've learned the hard way not to anger them."

Before Erac could react to this, the broad door in front of them opened. A well-built slave with lively brown eyes bowed in front of the princess.

"My lady. I hope you are well?"

"Thank you, Daran, I can't complain. What about you? I hope your masters weren't too strict with you after our last encounter. Is my brother ready to receive his guest?"

The slave chuckled. He seemed to enjoy the harmless subtle flirting. "My masters always give me what I deserve, so don't worry about me. Regarding the king—he's ready, as far as I know. But we better hurry. There's a storm brewing."

With these ominous words, the young man turned around and led them into the royal wing. Anesha smiled slightly nervously at her companion.

"Your Majesty, the king will see us now."

In silence they followed the appealing slave, and Erac wondered if Vespia had lost her mind completely, or if she only employed brainless idiots. Writing Daran off as a lapdog was a major blunder. For somebody who was supposedly nothing more than a spoiled creature of luxury who was pampered by his masters, the young man was way too confident. He moved through the royal chambers without shyness, and the way he had spoken to Anesha showed clearly how high up the food chain he was. Only a few slaves would dare to talk to somebody as highly ranked as the princess in such an audacious manner. Therefore, Daran had to be aware that his masters were even more powerful, which meant he wasn't even half as dumb as he had Vespia believing.

Erac's mind raced. Suddenly the information he had dismissed as worthless only a few hours ago appeared in an entirely new light. Daran had managed to trick Vespia, most probably to make more profit. The more stupid he acted, the longer it took to get any worthwhile information, and according to the bills Erac had reviewed, the slave was getting money for even the most trifling gossip. It seemed as if he was a shrewd, intelligent opponent, which also meant his information was more valuable than Erac had initially thought.

Erac wondered how much, if anything, Daran had told his master about the recruiting—and how it was to enjoy him in bed. Even when wearing a simple tunic and just leading the way, he radiated a beguiling carnality that had to arouse any onlooker. He was obviously a man who felt comfortable in his skin and who was aware of the admiring stares of others. It was no doubt a special pleasure holding him, especially since he was able to satisfy two masters at once.

The king of Medelina called himself to order rigidly. He wasn't here for his personal pleasure, but to find out how the political circumstances had changed. And this alluring slave, whom he had just stripped naked and done some very naughty things to in his thoughts, was the key to it. Even if—or because—he had told his masters about Asnari and her offer, his reports could still be highly useful. Castolus was no fool; he knew how the game was played, and he would never pass up a chance like that. It was up to Erac to use the situation to his advantage.

From one of the chambers, a clash resounded, followed by a colorful curse in the language of the North. Erac wasn't able to understand it all, but the content was quite clear. In front of him, Daran murmured, "And here we go again."

A deep, rather pleasant voice tinged with fury started to chide. "Damn, Casto, this was hardly necessary."

A second, slightly higher pitched and more melodic voice, answered in acid tones. "Yes, it was. There seems to be no other way for me to get through to you, Barbarian. No matter what you say, the partners of the Confederation are important for Ummana, and I really want to show their representative some respect."

"We don't have time for politeness and the finer points of Ummanian tactics. Canubis and I want to be back home before the winter storms set in, which means we need to leave in about two months."

"And how am I supposed to get the government affairs in order in such a short time? I've already explained it to you, Barbarian. I have a duty toward the citizens. I have a duty toward the business. We can't just pop out of nowhere, literally cut off all established centers of power, and then skulk off like thieves in the night."

"I already told you, we're fine establishing Anesha as your successor."

"Which won't be easy, as I've tried to make you understand more than once. It's definitely going to take more than just two months, especially if we don't want to hazard the consequences of such hastened actions. Are you even listening to me?"

"Not when you're complaining. You know my will, so obey."

The last sentence was spoken in a manner that didn't allow for the least bit of defiance. Anesha turned to Erac with an apologetic smile on her lips.

"I'm truly sorry, Your Majesty. My brother and Lord Renaldo haven't been married for long and still suffer some—problems."

Erac nodded reassuringly. He was glad nobody had noticed how well he had been able to follow the skirmish. Interesting, indeed. So the king was under quite some pressure. And the idea to establish Anesha as the new queen in his place was logical and coincided with Erac's interest. The princess wasn't an easy opponent to begin with, but it would take her a few years to reach the height of her power. Until she came of age, she'd need strong allies to help her on her way to the throne. And even though the barbarians were an impressive military force, as soon as they left the city, it would be the rich families and the guilds dictating politics again.

The possibilities opening up in front of him made Erac slightly dizzy. He had to control himself to ban the triumphant gleam from his features and to let his voice sound neutral.

"Don't worry, Princess. I know all too well. During the first two years of our marriage, my wife and I had about three normal conversations. If it's inconvenient, I can come back later."

There was a trace of relief in the princess's otherwise unperturbed voice.

"I don't think this will be necessary, Your Majesty. Daran, can you announce us, please?"

The young man obeyed immediately, the mocking gleam gone from his eyes. Now he really seemed like an average, obedient slave. Vespia hadn't exaggerated when talking about the warlords' wrath.

WHEN ERAC stood in front of the King of Ummana, he had to be careful not to stare openly. Vespia had told him about the unearthly beauty of the Angel of Death; she had even mentioned that Castolus had grown into a fine man, but Erac had dismissed her report as infatuation. Now he had to admit she had downplayed.

The young king was leisurely dressed, wearing soft linen trousers and a tunic, both dyed in a dark blue hue. Stout muscles on his arms hinted at the strength of his body, his clear blue eyes shone like diamonds in the sun, and the wheat-blond hair was held back by a leather band, but some wayward strands dangled around his exquisite, even face. Castolus had obviously become a handsome and self-confident man, who wore his power like a second skin. Underestimating him as an opponent would be a lethal mistake.

As impressive as the son of Isiris might have been, his husband outdid him easily. Lord Renaldo wasn't only taller than the king, his entire attitude showed clearly who the leader of Ummana was. The gray eyes of the Angel of Death were as calm as the sea on a windless day. And like the sea with its impenetrable depths, they hinted at how dangerous he really was. Unlike Castolus, the warrior was only wearing a dark blue tunic, but the way he moved betrayed the experienced fighter. Watching the Angel of Death, Erac got the impression of a cat of prey dozing in the sun while waiting for the hunt to begin."

Seeing all this unbridled strength, dominance, and danger united in a man who truly possessed the face of an angel made the situation unnerving. Erac could now better understand why Vespia was so afraid of the barbarians. He had to keep himself from kneeling in front of the mercenary.

The attitude of Anesha and Daran was telling as well. The king's sister was overly polite toward the Angel of Death, and the slave neither made a sound nor dared to look up while he poured everybody a cup of wine. Only the king seemed unfazed by his mate's oppressing presence. Even though they had just had a lively fight, Castolus seemed almost relaxed, as if he had enjoyed the skirmish. Now the king turned to Daran with a smile.

"You can leave now. I'll ring for you should we need anything else."

The young man bowed graciously and left the room, but not without paying Lord Renaldo his respect. When the door closed behind the slave, Casto became all businesslike.

"Welcome to Ummana, Your Majesty. I'm very glad you found the time to pay us a visit."

The subtle reproach did not escape Erac, but he, too, was a master of political small talk.

"You know what it's like, Your Majesty. Business keeps us busy. We're experiencing a very promising phase at the moment, and it's important to strike while the iron is hot."

"True indeed. May I introduce my husband, Lord Renaldo, the Angel of Death?"

Erac bowed low to the warrior. "Your reputation is well known all over the Plains, your lordship. But I do have to admit, your enemies don't do you justice. They always talk about the blood dripping from your hands, but they forget to mention your unearthly beauty."

An amused glint highlighted the angelic face.

"That's probably because they're preoccupied with dying when they meet me. Although, if you talk to my husband, he'll only mention my beauty briefly and elaborate on my character flaws at length. Like everything else in life, it depends on one's point of view."

"I'd never dare doubt your character, my dear husband."

The king's voice had now a playful undertone. He seemed to be amused. Both men exchanged a glance that made shudders run down Erac's spine. The heavy atmosphere in the room had turned into something a lot more carnal all of a sudden and made him fantasize again, this time about the king and his naked body. Before the situation could become too uncomfortable, Castolus went back to business.

"So what made you decide to finally pay me a visit, King Erac?"

The sudden change of subject, as well as the, by Ummanian standards, unusually direct approach, threw Erac off-balance for a moment. But he quickly regained his composure and decided to adapt. Now was not the time to be intimidated by a few sharp words.

"As you can imagine, Your Majesty, we've been observing the political circumstances in Ummana very closely and with a great deal of worry ever since your unfortunate disappearance. I have to admit, your sudden return has taken us by surprise, which is the reason we hesitated to pay our respects personally. But now I'm here so we can discuss your future plans concerning the Confederation."

"I wasn't aware there is anything to discuss. The contracts among the members of the Confederation are indisputable and don't expire at a given time."

"Of course I'm aware of that, but things have changed during your absence. Medelina has grown stronger, and our revenues are constantly increasing. We've left the other cities far behind and would like to see our new position honored within the Confederation as well."

The king's lips contorted into a smile that did not reach his eyes.

"To put it bluntly, you want more power. But no matter how economically virile you've become, you'll never be able to challenge Ummana."

Erac nodded in agreement. There was no arguing that point. "You're of course right, Your Majesty. Ummana's unique location is unrivaled. Still, you have to admit, Medelina is no longer on the same level as cities like Alemba, Wa'na Atoka, or even Kre. We only want what we deserve."

The king seemed to ponder this for a moment.

"What do you think you deserve? What kind of concessions are we talking about?"

"Fiscal advantages for the traders from Medelina. Our business is booming, and with certain deals we could become even more successful. Also, the representatives of the guild of traders have asked that their goods get privileged status when transported by the caravans. And we want more voting weight within the Confederation."

"Those are no trivialities you're asking for, King Erac. You want me to treat you specially and thus worsen the position of the other cities even more. This seems a little unfair. If anything, I'd have to do the opposite, don't you think?"

Erac allowed a derisive snort to escape his lips. "You're joking, aren't you, Your Majesty? We both know Ummana doesn't work that way. My demands aren't exorbitant and, even more important, they're negotiable. I'm aware that in these times everything has its price, but I'm positive we'll be able to find a satisfactory agreement." He threw a calculating sidelong glance at Renaldo before he went on. "And in short time, should you wish for it. Medelina, too, is interested in getting this wrapped up as soon as possible."

The gray eyes of the Angel of Death lit up dangerously when he heard Erac's derisive tone. Until now he had kept in the background, but it seemed he was willing to devour Erac wholly for his words. Before the warrior could say anything, Castolus shifted slightly in his seat. The powerful warlord exchanged another long glance with his mate, then he stepped back again. Inwardly Erac breathed a sigh of relief, while at the same time, his politically trained mind started assessing the relationship between the king and the barbarian anew.

Renaldo might be the dominant partner, but this did not mean Castolus had no authority of his own. How this could be an advantage during negotiations he had yet to find out, but one thing was already for sure: even though the king was in a difficult situation, it wouldn't be easy to get the better of him. Castolus was a shrewd negotiator who, without doubt, had a few aces up his sleeve. Erac deemed it wise to retreat for the time being.

"Those are my demands. I assume you want to think about them. I'm looking forward to hearing your counterproposals."

For a moment a hungry glint appeared in the king's eyes. He was obviously eager to start their game. With a smile as false as the friendly tone in Erac's voice, he ended the private audience.

"You're right, Your Majesty. I do have to discuss your demands with my counselors. It's very thoughtful of you to give me that time. What do you think, shall we have our first official meeting the day after tomorrow? By then, I'll surely have made up my mind."

"You're very kind, Your Majesty. I'll see you in two days."

Erac bowed formally to the king and his mate. Then Anesha, who had been uncharacteristically quiet, escorted him out of the room. When the doors to the royal wing had closed behind them, Erac scrutinized the young woman. It was time to dig a little deeper. After all, he was facing the potential new queen of Ummana.

"It seems you're intimidated by the Angel of Death."

It was a simple statement, made in a light tone. Anesha could have easily ignored it, but to his surprise and joy she reacted to it.

"Of course I am. Only a complete fool wouldn't fear the god. It would be good for you if you followed my example."

"I do have to admit, the barbarian is forbidding, but I can't imagine he's as dangerous as everybody claims."

Anesha shuddered.

"You can only talk like that because you've never seen him angry. I witnessed what Lord Renaldo is capable of when he gets irritated. If I'm really lucky, the nightmares will stop one day. But that's not the worst. Do you know what is truly horrifying? No matter how furious Lord Renaldo might be, his brother is definitely worse. The Wolf of War is the true power here in Ummana, and nobody can reach him. I can only repeat what I've already told you. Be careful. The rules of the game have changed, and the game itself has become more brutal."

Erac bowed. Anesha's frankness was both disturbing and reassuring, because although she was afraid of the barbarians, she was also willing to cooperate with him—or at least negotiate about it.

"Thank you for the warning, Princess. Do allow me to invite you for a light lunch tomorrow. I've brought my personal chef from Medelina, and he's truly an artist."

"Who am I to say no to such an offer? Thank you for the invitation, Your Majesty."

"I'm honored by your acceptance. I'll expect you tomorrow, Princess."

IN THE king's chambers, the Emeris had gathered. Their eyes homed in expectantly on Anesha when she returned.

"Did he buy it?"

Renaldo's voice was sly. He was sitting on one of the lounges, his right hand resting heavily on his lover's nape. Anesha grinned triumphantly.

"He swallowed the bait hook, line, and sinker. I'm invited to a private lunch tomorrow. If things go well, we'll have him then."

"You did well, sister."

Anesha winked at her brother conspiratorially, purposely ignoring his sour tone.

"Don't tell me you had doubts! Besides, you prepared the field perfectly for me. Your fight was so convincing, I was worried for a moment everything would blow up because you were arguing for real."

Renaldo pressed a gentle kiss on the king's cheek.

"We do have lots of practice. And it's hard holding back once you're in the flow."

Canubis chuckled. "Who'd have thought your constant bitching and fighting would come in handy one day? I'm more than pleased. It seems we can go home as planned."

The Emeris relaxed visibly. None of them had any inclination to spend the winter in the Twin Cities. Even Aegid and Kalad, who felt at home in the hot climate, were already missing the tranquility of the Valley.

The two desert warriors got up. "We'll go and tell Daran. He'll be happy."

"Tell him he did very well. I'm pleased."

Renaldo's voice was warm. He rarely praised anybody, but his brothers-in-arms' slave had earned it.

Kalad saluted his god. "We'll pass it on."

"I think we'll leave as well. It's getting late, and I haven't had my bath yet."

Hulda got up and, together with Wolfstan and Noran, followed the desert warriors. Canubis placed a hand on his brother's shoulder.

"That was really good. I hope we're on our way home soon."

Noemi kissed her brother-in-law and Casto on the cheek; then she took her husband's hand. The king and his mate were alone.

RENALDO PULLED Casto close and nibbled the soft skin on his neck.

"That went a lot better than we had hoped for."

Casto leaned into his lover's embrace. "It's always nice when a plan works out."

His voice sounded like a purr, he was so pleased with the whole situation. The Angel of Death put him at arm's length and studied his face intently.

"You've got to enlighten me. Why did you insist on Daran serving us? He did a great job, but I don't understand why it was so important to have him there."

The magnetic eyes darkened slightly. It was obvious how much Casto resented the question. When he finally answered, he sounded cautious, as if he was afraid of something.

"It was a trick. Erac knows Daran is his informant, and what he's gotten from him so far surely hasn't made him happy, since it was more or less worthless. I bet he has contemplated to terminate the business relationship. Now he has seen that this supposedly brainless luxury toy, whom he has fed quite the fortune up until now, is a shrewd and greedy tactician. When Daran meets Asnari the next time, I can guarantee Erac will be there as well to pressure him, which is exactly what I want. This way I'm in control of all the information and can influence negotiations to our advantage."

Renaldo's eyes had widened and admiration showed on his face, only to be replaced by suspicion.

"It makes things more dangerous for Daran, doesn't it? What if Erac suspects you pull the strings?"

Casto shrugged, seemingly unfazed.

"He's doing that anyway. He'd be an idiot if he didn't even consider the possibility. But the information he's going to get from Daran will be so good, he'll forget everything else about it and throw caution to the wind. He didn't come to Ummana for fun, and he knows he has to offer me a lot in return for the favors he's asking for. If he thinks he knows my weakness, it's easier to get the better of him."

The king fell silent, and Renaldo once more offered his thanks to the Mothers that this dangerous man was his heart and therefore on his side. Having Casto as an enemy was not a pleasant thought. And just when the Angel of Death started wondering how ruthless his mate really was, the king started talking again.

"The only thing bothering me is that I'm putting Daran in such danger. He's been brilliant until now, but he's not used to this game, and I don't know how far I can push him. My whole plan depends on how convincing he can be. That's a lot of responsibility for somebody whose biggest problem normally is evading his masters' advances."

Renaldo stroked his lover's back soothingly, glad Casto was preoccupied staring at his fingers and wasn't able to see the knowing grin playing around his god's lips. Even though the king had just spoken snidely about Daran, Renaldo still knew he was truly worried for the thief's safety, and not just because he was crucial to the plan, but first and foremost because Casto really liked him.

"Stop pondering! Daran is a lot more cunning than he seems, as you well know. And the Mothers are watching us as well. Everything will be fine, I'm sure of it, and then we can turn our backs on Ummana and go back home."

Casto sighed.

"It's about time. I miss the Valley."

"My own! Don't think I'm unaware of the sacrifice you've made. I only wish you didn't have to do it."

With a grave expression, the king looked up at his mate. All ruthlessness had gone from his features, and he only seemed tired.

"It was the best solution. I swore fealty to you. What are the inconveniences I had to endure compared to the lives we saved? And after all, it was a good thing I returned to this place. When I leave the Twin Cities this time, the demons of my past will stay back as well. I owe this to you, Barbarian."

Again Renaldo kissed the young man, full of love and a desperate hunger that grew whenever Casto showed signs of weakness.

"I love you so much, my own. Your pain is like a knife in my chest."

"You don't have to protect me from the world, Barbarian. All I need you to do is be there to catch me when I fall."

"I always am. And now, come here. I wish to possess you."

Groaning, Casto allowed the Angel of Death to take off his clothes and carry him to the bed. He gave in to the warrior's demands till late at night, full of joy that his days in the Twin Cities were almost over.

NORAN WAS sitting on one of the lounges in his chambers, a cup of Ummanian wine in his hands, staring contemplatively into the deep red. He, too, was relieved that they would soon return home. Too many things had happened in Ummana that he'd never remember it with joy. He was glad he had finally apologized to his god, but the indifference with which Renaldo treated him now still hurt. Canubis, too, acted with apathy, but their relationship had never been as intense. The Wolf of War was too aloof, too godlike. It was a lot easier to establish ties with Renaldo, even though he was the less contained one.

A soft knock disturbed Noran's train of thought. Frowning, he went to get the door. He had no idea who could possibly want to visit him at this late hour. To his surprise it was Sic who stood in front of him, his gaze cast down.

"May I disturb you for a moment, Master?"

With difficulty Noran managed to shake off the rigor that had taken hold of him when he beheld his most precious treasure. Being this close to Sic again was more than he had dared to hope during the weeks following his rescue.

"Of course. What can I do for you?"

Hesitantly Sic held out the box in which Noran had put the master disc. The smith's heart sank as he took it.

"I thank you for the present, Master, but I can't accept it. Seeing it reminds me too much of the past months, of what you did to me. And of what I did, of my fault. I simply can't stand having this—thing—close to me. I'm sorry."

The young man turned away quickly. Still, Noran could see the tears streaming down Sic's face, and his stomach constricted with guilt.

"Sic! I'm the one who should be sorry. I shouldn't have bothered you with it. But I wanted you to know how proud I am of you. You exceeded all my expectations."

Sic, who had been ready to flee, turned around slowly.

"Really, you're proud of me?"

He sounded so disbelieving and at the same time full of hope, Noran wanted to hit himself.

"I am. I know I never told you, but I always knew you were destined for greatness. And look at you! You're a master in a city famous for its high standards. You couldn't have done any better."

A shy smile crept onto Sic's features. For a moment he didn't seem to know what to do; then he abruptly bowed to Noran and left his rooms without another word.

For a long time, the master smith stared at the spot where, just now, the love of his life had stood. He knew he had no right whatsoever to even hope for Sic's forgiveness, but he still fantasized how it would be if he could woo the young man properly. It was a cruel irony that he finally understood how worthy Sic was of his love when he was no longer in control of the situation. On the contrary, he, Noran, had to prove his worth. A task he had thoroughly failed. It was a shame he would carry till the end of all times and probably beyond, a shame that would forever stain his soul.

He emptied the wine in one go and stored the box with the master disc in one of his trunks. A golden reminder of his own shortcomings.

4. SAR'REFF

Daran looked around in the gloomy tavern that was his meeting place with Asnari and wondered how things could have gotten so messed up. It was, of course, his own fault. He just should have kept his head down and been an obedient slave to his owners. But in an attempt to please and impress them, he had maneuvered himself into a tight corner, namely this stinking place where he would once again meet Asnari and, most probably, Erac.

After the King of Medelina had his private audience with Casto, the blond had warned him Erac would be present at his next rendezvous with Asnari. What he had forgotten to mention was that the king was a pervert, a bully, and to top it off, highly intelligent. It took all Daran's wits to turn down his advances, ignore the threats, and outthink him during their regular run-ins. To make things worse, Casto had set it all up on purpose, which of course had not escaped either Daran or his masters. Unfortunately Kalad and Aegid were less than pleased to know their exclusive possession was flirting with his target to get what Casto wanted.

And Casto wanted a lot, if not everything. To make Daran's mission as a double agent a success, Casto had been quite explicit about his plans so that the thief knew enough to be able to interact with Erac smoothly. At their first meeting, the king of Medelina had tried to intimidate Daran by acting all high and mighty and accusing him of only being after the money with nothing to offer in return. It had been hard work to set up a personality Erac could accept as plausible and would trust about the information he was fed. By now things were running more or less smoothly, and the negotiations were progressing fast. Daran didn't even have to tell outright lies, he just had to bend the truth slightly now and then. At the moment Casto was trying to make Erac accept and, more importantly, back up Anesha as his successor, although she was still underage.

Of course Erac already had a secret agreement with Anesha to help her on her way to the throne, but in order to squeeze some special concessions out of Casto, he feigned resistance. Which was exactly what the heart of the Angel of Death wanted. The goal was to get Erac so wrapped up in the petty points he wouldn't notice when Casto made him swallow the big toads. One of them was to permit a group of about fifty members of the Pack free access to all of Medelina, so they could find and kill all followers of the Good Mother who were hiding there. The second, even bigger one, was to ratify a law that obliged the members of the Confederation to outlaw the religion of the Good Mother and to put anybody who practiced it to death.

This was the real reason the Pack had come to Ummana, and it was up to Daran to distract Erac enough so he wouldn't find out about it until it was too late. It was like playing cat and mouse, only sometimes the juiciest mouse could suddenly turn into a ferocious cat, and nobody could ever be entirely sure whether they were predator or prey. In the end the winner was the person who could plan the furthest ahead and anticipate the opponent's movements correctly. Basically, Casto had to guess Erac's intentions, and so far he had made not one mistake.

Daran had tried to keep ahead of the game as well, since he played an important part in it, but had given up after a truly head-splitting migraine, which was cause for another major row between his masters and the heart of their god. How Casto managed to keep track of every move he and Erac had made and of every new feint that had been introduced remained a mystery to Daran. He had stopped pondering what Erac might think they thought he knew or wanted them to think. He just clung to his mission, which was to make the king of Medelina believe Casto was in a tight spot concerning Anesha's ascension to the throne.

The door to the shabby tavern opened and Asnari entered, followed closely by Erac. A saucy smile appeared on his lips when he beheld Daran.

"My cute little spy. You look even more alluring today. Tell me, what did those two barbarians do to you to make you so irresistible? You're glowing from the inside."

The thief blushed against his will, which fortunately only served his cover. He resented sharing such juicy details with anybody, but he had no choice. With a sour smile, he started to work.

"My masters are very experienced in matters concerning the bed, and they love to teach me. I didn't get much sleep yesterday, but the lessons were—satisfying."

"You really are a bad boy. Now you've got me all excited when I should be focused on your report. Do you have any idea what I should do?"

This was Daran's cue. There had been a long and heated discussion about how far he would be allowed to go with Erac, and in the end, his masters had agreed that a hand job was acceptable. Not that Daran enjoyed what he had to do—quite the contrary, in fact—or that Aegid and Kalad wouldn't make him pay as soon as he got back to them, but controlling Erac was a lot easier when he was sexually satisfied. So the young man stepped forward and helped the king of Medelina to let off some steam.

Compared to his masters, the king was rather sparingly equipped and did not show the same untiring stamina that made Daran pass out when he was going at it with the desert brothers, so the matter was concluded rather quickly. When Erac was satisfied, the thief wiped his hands clean and got down to business.

"King Castolus wasn't too happy about your last offer. Lord Renaldo keeps nagging him to wrap this up so we can go back home, but Casto resents becoming the obvious loser in these negotiations. The mood is rather difficult at the moment. They're sleeping in separate beds, and the smallest things can make both of them explode. Perhaps you could throw Casto some bone that can soothe his anger? It would make life a lot easier for all of us. If this goes on, he may decide to stay in Ummana out of sheer stubbornness."

It was a well-placed threat, since Erac wanted the king and his fearsome entourage to leave as soon as possible. His eyes narrowed.

"Do you really think he might stay?"

Daran shrugged. This was the easy part; it was just telling the truth.

"With Casto, nobody knows. I mean, he's able to live with the Angel of Death, which should tell you a lot about him. His backbone is made of iron, and once he's made a decision, it's almost impossible to convince him otherwise. We all want to go home, but if Casto gets too pissed, he may blow it off. And staying here will make *all* the Emeris real cranky."

Erac went through his options with the swiftness of a trained politician. He could prolong the discussion and perhaps get an even better result than he had anticipated, but at the same time, he risked losing it all. If the barbarians stayed in Ummana throughout the winter, there was no telling what would happen. Another downside was that he would have to stay in the Twin Cities as well to keep an eye on any new developments, especially with the other members of the Confederation.

Or he could do what Daran had suggested and throw the king of Ummana a bone. What did it matter if he made some minor concessions about one small law and a few barbarian warriors in his city? He would have the future queen of Ummana in his debt, and her brother and his terrible allies would be a long way off.

If he played his cards right, he could gain quite the influence in the Twin Cities, which would strengthen Medelina's standing even more. Erac's mouth watered when he pictured a grateful Anesha doing his bidding. Waking from this delectable dream was hard, and he had to concentrate to accomplish the task.

"I will see what I can do. As always, your services have been magnificent. Unfortunately this is the last time we'll see each other, since I'm planning to wrap this whole thing up tomorrow. So if you have anything else to say, please do it now."

Daran readjusted his face into a well-calculated mask of greed and unbridled self-confidence.

"Well, you've paid me good money so far, but I don't think you've honored my special services yet. Wouldn't that be a nice parting gift?"

A brief smile flashed across Erac's features when he was confronted with such a cheeky demand.

"I'd really love to have you for myself, but I guess your masters wouldn't sell you, no matter what I offer. Your greed and straightforwardness are so refreshing. How about I give you this necklace?"

Erac produced from his pocket a heavy golden chain with five emeralds embedded in the loops.

"Green suits you. It heightens the color of your eyes. Allow me to put it on you."

Inwardly repulsed, Daran lifted his braid so Erac could close the jewelry around his neck. It came to rest about two fingers below his collar, which was a skintight fit. Feeling Erac's fingers on his bare skin made Daran's flesh crawl, and he only endured it because he knew it was for the last time. Nevertheless he was looking forward to a long, hot bath to scrub off the stench of this unpleasant man.

"There, you're so beautiful. Thank you for your services—all of them."

Finally the king of Medelina let go of his informant. When he left the tavern, Daran prayed this had really been the last time he had to look at that smarmy, despicable smile.

Unnoticed by the thief, a shadow next to Erac stirred. The king of Medelina nodded toward the door.

"Get him. And make it look like an accident. We don't want the barbarians to be all over us."

The shadow nodded and went after Daran.

DARAN DIDN'T know when he realized he was being followed. After he had gotten out of the tavern, he briefly and unsuccessfully tried to get rid of the necklace, but the clasp had a complicated mechanism that wouldn't budge easily. Kalad and Aegid would be furious, of course, seeing him wearing jewelry from another man, but he'd have to endure their wrath. After another futile attempt, he hurried on, eager to get back into the palace.

It was shortly before he reached the little alleyway leading directly to the bridge at the western side of the palace that his inner alarms, honed in the streets of Kwarl, started shrilling like crazy. Even though he had led a numbing life of luxury during the past few years, he was still able to sense the presence of somebody else behind him. And that somebody wasn't just following him, but stalking him. Daran considered his options and decided to run.

Glad for the merciless training his masters had forced on him, he relied on his endurance to outrun his pursuer. And at first his plan seemed to work. The footsteps, which had been uncomfortably close, started to fall back. But when Daran reached the end of the alleyway, the bridge already in sight, he could feel the other one suddenly closing in. He just knew he wouldn't make it; still he gathered all his strength and sped up once more. It was no use. Cold, strong hands grabbed his braid and jerked him back so brutally he almost toppled over. Before he could regain his balance, the ugly necklace Erac had given him tightened around his neck, the sharp edges digging into his flesh and squeezing his larynx.

Daran reached up and tried to loosen the golden noose, but to no avail. If he wanted to survive, he had to switch tactics. Lifting his foot, he smashed it down on his attacker's boots with every ounce of strength he had left. The man at his back grunted, and his grip weakened for just a second—which was all Daran needed. His right elbow landed a direct hit in the man's solar plexus, and the back of Daran's head connected with the attacker's face, causing his nose to break with a crunching sound. The tight grip around his throat finally vanished, and the thief scrambled away from the attacker.

Daran gulped in the precious air with desperate gasps. At the same time, he tried to get back to his feet and to the bridge, which seemed to be at the other end of the world. His head felt dizzy and his knees were wobbly.

Behind him, the grunts indicating pain had stopped, and Daran didn't have to turn around to know his attacker was back on his feet. He tried to speed up, but a heavy hand landed on his shoulder, spinning him around so fast he crashed to the ground. Then the shadow man was looming above him, the cold glint of a dagger catching Daran's eyes. Even though he was facing certain death, the thief didn't want to give up. He concentrated, waiting for the cold steel to come down on him so he could try to duck away from it. The muscles in the raised arm holding the weapon tensed, ready to deal the final blow, when suddenly an even darker shadow appeared.

Daran saw long, elegant fingers close around the attacker's wrist and squeeze so tightly he let go of the dagger. Again the man grunted, and the thief wondered why he didn't cry out in pain, because by the look of it, all the bones in his hand had been pulverized. There was another gut-wrenching sound when the Angel of Death's fist connected with the man's head and sent him down. Daran looked up at his rescuer, still slightly dizzy from lack of oxygen.

"What are you doing here, Lord Renaldo?"

"Looking after you. I'm really sorry, Daran, but this bastard managed to give me the slip."

"You were following me?"

Renaldo bent down and helped him up.

"Think about it. Do you really believe your overprotective masters would have let you go all on your own?"

The thief felt the corners of his mouth twitching.

"I thought it was strange. So they didn't suddenly decide to trust me. I'm glad, otherwise I'd be dead now."

"Can you walk on your own? I want to take this one with us. There are some questions he has to answer."

Spooked by the grim tone, Daran hurried to get on his feet.

"Of course. Thank you for saving me, Lord Renaldo."

The demigod grinned and even bowed slightly.

"It was my pleasure. Now hurry, we need to get away from here."

BACK IN the palace, Daran and Renaldo were greeted by Kalad, Aegid, and Casto. When the desert brothers became aware of their slave's condition, they were all over him like two mother hens with only one chick between them.

"Daran, are you all right? What's happened?"

Kalad was holding the thief's face in his hands while Aegid was frantically searching him for wounds.

The young man tried to soothe them. "It's okay. I'm fine. Lord Renaldo came in time to save me."

The Angel of Death looked at his brothers-in-arms with a serious expression. "Take him with you and let Noemi have a look at him. He was almost choked to death. But you can be proud of him. He fought back like a real warrior."

"I told you this was too dangerous for him." Aegid glared at his leader, who stayed calm despite the insubordination. Before things could get out of hand, Casto intervened.

"It's fine, Aegid. Kalad. This was Daran's last mission. He's back with you now, so why don't you go and take care of him while my husband explains to me how things could get out of hand like they did. And who our guest is."

Spoken with calm authority, the words did not fail to impress the warriors. They took Daran in their arms and gently steered him toward their chambers. The king turned to the Angel of Death and his unfortunate prisoner.

"Who's this?"

Renaldo lifted the man's head up.

"I had hoped you would know. He was after Daran, and he managed to give me the slip. Definitely a pro."

Casto studied the unconscious man. He didn't know him and doubted that he had ever seen him before. A face like that was memorable. The man was at least as tall as Casto, with skin that seemed to change color from a dark bronze tone to a faint golden hue whenever the light of the candles hit it. He was on the slim side, with not an ounce of fat to soften the harsh lines muscles and sinew drew on his skin. His face looked like an odd mixture of all the different tribes on the continent. The slanted eyes and razor-sharp cheekbones from the Eastern and Plains people, the generous mouth with a prominent lower lip from the Western tribes, the arched nose with small nostrils from the South, and the long, thick hair from the Northern countries. Like his skin, his hair seemed to change color constantly. When Casto concentrated real hard, he thought he could catch a glimpse of gray underneath the alternating hues, but he wasn't sure. Something about the man was odd; he seemed as if he did not belong to the world, as if he was something alien, a wrong note in an otherwise flawless tune. Despite all that, Casto had the nagging feeling that he somehow knew this man. His presence was familiar, although the king couldn't quite put his finger on it.

"I haven't seen him before, but I think I should know him. It's strange."

Renaldo was by now used to Casto's special ways and knew he had to be patient, but he was still angry that the stranger had managed to get away from him and, even worse, almost killed one of his own. So his retort was sharper than he had intended.

"You think you should know him? Be sure, damn it. This is important. After all, he was sent by Erac."

"This much I anticipated. In fact, I'd have been disappointed if he hadn't tried anything at all."

"You knew this would happen?"

Renaldo was temporarily rendered speechless. During the tactical games of the past weeks, he had gotten to know a different, almost terrifying Casto. He was able to deal with the short-tempered, hot-blooded, and stubborn side of his lover; it was, in fact, one of the things he liked about him. But the way the king had calmly and ruthlessly made his moves against Erac was unnerving him. It was the way Casto had been ramming the metaphorical knife into his opponent's back without batting an eyelash, using his resources, human and otherwise, with cold precision. He, and even Canubis, had been one of those resources, and realizing what his heart was truly capable of made even Renaldo shudder. Now his lover's irritation was showing clearly in the blue depths the Angel of Death had once thought he knew.

"Of course I did. Sending you after Daran was not just to pacify Aegid and Kalad. It was to ensure the thief's safety."

"A close call. We really need to find out who this man is."

"So you don't plan on killing him?"

"Initially I wanted to, but after seeing him at work, I want to get to know him. What would you do with him?"

Casto shrugged his shoulders.

"I don't really care. Daran is safe, and it doesn't hurt if Erac is missing one of his servants. Could even make him nervous, which suits me just fine."

"I love it when you show your cold heart to me."

Renaldo grinned broadly when his mate punched him on the shoulder.

"I can do without your sarcasm. Let's get Noemi so she can wake him up."

IN THE chambers of the desert brothers, Daran enjoyed the ministrations of his masters. They had undressed him and were now taking off the despicable necklace. When it came loose from his neck, Daran breathed a sigh of relief. He had deeply resented wearing it. Kalad and Aegid stared heatedly at him.

"I'm really sorry, Masters, that I had to accept this. I tried taking it off myself, but…." Daran realized his owners weren't listening to him at all. Instead their eyes were glued to his throat as if he were sprouting a second head there. Tentatively he reached for his collar—and froze. The leather was in shreds. It took Daran two more heartbeats to understand what this meant; then he bent forward and threw up.

If it hadn't been for the collar, the razor-sharp edges of Erac's deadly parting gift would have cut his larynx like a hot knife plunging through butter.

And he had touched that man most intimately. He had allowed him to put the necklace on him. Daran felt hot tears pricking in his eyes. He was definitely not cut out for the shady aspects of Ummanian politics. Aegid lifted him up and carried the trembling thief to the bathroom. Kalad stayed back to clean up, which Daran tried to prevent.

"Please, Master, I can do that myself. I'm sorry I made such a mess."

"Shh. You're not fit to do anything right now. Let us take care of you, little thief. You know it's our pleasure."

Aegid's grip was firm, and Daran was way too shaken to argue with the giant, especially when he knew he stood no chance. Grateful, he rested his head on the firm, reliable shoulder and breathed in the familiar scent of his owner.

"Thank you, Master."

"THIS IS strange."

Noemi stared at the unconscious form of Renaldo's prisoner, her brows furrowed in thought. Her husband, brother-in-law, and his mate were watching her intently but did not dare interrupt her musings. She closed her eyes again and reached into the man's body, trying to discern it as she was used to. But there was nothing—or at least nothing she could understand.

Whenever her power sought a way in, it was immediately thrown out violently, as if it was repelled. The witch turned to the three waiting men.

"Whatever he is, it's definitely not human. He looks like one, but the body is made of—different things—and his mind…. Let's just say at the moment he's this side of insanity. Poor thing. It's as if he doesn't belong here."

"Do you think he'll wake up soon?"

"I don't know, Renaldo. Possibly. Perhaps. But I doubt you'll get any information from him. As far as I can tell, and admittedly that's not much, he can't even speak."

"Damn. And here I thought I'd found another worthy addition to our ranks."

"Don't dismiss him yet, husband mine."

Casto was biting his thumb in deep thought.

"Noemi, what did you just say about him?"

"That he's going to wake up, perhaps?"

"No, the other bit. Before."

The witch seemed puzzled, but Renaldo motioned her to speak, sensing his heart was on the verge of discovering something.

"I said he's not human. And that he feels out of place, as if—"

"As if he's from somewhere else!" Casto snapped his fingers. "I knew the feeling was familiar! I'm really stupid."

"Casto, what are you talking about?"

It was the first time since they had gathered that Canubis spoke. He wasn't pleased about what had happened to Daran and didn't try to hide his impatience. Casto loftily ignored the warlord's bad mood and answered as if nothing was amiss.

"Lys. He's the key. He may look like one, but he's not a horse, and he always feels a little out of place, as if he doesn't really belong here. Whoever this guy is, I bet he's like Lys."

The others stared at him as if he'd lost his mind. Renaldo in particular was dubious. Although Casto was his mate now, he hadn't been very forthcoming with details about Lys so far. And the Angel of Death hadn't pressed him, because he didn't want to make the black stallion angry. Lys hadn't completely forgiven him for the incident with Casto yet, and Renaldo was wise enough not to challenge the steed. He had contented himself with the knowledge that Lys and Casto were like brothers, which made the beast an ally. It also meant he and Canubis had no clue what the stallion really was.

"And what is Lys, exactly? You've never told us." Like Renaldo, Canubis was dying to find out more about Casto's exceptional ride.

The young man sighed. "I guess it's time to tell you." He closed his eyes for a moment, a faint smile tracing his lips. "I called Lys here. Since this is about him, it's only fair he's present."

Canubis nodded in agreement. Ever since Casto had almost died, Lys refused to stay in a stall and instead moved around freely. This had caused some heated discussions with the stable masters here in Ummana, but they had finally agreed to let the proud stallion roam around as he pleased.

Light hoofbeats at the door announced Lys's arrival. Casto opened the door and greeted his brother by pressing his forehead against the stallion's blaze. The guards at the entrance to the royal wing had let the horse pass without hesitation. They were used to much stranger things.

After greeting his brother, Lys focused on the man on the ground. His soft snout skimmed over the stranger, and warm breath blew on his face. The assassin opened his eyes. For a moment he seemed bewildered as to where he was, but then Lys made a snorting sound that caught the man's attention. He froze in place, staring at the stallion with tears in his eyes. Casto smiled.

"My guess was right. He's like Lys."

"Can you understand him?" Renaldo was eager to get some answers.

"Not him, no. But Lys does, and he's translating for me."

"What does he say?"

Canubis's patience was wearing out quickly. This time Casto hurried to do the warrior's bidding, since he didn't want to be subjected to his wrath.

"The man's name is Sar'reff. It means 'shadow.'"

Casto hesitated and listened intently.

"Well, not really shadow, not of a thing or person, anyway. More like—the memory of a thought. That kind of shadow."

"So, Sar'reff, why did you try to kill one of our servants?"

The man looked at Lys.

"He doesn't understand why you're upset about this, but he did it because Erac had told him so. Erac feeds and clothes him and gives him shelter. That's why he obeys his commands."

"Seems fairly simple to me." Derision tainted Renaldo's voice.

Casto sighed again. This was going to be difficult.

"You don't understand, Barbarian. Sar'reff has come to this world like Lys did. He followed a calling, a pull, so to say. There's no time or concept of space where those two come from, and when they entered Ana-Darasa, they had to submit to the laws the Mothers have established. For creatures of chaos, this is so hard it can drive them insane. They take the shape that is closest to what they are, and then they follow the pull to their anchor. In Lys's case, I'm the anchor, but Sar'reff couldn't find his. As soon as he had taken form, he lost the connection. Lys thinks this is because the shape is inferior."

"You mean there was a mistake when it was built?"

Noemi was fascinated. Casto chuckled. "No. Lys views the human shape as inferior and defective. He pities us for not being like him. He's quite conceited."

The stallion shook his long, dark mane. To Renaldo it almost seemed as if he was mocking them. Casto carried on.

"Anyway, without his anchor, Sar'reff was lost. He started roaming the world, trying to find the pull again, but so far he hasn't been successful. The longer he stays here without the one who called him, the weaker he becomes, both physically and mentally. He was almost completely insane when Erac's grandfather found him and took him in. The family has provided a certain continuity that has helped Sar'reff to pull through, but he's not at his best, probably never will be again."

"Wait a moment." Noemi was the first to understand the real problem. "If he's looking for his anchor, and that anchor is a human and he's been here for at least a century, then the anchor must be dead already. Isn't that so?"

Casto rubbed his temples. Things were getting complicated, even though the barbarians were more likely to understand than anybody else he'd ever met. Suddenly he regretted not having explained things to Renaldo earlier.

"Could be. But there's also the possibility that the person hasn't been born yet. As I said, these two come from a place where time doesn't exist. Sometimes they get the effect before the cause. And Lys is right, Sar'reff is weak. It can be that the anchor is already here, but he can't sense him or her. This is really messed up."

Though this statement was deeply fascinating, Renaldo's mind was momentarily distracted by another thought.

"How old are you, Lys?"

The black demon whinnied so softly, it almost sounded like a snicker.

"Lys is about a thousand years old. Or, to be more precise, that's how long he's been on Ana-Darasa."

Noemi and the two warlords stared at the stallion with new respect. Until now they had regarded Lys as someone who belonged to Casto. An intelligent beast, but still a beast. Now they realized for the first time that the Emperor of the Storms was a person in his own right, albeit in an unusual shape. Canubis regarded the powerful steed closely.

"He hasn't gone mad."

"He's strong. Very strong. In human terms, you would call him a king. But although he's so powerful, it was still hard for him to wait for my birth. All he had was the pull to hang on to, and Sar'reff has lost even that. He's lost in the truest sense of the word."

"So what shall we do with him? Listening to you, it seems the kindest thing would be to put him out of his misery." Canubis didn't mean to threaten Sar'reff; he was just being objective.

Casto shook his head. "I don't think we have to go so far. Being with Lys will help him stabilize, and perhaps we can even find his anchor. Plus, I would love to take him away from Erac. The king of Medelina has yet to pay for attacking Daran."

"I'll leave that to you, Casto. Except for the incident tonight, things have gone smoothly, and I expect you to wrap this all up within the next few days. We're all anxious to go home."

Canubis slung his arm around his wife and left the room. Lys gently nudged Sar'reff in the same direction, leading him out of the royal wing and into the stables. Renaldo hugged his mate from behind, his chin resting comfortably on the blond head.

"Let's go to bed, my own. It's been a long day, and even though there are quite a lot of things I'd like to discuss with you, I'd rather we do it after a good night's sleep."

For once Casto complied without further discussion. The constant maneuvering against Erac had taken its toll, and almost losing Daran had shaken Casto more than he liked to admit. Putting off the inevitable fight with Renaldo until later sounded like an acceptable deal.

5. SACRIFICE

"My own, why are you looking so dejected? Everything went according to plan, didn't it?"

While saying those words, Renaldo took his lover in his arms. Sighing, Casto snuggled closer. Of course, the Barbarian was right. The past three weeks—and especially the last four days—had been tiring but successful.

Yesterday King Erac had returned to Medelina, giddy about having beaten Castolus in their game of politics. Who cared if he had had to make some minor concessions to gain his victory? Medelina was now the most powerful city in the Confederation, right after Ummana, and business was sure to thrive with all the benefits he had negotiated.

He would have members of the Pack patrolling the streets of Medelina in search for followers of the Good Mother, and those who were captured would be publicly executed, but their presence had started to annoy him anyway and, as Castolus had pointed out, this way his own men would be free to protect the city from all the vultures the additional wealth would bring. Those who had accepted bribes from the priests were, without a doubt, going to protest loudly, but the new law stated they would then lose their heads just like the followers. The prospect of getting rid of some of his political enemies so easily almost made Erac orgasm on the spot. He was a little miffed about having lost his watchdog, but some things couldn't be helped, and it wasn't as if he couldn't find a replacement, especially after the man had failed to put Daran out of the equation.

Having the new queen of Ummana in his debt was also a nice touch. With Erac's backing, Castolus had managed to get Anesha on the throne against the resistance of the big families. For the first time in the history of the Twin Cities, a leader who hadn't come of age yet would rule.

The barbarians had already started preparations to leave the Plains before winter set in, which meant Erac had to deal with Anesha only. An easy task, since the queen hadn't yet developed the foresight that comes with experience. Even though Anesha was intelligent and cunning, Erac was sure he was in the more favorable position at the moment.

The King of Medelina had left Ummana in a state of such utter self-righteousness, he never once suspected he could have been the one who had been outsmarted. This was the art of manipulating your opponent, to the point that they were grateful for having been used. Casto had demonstrated his skills in this area most impressively. Renaldo caressed the king's naked back.

"You had this worm dancing to your tune all the time. I'm bursting with pride, my own."

"I only followed my instincts. To be honest, I'm a little worried that I'm capable of doing such a thing."

"I'm not. You're a king, heart of a god. You're destined to rule, to be different and better. Canubis and I are glad you're part of our family."

A pained grimace showed on Casto's face.

"What I did was hardly honorable."

"You deceived a fraud. I can find no fault in that. You've protected your family. Stop pondering it. In only a few weeks we'll be back home, and you can forget about this nightmare."

Unhappy, Casto looked up at him.

"But it's not over yet."

"What do you mean?"

"The nightmare. It's not over for me. Not yet. I still have to make a decision I've been dodging for weeks now. And no matter what I'm going to do, there will be pain."

"What in the Mothers' names are you talking about?"

"Sic."

This one word was enough to shut Renaldo up. He did not have to be a genius to deduce what Casto was brooding about. The same thoughts had crossed his mind as well. His heart spoke.

"He's so happy here. Jago and Cassia have become his family, he's found friends, his talent is finally recognized, and he's become a rich man. Every time we meet, I can see him thriving more. How can I ask him to return to the Valley with me, where he's nothing but a prisoner without a family and love?"

"You know that's not true. We are Sic's family. You're his best friend. He's a free man."

"Still, the Valley is the place where he has gone through the worst time of his life. It's the one place where he won't be able to evade Noran. He's still in love with him, and it's eating him up inside. Can you imagine the pain he'll have to bear when he comes with us?"

"It's his decision. Did he say he wants to stay here?"

Renaldo sounded anxious. Both he and Canubis would prefer if Sic came back to the Valley with them. Noemi had forbidden them to order the Luksari, and because of the blunder they had made, the two warlords had acquiesced to Noemi's demand. It was Sic's decision whether he wanted to stay in Ummana or not.

Casto sighed. "Not directly, but I can see how happy he is here. He'd never stay if he thought I needed him. So it's my duty to let him go. The thought alone makes me gag."

Renaldo shuddered. He was aware of the dilemma his heart was going through, but he didn't know what to tell the young man. The savage part of him that wanted to have Casto all to himself was ecstatic to know the greatest rival for his heart's affection would be a continent away. But the other, gentler part of him, which loved Casto so much it caused him physical pain, couldn't stand the idea of seeing him suffer. Not to mention that it would be a good thing to have a Luksari in the Valley.

"You're a good person, Casto. A true friend. I'm sure you're going to do the right thing."

The young man stared at him sadly. "Then why do I feel like my heart's going to burst?"

Renaldo didn't know what to answer.

"WHAT'S THE matter, Sic? You've hardly eaten anything. Are you feeling unwell?" Cassia regarded the young smith with worry.

Despondently he shook his head. "I'm fine. I just had a talk with Casto."

"And?"

"He's told me the lords are planning to return to the Valley come next week."

Silence descended on the table. Cassia and Jago weren't able to hide their shock. They had known this day would come, that the barbarians wouldn't stay for good, but it was still unpleasant, especially for the tiny midwife who had nurtured hopes the plan she had developed with Noemi would be successful.

"So you're going to leave us." Jago tried to sound casual, sensing how emotionally high-strung his guest was.

Sic was intently studying his plate. "Not necessarily. Casto says I'm allowed to choose. Lord Renaldo and Lord Canubis have given their consent. If I wish to, I can stay here."

"Then why are we moping instead of celebrating?" Cassia was suspicious. Something in Sic's tone did not sit well with her. "You're not telling me you're seriously contemplating going with them, are you?"

Now Sic raised his head. His voice was insecure and betrayed the conflict he'd been struggling with ever since Casto had spoken to him.

"I don't know. The offer was unexpected. I never thought I'd have a say in this."

"Then be grateful, tell the barbarians good-bye, and start your new life here, just like you deserve." Cassia's voice was growing sharper with every word.

The smith's shoulders slumped forward. His hostess's aggressive behavior didn't make it easier for him to make a decision.

"It's not as simple as it seems, Cassia. I don't know if I can leave Casto alone. He's the first true friend I ever had. And I owe him more than you can imagine. Despite that, I've sworn to my god to look after him."

"But if you go back with them, the despicable monster who made you suffer so badly will be there as well. How can you even consider returning with them?" The tiny midwife got up, her eyes glinting in fury, her voice shrill.

"They have hurt and humiliated you. They have treated you like garbage. The way I see it, you don't owe them anything. You'd be an idiot to stay with such a bunch of heartless thugs."

"Cassia, calm down. I think it's better if I talked to Sic. Why don't you go and look after Heljia?"

Jago's voice was soft, soothing. He gently nudged his enraged wife toward their sleeping chamber. Initially it seemed as if Cassia would snarl at her husband as well, but then she straightened up and left the two men.

Jago apologized to Sic. "I'm sorry. She loves you a lot, which is why it irritates her so much."

Filled with regret, Sic stared at the place Cassia had just left. It pained him to hurt his benefactress so deeply and made it even harder to arrive at a decision.

"I'm sorry for causing you so much grief. I didn't mean to."

"It's fine, Sic. I assume you don't know what to do yet?"

"No. My mind is ecstatic about this once-in-a-lifetime chance. I know I can't do better than staying here, with the people who love me, in a city that has already made me rich. But my heart grows heavy when I think I'll never return to the Valley. Most of the time I was happy there, even if you find it hard to believe. And as I said, Casto is my friend. He told me he'd be glad if I stayed here and was happy, but I could sense how much it cost him."

Jago took the hand of this exceptional young man and wondered why fate hadn't treated him with more kindness. Sic was such a good and kind person, and despite his unbelievable talent, he was still modest and unpretentious. He deserved to lead a normal life, to know happiness. But normalcy was something the inhabitants of the Valley didn't seem to know. The best example was Casto, who had integrated so perfectly into this group of terrifying people. He was as far from normal as humanly possible.

"Casto is a good friend. He wants the best for you. Obviously he thinks staying with us will do the job, otherwise he wouldn't have brought it up."

Sic sobbed in despair. Knowing his friend had given so much thought to him only increased his conflict instead of ending it.

"I simply don't know what to do. I'm happy here, very much so. And I love you, as well as my work. I just can't decide."

Jago slung an arm around his young friend.

"You still have a week's time, Sic. Lie down, sleep a night, think about it carefully. And be assured, no matter what you decide to do, we love and support you. You can rely on us."

Sic started crying from the bottom of his heart. Whimpering, he let Jago sway him while the severity of his choice weighed him down like an oncoming storm.

THE NEXT four days, Sic barely left his room. He didn't eat and wasn't able to sleep. All the time he was brooding about what he should do. When he finally reached a decision, he was mentally so exhausted he slept for an entire day. Then he was prepared to speak with Casto.

The king was waiting for him at their usual meeting point in the gardens. He looked as tired as Sic felt, and the smith felt a pang of guilt for leaving his friend alone. When he approached him, the blond smiled weakly.

"Sic. How are you?"

"Tired. Insecure. Frightened. You can choose one."

"So you're going to stay here?"

Under his breath, Sic cursed Casto's empathy.

"Yes. I'm going to stay here." He hesitated a moment, unable to deal with the pain he had glimpsed in his friend's eyes before the king regained his composure. "I'm sorry, Casto. I know I'm leaving you alone. And I know I'm a jerk for doing so. But I've been thinking about this so long and hard, my brain almost got tied in a knot. I'm not used to making my own decisions, and for my first one to be such a major thing—it's not fair. Apparently life seldom is, as the two of us have learned the hard way. I know you don't really want to let me go, but that you will if I decide so. And I can't say I wasn't tempted to return with you. I consider the Valley my home. I'd be safe there, you'd be there. And so would Noran. Do you remember when we discussed how I still love him despite everything he's done to me? How you scolded me and called me an idiot? You were, of course, right. But emotions are a strange thing, and apparently I'm unable to control mine. Part of me still yearns for him, although another part tells me to forget about him as soon as possible. Therefore, as much as I would love to stay with you, to spend my life basking in our friendship, to maintain my sanity and to finally break free from those invisible chains, I need to stay here. I hope you can understand."

Sic glanced at his friend, who stared at him as if he'd seen him for the first time.

"I've never heard you say so many words in one go. You really thought this through, didn't you?"

Sic nodded feebly. Casto threw his arms around him.

"I fully understand. Admittedly, I hate leaving you behind. It makes my stomach churn and my heart burst. But more than anything else, I want you to be happy, to find the serenity you deserve. Losing you to Jago and Cassia is something I can learn to live with. They're good people. I may wish things were different, but I can understand your reasoning, and I will respect your decision. Just promise to write me regularly, won't you?"

Sic couldn't believe his ears. He had half expected Casto to pressure him into changing his decision, to use his manipulative talents to make him yield. When he looked at his friend, he understood Casto had contemplated exactly this and had refrained from doing so because he loved him. Sic hugged him silently, trying to convey with his body what words could never hope to express.

"NORAN, DO you have a moment? We need to talk."

"Surely, Hulda. What's the matter?"

The beautiful assassin entered her friend's rooms with a dark expression.

"I've just spoken to Casto. Sic won't come back with us, but stay with Cassia and Jago."

All color drained from Noran's face when he heard those words he had been dreading for a week now. Groaning, he slumped on a chair. His head fell forward as if he had just received a terrible blow. He sounded disbelieving.

"This can't be. Please tell me this isn't true."

"I'm so sorry, Noran. So unbelievably sorry."

Hulda embraced the burly man and caressed his head. She knew better than anyone how much Noran had hoped his former slave would return to the Valley with them.

"Casto has told me the decision wasn't easy for Sic, but he thinks it's for the better."

A sound like a lethally wounded boar would make was the only answer.

"Hulda, I can't lose him like that. I haven't repented my sin, I haven't even begged his forgiveness. What am I supposed to do?"

"I honestly don't know. I'm sorry, Noran."

Soothingly the mother superior stroked the master smith's back. She suspected this was part of the punishment Noran had to endure for the things he'd done, but she'd rather bite off her own tongue than saying it. There was nothing she could do for Noran, so she just lent him her shoulder as a friend.

THE NIGHT before the Pack left the Twin Cities, nobody got much sleep. Renaldo and Canubis were ecstatic to finally go home, having gotten their revenge on the Good Mother's followers. Noran was trying to get drunk and failed miserably. Casto and Sic spent the last hours together, not talking much, just enjoying each other's company. Lys was still busy helping Sar'reff to get a grip on reality again, a task that had been keeping him occupied for the past weeks and would do so for a long time to come. Daran still had his hands full comforting his masters, who hadn't quite gotten over the fact they had almost lost him. And Anesha was basking in the triumph of her complete victory.

6. A KISS

Before the sun had time to tint the sky pink with her first rays, the barbarians from the North gathered at the stables for their departure. Cheerful anticipation filled the air; most of them were happy to finally go home again. Queen Anesha was standing in a group with her brother and the divine brothers to talk about some final detail, but it was comparatively idle chitchat since they had cemented her claim to power during the last weeks.

That she was related through her brother to the leaders of the most powerful army of mercenaries in the world had helped. Officially, Anesha now had absolute power over Ummana and the Confederation. Unofficially, she was still dependent on the brothers, at least until she managed to form her own alliances within the city. As long as she was tied to the Pack, she would see to it that the followers of the Good Mother would get no chance to set foot in the Twin Cities or anywhere in its sphere of influence. Regarding business, she already could do as she pleased, and Casto had even decided to allow his sister to act as a trustee for his private fortune. Having such a large sum to back her actions up, Anesha had an easy start as queen and would surely make her brother even richer than he already was. In the Valley the money was of little significance, and so it made sense to at least put it to some use.

Casto knew his sister well, and he was aware she had been scheming behind his back all along, but since her goal and his had been the same, namely getting her on the throne, he had let her be. Briefly he had contemplated putting her a little off by revealing how much he knew, but he decided to refrain. He was going home, and that was all he cared about, even though he had to leave his best friend behind.

Renaldo sensed the distress of his heart and placed his hand on Casto's nape. He, too, was sad to leave the young smith behind, but he knew how much sorrow they spared themselves. Even though he was a Luksari, for all they knew Sic was still mortal. In only a few years—forty, perhaps fifty if he was lucky—the smith would take Ana-Isara's hand. It was better losing him now, when he was still alive and time hadn't had the opportunity to forge bonds between them that, when broken, would leave wounds almost impossible to heal. Wisely he refrained from sharing those thoughts with his heart. Casto was too young to understand what it truly meant to be immortal. Renaldo was intent on keeping this shocking revelation from the king as long as possible.

With eyes clouded by pain and grief, Noran stared at the palace, his horse standing next to him. He still couldn't believe he would actually lose Sic. Hulda watched him with pity, but when she wanted to approach the smith, her husband stopped her.

"Leave him alone. It's difficult enough as it is."

Before Hulda could make up her mind whether to follow her mate's counsel or ignore it, Canubis gave the signal, and they all mounted their horses. With the divine brothers and Casto leading the baggage, the Pack left Ummana as swiftly as it had entered the city only a few months ago.

Anesha watched the barbarians as they made their way through the still empty streets from the highest tower of her palace. Aktan stood next to her, glad the intimidating, dangerous strangers were gone and a little uneasy in the presence of the new queen, whom he already knew as a dangerous schemer. When the female turned to him with a seductive little smile playing around her lips, Aktan's heartbeat sped up.

"How's he doing?"

Cassia was carrying Heljia through the kitchen, her eyes glued to her husband. Jago shrugged.

"He hasn't talked much. Stayed behind his anvil the entire day and worked like crazy. But that was to be expected. It's only the first day since they left, and they were all the family he had known until he came here."

"He hasn't eaten anything today. When he came home, he vanished right into his room. Well, he did give Heljia a kiss, but nothing more. I'm worried."

"I'm sure he's going to be fine, my beloved. This was so hard for him, and it took all his courage to tell Casto good-bye. You can't expect him to be all jolly as if nothing had happened. It will take time. I guess we just have to be patient. After all, he chose us."

Cassia smiled a tiny bit triumphantly. Except for Noemi and perhaps Casto, she didn't care too much about the barbarians. In her eyes they were nothing but a bunch of savages who bent the world to their liking. It was a good thing Sic had severed all ties with them. And as soon as he got better, she could start finding him a nice, decent mate. Everything would be perfect.

Together, Jago and Cassia put Heljia to sleep before they went to their chamber. They were just dozing off when the first scream pierced their ears.

AFTER A long, tiring day during which Sic had tried to numb his thoughts with bone-wrenching work and the deprivation of food, he had fallen onto his bed, exhausted but unable to find rest. Not even the sight of Heljia had managed to soothe his raging emotions, and so he had retired almost immediately, knowing Cassia was worried sick about him but unable to put up a front for her sake.

He must have dozed off, because he suddenly felt the warmth of a forge on his face and woke with a start. Surprised, he noted he was in the Valley, in Noran's smithy. Slowly he got up and looked around. It was very quiet; except for him, nobody seemed to be there. His naked toes tripped over a piece of metal. It was the chain with which he had been bound to the forge during the last months. The collar lay next to it, broken. Shuddering, Sic felt for the padded scar around his neck that even now that he was a free man told the whole world he had been marked as a traitor. Uneasily his gaze darted around the smithy. Everything was familiar, but also strangely blurred, as if he wasn't really there.

"You aren't. But this is the only place where you feel truly safe, and I want you to relax."

The voice was melodic, high, a female tone, and Sic knew even before he turned around and beheld the pale face surrounded by white hair that the Empress of the Dead had come to him. His stomach turned to ice while he sank to his knees. He had been waiting for this moment ever since he'd taken the cloak pin from Casto's trunk and given it to Damon. The only surprise was how long the mistress had waited to punish him.

"Why are you so afraid, Sic?"

He bit his lips to stop the trembling, then spoke in a quivering tone.

"Because of me your son almost lost his heart. I've betrayed one of your own and played into the hands of your archenemy. I don't even dare to imagine the extent of your wrath."

The goddess seemed to be musing about his words for a moment; then the bloodred lips parted in a reassuring smile.

"You're right. Because of you there was quite a commotion in the Valley. But if I'm not mistaken, my son, as well as his heart, have forgiven you. And Noran gave up his right to forgive you when he punished you like he did. Don't you think it's enough already?"

Tortured, Sic looked up at the alluring goddess. Before Ana-Isara, no pretense was possible.

"How can it ever be enough? I brought shame on myself. I don't deserve forgiveness. How can I accept Casto's friendship, knowing I almost killed him?"

Ana-Isara leaned down to the young smith; her cold fingers caressed his hair.

"How can you deny his friendship? Casto is a proud man, one who doesn't open up easily, but you have his trust. Don't you think it's a little arrogant to cast such a gift aside?"

"But I'm not worthy! Besides, what does it matter now? He's gone and I'll probably never see him again."

"Thankfully that's not your decision, Sic. Even my son has opened his heart to you, something that's never happened before. It's time to forgive yourself. Given the circumstances, you couldn't have acted otherwise. You made the best out of a difficult situation. My sister and I can't find anything wrong in that."

Tears flowing down his cheeks, Sic stared at the Empress of the Dead. Her words were meant to soothe, but he could sense there was still something unpleasant to come.

"What will be my punishment, Mistress?"

Ana-Isara smiled again, this time with a trace of malice in the night-dark eyes.

"I'm not going to punish you, young smith. Quite the contrary. I'll make you part of the family."

It took a moment until Sic understood what the goddess meant, but then he retreated hastily, all color drained from his face.

"Please, Mistress, don't do that to me! It's bad enough to spend one lifetime in unrequited love. An eternity would be unbearable."

"Oh, Sic." Ana-Isara pulled the smith into her embrace, her voice like the sweetest honey in his ears, meant to break his resistance. "Love has never left you. You took it with you to the darkest places and kept its flame alive. I don't know anybody except you who could have done such a thing. I promise, if you give it one more try, you'll never be disappointed again.

"You showed great courage when you were willing to sacrifice your life for that of your tormentor. Now show the same bravery and live—with my blessing."

The bloodred lips tried to kiss Sic on the forehead, but somehow the young smith managed to evade the goddess. Blinding light surged around him and threw Ana-Isara off. Sic panted.

"I've already decided not to go back to the Valley. I did so to find at least a minimum of peace. It was the hardest decision I've ever made, and now you come here and want me to rescind it? How can you be so cruel?"

The Empress of the Dead stared at Sic with a hint of something he couldn't quite grasp. Her voice was still level when she answered him.

"I'm not cruel. I'm Death, and all I know is justice. It's my nature. But I have learned the meaning of regret, and you can trust me when I tell you, I'm really sorry for what happened to you. Some of it was necessary for both you and Noran to become what you need to be in order to be useful to my sons. But those months when he tortured you for the sheer fun of it—I did not intend that. It was a perversion of everything my sister and I hold dear."

"Then why? Why didn't you stop my master? Why didn't you help me?"

Ana-Isara sighed. Her white hair flew up as if caught in a breeze. When she finally spoke, it was in measured tones.

"There is no answer I can give to you that won't leave you either mad or confused or both. So let's just leave it at that: I made a mistake and I'm sorry for it. I'm even asking your forgiveness."

Sic glared at her. He was so angry, he'd almost forgotten he was talking to a goddess.

"You're asking my forgiveness, but you won't change your mind, will you?"

"No. My sons need you, need your power, need what you are. Forcing a Luksari is not a wise thing to do, but my hands are bound. You're the one destined for them, and I won't allow you to decline."

When she saw Sic's expression, her gaze softened.

"Please, Sic. All I'm asking for is another chance from you. This time there won't be any mistakes, I swear. You were never entirely sure whether you should really stay behind. That was because, deep in your heart, you know where you belong. Isn't that right?"

Sic closed his eyes. Something deep inside him stirred, a power that had been dormant all his life. For the first time, he understood what it meant to be a Luksari. It meant being able to refuse the wishes of someone as powerful as a creator goddess. It meant controlling powers so great they had best stay untouched. All Luksari were by nature calm, open, and friendly to the point of neglecting themselves. If they weren't, they would destroy the very fabric of creation. Sic listened to what his nature told him to do.

Ana-Isara watched him closely. She and her sister had created the universe and everything within, but the Luksari were not part of it. Not even Ana-Aruna, who had spent more time with them than anybody else, truly understood them or the extent of their power. Meeting Sic had come as a pleasant, albeit unexpected, surprise since they both thought the race had died out long ago. Unfortunately the young smith was also bound by fate to her sons, and so she had to hope he would decide to fight at their side. Because even though she had told him otherwise, there was no way she could force him if he refused.

Now the young man got up and looked her directly in the eyes. For the fraction of a heartbeat, Ana-Isara was allowed a glimpse of what lay beneath the open, friendly face, and she couldn't suppress a shudder. Then the image was gone, leaving behind only an insecure, frightened boy who had already endured more than others did in two lifetimes.

"Since there's no helping it—do what you have to do."

The red lips parted invitingly, and once again the cold arms embraced the young man. He felt a slight sting when Ana-Isara pressed her kiss on his forehead.

"Thank you, *ana ligtos wanda*. Trust in love, and, only once more, trust *him*, and everything will be fine. This I promise as the creator of the worlds you're walking."

A breeze caught the white strands again. Sic felt them scraping over his skin like cobwebs and then Ana-Isara, the Empress of the Dead, was gone.

The fire in the forge flickered. The pain set in.

"WHAT'S THE matter with him?"

Jago was trying to soothe the wailing baby in his arms, whose high-pitched screams were almost indistinguishable from those of Sic. Cassia was bent over the flailing young man, trying to examine him and not get hit at the same time.

"I don't know. He doesn't seem to be hurt, but his skin is boiling hot and he won't open his eyes."

"Poison?"

Cassia shook her head.

"I don't think so. At least none I've ever heard of. If only he would wake, I could try to give him something against the pain."

Jago stared at the twitching body of his young friend. Even when he had first met him, he'd known Sic was special. And the master smith had the nagging feeling that what was happening now had more to do with the barbarians than could please him. Cassia was still trying to wake Sic when her husband suddenly yanked her back so quickly she almost toppled over.

"Watch it, Jago! What did you do that for?"

He pointed with his chin, his tall frame trembling slightly.

"Look!"

Cassia's eyes followed the direction indicated by her mate, and she too froze. The thick scar around Sic's neck had turned almost black and was fading while they watched, leaving behind nothing but unmarred skin. Cassia bent forward again.

"He's healing. All the scars are vanishing. Not even Lady Noemi was able to do that!"

The couple looked at each other in awe. Only a goddess could accomplish such a difficult task.

"Well, Casto did say the Mothers are always with them. Perhaps he's finally rewarded for everything he had to endure?"

Cassia doubted this but didn't know what to make of the situation either. She stroked Sic's skin, which was slick from sweat. He seemed to calm down a bit; the convulsions running through his body eased slightly. Unfortunately it was only a short reprieve. The next moment his back arched up, his fingers dug into the fur like claws, and the scream he gave sounded like it was torn from his lungs with hot pokers. Cassia wanted to at least comfort him, if she could do nothing else, when she became aware of the light surrounding Sic's frame. It was growing rapidly in intensity, and before she knew it, she and Jago had to shield their eyes not to be blinded by it. Sic's hand under her fingers felt thin like paper, as if it was losing its integrity. Cassia panicked.

"Sic! Stop it! Stay with us! Don't you dare go!" Her voice was shrill, joining the still-wailing Heljia and Sic's unearthly cries.

Jago tried to snap her out of it. "What's happening, Cassia?"

"He's losing his shape. Probably to escape the pain. But I don't think he should be doing that."

"Are you sure?"

"How can I be sure? I'm a midwife, not a witch. But if you ask me, I'd say he needs to stay in his human shape."

Jago nodded. Years of marriage had taught him to rely on his wife's intuition. It was never off.

"Then how do we anchor him?"

"I've no idea. Try shaking him harder. You're stronger than me."

Cassia took the baby, and Jago bent over his friend. The light surrounding him was not only blinding but also hot, like a protective cocoon. And the skin he was touching was almost gone. Just a few moments longer, and Sic would be nothing more but a beam of light in the dark. Jago was desperate enough to slap the young man in the face. For a few frantic heartbeats, the master smith thought it had worked, for the light dimmed a bit, and Sic even seemed to focus on him. Then suddenly a new wave of pain overwhelmed him, sending the light glaring.

Cassia pushed him aside. With Heljia in her arms, she bent over Sic, holding the infant out to him. Her voice was soft, nothing more but a whisper.

"Sic. I have Heljia here. She's crying. She needs you. Can you take care of her?"

The smith's body jerked and then lay still. Fingers almost indistinguishable from beams of light reached out for the mewling baby. When their hands connected, Heljia stopped crying. She gurgled happily and admired the streaks of light dancing around the room, chasing the shadows away. Sic gradually calmed down, never letting go of Heljia's hand.

Cassia breathed a sigh of relief.

"I think it's fine now. You can go and get some sleep. I'll stay here with these two."

Jago followed his wife's advice, glad they hadn't lost the young smith.

SIC AND Heljia slept in the following morning, huddled together like two kittens waiting for their mother. It was almost noon when the young smith entered the kitchen with the baby in his arms and a guilty expression on his face. Jago and Cassia stared at him expectantly.

"I take it you're feeling better now?" Relief colored Cassia's tone. She was more than happy that Sic seemed to be normal again. Her guest smiled awkwardly at her.

"Yes, I do. I'm so sorry for what has happened. And I'm grateful. You saved me last night."

"You're welcome. Now tell us, what did we save you from?"

Sic avoided Cassia's glare. She wouldn't be happy about what he had to tell her now.

"Ana-Isara came to me last night. She gave me her kiss and marked me as one of the Emeris. I'm afraid I can't stay here after all."

"How could she do that? Why did you allow it? You've worked so hard for your freedom—you endured so much. How can this goddess take it all away from you again?"

Sic smiled sadly. "Because her sons need me. For reasons I don't understand, I've been chosen to fight at their side. I don't like it any more than you do, perhaps even less, but in the end, I had no choice. My vows were still binding me to Casto even before she came, but now I'm obliged to follow them."

While saying this, Sic opened his tunic to reveal his torso. The scars were indeed all gone, a miracle and a blessing in one, but right over his heart, two symbols were carved into his flesh, shining from it darkly as if to mock Cassia and Jago.

"The one right above my heart is the rune of the Mothers, their sign. The other one is my sign, a rune that means 'light.' Not very imaginative, but I guess a creator of worlds doesn't have to mind the fine details. At least it's straightforward."

"Light is indeed fitting. You should have seen yourself when you were out of your mind. You tried to become light."

"Again, I'm sorry about that. Without you and Heljia, I'd be gone by now. It was just too much, and my mind tried to escape the only way it knew would work."

In the silence following these words, Heljia gurgled happily in Sic's arms. Her tiny fingers had closed around his thumb with surprising strength, and she tried sucking on it with her toothless gums. Her mother smiled gently at this beautiful picture.

"So what are you, Sic? If you don't mind me asking."

"No, it's fine, Cassia. I'm not sure myself, but Ana-Isara called me a Luksari. I've no idea what that means, but I've gotten a glimpse of what I'm capable of. Afterward, I had no choice but to agree to her proposal. Even now I'm terrified by what I've felt. It really is better if I return to my gods. I could never forgive myself if anything happened to you."

Jago took Sic in his arms. He hated losing him to the barbarian, although he felt deep inside it was for the best.

"We're going to miss you. I guess you want to depart as soon as possible?"

A soft sob escaped Sic's throat.

"Yes."

"Then we'd better start packing. We'll be sending your money with the next caravan, since it'll take some time to get back the investments. It may be spring till you have it. Is that all right?"

Sic took a step backward, Heljia still in his arms.

"No, it's not all right. I want you to keep that money. I won't need it in the Valley anyway, and you will put it to good use."

"Sic, you can't!" Cassia shook her head violently. "We won't take any money from you. You're family. We simply can't accept this."

"I know, Cassia, but I'm begging you to do it. Casto once told me that in Ummana everything can be bought at a certain price. Since I can't be here to watch Heljia grow up, let this be my parting gift for her. I'm betting my fortune on her future."

"Sic."

Jago didn't know what to say. His exceptional friend patted his shoulder.

"I almost forgot. Casto has given me a house—or rather a palace— here in the inner city as well. I'll leave it to you. Even though I can't imagine you living anywhere but here, it might be nice to have a little more room when this little lady grows up."

"You know this won't make us suffer less, don't you?"

"Yes, Cassia, I know. Neither does it make leaving you any easier. I just want to ensure Heljia's happiness in the future. And yours, of course. So please accept what I'm offering and allow me to feel a little less guilty."

The tiny midwife hugged him desperately, whispering frantically in his ear. "There's no need to feel guilty. Of course it hurts. It always does when you decide to love somebody. It's part of being alive, of having a family. And we don't regret having chosen you as a part of our family. We're proud of you, and we want what's best for you, even if it means you can't stay with us."

"Thank you, Cassia. Thank you for welcoming me into your family. You've given me hope when I was at a low point. I'll never forget you or what you did for me. Never."

And so, after many sweet words of love and assurance, Sic left the Twin Cities in order to return to his other, old family in the North.

Exclusive Excerpt

Braving the Storm

Gods of War: Book IV

By Xenia Melzer

Though some struggles have ended in victory, ease and contentment are not the fate of the gods of war. Instead, they must contemplate the sometimes terrible and frightening nature of their powers—and the effect those powers have on the men they love.

After their campaign in Ummana, the gods of war return to the Valley with their ranks finally complete. Sic is the eighth Emeris to join Renaldo and Canubis in their war against the Good Mother. Even so, they must wait for their powers to manifest, and trials lay ahead.

It is only when a tragedy befalls Aegid, Kalad, and Daran that Sic learns the extent of his abilities as a Luksari. What he achieves will change Daran forever—and set him up for trauma that leaves him doubting his relationship with Aegid and Kalad. Daran must affirm his commitment to his lovers and his new status among them through blood and violence.

Meanwhile, Renaldo's true power sends Casto fleeing in disgust, and at the worst possible time—because the Good Mother is plotting her next move.

Coming Soon to
www.dsppublications.com

BACK AND BEYOND

1. BITTER TRUTH

IT WAS the third day since their departure from Ummana. Canubis had taken the first watch, eager to have some time on his own, alone in the darkness with nothing to distract his thoughts. He still didn't know whether he should be pleased about this year's unusual campaign or if he should write it off as a failure. Their original mission had been a success, no doubt. Not only had they gotten their revenge on the followers of the Good Mother in Medelina, they had also seen to it that the lives of those worshipping the old hag in the vicinity of the Confederation were going to be a lot more uncomfortable from now on. It was all thanks to his brother's heart, and this was where the problems started.

Canubis liked Casto, not just because he was Renaldo's missing part, but also for his stubborn and unbending personality. The young man was worth liking. He was also a king who had shown impressively what he was capable of at any time of the day. Canubis didn't feel threatened. It was his nature, after all, just like Renaldo's nature was the fire, wild and untamed. He was worried, though. It was hard to read Casto, and he still wasn't entirely sure if he could rely on the capricious blond like he had to.

Then there was all that trouble with Noran. The Wolf of War had silently watched the affair Renaldo had with the master smith shortly after he joined them. Since he himself had rarely said no to anybody before he met Noemi, he didn't have the right to interfere. When Noran had hooked up with Arja, Canubis had still held back. From his point of view, it had been a minor incident with little to no significance whatsoever. Well, he had been wrong about that one. Now he had to deal with an Emeris who was so riddled with guilt, he was hardly capable of performing his duties. Canubis wondered whether he should have a word with Noran. On the other hand, Hulda seemed to have taken this in hand. Interfering with her was unwise, to put it mildly. Besides, leaving the whole business to her made life easier for him.

Their latest addition, the demon called Sar'reff, was another problem he hadn't decided how to deal with yet. His sudden appearance had at least shed some light on Lys's nature and so far, that was the best he could say about him. Canubis wasn't too keen on having two alien creatures who did not answer to his power inside the Pack. There was nothing he could do about Lysistratos since he was irrefutably linked to Casto, but the other one was a different matter. Noemi thought it was a good thing to have him here, a notion her husband didn't share. If push came to shove, Lys would always side with Casto, and the blond was unpredictable. Most likely, Sar'reff would follow the stallion's example since he hadn't found his anchor yet. And probably never would—putting him out of his misery might even be an act of mercy, just as he had suggested.

Losing the Luksari had been a low blow. Given the circumstances, they had to be grateful for getting out of their debt toward the young man almost unscathed, but the whole thing still left a bad aftertaste. Of course it was hard to recognize a Luksari—not even Ana-Aruna was always dead on—and there had been that damned spell, but still. He and Renaldo had not only not recognized what Sic was, they had also subjected him to their wrath and left him to Noran. It was the worst blunder Canubis had ever made in all his years as a leader. And now, of all times, when they had gotten so close to finally completing their ranks. It was infuriating. And stupid. If only….

One of the wolves who had been lying at his feet perked up. A single rider was approaching. The Wolf of War drew his sword, his eyes pierced the darkness.

"Whoever you are, come out and show yourself or I'll kill you."

There was a rustling in the bushes and then a thin, familiar voice answered.

"Please, don't do that, my lord. It's me, Sic."

The smith emerged from the shadows, leading an unhappy horse toward the warlord.

"I'm sorry, I didn't mean to sneak up on you, but this one here isn't used to the wolves and she's kind of edgy."

Canubis indicated the predators to leave them alone and take up their posts a little farther from the camp. Once the wolves were gone, the mare calmed down enough for Sic to step closer.

"Thank you, my lord."

"Sic, what brings you here? I'm thrilled to see you, but, to be frank, I expected to never meet you again."

The young man evaded his gaze.

"Can we go to the camp? I'd better show you."

Canubis furrowed his brow but followed the smith back to the fire in the middle of the camp. He could tell there was something strange about the young man, probably the awakening of his Luksari nature. At the fire, Renaldo was waiting for them. He had felt his brother's surprise and was curious about the reason. When he beheld Sic, his eyes widened.

"Sic! What are you doing here?"

The Luksari stepped into the light, his eyes shyly cast downward.

"Some things have happened and now I want to ask your permission to return to the Valley with you."

"Something bad? You don't look very happy."

Thrilled about the prospect of getting Sic back, Canubis had to concentrate not to show his excitement. The smith looked so crestfallen, his reason for returning had to be something serious.

"After you had left, I had a visit from Ana-Isara. She kissed me."

Stunned silence followed these words, then Canubis rushed forward. "Show me."

Demurely, Sic took off his riding coat and opened his tunic. The warlords stared at the black runes glowing on the unmarred skin, unable to believe their own eyes. Here stood the last Emeris, the one they had been waiting for so long—it was too good to be true. Renaldo reached out to touch the signs with an expression of sheer awe on his regal face.

"This is so amazing. And so perfect." He hugged the smith gently. "Welcome to the family, brother. It's good to have you finally here."

"My brother is right—I'm glad we're now complete. Welcome, Lord Sic."

The oddly formal words made Sic realize how drastically and completely his life had changed. All of a sudden, he felt exhausted.

"I'm very tired, my lords. May I rest?"

"Of course. This must have been difficult for you."

Canubis patted his shoulder. "Go and have a good night's sleep. We can talk tomorrow."

"Casto will be thrilled. I can't wait to see his face."

Renaldo radiated happy excitement that made Sic feel even more miserable than before. Then again, seeing Casto was the one thing he was actually looking forward to. He went to lie down and hesitated. On their journey to Ummana, things had been painful but clear. He had helped the other slaves to set up camp, served Noran as his personal toy, and then slept on the ground in the master smith's tent. It was not a place he wanted to visit right now so he directed his steps toward the area where the common slaves slept. A heavy hand on his shoulder stopped him.

"What do you think you're doing?"

Renaldo sounded apprehensive.

"I wanted to lay down. But if there's anything you want me to do, my lord...."

"No! You don't have to do anything. And you're most certainly not going to sleep with the slaves. Come with me, you can have my place."

Sic was close to panicking. Having the aloof Angel of Death treat him like a treasured friend was too much after all the strain he had to endure. Desperately he tried to find a way out while Renaldo was already dragging him toward his own tent. He shoved the struggling smith inside, pressing a finger to Sic's lips.

"Shh. Casto's sleeping, so try not to make too much noise. My furs are right next to him. Now take off your boots and rest. We'll talk about everything tomorrow."

Sighing, Sic obeyed the commands of his god, too tired to argue with the empty air for Renaldo was already gone. Casto was sleeping soundly, his soft blond hair surrounded his face like a halo. He looked very young and vulnerable in his sleep, nothing like the stubborn, arrogant, and short-tempered man Sic had come to call his friend. When it came to hardships, they both had gotten more than their fair share. Being with Casto again was the only good thing he'd gotten out of the bargain with Ana-Isara. He was still afraid of her sons, and he dreaded having to deal with Noran again. It was too confusing, too painful. If he had still been a normal human, he could have evaded the master smith somehow, but now that he was an Emeris as well, there was no way he could ignore him. Sic would have to address his issues with his former owner, the sooner, the better. The mere thought terrified him.

Well, there was nothing he could do right at the moment, so he took off his clothes, made himself comfortable on the furs, and was asleep before he even noted the velvet softness of his covers.

THE NEXT morning Sic woke with a start. Casto was looming over him like a hungry vulture, his face only a hand from the smith's nose.

"So you're finally awake. I thought you'd sleep the entire day. Why didn't you wake me when you came here?"

Sic smiled weakly. Talking to his friend again made him feel all tingly inside.

"Because a certain god who has the means to make my life unbearably miserable has told me to let you sleep."

"Why would you listen to him? He's like a mother hen, so just ignore him."

"I can't do that, as you well know. I don't have your guts."

"I'm not that brave either, just annoyed as hell. He's really getting on my nerves. Now back to the issue at hand. Why are you back? I mean, I'm thrilled, don't get me wrong, but I do remember your reasons for staying in Ummana, and they were substantial. So what made you change your mind?"

Sic's face darkened.

"Not what. Who. I got a visit from the Empress of the Dead. Seems like we'll be staying together for quite some time."

It took a few moments for the words to sink in and when they finally did, Casto's face was a sight to behold. Different emotions flickered across his features, among them joy, pity, regret, and fear. It moved Sic deeply to see how completely his friend understood him and how he was feeling with him. Finally, the king hugged the smith, his voice was a harsh whisper.

"I can't say I'm sorry. I know how hard this must be for you. But I just can't say I'm sorry. I'm too glad."

"I know. And you're the only one permitted to say so."

They were still basking in this intimate moment when Renaldo came barging in. Sic couldn't remember ever seeing the god so jittery with excitement.

"What are you two waiting for? There're lots of people out there who wish to welcome the new Emeris to the Pack. So get going. Get going."

"Easy, Barbarian. Sic has just woken up. He hasn't had breakfast yet."

"He can eat later. Now come!"

Renaldo grabbed Sic by the hand, dragging him into the morning light like an impatient toddler would his mother. In front of the tent, they were all gathered. Up front were Noemi and the Emeris: Hulda, Wolfstan, Kalad, Aegid, and Noran, although the master smith stayed back when the others approached their new brother. Behind them came the warriors and then the slaves. They all wanted to greet, or at least catch a glimpse of, the last Emeris. Sic was buried under an avalanche of hugs, kisses, and salutations. It was Canubis who saved him in the end.

"It's enough! Sic has gone through a lot and we still have to get back home before the winter storms set in. So while he eats his breakfast, it would be nice if you guys could pull down the camp and prepare our departure."

THE JOURNEY back to the Valley was peaceful; no highwayman was crazy enough to go after the heavily armed baggage of the divine brothers. Sic spent a lot of his time with Hulda who introduced him to the rules that would shape his life as an Emeris from now on. If he wasn't with the beautiful killer, he rode next to Casto. Most of the time they kept their silence, simply enjoying each other's company as well as the fact that they didn't need words to understand each other. In the evenings, when the slaves erected the camp, the Angel of Death took Sic aside to teach him the basics of fighting. Sometimes Aegid and Kalad would accompany him and act as dummies. Renaldo was satisfied with Sic's progress.

"You're a fast learner, Sic. And you're talented. Soon you'll be able to stand your ground in any fight—except against me, of course."

Sic had bowed demurely for receiving such praise.

"You're very gracious, my lord."

Renaldo put his hand on the young man's shoulder.

"You know you don't have to call me 'lord' anymore? At least not all the time."

"Yes, but I have to get used to the thought first. Not long ago, I was worth even less than the dust beyond your feet. My sudden ascent is still confusing me."

The powerful warrior laughed out loud.

"You're not the first one. Believe me, you'll get used to it. In a hundred years' time, we'll think about this day and have a good laugh."

At the mention of his immortality, Sic still felt uneasy. He didn't want to imagine what it felt like to have all the time in the world. Right now, he didn't want to think about anything at all.

When they were only a few days' ride from the Valley, Canubis sent a messenger to announce the happy news about their latest addition.

"We want the last Emeris to have accommodation befitting his rank," he had told his brother with a broad smile. Renaldo had reciprocated the smile. Both gods were in an exceptionally good mood since the time of waiting was finally over for them.

The welcome to the Valley was as effusive as could be expected in view of such good news. Cornelia and Bantu had prepared an elaborate feast during which Sic was officially introduced as the eighth Emeris. A shower of gifts rained down on him and his spartan rooms in the main house filled up quickly, a fact he mainly owed to Aegid. The intimidating giant had excellent taste and was eager to decorate Sic's new home.

More important to Sic than the pleasant housing was the small forge Renaldo had built for him adjacent to his chambers. Through a newly installed door, he could enter his working space any time he wanted. Since his rooms were facing west, away from those of the other Emeris, he wouldn't disturb them even when he started working early in the morning or stayed late in the night. Sic was so happy about this, he even managed to forget about Noran for a couple of minutes each day.

The master smith kept away from him—even coincidental meetings were rare—although Sic longed to see his master's face. He hated himself for still loving the monster that had hurt him so much. The contradictory feelings tore him up inside, constantly gnawing on him, making his thoughts go round and round without ever coming to a solution. Even the peace in his smithy was disturbed by this emotional rollercoaster.

Only during the training sessions with the Angel of Death did he manage to forget. The god was working him so mercilessly, he had trouble standing on his own two feet after each lesson. This overwhelming exhaustion helped him to stop his useless pondering at least for a while.

Another reason for worry were the slaves he had received during the feast as part of a welcoming gift. The two men and three women still saw the traitor he had been at his departure in spring and acted accordingly. Not being able to bring himself to punish them didn't help his case at all. He was still musing how to solve this problem on his own, because he would rather die than ask any of his new brethren for help, when Casto took matters in hand. How his friend had found out about it, Sic didn't want to know, but it reminded him never to forget that there was a lot more to Casto than met the eye.

One day his capricious friend waited in front of Sic's door with an elderly slave at his side.

"Sic, may I introduce Gweris to you? She's been working for Renaldo for ages and from now on, she's going to take care of you. You're so busy at the moment, nobody can expect you to keep your slaves in line as well. Gweris is going to do that for you."

The slave bowed to him respectfully; her voice was a soothing, congenial alto.

"My Lord Sic."

"Gweris. I'm honored to meet you. Please, come in."

The slave entered the room. Her friendly, green-brown eyes narrowed when she took in the chaos inside. Her voice was stern when she talked to her new owner.

"Where are your slaves, Master?"

Sic blushed.

"To be frank, I don't know."

A last, scornful glance, then Gweris pushed the two young men out of her way.

"I understand. I'm going to take care of this."

Her tone of voice indicated that those at the receiving end of her wrath would regret their abhorrent behavior quite deeply. When she was gone, Casto's shoulders slumped forward.

"I admit, she's a bit scary, but she's also the best."

"Scary? You're kidding me, right? I almost lost control of my bladder, that's how terrified I am. Have you seen her eyes? She's almost as bad as Cassia. I think Gweris has only spared me right now because she was too busy being furious about my slaves. How can anybody own a woman like her?"

Casto grinned.

"Because she chooses her masters, which is the reason I brought her to you. Even Renaldo treads carefully around her. She's going to bring your servants to heel."

Embarrassed, Sic glanced at the ground.

"How did you know?"

"I'm your friend, Sic. And a king, heart of a god, and not stupid. I can sense it when you're upset. This is a problem with which I can help you, so I did."

The underlying message in these words was clear. The king also knew about Sic's other problems even though he wasn't able to offer useful counsel. His voice was very gentle.

"Perhaps you should talk to somebody who understands what you've been through. Once you think you're ready, I'm sure Cornelia will gladly listen to you."

Lost for words, Sic embraced Casto. He thanked the Mothers for blessing him with such a wonderful friend. It was up to him to prove that he was worthy of such grace.

XENIA MELZER was born and raised in a small village in the South of Bavaria. As one of nature's true chocoholics, she's always in search of the perfect chocolate experience. So far, she's had about a dozen truly remarkable ones. Despite having been in close proximity to the mountains all her life, she has never understood why so many people think snow sports are fun. There are neither chocolate nor horses involved and it's cold by definition, so where's the sense? She does not like beer either and has never been to the Oktoberfest—no quality chocolate there.

Even though her mind is preoccupied with various stories most of the time, Xenia has managed to get through school and university with surprisingly good grades. Right after school she met her one true love who showed her that reality is capable of producing some truly amazing love stories itself.

While she was having her two children, she started writing down the most persistent stories in her head as a way of relieving mommy-related stress symptoms. As it turned out, the stress relief has now become a source of the same, albeit a positive one.

When she's not writing, she teaches English at school, enjoys riding and running, spending time with her kids, and dancing with her husband.

Website: www.xeniamelzer.com
E-mail: info@xeniamelzer.com

CASTO
GODS OF WAR
XENIA MELZER

Gods of War: Book I

All is fair in love and war. Renaldo has lived happily by that proverb his entire life. But he has finally met his match, and he's about to discover how unfair love and war can be.

When demigod and warlord Lord Renaldo takes a beautiful stranger captive during an ambush, he is delighted to have found a distraction that will keep him entertained during the upcoming siege. Little does he know, Casto is keeping more than just one secret from him. Slowly, Renaldo gets sucked into a turbulent roller-coaster relationship with his mysterious prisoner, one that begins with hatred and soon spirals into a whirlwind of conflicting emotions. And when it seems that things can get no worse, an old enemy stirs right in the heart of his home.

Determined to keep Casto by his side, Renaldo has to find a balance between the capricious young man and his own destiny as a ruler and god to his people.

www.dsppublications.com

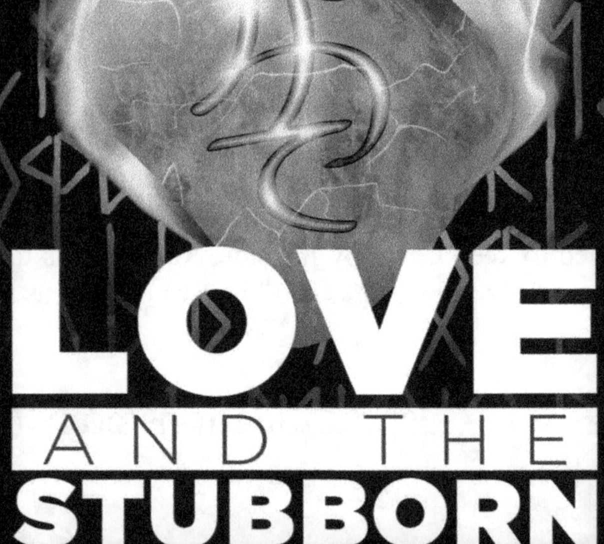

LOVE
AND THE
STUBBORN
GODS OF WAR: BOOK II

XENIA MELZER

Gods of War: Book II

All is fair in love and war. By now, Renaldo has found out the hard way how utterly stupid this statement is once you've met your match. And Casto won't give an inch in their ongoing war for love.

After a tumultuous start to their relationship, Renaldo and Casto seem to have finally reached calmer waters. But just when Renaldo starts getting comfortable and thinks he can relax, things get out of hand again. His old enemy, the Good Mother, is dangerously close to defeating the divine brothers by reaching out to what is most dear to him. Casto still clinging to his stubborn pride is all the plotters need to drive him and Renaldo apart. Burdened by the secrets of his past, Casto fights with everything he's got not only to save his life, but also to secure his future happiness. Facing the destruction of everything they have built together, Renaldo and Casto must choose between pride and love.

www.dsppublications.com

For more
great fiction
from

DSP PUBLICATIONS

visit us online.

WWW.DSPPUBLICATIONS.COM

www.ingramcontent.com/pod-product-compliance
Lightning Source LLC
Chambersburg PA
CBHW070425120726
47910CB00003B/655